RELAY PUBLISHING EDITION, AUGUST 2023

Ava Richardson is a pen name created by Relay Publishing for co-authored Fantasy projects. Relay Publishing works with incredible teams of writers and editors to collaboratively create the very best stories for our readers.

Cover Design by Joemel Requeza.

www.relaypub.com

RISE OF THE DRAGON RIDERS

Dragon Tongue

Dragon Scales

Dragon Fire

Dragon Plague

Dragon Crystals

Dragon Wars

RISE OF THE DRAGON RIDERS : BOOK SIX

AVA RICHARDSON

BLURB

The Blight must be stopped, no matter the cost...

Cora and her bonded dragon Alaric have managed to slow the Blight, a sinister plague striking both dragons and their riders. But both the sickness, and the evil mages who control it, are still a threat to the Kingdom. If Melsuine seizes the magic in the Heart of Tenegard, there will be no stopping them.

With the help of the gruff Lenire and newly awakened Faron, Cora and Alaric harness one of Melsuine's own creations to reach the Heart of Tenegard before their enemies. But their success is short lived, when a new battle costs them dearly.

To end the Blight, Cora and Alaric must join all Tenegardian magic together, and cut to the core of the bond between dragons and their riders. To protect her Kingdom, Cora will pay any price.

But can she sacrifice the one thing she can't bear to lose?

MAILING LIST

Thank you for purchasing *Dragon Wars*
(Rise of the Dragon Riders Book Six)

If you would like to hear more about what I am up to, or continue to follow the stories set in this world with these characters—then please take a look at:

AvaRichardsonBooks.com

You can also find me on me on
www.facebook.com/AvaRichardsonBooks

Or sign up to my mailing list:
AvaRichardsonBooks.com/mailing-list

CONTENTS

Chapter 1 1
Chapter 2 11
Chapter 3 23
Chapter 4 35
Chapter 5 47
Chapter 6 56
Chapter 7 67
Chapter 8 77
Chapter 9 89
Chapter 10 98
Chapter 11 108
Chapter 12 115
Chapter 13 127
Chapter 14 135
Chapter 15 146
Chapter 16 156
Chapter 17 164
Chapter 18 175
Chapter 19 185
Chapter 20 192
Chapter 21 203
Chapter 22 212
Chapter 23 222
Chapter 24 234
Chapter 25 245
Chapter 26 257
Chapter 27 265
Chapter 28 279
Chapter 29 287
Chapter 30 296
Chapter 31 308
Chapter 32 319
Chapter 33 329
Chapter 34 338

Chapter 35 347
Chapter 36 357
Chapter 37 366

End of Dragon Wars 373
Thank you! 375
About Ava 377
Sneak Peek: Pack Dragon 379
Also by Ava 387
Want More? 395

CHAPTER 1
CORA

A sharp gust of frigid wind cut between the mountain shelves, and Cora was almost hurled from her saddle.

Hold on!

Alaric, her dragon, warned her, using the telepathic connection they shared, and despite the wail of the wind that battered her chapped cheeks, his voice was clear and determined.

Another gale swept between the mountain peaks, threatening to blow Alaric off course, and Cora clung tighter to her saddle, desperate to stay in her seat. *Where did this storm come from?*

I don't know. We should get back to camp and warn them before the worst of it arrives, Alaric said.

Sudden wintery storms were something Cora was still learning to contend with this far into the mountains. The weather was unpredictable, but at least she'd come better prepared this time. She pulled her hood up and gripped the pommel of the saddle harder with her hands, trying to generate some heat inside her gloves. Melusine, the sorcerer who was determined to use the Blight to destroy the source of all Tenegard's magic, was out there plotting, and Cora wasn't about to let a little cold snap deter her. She had to beat Melusine to the Heart of Tenegard if she had any hope of preserving the country's magic and waking her partner, Faron. Along with the rest of the dragon riders who'd fallen prey to the Blight-induced sleeping sickness, he still lingered in unconsciousness.

We will *beat her there*, Alaric assured her, reading the anxious tone of her thoughts. *But there is nothing we can do about this coming storm. Not even Melusine has mastery over the weather.*

Maybe if it was only Melusine they were fighting, Cora would be more certain of their success, but Melusine now had Zirael on her side—the wizened sorcerer who'd come to Tenegard to reclaim control of the Blight. One enemy was hard enough to deal with, but two powerful sorcerers and a mystical creature of destruction were pushing it, even for a group of dragon riders.

We should turn back, Alaric said, cutting into her thoughts again. As his words faded, a blast of cold air whipped past them. Alaric slowed dramatically, fighting against the current, and Cora's stomach dropped. She opened her mouth to scream but no words came out, just the howl of the wind as Alaric was forced into a dive.

He twisted between sharpened cliff peaks until he was able to unfurl his wings again. The moment he did, he pierced the side of a rocky cliff with his hooked claws. Cora bounced hard in her seat as she scrambled for purchase, hugging her legs against the smooth scales of Alaric's back. Her fingers were locked in place, curled around the edge of the saddle. She lurched forward, almost pressing her face against the midnight blue scales to avoid slipping and falling off into the dark canyon below. Alaric clung to the jagged peak, his massive wings fluttering and snapping like giant flags against the stone.

Are you okay? he asked.

You were right. We should have turned back earlier.

We couldn't have known how bad it would get.

Let's drop to that clearing, Cora said, pointing to a low-lying space between the cliffs. Alaric twisted his massive head around toward where she was pointing. *We've come this far. I think it's worth one more reading to confirm whether or not we should continue here tomorrow.*

We have *been making good progress in this direction.* He shifted against the peak carefully, his claws grabbing onto sharp ledges, sending handfuls of jagged stones skittering down the cliffs. Alaric had once promised to never let her fall. She didn't think she should test that promise now, so she clung even tighter as he maneuvered for takeoff. In their current position, a poorly timed gale might force them back against the cliff and Cora would be crushed. She closed her eyes as a chilling gust snapped at her. Tiny ice crystals scratched against her exposed skin. Over the constant wail of the wind, she could hear the scuffing of Alaric's scales against the stone. She opened her eyes. The midnight blue shimmered against the dark gray granite.

You trust me, right?

Cora frowned at his tone. *Of course.*

Then grab onto something.

Alaric dove backward off the cliff face and the ground rushed up to meet them. For a long moment they were simply free-falling, then Alaric twisted midair, keeping his wings tight against his body to avoid shearing them against the spiked cliffs that jutted up around them. They plummeted through the sky, descending so quickly Cora could suddenly make out the terrain of the clearing below.

A bubble of nerves shot up from her stomach, colliding with the back of her throat so hard Cora thought she might be sick. But then Alaric unfurled his wings and they slowed, coasting over some tall, spindly pines before setting down in the midst of the clearing.

The moment they were on the ground, Cora slid from Alaric's back. Her legs felt like soup. With nothing of substance to hold her up, she plopped down on a rock to catch her breath.

"Are you all right?" Alaric asked out loud. The clearing was bordered by evergreens on both sides, creating a windscreen. Down here they were safe from the gathering storm, at least for a moment, and now that they weren't competing with the wailing mountain wind, they could hear each other easily.

Cora laughed and got to her feet. Her limbs were still shaky but the thrill of the flight had mostly worn off. "For a moment there I wasn't sure."

She removed one of her gloves and reached for him. Her fingers brushed the stubby scales of his snout, warmed by his heated breath. In his dark eyes she could see her own reflection. The wind had picked at her braid, leaving loose hairs sticking up in all directions. She tried to smooth them away with her other hand but only made it worse. "Come on," she said, inclining her head toward a patch of loose gravel. "Let's get to work."

Alaric followed her, his heavy tread making the small stones tremble. Cora knelt down, removed her other glove, and pressed her bare hands against the earth. She always got a better read without her gloves. As she let her magic seep into the ground, Alaric's energy burst through her. Their combined magic sank deeper and deeper, crawling between dirt and stone, searching for that familiar pull from the river. After the last crystal deposit they'd found had been contaminated by the Blight and turned into an army of hounds, Cora had been forced to return to their old method of manually tracking the magical river back to the Heart of Tenegard.

It was slow-going and draining work, leaving her and Alaric exhausted by the end of each day, but at least their repaired bond made the task easier than it had been back when the Blight was feeding off their magical energy. She was grateful for her renewed connection with Alaric and the use of her full magical strength, especially now, but thinking of all the damage Melusine had caused still made her furious.

Cora channeled that fury and sank her fingers into the dirt, pushing her magic farther and faster. She closed her eyes, sensing the path with her mind, searching for any sign of the river when it suddenly caught her like a hook around the waist. Her magic lurched into the swarm of energy and her glee at having successfully found the river was momentarily eclipsed by the strength of the magic that swarmed her. It was like trying to navigate the most dangerous of rapids. Cora's magic was dragged along, sinking into the uncontrollable torrent.

Cora, Alaric demanded. *Come back!*

The sound of his voice in her head was like an anchor point and she reached for it. Her magic twisted, spiraling around her as if it had been caught in a whirlpool. The force of the river had always been overwhelming, but she was certain lately its strength was increasing.

Cora!

As if he'd grabbed her by the back of the tunic with his teeth, Cora felt Alaric's magic yank her from the river's grasp. The strength of their bond surged around her, and Cora's eyes flew open. She was lying flat on her back, staring up at the looming mountain peaks and the darkening sky, the force of extricating herself from the river having knocked her off her feet.

A dark, pearly dragon eye came into view, blocking out the storm clouds.

"Looks like we found it," Alaric said, peering down at her.

Cora laughed. She couldn't help herself. She struggled to sit, and Alaric propped her up using his tail. "It's getting stronger, right?" Cora asked. "It's not just my wishful thinking?"

"The signal from the river is becoming clearer," he agreed. "Plus, the influence of the Heart's magic is starting to show in the land."

Cora glanced around. He was right. This far into the mountains, at this altitude, the clearing was unusually lush. The evergreens shielded green grass. Rich soil sprouted wildflowers from between rocky crevices. And a thick layer of earthy moss clung to the sides of great granite boulders.

"I'm trying not to get my hopes up, but I think we're getting close." Cora leaned back against Alaric's tail, letting herself relax for a moment. With every pause, every break, Cora was acutely aware of the fact their enemies were regrouping. It had been almost a fortnight since Melusine had fled their last battle. In that time, Cora had been banished from the capital for refusing to send the dragon riders to war with the neighboring nation of Athelia. Under Councilor Northwood's command, Tenegard was gearing up for battle—one Cora was certain was unjust.

In order to maintain some control over the movement of the dragons, Cora and Strida had divided the remaining healthy dragon riders, forcing them to choose who they would fight for. Those who had chosen to stay allied with Northwood and the council stayed under Strida's leadership, dividing their time between the dragon-rider school and the capital. The rest had followed Cora into the mountains.

"Our progress is heartening," Alaric agreed.

"Especially considering the anxious state of the dragon riders this morning." When Cora and Alaric had set out just before dawn, she'd sensed the tension brewing in camp. The hushed conversations. The cutting glares. Cora knew when someone was talking about her.

Though she'd left the school with about twenty dragon-rider pairs at her side—by their own choice—there was still a lot of discontentment to deal with.

"What are you worried about?"

"That the dragon riders who followed me are starting to regret their choice."

"Why would you think that?"

Cora's lips flattened into a thin line. "You really haven't noticed them all muttering to each other every time I walk by? They're impatient. They're starting to doubt me. My constant absence is only fueling their discontent."

Alaric leaned down and nudged the top of her head gently with his snout. "A few of the dragon riders might grumble, but that's only natural, especially given what they've been through recently. Combine that with the stresses of training in a mountain camp and a little frustration is to be expected."

Cora hummed. It had been a stressful couple of weeks. They were constantly patrolling base camp for signs of attack, whether physical or magical, and keeping up with their training for the next inevitable confrontation with Melusine and the Blight. It was a lot to ask without any of the comforts of the school. Still, the weight of discontent was starting to get to her, and Cora wished she could risk communication with Strida or Octavia. There was a communication anchor in Alaric's saddlebag, but Cora had agreed only to use it if absolutely necessary in order to protect their schemes from being discovered. She couldn't upend everything just because she was overwhelmed. That didn't stop her from daydreaming Faron might come flying over the mountain ridge, having miraculously woken from the sleeping sickness. She always regretted letting her mind wander in that direction. Though she missed him terribly, it hurt to have to drag herself back to reality.

"We should go," Alaric said. His snout turned to the sky, his nostrils flaring. "Snow is coming."

Cora shook off the chill of their flight by a dinner fire. No matter how far she and Alaric traveled, tracking the magic river, they always returned to base camp each night to regroup. They'd settled north of the last remote village where Cora and Lenire had tracked a crystal deposit and then subsequently fought Melusine and Zirael's hound creations with the help of the dragon riders. Cora didn't want to intrude on the village any longer, but the proximity meant the area was familiar.

"Cora?" a voice called as she flexed her fingers above the heat of the flames. She turned in time to see Emmett approaching. Once Northwood's lackey, the capital-liaison-turned-ally had accompanied Cora's group of riders to the mountains. Though he wasn't adept at dragon riding, Emmett had other *talents*.

"What now?" she asked, noting the rolled parchment he carried in his hands.

"By my latest numbers," Emmett said, launching into a report, "we're running short on some important provisions. I've spent the day setting up a supply arrangement with the nearby village—"

"I didn't want us to bother them again," Cora interrupted.

"You probably also don't want us to starve," Emmett said without missing a beat. He grumbled something about unpredictable backwoods access to military necessities, but they both knew there was nothing that could be done about that. The council considered them traitors. There would be no aid coming from them. "I've also dispatched regular hunting parties, so between that and the supply arrangement, I've been able to loosen the limits on our rations."

“Thank you for doing all that,” Cora said sincerely. Tensions were already running high. The last thing she needed was her dragon riders thinking they were going to starve.

“It ought to pacify the troublemakers at least,” Emmett said.

I don’t think they like being called troublemakers, Alaric cut in privately.

“They’re restless,” Cora said to Emmett while silently agreeing with Alaric. “They made a difficult choice to follow me into the mountains. It hasn’t been easy. But I am impressed by your resourcefulness.”

Though Emmett was clearly pleased by the recognition, a commotion in camp caught his attention, and Cora took the opportunity to slip away. She stepped between the myriad of tents that had popped up, pausing only when she reached her father’s small fire. She sank down onto a log, letting the weariness of the day overcome her.

“You’re back!” her father said, emerging from his tent. Viren Hart had joined them in the mountains upon learning Cora and her dragon riders had abandoned the school, and she’d never been more grateful for his sturdy, reassuring presence. He scooped her a bowl of stew from the pot that bubbled over the fire. “When did you get in?”

“Just a few minutes ago,” she said.

“You look tired.”

Cora mustered a smile for him but she couldn’t hide the way her shoulders sagged. She wanted nothing more than to stretch out and sleep right here.

“Any luck out there?”

She nodded, chewing through a potato. “We’re still on track. The river’s presence is getting stronger.” Her father opened his mouth to respond as Cora looked up. Then he closed it without saying anything. Cora could sense his hesitation. "What is it?"

"Nothing really. It's just that one of the dragon riders was complaining earlier. They wanted me to talk to you."

Cora felt the spoon slip from her fingers as a wave of weariness settled over her.

"But it doesn't have to be now," Viren assured her.

Cora massaged her eyes with one hand. Letting the complaint fester would only make it worse. When she took her hand away, Lenire strode right into her father's camp and sat beside her. "I have something to tell you."

She sighed. "Can you at least wait until I'm done eating?"

"I think I figured out how to wake the sleeping dragon riders."

Cora dropped her entire bowl of stew. "What?"

"There's only one problem," he said, unfazed by the dinner congealing on his boots. "We have to sneak back into the school in order to try it."

CHAPTER 2

CORA

"What do you think our odds of getting in undetected are?" Lenire asked.

Cora tightened Alaric's saddlebag, ignoring her exhaustion, as she glanced at Lenire. He was one of the few people who knew the truth about the arrangement between her and Strida. "I don't think we'll exactly be welcomed back with open arms considering they think I'm a traitor now, so it's in our best interest not to get caught. The school might even have orders to detain us if we're spotted on the grounds."

"Do you really think they would do that?" Lenire said. "To you of all people?"

Cora lifted her shoulder. Leaving the school and dividing the dragon riders had been one of the hardest things she'd ever had to do. "I wouldn't put it past Northwood to order such a thing. He already banished me from Kaerlin. He probably wants to make sure I don't have any contact with the remaining riders."

A cold, shifting wind slithered down from the mountains and Cora shivered. The storm she'd flown through with Alaric was on its way.

"We should get going," she told Lenire. "Before this weather catches up to us."

Lenire pulled on a pair of fur-lined gloves before hiking himself onto Yrsa's back. The iridescent dragon was more serpentine than the dragons from Tenegard. She was lean where Alaric was bulky, and her feathery mane and tail made her a swift flier.

As Cora studied Yrsa, she felt eyes on her. Slowly, she turned, studying the other dragon riders. Most were busy preparing for sleep or securing their shelters for the coming storm.

Over there, Alaric said.

Cora turned in the direction he indicated, her gaze immediately landing on Renka. The girl was tall, with short black hair that cut sharply just below her chin. She leaned against a tree, arms crossed, shaking her head.

If Emmett's so-called troublemakers had a leader, it was definitely Renka. Cora took a deep breath to steady herself, but Renka launched into her protest before Cora had even finished inhaling.

"So you're leaving *again*? Just like that." Renka pushed off the tree, marching toward her and Alaric. She stopped a few inches from Cora. Any closer and she would have been standing on Cora's toes. "Why did you even ask us to choose?"

Cora licked her lips, preparing her answer. "I don't—"

"If you're going to do everything yourself, why do you even need other riders?"

The camps nearest them had fallen silent, and Cora felt a dozen more eyes on her back. The others were listening now. "I know it seems that way—"

"It *is* that way."

Cora sighed. She didn't want to raise people's hopes until she was certain she could wake the sleeping trainees. If Lenire's plan failed, she was going to feel wretched enough. She didn't need to carry the sadness of all her dragon riders as well. "Look, Renka," Cora said, turning away from the crowd, attempting to keep their conversation private, "I can't tell you what I'm doing. Only that it's desperately important."

"But it's okay for this newcomer to accompany you?" Renka responded loudly as she gestured to Lenire. Any hope Cora had of settling this dispute quietly drifted away with the wind. "We barely know him and yet you repeatedly ask for his help instead of that of your own students. Except for the handful of lessons he teaches, we rarely see him, much less talk to him."

Cora glanced over her shoulder. Lenire had been teaching the riders bits and pieces of Itharusian dragon lore, though clearly they weren't all that impressed with his presence. Lenire shifted in his saddle, the muscles in his cheek twitching. Renka couldn't see past his stony expression, but Cora could read him well enough to know he'd been hurt by the comment.

"Do you even care how we feel?" Renka demanded of them both.

Cora, biting back the impatience that boiled in her gut, placed her hand on Renka's shoulder. "Lenire's magic helped us fend off the Blight, which we otherwise had no weapon against. And it's his magic that now bolsters the shield around the school."

"Why do you care about the school? You left it behind, remember?"

Cora bristled. It wasn't a choice she'd wanted to make. She gathered her thoughts before they could spin down that thread of regret. "What I'm trying to say is that Lenire's Itharusian magic might help in another situation where our own has failed. As I'm sure you're learning for yourselves, Itharusian magic is tricky. Since I have the most experience working with him, I'm not about to risk sending raw beginners on a mission like this."

Cora had experienced the dangers of Itharusian magic herself once when a spell of Lenire's rebounded and almost killed him. She didn't want any more blood on her hands. Especially that of these young riders.

Renka scoffed, her breath fogging in the mountain air. "You know, if you could have just let go of a little control and let others have a hand in running things, maybe we never would have had to leave the school in the first place."

Every muscle in Cora's face tensed. Her pulse beat so hard in her neck she was certain everyone could see it. "Renka, I don't have time for this right now. We have to go."

"You do that," Renka said, backing away while shaking her head. "We're used to being on our own."

"We can talk about it if you want," Lenire offered.

"I don't really want to," Cora said, squinting into the darkness. "Renka's angry. They all are. But I can't fix that *and* save Faron and the other sleeping riders." She threw her hood back. The night was clear this far from the mountains, with no trace of the winter wind or snow. She could see the stars above them and even the first faint glimmers of light from the school. "We're almost there," she said, mostly to Alaric. "We should probably start looking for a place to touch down. We'll have to walk from here if we want to avoid being spotted from the air. I'm sure they have patrols going."

Alaric descended into the trees, splintering branches as he touched down. Yrsa landed beside them. She was more delicate, her landing softer. As Cora slid to the ground, Alaric opened his jaws and dropped the sack he'd been carrying. It shifted and snarled, and when Lenire stepped forward to rip the sack away, Cora stepped back, covering her mouth and nose with her hand. This was the last remaining hound from their battle with Melusine. It smelled of putrefied flesh, each mottled chunk of its body trembling from within its knotted bindings. The dragon riders had secured the creature with thick black rope, which Lenire had spelled with Itharusian knots. There was no way the hound could get free but Cora's hand still drifted to the hilt of her sword at her waist.

"How are we getting this thing inside the school?" she asked, already considering which portion of the shield would be the best one to dismantle. Because the creature was fueled by a crystal heart that contained a small piece of the Blight, it would definitely trigger the school's protective shield.

Lenire waved his hands over the creature, tying more of those invisible knots. "We're not. Taking it inside the school is too risky. Someone will notice."

Cora frowned. She didn't quite understand how this was going to work, but she trusted Lenire and his magic. Plus, a part of her was so desperate to wake Faron that she was prepared to agree to anything.

At the look on her face, however, Lenire said, "The dragons will keep watch over the creature out here. You and I will sneak inside."

Cora nodded in silent agreement and the two of them set off through the trees, hurrying toward the school. They approached the shield from behind the dining hall, combining their Tenegardian and Itharusian magic to lower a section small enough for them to squeeze through. At this time of night the dining hall was likely to be empty, but just in case it wasn't, the sheer size of the building would hopefully hide their arrival. They ran across the grounds, stopping at the edge of the dining hall, cloaked by its shadow.

"Which one is Elaine's cabin?" Lenire asked.

"That one there." Cora pointed to a small building near the infirmary. Elaine was her father's new wife, Faron's aunt, and the healer in charge of the afflicted riders. She was also the only other person on the school grounds who actually knew the truth of Cora and Strida's forced separation.

Lenire drew his hood over his head and crept along the shadow of the building. Cora did the same, staying away from the glowing candles that burned in the windows of the student dorms. They reached Elaine's cabin without interference and Cora knocked twice. There was movement inside, like someone kicking off sheets, then the thump of footsteps. Cora pulled her hood down as the door swung open. Elaine's expression registered in the flickering light of the candle lamp she carried: first elation, then fear. She snatched Cora by the front of her tunic and hauled her into the cabin, doing the same with Lenire a moment later.

The door shut with a soft *snap*, then Elaine was hugging them. "By the stars, what are you doing here? Don't you know how dangerous this is? Northwood's declared you all traitors to the nation. You'll be detained if you're discovered."

Cora gave Lenire a look. She'd been right about Northwood.

"We're here to wake the sleeping dragon riders," Lenire said, not wasting another moment.

Elaine's worry melted into astonishment. She collapsed on the edge of her bed. "But how? We've tried everything."

"Everything but the Blight itself," Lenire said. Cora sat next to Elaine while Lenire pulled up a chair from the small dining table. "We've brought one of the hounds with us. Its crystal heart is powered by a small fragment of the Blight. If we destroy it, I think it will result in a burst of magical energy."

“We’ve destroyed those crystal hearts before,” Cora pointed out to him. “That’s how we defeated the hounds. There was never any burst of magic.”

“I don’t mean the crystal,” Lenire explained. “I’m talking about the actual fragment of the Blight.”

Cora looked to Elaine, but the healer’s expression showed nothing but confusion.

“That small piece of Blight is connected to the main bulk of the creature.”

Cora nodded. “Right.”

“And when we destroyed the hounds in the past, that small fragment of the Blight was free to rejoin the rest of the Blight. There’s a bond there. I’m talking about breaking *that* bond.” Lenire stood, pacing before them. “Do you remember the way Itharusian magic recoils when broken?”

Cora swallowed hard. She’d been there when Lenire’s spell had rebounded. In fact, she’d been partly responsible for the spell breaking and the damage that had followed. Lenire had barely survived the burst of magic.

“I think breaking the bond between the Blight fragment and the rest of the creature will result in a similar burst of magical energy. And if we theorize where most of that energy has been coming from lately, then the magic it expels should be—”

“The Tenegardian magic that was stolen from the dragon riders!” Cora said, jumping to her feet. Something clicked in her mind and Lenire’s plan suddenly made perfect sense.

“Exactly.” The corner of Lenire’s mouth flickered into an almost-smile. “You said the sleepers’ condition is a result of depleted magic. I say, we break the bond of the Blight fragment and take that magic back. Then Elaine can use a healing spell to channel the magic into the afflicted dragon riders."

"Do you think it's enough to wake them?" Cora asked, turning to Elaine.

Elaine was silent for a moment, then her brow arched. "You know, it just might work." She was on her feet in an instant, retrieving fresh healer robes from a trunk at the end of her bed. "But you two can't go out there looking like that. Someone is certain to recognize you and then any hope we have of waking the riders is gone."

She tossed a set of robes to each of them. Lenire shucked his traveling cloak, pulling the robes over his head.

"What's that?" Cora asked as Elaine began mixing a concoction of liquid into a bowl.

"A glamour. It's weak but if you can avoid touching your face it should hold long enough to get you inside the infirmary undetected." She wiped the liquid across Cora's face before doing the same with Lenire. When Cora looked at him she was looking at a stranger. Then the glamour twitched and more of Lenire's true face shone through.

"Come," Elaine said, ushering them to the door. "It won't hold long. We have to hurry."

They raced down the trodden path from Elaine's cabin to the front of the infirmary. Elaine halted them at the door, looked them over once, then plastered on a smile as she stepped through the door.

Inside, the lights were dim. Two young healers roamed between the cots, working the overnight shift. They looked up curiously the moment Elaine entered. "Is everything okay?"

"Yes," Elaine said. "Of course. I've had a couple new colleagues arrive. I thought they might work the evening shift to acquaint themselves with the riders. I'd prefer to show them the routine myself," she continued, ushering the other healers to the door. "We'll take it from here. You two take the evening for yourselves."

Elaine practically shoved the last healer out the door, holding it closed as if they might try to barge back in. "Let's make this quick," she said, turning around.

Lenire was already rolling up his sleeves. He closed his eyes, then sank his arms into the empty space in front of him. It looked as if he was reaching through a hole cut into the world, the same way Melusine did when she transported herself across long distances. Then suddenly the muscles of his forearms tensed and he pulled a thick black rope from the invisible space. It reminded her of the bonds that secured the hound.

Cora was surprised she could see Lenire's magic at all. She couldn't normally see his Itharusian knots, at least not without the disk he'd once used, but then she realized the black strands were the fragment of Blight he'd taken hold of. That's why she could see it.

As Lenire yanked on the rope, black smoke began to spiral around his fingers. His hands shook, his teeth clenched. As the smoke gathered, Cora could see the black rope thinning, like the connection was being stretched. Whatever Lenire was doing looked to be working.

"What can I do?" Cora asked.

"Get ready," he said, the words hissed between his teeth. "I'll need you to help me direct the magic when the bond breaks. Keep it from escaping the infirmary. And Elaine, be ready to receive and channel the magic into the sleepers."

Cora took a step back and cast a shield of air. It encircled them, blocking off the door and all the windows. Elaine also readied herself, palms up like she might catch the magic in her hands.

Lenire took one hand off the rope. Cora recognized the motions as he cast an invisible knot of his own around the rope. Then he pulled hard and that thinning area in the rope bulged and bucked. Lenire was cutting off the connection. He pulled his knot tighter and tighter, winding the invisible string around his hand. And then, all at once, the knot severed the connection, and Cora collapsed her shield into a smaller shell, catching the burst of magic.

Her feet slid back against the floor as the power of the explosion threatened to break the shield, but Cora managed to funnel the magic to Elaine by making a small hole in the shield. As the magic spilled into her hands, Elaine twisted it into a healing spell, dispersing the magic throughout the room. Energy crackled around them as the magic seeped into the sleeping dragon riders. In the silence that followed, goosebumps stretched up Cora's arms. She shivered, stepping between the cots, watching Faron's unconscious form. His chest rose and fell. His breaths were as steady and even as they'd always been. Nothing had changed.

Cora, Alaric called.

She lifted her hand to her mouth, containing the sob that sat on the back of her tongue. *I don't think it worked.*

It's okay. We'll try something else.

But then Faron moved.

Cora surged forward, watching Faron's hand shift. Then his eyes blinked open, scanning the room, scanning her face. Cora knelt by his side and the sob finally broke free. "By the stars, you're awake!"

"What happened?" Faron asked dazedly, sitting up on his elbows. "Where am I? Who …" he began, looking at her with confusion. "Who are you?"

Cora's stomach dropped, then she gave a shaky laugh, remembering the glamour Elaine had cast over her face. Cora took the edge of her robe and wiped the glamour from her face, scrubbing her cheeks and chin.

"Cora?" Faron whispered.

The sound of her name was like music, and she threw her arms around him, lingering in the moment for as long as she could. All around them dozens of riders began to wake, and from outside, Cora heard the panicked grumbles of the dragons who'd also been caught in the sleeping sickness.

"Cora," Lenire said, hurrying to her side. "Your glamour?"

"I rubbed it off."

His own glamour was waning. "We have to go."

He was right. Waking the riders and the dragons was bound to draw attention. Soon the infirmary would be swarmed with confused but elated dragon riders who would fly to the capital to deliver the news to Strida and the council. They had to be gone before they were spotted.

Faron's hand wrapped around her wrist, his grip surprisingly strong considering how long he'd been unconscious. "Don't go."

"We can't stay. I know you don't understand. I'm sorry."

Faron's grip tightened. "Don't leave me."

The front door bucked as someone crashed against it. "Elaine?" voices called.

"Cora, let's get out of here!" Lenire hissed, peeking out the window. He rushed back to her side.

The front door shuddered again.

“Cora!” Faron demanded.

She turned to Lenire. “I can’t leave him.”

“Then he’s coming with us.” Lenire bent down, threw Faron’s arm over his shoulder and hauled him to his feet. Cora slipped under his other arm.

“Hurry!” Elaine said, appearing behind them. “The back door. Go!”

Cora and Lenire dragged Faron’s weakened body across the infirmary, slipping out the back just as the front door burst open.

CHAPTER 3
CORA

Faron collapsed outside Elaine's cabin.

"Get him inside," Cora hissed at Lenire, shoving the door open and grabbing Faron under the armpit at the same time. They hauled him across the floor of the cabin, his body as limp as a rag doll.

"Faron?" Cora said, kneeling on the floor next to him. He groaned, his face as pale as the mountain snow she'd become so accustomed to. Cora pulled her healer robes over her head, tossing them aside. "Faron, it's me," she said, cupping his cheek with her hand. "Can you hear me?"

The door flew open behind them and Cora whirled around, her sword half-drawn before she recognized Elaine.

"Get him on the bed," Elaine ordered immediately.

"What about the other riders?"

"I've filled Nadia in and left her in charge for now. She's monitoring the recovery process."

Cora and Lenire half-dragged, half-carried Faron to the bed. Lenire moved to the window while Cora sat on the edge of the bed, clasping Faron's hand.

"There's a lot of movement out there," Lenire said. "I don't know how we're going to get back to the dragons."

"We'll have to figure something out." Cora lifted Faron's limp hand and pressed it to her lips. "Faron," she whispered before turning to Elaine. "What's wrong with him?"

"The healers' ministrations might have prevented a full coma once the effects of the Blight were reversed, but his body is still a shell of what it once was. His magic was restored, but he doesn't have the physical strength to support it. Basically, we overwhelmed his system."

"But he'll be okay?" Cora asked her.

Elaine's smile was brief but reassuring as she set to work. While Elaine wielded her cold healer magic, Cora joined Lenire at the window, peeking between the drapes. Now the unconscious riders were awake, there was a steady stream of movement to and from the infirmary. "I didn't really think this through," Cora said, letting the drape fall back in place.

"Neither did I," Lenire admitted.

"The whole school's probably awake by now."

Faron sucked in a sharp breath, sitting up suddenly. Elaine caught him by the shoulders, settling him back against the pillow. "What happened?" he asked.

"You passed out," Cora said, returning to his side. "How do you feel?"

"Sort of like a dragon sat on me."

Cora chuckled. She'd imagined this moment more times than she could count, but none of her daydreams had ever truly done it justice.

"You're going to feel like that for a few days at least," Elaine said, fussing with the blankets over Faron's legs. "Some of the effects might take weeks to wear off. After being unconscious for that long, you're going to be weak. And it will take time for your muscles—and your magic—to recover to full strength."

"Effects?" Faron said, flexing his hands. "Will someone tell me what happened?"

Between Cora and Elaine, they managed to catch Faron up on everything he'd missed: Melusine's treachery and their defense of the school, the creation of the hounds, meeting Lenire and Yrsa, and pursuing the Heart of Tenegard, even when it meant dividing the dragon riders.

"And the others?" Faron asked Elaine.

"Are under Nadia's care."

Cora inclined her head and Elaine followed her across the room. "We can't stay much longer," she said, her eyes drifting back to Faron. "Every moment we risk being seen here."

Elaine sighed. "He should really avoid exerting himself or taking unnecessary risks. That means staying where a healer can take care of him."

"When do we leave?" Faron called. He shifted, sitting up, but he winced and then wobbled sideways. Lenire had to stop him from pitching off the edge of the bed.

"Faron—" Cora and Elaine said at once.

"I've spent enough time lying in bed," he said, kicking off the sheets Elaine had tucked around him. Clearly, he was frustrated with everyone fussing over him. "Don't think for one second I'm going to stay here while you go after Melusine."

Cora turned back to Elaine. "I can't leave him behind," she muttered.

"I know," Elaine said, frowning. "And that boy is so stubborn he'd just turn around and follow you if you did. That's why I'm coming with you."

Cora couldn't help but smile at that. She took Elaine's hand and squeezed it. "We're glad to have your company. Dad will be pleased too."

At once Elaine broke away and began gathering her things, packing salves and poultices into a travel bag.

"Sounds like we're going to need a distraction if we hope to get out of here undetected," Lenire said.

"About that," Cora began, hurrying to Faron's side and helping him sit up on the edge of the bed. "I have an idea, but you might not like it."

"Let's hear it."

"We get Yrsa to fly to the opposite end of the school since she's the fastest of the dragons. If she causes a distraction over there, it should attract almost all of the riders. While they're investigating, we get Faron's dragon, Wyn, to fly us all back to meet Alaric. She'll be weaker since she's just woken, but it's a short flight. The only trouble is if—"

"Yrsa gets caught," Lenire finished for her.

Cora grimaced. "The riders here won't take kindly to her presence. If they spot her, you'll have an even bigger target on your back."

"It's not like I'm very high on the likability scale right now anyway," Lenire quipped. "Yrsa can do this. I know she can." He stepped away, presumably to relay the plan to Yrsa. He turned suddenly. "She wants to know what kind of distraction."

Cora's mind drew a blank.

"Fire," Faron grunted.

"What?" she asked, looking down to where he hunched over the side of the bed.

"If you want to make a scene, use Dragon Fire."

Lenire nodded. "One fiery distraction coming up."

Cora knelt beside Faron. "Hey, can you tell Wyn to meet us here?"

He nodded, cradling his head as he mentally reached out to his dragon. Once they managed to slip past the school's defenses, Wyn was likely going to need assistance flying the distance to the mountains, and she was glad both Yrsa and Alaric were here to help. Cora ran her hand over Faron's bare forearm and it struck her suddenly how he was dressed. They couldn't take him to the mountains like this—in nothing but pants and an undershirt. He didn't have boots for his feet, never mind the appropriate attire for the frigid weather.

"I'll be right back," she announced.

Lenire whirled around. Elaine stopped packing. "Where are you going?" they demanded at almost the same time.

"Faron needs proper clothes. And I doubt you're keeping his size in your trunk," she said to Elaine.

"Please be careful," Elaine replied, still plucking her own supplies from shelves and drawers.

Cora nodded, throwing up her hood. Faron grabbed her wrist before she could hurry to the door. "Bring me my sword," he requested.

"I will," Cora promised, and then she was gone, racing out into the night. She kept her head down as she weaved her way through the shadows to Faron's old cabin. Luckily, it wasn't far, and the few riders she passed were too preoccupied with getting to the infirmary to pay much attention to her. The bigger problem out here was Cora had no concept of what was going on with their distraction plan.

Alaric?

Yrsa's on her way to the woods opposite my location.

Good. How much time do you think I have?

As a dragon flies? Not long.

Cora ran faster, sparing a quick second to check over her shoulder before bounding up the steps to Faron's cabin. Despite the risk, she left the door wide open, needing what little starlight spilled across the floor to see. She fumbled around the room, stuffing clothes into an old rucksack. She found a pair of sturdy boots under Faron's bed and his sword sheath hanging from a post by his bed. She strung the weapon over her shoulder. On the back of the door she found a thick traveling cloak.

Cora, hurry! Alaric said, his tone insistent.

I'm done, she said. *Heading back now.*

She hurried through the open doorway, skidding to a halt as a dragon came charging around the corner of the cabin carrying something in its mouth. Cora froze, staring up at it with her mouth open, before she recognized the coloring of the scales. "Wyn!"

"It's good to see you, Cora," Wyn replied after dropping the saddle she was holding in her mouth. Suddenly, a stream of fire sliced through the night sky like a massive torch. Cora and Wyn stared at the flame as it crackled in the distance. "That's Yrsa," the dragon said.

With trembling limbs, she sank low enough for Cora to throw the saddle over her back and cinch it down.

Cora tossed the rucksack into Wyn's saddlebag, then heaved herself into the saddle. Wyn lifted off with a few struggling flaps of her wings and coasted down to Elaine's cabin. With her massive tail, she rapped on the door. It flew open a moment later. Elaine and Lenire came stumbling out with Faron between them.

Cora reached down. "Did you see the—"

"Fire? Yeah," Lenire said, helping hoist Faron onto Wyn's back. He pushed and Cora pulled. "Yrsa said a team of dragon riders have pursued her into the woods."

"But she's okay?"

"For now."

Cora got Faron settled behind her, then tossed his cloak over him. Elaine scurried up next with Lenire's help. Then Lenire passed up Elaine's carefully packed bag of healer supplies.

"Let's go," he said, grabbing hold of Wyn's wing and hauling himself into place. Wyn lifted off, gliding into the night to rendezvous with Alaric.

The storm had come and gone by the time they made it back to the mountain base camp. Touched by the gray light of dawn, Cora could make out the thin layer of powder that now coated the firepits and tents as she descended from her saddle. Lenire slid down next to her, his boots crunching in the snow.

Alaric dropped the sack he'd been carrying, and Cora jumped back as the hound creature rolled free. What was once a snarling menace was now a twitching mass of half-living flesh. Frankly, Cora was surprised to see the creature alive at all, but judging by Lenire's curious examination, he'd expected it.

"We didn't destroy the crystal heart of the creature," he said when she asked. "Only the Blight's control over the fragment that remains inside. Whatever magic still remains is enough to sustain it."

"You mean Melusine and Zirael's magic? They created this thing."

"It's harmless now," Lenire assured her. "Without that thread of control, the hound isn't capable of self-animation."

Cora hummed uncertainly. She'd been through too much with Melusine to trust anything of her design.

"Weren't you the one who insisted we keep the hound in the first place in order to see what could be learned from it?" Lenire said.

Those *had* been her words, shouted in the heat of battle. Now Cora wondered if it was better to dispatch the creature. It had served a greater purpose than she'd ever intended—waking the dragon riders. Expecting any more from it was a foolish idea, but she could tell by the look on Lenire's face that he was eager to explore the capabilities of the hound. "Just keep it tied up," Cora said. "I don't want to see this thing left lying around unguarded."

"Of course," Lenire agreed, bending down to secure the knots of the ropes that still bound the hound's limbs. As he did, Cora glanced up in time to see Faron slump off Wyn's back, stumbling the moment he hit the ground. Wyn twisted sharply, using her massive head to keep Faron on his feet.

Cora rushed to his side. Elaine was already there, hands pressed to Faron's cheeks, likely using that cold healer magic to assess his condition. Faron attempted to shrug her off.

"I'm fine," he insisted.

"You're not fine," Elaine grumbled. "You've over-exerted yourself flying all this way."

Now that Cora got a good look at him, he was almost as gray as the dawn. His face was hollow and skeletal, dark circles beneath his eyes. "I'll be okay," he said, gasping the words. "I just need to sit for a moment."

He stumbled back against Wyn, then slid to the ground.

Wyn isn't faring much better, Alaric added privately. *It took every ounce of her strength to keep pace with us on the flight back.*

Cora gave him a discreet nod of acknowledgment. Dragons shared a telepathic connection, so if Wyn was struggling, Alaric and Yrsa would have picked up on it. Wyn settled next to Faron, letting out a mighty sigh of relief.

"We should get him to the infirmary tent," Elaine said.

"Wait," Faron interrupted, pushing himself to his feet and wobbling as he did. "Look, I'm fine." He gestured to Wyn. "We're fine. Good enough to join the other riders for training exercises this morning."

"Absolutely not," Elaine said. "I know you don't want to be coddled, Faron, but I am putting my foot down on this. You are too weak to even consider it."

Faron's cheeks pinked. Whether it was from anger or embarrassment, Cora was glad to see a little life come back to his face. "We just need some practice to get us back into shape. That's all."

"No, Faron," Wyn said out loud for everyone to hear.

Faron twisted, almost tipping over before he caught himself against her side. "Not you too?"

"Elaine is right about this. It's too dangerous for us to participate in training exercises right now. We barely managed the flight to the mountains. Our magic is exhausted. Our energy is depleted. We need more time to recoup our strength now that we are finally awake."

Elaine's brow lifted as Faron opened his mouth to argue. Cora could tell she wanted to say, *I told you so*.

Instead, it was Alaric who spoke, gently backing Wyn up. "I know you don't want to hear this, but the herd would never allow a dragon to fight in such a depleted state."

Faron rubbed his hand along Wyn's scales. "We've been asleep so long; we've wasted so much time."

"Which is why we can't risk you or Wyn before you're ready," Cora said, reaching out for his hand. "I just got you back. I don't want to lose you again because we foolishly rushed your recovery."

"You won't lose me," Faron promised, his hand tightening around hers. "Not this time."

Cora was comforted by the strength of his grip. "That's what I'm counting on." She tugged a little. "Now, come. Let's get you settled in the infirmary."

Cora escorted Faron to the tent and waited while he was doted on by Elaine. Even after he was settled and asleep on a cot under a pair of thick furs, Cora sat with him, holding his hand the way she had for so many days back at the school, only this time she knew he would wake up. Eventually, duties called her away and she left to train and track the river, though she returned earlier than she'd intended, eager to check up on Faron. To her surprise, he was awake and there was more color in his cheeks. He sat outside the infirmary tent, a bowl of stew in his lap.

"Elaine only let me out of the tent because I agreed not to attempt anything dangerous," he said the moment she sat down.

"I'm glad to see you up and eating."

"Apparently, that's all I'm good for."

"Hey," Cora said, reaching out for him. Her fingers whispered across his cheek.

"I know I can't join you yet, but I wish I could at least help lead the recruits in your absence. It's unnerving being confined to the ground. What use am I going to be to you if I'm stuck here eating stew and being smothered by fur blankets?"

Cora couldn't help the smile that tugged at her lips. "A few more days at this altitude and you're going to be grateful for those furs." She stood. "Come with me."

Faron looked around, almost as if he expected Elaine to appear and protest. "Where?"

"I have an idea."

Cora took his hand and led him across the camp, doing her best to avoid the stares and muttered words from Renka and the other *troublemakers*. Faron's arrival had been a shock to most, and news that Cora and Lenire had woken the dragon riders had spread like wildfire through the camp.

"What are we doing here?" Faron asked when they reached the edge of the pit they used to house the hound. Below, Lenire was attempting some kind of Itharusian spell on the creature. To Cora's surprise, it was now wandering aimlessly around the pit, bumping into walls. If Cora didn't know any better, she'd say Lenire was trying to cast his knotted strings around the hounds' limbs. Maybe doing so gave him some sort of control over the beast.

Intrigued by Lenire's experiment, Faron climbed down the side of the pit. Cora followed closely. With her back turned, she didn't notice the moment Lenire lost control of his spell. But Faron did, and he grabbed her, yanking them both to the ground as the magical energy ricocheted around the pit before being caught by Lenire.

"What *was* that?" Faron asked a moment later.

"A rebounding Itharusian knot," Lenire said. "Sorry about that." He reached down to help them both up. "You've got good reflexes for someone who has just woken from a Blight coma."

Faron snorted, but Cora smiled, dusting off her pants as she grinned at Lenire. "I think I just found you an assistant."

CHAPTER 4
OCTAVIA

A company of soldiers crossed through the woods right where Octavia was hiding. She ducked down against a fallen log, the musty scent of rotted wood filling her nose. The clatter of chain mail and the thunder of dozens of feet marching in time echoed between the trees. The sound drummed inside her chest until her heart beat to the same rhythm.

Don't move, Raksha warned her. *Another company is coming.*

Where did this group come from? Octavia replied using their telepathic connection. Thankfully, her dragon was sheltered in a cave farther along the border. It was perched halfway up a cliff, giving Raksha a perfect view of the wooded tree line below. *There hasn't been a patrol in this area for days. Do you think someone spotted us?*

They have supply wagons with them. I think these are the troops we noted a few days ago during our scouting mission.

They made good time, Octavia grumbled.

She and Raksha had been scouting up and down the Tenegardian border for the better part of two weeks, looking for the best place to cross into Athelia, in hopes of making contact with members of the senate. Though she could clearly see the border between the two nations, there had been three major problems. One, as far as they knew, Melusine was also hiding out somewhere along the border. The last dragon rider to cross her here had been badly injured. After helping Cora defeat the hounds, Octavia knew better than to take on Melusine alone. Two, like the company that had just arrived, Northwood's soldiers were now being stationed along the border. If they caught Octavia or Raksha, they would face the full wrath of the council after having been banished. And three, the weather had been uncharacteristically nice, making it impossible to disguise their flight. A night flight would have made the most sense, but flying in pure darkness was already hazardous for a dragon, even more so when they were unfamiliar with the terrain. Octavia had no idea what they would be facing in Athelia, so the last thing she wanted to do was go in blind.

Finally, this morning, Octavia had woken to a light drizzle of rain and a welcomed layer of grisly, gray cloud cover. This was their chance to make their escape, though the sudden arrival of more of Northwood's soldiers was an unwelcome obstacle.

There's been no sign of Melusine. I think we still need to take our chances crossing even with the troop activity, Octavia said, inching forward on her forearms through the mossy bed of foliage. The ground was damp, her blonde braid dragging through the mud as she crawled. Octavia flipped it back over her shoulder, pausing to watch the patrol. The wagons rumbled nearer and the lines of troops snaked out of the trees, halting to set up camp. Raksha was right. Northwood's forces were here to stay. Pretty soon the woods would be swarming with soldiers foraging for supplies. They needed to move while they still could.

Octavia ducked behind a tree, using it as a shield.

They're going to see us, Raksha said. *There's no way to avoid it now. At least until I can get us high enough that the clouds provide cover.*

I don't think we can wait any longer. The weather is unpredictable. It could be days before we get this chance again.

There was more risk now Northwood's army had arrived, and they'd certainly be in trouble if they were caught. But if the Athelian soldiers spotted them crossing on a clear, sunny day, they would likely try to shoot them down. And if one side started shooting, both sides would. Octavia didn't want to be responsible for instigating the fighting between the two armies. She wouldn't be able to reason with the Athelian troops or the commanders along the border. Once they saw a dragon, they would consider her the enemy. What she needed to do was ride the cloud cover all the way to Erelas, the Athelian capital. Once there, she could begin her investigation into Athelia's connection to Melusine and go directly to the senate to plead for peace between their nations.

Octavia crouched behind a row of bushes, using the squeaky churn of the wagon wheels to disguise the tread of her boots through the mucky puddles that covered the forest floor. She only had one goal now: don't get caught.

She'd rather not have to contend with the Tenegardian military presence, but the fact that Northwood's soldiers were only now arriving irritated her a bit. It proved Northwood had been telling the truth after all when he denied her accusation of deploying troops to the border without the council's approval. All her efforts as a member of the council had been wasted. The only thing she'd managed to do was give Northwood and his supporters the perfect excuse to be rid of her. The bitterness of her thoughts must have caught Raksha's attention because a sweeping wave of reassurance trickled down the dragon bond.

I know you're still angry about that, Raksha said. *But the soldiers only now arriving do give us one important piece of information we didn't have before.*

What's that? Octavia asked, checking over her shoulder before she darted for the cover of another thick tree trunk.

We now know Serafine lied about the Tenegardian soldiers already being here and the reason your request for help from the Athelian sorcerers was denied.

You're right, Octavia replied, her thoughts drifting to the memory of the young Athelian senator she'd secretly spoken to using North-wood's communication device. *But why would she have lied? What purpose would it have served?*

I don't know what her reasoning was, but at least we know where we should begin our investigation.

Determined now to get to the bottom of Serafine's deceit, Octavia hurried through the woods, ducking low hanging branches. She kept her arms up, batting away water-lined leaves, when a voice rang out behind her.

"You there! Stop!"

Octavia did, skidding to a halt in the mud. She turned, her heart beating in her throat. Half-a-dozen Tenegardian soldiers had broken rank, crashing through the trees behind her.

All Octavia saw was the silver flash of their swords, and then Raksha was shouting inside her head. *Run, Octavia. Run!*

She didn't need to be told again. Octavia dashed between the trees, disobeying the soldiers as she made a break for the cave where Raksha was hiding.

"Halt!" a thunderous voice screeched after her. "By order of the Tene-gardian military!"

Oh, they're angry, Octavia said. She used her magic, letting it slither into the ground, digging up the earth behind her. She left massive divots in her wake. She spied over her shoulder long enough to see some of the soldiers get tripped up in her trap. Others hurdled the holes and kept running.

Octavia moved faster, whipping between the trees so quickly she was hardly looking where she was going. She clipped her shoulder on a gnarled branch and bit back the cry of pain.

Then, suddenly, something caught her ankle like a hand had reached out and grabbed it. It was a thin rope that had been thrown by one of the soldiers, wrapping around her leg. She fell hard, smashing into the earth with her chin, and for a second all she saw was sparkling stars. They winked behind her eyelids as a searing pain coursed through her jaw and pulsed at the back of her head like a lost heartbeat.

"We've got her!" one of the soldiers shouted. "She's down!"

Octavia dug her hands into the mud, pushing with all her might to right herself, but her head hurt and her ears rang and she wasn't moving fast enough. They were going to catch her.

I'm coming to get you, Raksha said.

No, Octavia argued. *Don't give yourself away. Right now, they probably think I'm some Athelian spy. They have no idea I'm a dragon rider.*

She rolled over, summoning an air shield as the soldiers approached. It rattled through the trees as she cast it away from her, stripping the branches of their leaves. It blew the soldiers back long enough for Octavia to kick off the rope and struggle to her feet. She started moving again, but stumbled into the first tree, holding it for support.

Her vision swam and, as a spell of dizziness caught her, she sank to her knees.

Behind her twigs cracked, the heavy tread of the Tenegardian soldiers growing closer and closer. This was it. They were going to catch her. She was going to have to answer to their superior. And beneath all the sweat and dirt that came from living outside these past weeks, they would recognize her as the supposed traitor Northwood banished. The exiled princess.

A massive roar echoed through the woods, sending a chill through Octavia's entire body. It was the most exhilarating and terrifying sound Octavia had ever heard, and her body reacted as if it had been given a charge of lightning. The dizziness subsided and a bolt of energy swarmed through her. It was Raksha's magic, filtering down the bond.

The Tenegardian soldiers had stopped at the sound of Raksha's roar, drawing their swords. The ground beneath their feet trembled.

"Dragon!" one of them shouted as Raksha burst through the trees, shearing massive branches clean off as she barged through the woods. Raksha growled at the soldiers and bared her teeth, each one long and pointed and white. The growl was so menacing, the soldiers actually began to retreat.

Octavia stumbled to Raksha's side and hoisted herself onto her dragon's back.

Hold tight, Raksha told her.

Octavia had just grabbed hold of the front of the saddle when Raksha exploded skyward. She smashed through the tree-lined canopy above, showering Octavia in a rainfall of feathery, green leaves.

So much for stealth, Octavia said as Raksha ascended upward. She didn't immediately head for the border but climbed higher and higher toward that hanging cloud ceiling. When they broke through it, Octavia took a gasping breath. The air was crisp this high up. As the ground below them disappeared in a fog of clouds, she let herself relax, but only for a moment. They were concealed from the soldiers below, but they still had to get across the border.

Raksha glided toward the invisible borderline between Tenegard and Athelia, and Octavia's next breath stuttered. If Melusine was watching the border, if she'd placed some sort of defensive magic upon it in order to catch dragon riders, they might be flying straight into a trap.

An anxious bead of worry clung to the dragon bond, each flap of Raksha's wings was fraught with uncertainty. Octavia scanned the sky ahead, looking for any sign of magical tampering. The shield at the school was visible from certain angles. She wondered if a spell left by Melusine would do the same.

Octavia's thoughts drifted back to Jeth Arenson and his dragon Zoya. Jeth was the spy she'd employed to gather information at the border for her. He'd taken some colleagues on his last mission, and they'd stumbled upon Melusine. Not only had she killed his colleagues, but she'd gravely injured Jeth and his dragon. The pair had barely managed to reach the palace in Kaerlin before collapsing. Tension ran through her. Octavia had sent Jeth on that mission. She was responsible for those losses. Her eyes roamed ahead again.

I think we're approaching the border now, Raksha said. They caught the occasional glimpse of the terrain below through the shifting clouds. Thankfully, it was never for more than a second, so the soldiers below would think Raksha's dark belly was nothing more than a thunder cloud.

I don't see or feel any signs of unfamiliar magic yet. They'd staked out this particular area for days, certain Melusine was no longer in the area, but that didn't eliminate a magical threat.

Raksha hummed in agreement, the sound rumbling down her throat and through her chest, the vibration passing beneath Octavia's legs. *If Melusine had left behind some sorcerous line of defense, I think we would have encountered it already.*

So we did it? Octavia asked. *We made it across?*

Octavia's momentary excitement passed down the bond, and Raksha indulged her happiness. *Welcome to Athelia.*

Octavia grinned, letting herself enjoy the moment, even though she'd been forced into making the crossing earlier than she would've liked. It had been a close call, but it was still the first win they'd had in the weeks since helping Cora destroy the hounds. Being banished from the council in Kaerlin had been a massive blow, hurting Octavia more than she let anyone know. Even Strida didn't understand the depth of the failure she felt. But today had turned into a good day. Today they were making progress. She didn't even care that those Tenegardian soldiers might have recognized her or that their departure from Tenegard was more conspicuous than they'd planned. She also didn't care that the soldiers would likely report back to Northwood about the dragon sighting. She was going to find her own path toward peace. The first step was understanding the link between Melusine and Athelia—since it was Athelian soldiers who had captured Octavia's informant Jeth at the border and taken him to Melusine to be tortured. The second step was uncovering why Serafine had lied to her. The senator had refused Octavia's request for aid weeks ago, claiming there were Tenegardian troops threatening Athelia at the border. But that wasn't true. After spending all this time staking out the border with Raksha, it was clear the Tenegardian troops had only started arriving in the two weeks since war had been declared. If she could accomplish those two goals while also making some true alliances in the senate, she might be able to convince them to stop this war.

Raksha soared above the clouds, gliding on the wind currents. *I think we're far enough past the border to dip down and get our bearings.*

Octavia was eager for her first true view of Athelia. *From what I remember from my studies, Erelas is not that far from the border. Certainly much closer than Kaerlin as a dragon flies.*

As they descended through the cloud cover, Octavia spotted the rolling green hills of the landscape. Muddy roads stretched beneath them, but it was the silhouette of the city on the horizon line that caught her attention.

That must be it. Raksha chuckled. *And here I thought we were going to have trouble finding it.*

It's huge, Octavia said.

Have you given any thought as to what you're going to say when we arrive?

Well, Octavia began. *I sort of figured I'd come up with something on the spot.*

Raksha chuckled again. Octavia could tell she was thrilled to be in the air. Sneaking around wasn't how dragonkind liked to handle their problems, and Raksha had grown weary of sleuthing along the border. The freedom was intoxicating, and Octavia basked in Raksha's good mood all the way to Erelas.

Where should we set down? Raksha wondered as her giant shadow eclipsed the buildings below.

There was no sneaking up on Athelia with a dragon, so Octavia opted for being fully transparent. If she wanted Athelia to trust her, they would have to do this right.

How about there, Octavia said, gesturing to a large courtyard where a company of Athelian soldiers gathered.

Looks like they cleared out the civilians just for us, Raksha remarked.

Just don't show them your teeth.

I won't unless they make me.

Octavia brushed at the mud caked to her clothes. *So much for looking presentable.*

What? You don't think they'll appreciate your mud-encrusted fashion choices? It's all the rage in the rebel circles.

Oh, ha ha, Octavia said, rubbing mud from her chin and picking bits of dirt out of the end of her braid.

Raksha circled the courtyard, descending slowly. A dive would make them think they were on the attack and Octavia didn't want that. They set down gently and Octavia slid from Raksha's back, taking a second to smooth the wrinkles from her tunic. Stars, she was a mess.

"Halt!" a soldier called. "You are trespassing on Athelian territory."

"We are here seeking asylum," Octavia called back, drawing on her best courtly formality. "We are outcasts in Tenegard and friends to Athelia." It was at least half true.

The soldier left his hand on the hilt of his sword but didn't draw it from its sheath. He approached Octavia, while the soldiers behind him remained at the ready. Judging by the amount of decoration and medals that hung from his uniform, he was their commander. "Historically, the dragon riders haven't been friends with Athelia."

"Well, this dragon rider is."

As the commander approached and she could see his face better, Octavia noted he was older. Perhaps as old as Northwood. His chin was covered in gray scruff, his forehead creased with wrinkles. She was grateful for his age, suspecting that's what gave him pause upon their arrival. Someone younger might have attacked without speaking first.

"And what does this friend of Athelia want?"

"My name is Octavia. I would like to request a meeting with Serafine, one of your senators. We have been in contact, and I would like an audience with her." Part of her actually felt like a traitor now.

Don't let yourself be swept away by those thoughts, Raksha said. *If posing as potential allies to Athelia will allow us to get close to the senator, we can uncover if she is working with Melusine and start to lay the foundations of peace. If Northwood and the council will not listen, maybe the other senators will.*

You're right, Octavia replied. She stood straighter, hoping to make her intent known.

"Strangers from lands that are currently arming their border for war against us aren't usually granted audiences with our senators." He smiled in a way that told Octavia he could be dangerous if pressed.

"And that is a good policy to have," she replied. "But as I said, I am here as an ally. I do not want war between our nations. Neither do the Tenegardian people. They should not be made to suffer for the decisions of a few. My hope is that together we can find a way to bring a peaceful end to the fighting."

The commander's gaze bore into her, like he was trying to stare through her. To see beyond her words. Octavia's fingers drummed against her thigh. What if he refused? Would she and Raksha be able to escape the courtyard before his soldiers attacked?

The commander stepped away to speak with his soldiers. One of them fumbled in his pocket for something that looked like a communication anchor. A quick discussion happened. Perhaps they were relaying her arrival to the senators.

I don't want to have to fight our way out of here, Octavia said.

Give it a moment. We don't know if that's what they're discussing.

Despite Raksha's assurances, Octavia took a few slow steps in the direction of her dragon in case they had to make a quick escape.

The commander turned around. "It appears that you are welcome here in Erelas. If you and your dragon would follow me."

Octavia and Raksha fell in line behind the commander. The rest of the soldiers followed at their flank. He led them to an upscale inn near a grand government complex. There was a haunting similarity to Kaerlin with the stone-worked courtyards and the fountains of sparkling water. But it was the buildings where Octavia really started to notice a difference, the architecture favoring thick, blocky lines and tall turrets from where soldiers scanned the streets below.

"Make yourself comfortable," the commander said, gesturing to the inn. "I will leave a detachment of soldiers behind for your protection or in case you should need anything before you meet with the senator."

Octavia understood what was happening. They were going to entertain the idea they were allies, but the soldiers were present to make sure she and Raksha never got *too* comfortable.

"Thank you for your hospitality," Octavia said, nodding her head and dropping into a quick curtsey. It would have been much grander in her palace dresses. Here, in her riding clothes, she probably looked foolish, but it worked and the commander departed.

Octavia turned to the inn. *Well,* she said to Raksha. *This is certainly the finest holding cell I've ever seen.*

CHAPTER 5

CORA

Alaric weaved between the tips of two giant pine trees, the conifers trembling as they soared past. Cora locked her legs against the saddle to keep herself from sliding, but just as her stomach dropped and her limbs began to float, Alaric straightened out. They'd started training before dawn, the remnants of night still lingering, painting the landscape navy. Alaric dodged a young dragon rider who came soaring up beneath them. They made a sharp dive to the left, and Cora heard the kid swear loudly, the sound echoing through the mountains.

That was close, Cora remarked.

I saw them coming, Alaric said. *Just wanted to give them a chance. I think it helps boost their confidence.*

Don't get cocky.

You don't actually think they could catch us, do you? He laughed, the sound vibrating through his entire body.

The beanbag Cora had tucked under her arm slipped but she managed to take hold of it again. The dragon riders were growing restless, so they'd had to get creative with training. This morning, Cora was the target. Well, technically the beanbag was the target, which made Cora and Alaric the current enemy. The training mission was simple: retrieve the beanbag by any means necessary. So far, it hadn't been going well for her riders.

As she entertained that thought, a pair of dragon riders approached from the front. Cora watched them raise their hands, magically summoning thick cloud cover.

Oh, this is a new trick, Alaric said.

Stay alert. I'd like to avoid any accidents.

Alaric twisted through the clouds, using his wings to bat them away. Dark shadows zipped around them. The dragon riders were closing in.

Cora stuffed the beanbag in her lap and cast a shield around her and Alaric. As she did, a spell crashed against her magic. It recoiled and Cora heard a yelp as the dragon rider had to retreat from their own spell.

As Alaric passed through the summoned clouds, they came face-to-face with Renka. Her lips were pursed, her gaze stern and focused. Alaric darted away and Renka dove after them. Her dragon was fast, but Alaric was faster, and he had more training. Alaric pulled out of the dive at the last second, forcing Renka to momentarily abandon her task as they regrouped.

Alaric zipped around a grove of trees, but Renka had doubled-back, and they narrowly avoided a collision. Cora felt the hairs on the back of her head ruffle and she knew they'd just missed a spell Renka had cast at them.

The girl didn't give up, though, and she resumed the chase. As Alaric rounded the other side of the grove, a familiar dragon slithered from between the trees. It was Lenire and Yrsa.

"Want to hand it off?" he called.

Cora launched the beanbag at him. Lenire caught it and zoomed off, ducking and weaving between the other dragon riders who were trying desperately to catch him. Cora turned to scan the training field. The sun was rising, a warm glow inching its way over the mountain peaks, bathing the tops of the trees in gold. Across the field she spotted Faron. He hadn't been permitted to join the training exercise, but Elaine had relented enough to allow him and Wyn to practice some basic flying drills in order to build up their stamina.

She watched them twist back and forth, going through the various offensive and defensive flying patterns. He looked strong this morning, his hair ruffling in the wind. Wyn kept them close to the ground, never more than a few feet between them and the snow-packed earth.

"Cora, watch out!" a voice shouted, and she hardly had time to turn around before Renka plowed into them.

Alaric snarled as he untangled himself from the other dragon, pushing off and soaring out of reach.

"She doesn't have the target!" Lenire called. He flew into view, holding the beanbag up for Renka to see, but the girl didn't stop her assault. Her dragon dove at Cora again.

Alaric managed to avoid the strike. *What do you want to do?*

Take us down. Take us out of the exercise.

Alaric did, and as Cora dismounted, she watched Renka and her dragon skid to a stop a few feet away. Renka dropped to the ground and immediately threw a spell at Cora. It missed but Cora felt the ripple of wind pass her. Faron came up behind her, and Cora conjured an air shield to protect them both.

"Hey!" she shouted as Renka's next spell crashed up against her shield. It bounced her back a bit, her boots slipping in the snow. "Renka, stop! That's enough."

Another spell hit her shield, so Cora recast it, determined not to let anything happen to Faron. He was still recovering. The last thing he needed was to be hit by a wayward spell.

Alaric stepped in between them, roaring so long and so loud that Renka dropped her arms and shivered. Even her dragon recoiled. Whatever had possessed Renka was gone. Instead, she glared at Cora. Lenire and Yrsa landed next to Alaric.

"She was tapped out," Lenire said to Renka, tossing the beanbag to her.

"Oh, I must have missed that," Renka said, obviously lying. She took the beanbag and climbed back on her dragon. "You did tell us never to let our guard down." Then her dragon leaped into the sky and the two of them rejoined the exercise.

"Let her go," Cora said as Lenire started to follow.

"She knew exactly what she was doing," Faron muttered darkly. "Is she one of the riders Emmett said is causing trouble?"

Cora frowned. "You've heard about that already?"

"Emmett's been filling me in." Faron caught her by the front of her traveling cloak and tugged her closer. "Are you okay?"

"I'm fine," she assured him as he brushed a few loose strands of hair behind her ear.

"If she's not going to follow directions, she's not going to make much of a dragon rider."

Cora sighed. "Renka's got a lot of … feelings about what happened at the school. I'm dealing with it. Or trying to."

"You don't have to do it alone," Faron reminded her. He pecked her on the lips.

Cora smiled in return, though she knew Renka's problem was with her alone. That made it her problem to fix. "I know," she said to pacify him. "Get back to your training so you can join us next time."

Faron squeezed her hand once, then set off with Wyn.

Cora turned back to Lenire as the sun finally crested the mountain peaks. "That's my cue," she said.

"You're sure you don't want help tracking the river?"

"It helps more to know that someone is here training with the dragon riders," she said. "And judging by the way that just went, they could use some additional supervision until the exercise is complete."

"Okay," Lenire said. "We'll keep at it."

"You'll keep an eye on Faron, too?"

"Don't worry, I'll put him to work."

"Nothing too strenuous," she called over her shoulder as she climbed up Alaric's back.

"I've got big plans for today!" Lenire shouted as Alaric lifted off.

Cora had no idea what Lenire had in mind, but as long as Faron was safe and he felt productive, she didn't mind.

Alaric swept across the field, lifting higher than the practicing riders, soaring over their exercise. Cora spotted Renka in the fold. The girl was watching her again. Alaric flew between two sun-drenched cliff faces, setting off in the direction they'd last located the river, and it was a long time before they spoke again.

You know it's not your fault.

Renka wasn't trying to go for anyone else. Just me.

Her anger is misplaced.

Is it, though? Disappointing the dragon riders that followed her was one of her biggest concerns. She wanted to be someone they could look up to. Someone they wanted to follow. So far, Renka was making it perfectly clear how she felt about Cora.

I think the girl and her dragon could do with a reminder about what it means to be a dragon rider. If we can't trust each other, we can't work together.

I think that's her problem, Cora said. *We're* not *working together. They've been cooped up in camp for weeks.*

That is still no excuse for her behavior.

I suppose not, Cora agreed as Alaric coasted toward a clearing. He didn't land, just hovered close enough for Cora to confirm this was the location of the last river connection. Then he pressed on, flying between craggy cliffs until they spotted another clearing.

This time Alaric touched down so Cora could confirm the river's presence.

She knelt, closed her eyes, and set her magic free.

"Do you feel that?" she asked Alaric, popping to her feet excitedly. The shock of energy was so intense Cora had barely let her magic sink into the earth before she recoiled. It was like being zapped by static. "It's getting stronger."

She scrambled up Alaric's back and settled into the saddle. They took off again, and Cora swore she could feel the river, even from way up in the sky, like a signal. It guided them forward, and the landscape beneath them turned green and lush.

Look at that, Alaric said, sinking until he could graze the tops of the trees with his claws. *The tree branches are bent.*

Cora looked where Alaric was gesturing. He was right. It was as if the river's magic was tugging on them, leaving them permanently shaped like a winding path. Using the trees as a guide, Cora could visualize the movement of the river far beneath the mountain's surface. A burst of energy surged through her, but Cora quickly realized it hadn't come from Alaric.

Did you feel that?

We must be getting close, Alaric said as he swept along the face of the next cliff.

As they came over the top of the peak, Cora caught a glimpse of a huge cavern in the next crag. *That's it!* she shouted inside her head. The Heart of Tenegard. The source of all its magic. *That must be it!*

Alaric flapped his wings hard, coming to a stop on a rocky peak. It was immediately obvious this was where the river had led them. The magical current they'd been following spiraled around them so palpably, Cora felt like she could reach out and touch it.

Alaric took to the air again, hurrying toward the opening of the cavern, but the closer they drew, the more resistance they faced. *It's stronger than the fiercest of headwinds,* Alaric said, his thoughts sharp and focused. He landed again, setting down on another rocky peak. *I can't get close to the source.*

They were so close, Cora could see into the mouth of the cavern. *Wait,* she thought to Alaric. *Maybe the resistance will be less if we approach on foot.*

Alaric scrambled down the side of a rocky ledge, but the resistance was still too much. Cora slid from his back. *Let me try alone,* she said.

I'll approach from behind. Alaric lifted off, making a sweeping circle above her. He dove back toward the cavern, and Cora watched as he was halted mid-flight by the resistance.

Cora darted down a steep bluff, then made her way toward the cavern. Hope bloomed in her chest. She reached a flat expanse of rock and started running. No sooner had the hope blossomed than it fizzled. Her legs suddenly weighed a thousand pounds, and she fought for every step.

Alaric struggled his way to her side. "Whatever enchantment is protecting the Heart is too strong."

"Perhaps we need some magic of our own," Cora said. She conjured an air shield, tossing it at the cavern, but the shield simply bounced off the protective defenses.

"Dragon Fire?" Alaric asked.

Cora nodded and together they directed a stream of raging fire at the mouth of the cavern. The spell didn't bounce the way she feared it might, so there was no need to duck out of the way of their own fire, but instead the defenses seemed to brush away the spell like it was nothing more than cobwebs. The flames fizzled into streams of smoke, drifting away on a mountain breeze.

"I don't think this is working," Alaric remarked.

"Maybe …" Cora said as an idea came to mind.

"What are you thinking?"

Cora cast a shield around her and Alaric, honing it until it was like a second skin around them. "Maybe we can shield ourselves and push through the barrier."

For a moment, Cora thought it might work, but then the shield dissolved as the cavern's defenses threw off her magic.

"If we can't get inside, can we at least shield the Heart?" Alaric wondered.

"You mean hide it?"

He nodded and Cora used her magic, first to conjure a layer of cloud cover that might conceal the entrance to the cavern. It blew away faster than she could cast the spell. Next she raised the earth, pulling dirt and rocks over the cavern like a granite wave, but even that didn't work, the rock crumbling to dust. Defeat rang inside Cora like a toll bell. They'd come this far and now nothing they tried was working.

"Cora, don't be discouraged," Alaric said. "This is a huge win. By finding the Heart, we've solved a major piece of the puzzle."

"I know," she said, trying to muster a smile. "And it feels amazing to finally have something to show for all our work tracking the river." This was the object of their quest. "But if we can't get inside, and if our magic does nothing more than bounce off it, how do we possibly defend it from Melusine, Zirael, and the Blight?"

CHAPTER 6

CORA

I *don't think we should tell the other dragon riders about finding the Heart,* Cora said as Alaric lifted into the sky. She could feel his confusion slither down the bond as they climbed higher and higher, twisting through the lingering mountain fog.

You don't want to share news of our success?

Not just yet, Cora explained. *After what happened this morning with Renka, it's obvious tensions are still high.*

But perhaps some good news would help cool those tensions, Alaric suggested.

Maybe. Or it might make the dragon riders even more restless. And I don't want to announce the discovery of the Heart and start a dozen wild rumors until we at least know what we're working with. At this point we can't even get inside.

Alaric kept his thoughts hidden, the place in her mind where she could usually hear his internal monologue going strangely blank. They crested a long ridge of cliffs, sweeping across the mountaintops. *Perhaps you are right,* he said after a while, his words careful and considered. *I didn't like the way Renka behaved this morning. It was foolish and dangerous and might have ended badly.*

Cora didn't think Renka would have actually been able to hurt her. Cora was a seasoned fighter, both with magic and without. Besides, it's not like she'd really tried to defend herself. All she'd done was throw up a shield. Then again, if Cora had truly fought back, Renka might have been injured. And she didn't want that either. She wanted her dragon riders to trust her, not fear her.

If we are to avoid another incident, Alaric continued, *we should prepare a proper explanation. And that will require more time and research into the cavern.*

I agree, Cora said, glad they were on the same page. Right now, they needed to get back to base camp, regroup, and come up with a new plan for getting inside.

I do think you should tell someone though. Lenire and Faron perhaps. Maybe Elaine. This is a heavy discovery to carry on your own. It's okay to share that burden.

The corner of Cora's mouth quirked. She had a bad habit of trying to do everything alone. That's what Alaric was trying to tell her.

You trusted Lenire and Elaine with the real reason you and Strida were dividing the dragon riders. I think you can trust them with this.

You're right, Cora said.

Alaric dove quickly, proving he was as agile as ever. Cora's stomach flipped and her arms grew weightless and she threw them out on either side of her, basking in a moment that felt like freefalling. She laughed as Alaric twisted and turned through the mountains. She hadn't really given herself a second to enjoy the discovery. To be excited their mission was finally coming to an end, she hadn't even congratulated herself on a job well done. Standing before that cavern had almost felt too good to be true, and then when they'd been unable to enter it, Cora's panic and worry and fear had returned, eclipsing any sense of relief.

But now, in this moment, Cora realized there was room for both. She could be worried about the Heart and relieved they'd found it.

She could take a moment to celebrate their win.

By the time they returned to base camp, the hot afternoon sun beat down, melting the lingering snow, and Cora was forced to shed the heavy shawl and fur-lined gloves she'd grown used to wearing in the mountains. Sweat clung to her neck, dripping down the back of her tunic. Cora wiped at it as she made her way toward her father's tent.

She stopped at the infirmary tent first, looking for Faron or Elaine, but neither of them were around. Cora was surprised by that. She was certain that after letting Faron practice his flying drills this morning, Elaine would have ushered him back to the tent for some rest and recuperation. She supposed she shouldn't be surprised Faron refused to lie down. He was eager to return to duty in any capacity. He'd probably talked Elaine into letting him go hunting or something.

When she reached her father's tent, she pulled the flaps of the tarp back to find he was also missing. She turned to the firepit where her father usually kept the coals hot. They were gray and chalky. Cora bent down and lifted the lid on the pot that was normally bubbling by the time she returned from the mountains. She poked her finger into the stew. It was sludgy and cold.

"Strange," she muttered under her breath. She rose and squinted into the sun, studying the camp. Had something happened while they were gone? Perhaps the school had sent word. Or maybe Strida had a message delivered from the capital. It could even be Octavia, reporting that she'd finally managed to cross into Athelia. Of course, any of those things could spell bad news.

Cora, Alaric cut into her musings. *Meet me at the pit. I think this is something you're going to want to see.*

What is it?

Just get over here.

Cora hurried in the direction of the pit where they kept the hound, and as she did, she realized she wasn't the only one on her way there. Excited whispers flitted through the camp as the other dragon riders started to converge on the area. Cora picked up her pace, almost sprinting between the meandering riders. When she arrived, huffing from the exertion, there was already a crowd at least three people deep. They surrounded the pit on every side, the excitement in their voices spiking with worry and the occasional short-lived yelp.

She spotted Alaric on the other side of the pit. He stood with Yrsa and Wyn, their hulking forms like three small mountains. *What's going on?*

Alaric gestured below and Cora fought her way to the front of the crowd. "Make a hole," she said, shoving riders aside. "Let me through."

Cora startled when she reached the edge of the pit, jerking back from what she saw. Below her, caked in mud, were Faron and Lenire. They stood in the center of the pit, eyes locked on the hound as it ran the perimeter. Its movements were sloppy, like it wasn't sure which limb to pick up first, and it stumbled every few feet. Instantly, it reminded Cora of Alia, the girl from the village who'd had her body possessed for a short time by the Blight.

"By the stars," she muttered to herself. The last she saw of the hound, it was barely animated, wandering aimlessly and bumping into walls.

Now it was moving purposefully again, like new life had been breathed into it, apparently under Lenire's direction.

"Cora!" Faron called, spotting her in the crowd.

"What's going on here?" she asked.

"Isn't it amazing?" Faron's grin widened. A surprised bubble of laughter poured out of him as the hound crashed against the wall of the pit. It righted itself, taking a moment to gather momentum before it propelled itself forward, even faster this time.

Exclamations of mingled awe and worry whispered through the crowd around her. Amazing wasn't exactly the word Cora would use for it.

"Can you get it to jump?" Faron asked Lenire who stood next to him, arms out and fists tight, like he was clinging to long strings. Whatever Lenire was holding was invisible to Cora, making her think it was some sort of knotted Itharusian spell. When Lenire had used the disk to help restore her bond, he'd cast a spell on her limbs to help guide her in ridding her bond of the Blight's influence. Perhaps he'd used a similar technique here to take control of the creature.

Lenire gritted his teeth, his eyes narrowed as he opened his palms and focused his invisible magic in the direction of the creature. It gave a pathetic little hop, its limbs barely coming off the ground, but Lenire and Faron were enthused.

"Let me try again," Lenire said. "I think I can do better." This time the hound jumped before stumbling and rolling in the dirt. Faron and Lenire grinned at each other.

Cora shook her head. "I'm not sure you should be messing with the creature like that. We might not fully understand what it's capable of." She still remembered the first time she'd encountered the creatures. Two of them had descended upon a mountain village, hunting for the crystal deposit. Luckily, Cora and Alaric had managed to keep them corralled in the market square. Even using all the magic to keep the hounds confined, they'd still caused untold destruction and injury. The last thing Cora needed was to give this thing another opportunity to hurt anyone.

"Does it look dangerous to you?" Lenire said, manipulating his hands so the hound paused beneath Cora. It rose up on its hind legs, scratching at the side of the pit, a flood of soft mewls issuing from its mouth. She didn't know if they belonged to the creature or if they were of Lenire's making. A shiver ran through her. She didn't like the idea of messing with Melusine and Zirael's creations. She wanted to learn from it, and she was grateful for the role the hound had played in waking Faron, but this was too much.

"No," Cora said. "And that's exactly the problem." Underestimating Melusine and her creations wasn't something Cora was going to do again.

"This is a major breakthrough," Faron exclaimed. He moved to the edge of the pit, and Cora bent down to speak with him. It wasn't exactly private, but it was better than shouting at each other. "With the hound severed from its creators' influence, Lenire found a way to actually pilot the creature."

"Pilot?" Cora said, her lips flattening into a thin line. "Don't you mean possess?" Cora knew a possession when she saw one. She'd had enough experience with the phenomenon recently.

"Well, yes," he admitted. "It's a form of possession. The connection with the main bulk of the Blight is gone, but Lenire is able to possess the harmless fragment of the Blight that remains inside the hound. The way he is able to manipulate it, gives us the ability to steer the hound."

Cora didn't know what to say, but the uncertainty must have been written across her face because Faron reached up and took her hand, threading their fingers together momentarily. "There's nothing to worry about. Let us show you."

With that he released her hand and took a step back, making room for Lenire to pilot the hound up the side of the pit. With its mangled claws, it scraped and scratched its way free, climbing the muddy bank. The crowd of dragon riders gasped, parting as the hound crested the ledge. The riders left a giant berth around the hound. All except Cora. She stayed exactly where she was, watching as the creature trotted around the edge of the pit.

They'd freed it from its prison all to prove a point, and though Lenire appeared to be in complete control of the creature, Cora's hand fell to her sword, wrapping around the hilt in preparation. She wasn't sure what she expected to happen, but she was ready in case the creature lunged unexpectedly. Even the most enthusiastic of spectators had shied away, moving to stand in the shadows of their dragons.

The hound approached and as it did, Cora caught a whiff of its putrid, rotting stench. Despite the animation, the creature was wholly dead. That didn't stop her from counting every one of the ragged teeth that jutted out over its swollen jaws. "That's close enough," Cora said, taking a step back to steady her stance. "*Lenire*."

At the last moment, the hound slowed its approach, dipping its head over its front paws. Then the entire creature laid down, almost on her boots. Cora could feel the energy radiating from it. It was mostly Lenire's Itharusian spell. She'd become accustomed to the feel of his magic these past weeks. But there was something else. Something eager to react. To serve. That had to be the remnant of the Blight, looking for some sort of magic to cling to.

"Look at the control he has," Faron said.

The only thing their demonstration had done was unnerve her and prove this creature could be used to get close to them. "How can you be sure it's safe?"

"Don't you see?" Faron said with a giant smile. "This puts us in command. For the first time we could be using the Blight to help our cause, instead of having it wielded against us."

Their intentions were good, yet Cora feared the unknown. She could tell Faron was crestfallen by her less than enthusiastic reaction, but she didn't care. Someone needed to be the voice of reason here. They needed to take this new discovery slowly.

"We wouldn't have attempted such an experiment without being absolutely certain," Faron said. He climbed up the side of the pit. Lenire scrambled after him, guiding the hound back to its feet. It began to duck past the riders, running between the tents like a dog begging for scraps. "I never would have put you in danger like that."

"I never thought you would," Cora assured him. "But magic comes with certain limitations. I guess I just wonder if we really know the limitations of this yet?"

"That's a fair concern," Faron said. "But those answers will only come with trial and error. And think of the possibilities. We could take the hound out for a reconnaissance run. Lenire could direct it to scout around the nearby village."

"I'm worried the sight of the hound might stir up fear in the villagers," Cora said.

Faron chuckled, squeezing both her shoulders. "We'll be careful to keep it hidden, of course."

"It would be a good test run," Lenire called over his shoulder. He'd stopped a few feet away, where he had a good sight line to direct the creature through the camp. "Low stakes. No real enemy activity."

"I don't know," Cora said, though she could feel herself softening to the request. This was the most lively Cora had seen Faron since waking him in the infirmary. She liked the excitement in his voice. She liked that he and Lenire seemed to be becoming fast friends. Maybe a quick loop around the village wouldn't hurt.

But just as she thought it, Lenire grunted, teeth bared, his legs bent and shaking as he struggled to maintain control of the hound.

"What's going on?" Faron asked, immediately running to Lenire's side.

"I don't know. I think it might have veered out of range. We haven't tried to control it at this distance yet." Lenire's boots inched through the mud, almost as if the creature was using Lenire's magic to propel itself forward without direction.

The hound crashed right through a tent, tearing apart bedding and dishware, forcing a couple of dragon riders to dive out of the way.

"Can you bring it back?" Faron asked.

"I'm trying," Lenire said, fighting the pull of the hound and his own magic.

"Here," Faron said, casting a spell of elemental dragon magic. He pulled a rocky pillar from the earth, giving Lenire something to grab on to. Lenire let go of his hold on the hound with one hand and used his free hand to cast a knotted spell around Faron's anchor. Together they managed to drag the hound back within range of Lenire's spell and the creature immediately toppled over, simply a mass of undifferentiated flesh without Lenire's guidance.

"Everyone okay?" Faron called.

"All good," came the chorus of replies.

Lenire was on the ground, heaving. Faron reached down to help him up. They looked at each other for a beat, then broke into laughter.

"Do you think there's a way to extend the range?" Faron asked.

"It might just be a matter of having more points of control," Lenire suggested. Clearly, they were both eager to attempt their experiment again. "Or maybe we could do something with an anchor point," he said. "That was a quick bit of magic you did there."

"By the stars, are you two listening to yourselves?" Cora interrupted. "After what just happened?"

"No one was hurt," Faron said.

"But they could have been," Cora said. "You both know firsthand the dangers that come from messing around with the Blight. I'm worried you might risk falling prey to it for the sake of some experiment."

"That's not what this is," Lenire tried to assure her. "I know the dangers and that means I know when I'm at risk."

"And I know my absence was difficult for you and you want to protect me," Faron said. "But this is a fight, Cora. We need to use everything we can to our advantage."

She shook her head. "I don't think manipulating the hound is a good idea."

They kept trying to convince her, talking over her and each other, the excitement and enthusiasm rising to a boiling point. Cora felt like her head was going to explode.

"There she goes again," a voice murmured. Cora looked over her shoulder in time to see Renka whispering to another rider. "Stepping all over everyone else's good ideas. Might as well put her boyfriend back to sleep if she's going to treat him that way."

Anger roiled in Cora's blood, and it took every ounce of control for her not to turn around and blast Renka off her feet.

"Cora?" Faron said, waiting for an answer.

She opened her mouth to respond, but she didn't know what to say.

She wasn't trying to control Faron, she just didn't want to see him hurt again, and the last time he encountered the Blight, he'd almost died.

CHAPTER 7
OCTAVIA

Octavia wasn't a fool. The guards in the square were watching her, and they were armed. She knew better than to think the Athelian military would leave a Tenegardian councilor and a dragon alone at an inn within walking distance of the senate building, but the thing that amused her was the fact Athelia thought they were being discreet. Since their arrival, a group of soldiers had been stationed around the inn and in the courtyard where she'd come to wander while waiting for Serafine to accept her request for an audience. This morning, more guards had been added to the roster. Some of them were even dressed in plain civilian clothing instead of that now familiar Athelian uniform.

She could tell they were soldiers by the way they carried themselves. Back stiff. Arms rigid. A hand always hovering over their concealed weapon. Even now, four different undercover soldiers swapped out positions around Raksha who was lounging in the courtyard under a patch of sun. The truth was these soldiers stood no chance against a dragon. Luckily, Raksha was not here to stir up trouble. They had nothing to worry about so long as their weapons remained at their sides and not in their hands.

A knock on her open door drew her attention. It was the Athelian commander she'd met upon arrival. Octavia dipped her head in greeting. "Commander Dolan. Please." She gestured to a chair by the hearth. Her accommodations were fitting for a visiting ambassador, giving her plenty of room to entertain company.

Dolan entered but didn't sit. He remained standing, the glittering accoutrements on his uniform reflecting the daylight that streamed in through Octavia's window.

"I trust you are enjoying your stay?" he said, joining her at the window.

"I am. And I trust your company of soldiers are enjoying their new posts?"

Dolan's lips curved at the corner. "You have to understand that the senate would have my head if I left you unattended."

Octavia had grown used to the faces of the soldiers who guarded her. She could have picked them out of a crowd if she had to. But Commander Dolan's was the most familiar of all. "You've already divested me of my weapons," Octavia pointed out. "How much damage could I do?"

"With a dragon at your beck and call?"

"She means Athelia no harm," Octavia said.

"Even if that is the truth, we Athelians are not so far removed from the happenings in Tenegard not to know dragon riders are often incredibly gifted. You do not need a sword in your hand when you have magic. We have many reasons to fear you."

"Is that how the Athelian people feel about the dragon riders? Are they afraid?"

"Wouldn't you be? You command creatures of myth."

Octavia chuckled. "I do not command Raksha any more than she commands me. The bond between a dragon and their rider is the deepest of friendships. She is not an animal I had to tame." Dolan absorbed that. "In fact, until recently, Raksha even held a place on the Tenegardian council."

"My grandmother used to whisper to me stories of the Tenegardian dragons. Stories her grandmother told her. Mind you, this was a long time ago, back before you were even born."

Octavia hummed under her breath. "And what did she say?"

"That the dragons were mighty but peaceful creatures. Until ..."

"Until what?"

"King Onyx."

Octavia's entire body flushed with an icy chill. "Onyx the Deathless," she said, almost to herself. Sometimes she managed to forget she'd been raised by that man. That she'd sat by while he tormented the citizens of Tenegard.

"We believed Onyx had twisted the dragons for nefarious purposes. That he was creating an army. And we trained and prepared for the day he would come flying across the border."

"He tried to create that army," Octavia said. "But we stopped him."

Commander Dolan hummed to himself. "You're different than I ever could have imagined."

"Not the snarling, fire-breathing demons you were told to expect?"

"No," he agreed.

Even if this was the only thing she accomplished during this mission, Octavia was glad to have changed at least one mind about Tenegard's dragon riders. But then something dawned on her. "That's why the courtyard has remained empty since my arrival," Octavia said, finally understanding. "You're keeping the civilians away."

Erelas was a larger capital than Kaerlin. She'd wondered where all the people were. Most of the shops had been closed, their doors bolted and windows dark. Now she knew why. They'd cleared out this square just for her and Raksha. And besides the staff who ran the inn, or the guards who stopped in for a meal, no one else had set foot on the property.

"It was a risk mitigation strategy."

"Wouldn't it be better for the people to see for themselves that we mean no harm? That Raksha is not a threat? My intention is to broker peace between our nations. That will be immensely harder if the people are fearful."

Dolan tipped his head back and forth, considering her words. "Let's see how your conversation with the senator goes. After that, I will talk to my higher ups, and perhaps we can consider reopening the square to civilians and letting businesses resume."

"She's agreed to see me?" Octavia asked, unable to keep the tremor from her voice. Suddenly reopening the square felt like a trivial request. She wasn't nervous per se, but she'd be left alone in this inn long enough to start agonizing over what she would say if Serafine ever agreed to the audience.

"She has in fact. That was the reason for my visit."

"Am I to go to the senate hall?"

"No," Dolan said. "It has been decided that Serafine will hold her audience here."

"That's why you've increased the military presence in the square!"

"Not much slips by you." His lips twitched. "I'll leave you to prepare." He walked to the door, pausing to add, "She's requested to meet you outside in the courtyard. With guards present." With a brief nod, he was gone, and Octavia started panicking.

The entire plan she and Raksha had come up with required investigating the link between Athelia and Melusine. Part of that now meant figuring out why Serafine had lied to them about Northwood moving troops to the border. But Octavia and Raksha also needed to earn her favor. If Octavia had any hope of determining whether Melusine was working with Athelia, she needed to have the freedom to investigate, and that wouldn't happen if Serafine was suspicious. She and Raksha would be locked up or tailed everywhere they went. And if they remained at odds, then peace between Tenegard and Athelia would never amount to anything more than words.

You better get down here, Raksha said, cutting through her spiraling concerns. *It's probably best if I'm not the first one to greet her.*

Octavia ran her hands down her front, smoothing the lines from her tunic. She missed her palace wardrobe, not for the fineries, but because of the confidence it gave her. But here she wasn't Octavia the councilor. She was Octavia the dragon rider. And she would have to find confidence in that. She put her shoulders back and marched from her room, down the winding staircase that led to the dining area, and out the front door of the inn.

Octavia joined Raksha in the courtyard, watching the procession approach. It wasn't much, just Serafine flanked by four Athelian soldiers, but in her dark robes, Serafine cut a stern, commanding figure, and Octavia leaned into her dragon bond, frantically clinging to any bit of reassurance Raksha had to offer.

It's no different than any other council meeting.

Right, Octavia said. *It's just a council meeting.*

"Octavia!" Serafine greeted her as soon as she was within earshot. The angles of her face were harsher in person, but there was a familiarity there Octavia couldn't place. It wasn't only the fact that she'd seen her on the other end of the communication device in Northwood's communication chamber, but for some reason Octavia had the sense that they'd met before.

"Good morning," Octavia said. "Thank you for meeting with me. I know you must be incredibly busy."

Serafine waved her hand and the soldiers who were trailing her stopped. She took a seat in one of the wicker chairs that filled the courtyard immediately outside the inn. Octavia did the same. "I apologize that you can't be allowed to address the full senate. Unfortunately, mages are not permitted inside the building."

"Oh?" Octavia said.

"Yes, they are forbidden, in fact. Since Athelian magic could all too easily be used to sway opinions, all senators are carefully screened for magical ability."

"That's quite impressive," Octavia said. Even without magic on his side, Northwood had managed to bully himself into a place of absolute power on the Tenegardian council. She didn't even want to imagine what he could do with a little bit of magic.

"Hmm," Serafine said, and Octavia felt the discussion shifting. "Commander Dolan has been keeping me informed of your conversations. He claims you come to speak of peace between our nations. Last we spoke, peace didn't seem to be something Tenegard wanted."

Serafine was hinting at the lie she'd fed Octavia. There had been no Tenegardian troop movements at the border. No war declared. But there had been Athelian soldiers on the wrong side of the border—soldiers who had aided in Jeth's capture and his colleagues' deaths. Of course things were different now, but back then Serafine had lied when she said Northwood was moving against them.

Play the game, Raksha whispered inside her head. They'd talked about this. About what cover story they would use with Serafine. Octavia asked herself what would be believable coming from a banished councilor. As far as Serafine was concerned, Octavia was here to broker peace but also to reclaim control of her country.

"I know it appears like the Tenegardian council is playing games with you," Octavia said diplomatically, "which is why I offer my allegiance."

"Dolan mentioned that you'd been banished."

"An Athelian sympathizer is what they called me." Octavia let her words sink in for a beat, hoping Serafine was buying her story of the jilted former princess.

"You speak of peace," Serafine said. "But how exactly do you intend to achieve such a thing?"

Octavia had thought long and hard about what she meant when she spoke of peace, and she had her answer ready. "In exchange for my allegiance, I'll need the senate's support in taking back control of Tenegard."

"Once we've won the war, you mean?"

"Yes," Octavia hurried to agree. She didn't actually intend to help Athelia win the war by working against Tenegard. There should be no winners and losers in this fight, only a ceasefire on both sides. But she could tell Serafine would reject the idea of a ceasefire when Tenegardian soldiers were still lining the borders, so Octavia would have to build to the idea slowly, once she'd garnered more senator support and investigated her other questions. But until then, she needed to sell the idea that she was fully committed to Athelia's cause. "Northwood cannot be allowed to maintain the control he has over the council nor Tenegard's military. He must be stopped."

"Not to mention that Northwood continues to make moves against the dragons, attempting to corral and control the dragon population," Raksha added.

Serafine's eyes widened at the sounds Raksha made. For the first time since Octavia met her, Serafine seemed genuinely caught off guard, that perfectly practiced I of control slipping. Octavia supposed having a dragon grunt and snarl at you would be unnerving. To Serafine's ears, that's all it was, so Octavia translated before the waiting soldiers grew uneasy.

"Ah," Serafine said once she'd understood. "He doesn't seem to understand the concept of an ally, does he?"

"Not quite," Octavia said. She tried for a smile but Serafine didn't return it. Instead, she crossed her arms, reclining back in her chair. There was still a wall between them, Octavia realized. One fraught with suspicion.

"How do I know you mean what you say?" Serafine asked.

Octavia swallowed hard, glancing at Raksha who gave a subtle nod. They'd also discussed what they would say should Serafine demand proof of their loyalty. Which of Tenegard's secrets could Octavia reveal without hurting anyone she cared about. Octavia knew the price of Athelia's help would be intelligence, and she was prepared to part with it. "Because I can tell you about the division that exists within the Tenegardian council. I can tell you which of the former rebel leaders still oppose Northwood. I can tell you which councilors are least invested in the war."

"Let's start with that," Serafine said, leaning toward her. "Give me a name."

"There's Strida," Octavia said. "She's recently replaced me as an advocate for the dragons and a representative for our dragon-rider school."

"You say she doesn't want the war?"

"None of the dragon riders do."

"But they will fly to Tenegard's aid should Northwood command it."

Octavia bit her lip. She couldn't be certain of that. "The dragon riders do not answer to Northwood." Giving these bits of information away felt strange, but Octavia needed to balance the truth of her story. If she wanted to get close enough to Serafine to figure out why she lied to her the last time they spoke, then she needed her cover story to be plausible. Though she still had to be careful not to give away anything genuinely harmful about Tenegard, or even Northwood himself. She wanted the man removed from power, she didn't want him dead.

"I can't help but notice that the information you've provided me is relatively low-stakes," Serafine said.

Octavia lifted a shoulder. "I need proof of your good faith as well."

Serafine reclined in her chair again, considering Octavia's words.

"But if it helps to convince you," Octavia said, "Strida is my partner, and I would never expose her to danger without very good reason."

Though it was clear she still wasn't completely convinced, Serafine nodded as if to say that Octavia had satisfied her for the moment. "I'm pleased that you've turned up." She got to her feet and the soldiers around them came to attention. Octavia rose as well. "As my act of good faith, I'll withdraw my soldiers from around your lodgings. You'll be free to move about the city."

"Thank you," Octavia said, wary of how easily Serafine had offered up that freedom.

"I do think we're going to make good allies." Before Octavia could agree, Serafine added, "So long as you can demonstrate your trustworthiness to me."

"How exactly do I do that?"

Serafine came closer, her words barely audible. "By spying on the pacifist movement among the public in Erelas. They will welcome you if you present yourself as a double agent. I already have my suspicions about who is helping them from within the senate, but beyond the government, they've eluded me."

Octavia hesitated. She hadn't intended to get mixed up in Athelia's own civil matters. She was here to investigate the link between Melusine and Athelia, discover why Serafine had lied to her, and to broker peace. Spying for Serafine felt like a dangerous way to prove her trustworthiness, and she couldn't help but feel that she'd been outplayed.

If she refused, Serafine would immediately be suspicious of her, and she might even revoke Octavia's freedoms, making it more difficult for her to get her own answers. If she agreed, she was playing right into Serafine's games. Games Octavia didn't yet have all the rules to. It was a complicated decision, but Octavia straightened her spine, pulling on years of royal training to maintain an even expression. "Very well," Octavia said, stamping down the disappointment she felt —she'd given up information about Tenegard and gotten nothing except complications in return. That was not at all how she'd intended this meeting to go, but if it was the only way to earn Serafine's favor, what choice did she have? "I'll see what I can learn from these pacifists for you."

"Excellent," Serafine said, glancing around to make sure no one overheard. "I'll call upon you again soon and we can talk logistics."

CHAPTER 8
CORA

It took both Faron and Lenire's combined strength to drag the hound back into the pit. Without Lenire's guiding magic, it really was just a mass of useless flesh, and the entire thing slumped back over the edge of the pit they'd dug, hitting the ground with a hard thump. The creature made no sound, and when Cora peered over the edge, its limbs jerked as if dreaming. It remained in that half-conscious state, posing no apparent threat.

"All right," Cora called to the remaining dragon riders who had lingered to watch the end of the experiment. "Clear out. Back to your tasks."

There was a muttered complaint from some of the riders who'd much rather watch Faron and Lenire mess around with the hound than collect firewood. Cora didn't care. She hurried them along. There were only a few good hours of sunlight left, and she was eager to use them to return to the cavern that held the Heart of Tenegard. She'd hurried back to base camp in order to tell her inner circle about her discovery, only to be sidelined by Faron and Lenire's experiment with the hound. But that was over now, thank the stars, and she had her chance.

"Can I talk to you?" she asked Faron and Lenire as they scrambled up the side of the pit once more. They both exchanged a guilty look, like they expected her to chastise them again about messing around with the hound this much.

"I know you're not a fan of this idea," Faron began. "But I really think if you were to give it a chance, you'd see the possibilities that are—"

Cora cut him off. "That's not what I want to talk to you about."

Faron's jaw remained open for a beat. Finally, he said, "It's not?"

Cora glanced around. "We've talked about the hound enough. I know we're not exactly on the same page about it, but I think we can let that topic rest for today. There are more important things I want to discuss."

"Hey," Faron said, catching her hand. He squeezed, pulling her attention back to him. It felt like it had been ages since Cora had Faron to worry over her, or even to bounce ideas off, and it almost startled a sob from her. "What's wrong?" he asked gently.

"Nothing's wrong, per se. Just a complication."

"Then who are you looking for?" Lenire asked.

"Elaine and my father. They should be included in this conversation."

"Elaine watched the experiment for a while," Faron admitted. He still hadn't released her hand, instead running his thumb over her knuckles. "But since she couldn't find any reason that I would be overexerting myself, she gave up trying to convince me to go back to the infirmary tent."

Over here, Alaric cut in. *Your father and Elaine went with a group to trade supplies from the village. They're returning now.*

Cora twisted in Alaric's direction. It was difficult to pinpoint him in base camp with so many dragons about. She spotted Yrsa first, her Itharusian coloring unique among the Tenegardian dragons, and where Yrsa went, Alaric usually followed. "Come on," she said to Faron and Lenire. "Elaine and my father are on the path from the village. Let's meet up with them and—"

"You found it!" Faron said suddenly, like he'd read her mind.

Lenire's head snapped around in her direction, his eyes wide. "The Heart? Really?"

Cora's mouth stretched into a thin line. It felt like less of a win considering she and Alaric had failed to get inside the cavern, but it was hard to be disappointed in herself when they both sounded so excited.

"We found it," Cora said, confirming that it was real.

"Why didn't you start with that when you first got back?" Faron exclaimed.

Cora gestured at the pit. "You two were a little preoccupied with this whole hound situation."

"I think this news outclasses what we were doing," Lenire said.

Faron barked a laugh. "I'll say." He was giddy, and even Lenire cracked a tentative smile.

As they hurried across the camp, a dark shadow passed over them. It was Wyn, flying low. Faron had likely summoned her for this conversation. She landed in a clearing up ahead, walking over to join the other dragons.

When they arrived, they found Elaine and her father waiting with Alaric, Wyn, and Yrsa, and Cora wasted no more time. She launched into her explanation surrounding the Heart: how they found it, the surplus of magic that surrounded the cavern, and her difficulties getting past it.

"My magic didn't work to break through the cavern's defenses," she finished. "But Alaric and I only have access to Tenegardian magic."

"The same magic that Heart is made of," Lenire said. His arms were crossed, his head lowered, deep in thought.

"Exactly," Cora said. "Maybe the Heart is able to fight off my magic because it's similar."

"So you want us to try?" Lenire said.

Cora nodded. "I think both you and Elaine should return with me. That way we can test both Itharusian and Athelian magic against the cavern. Maybe one of your spells will work better since your magic isn't drawing from the same source we're trying to access."

"I'm coming too," Faron said.

"Now hold on," Elaine began. "Your recovery is going well, Faron, but I'm not sure setting off into the mountains is what you should be doing just yet."

"You might need an extra set of hands," he argued. "Or perhaps Cora simply needed more magic. And I know you both think I'm going to keel over at any moment, but I've got magic to spare. I'm coming with you." He waited for either of them to argue. Cora glanced at Elaine but the healer merely shrugged. "In fact," Faron continued then. "Having more hands on deck to consider this magical situation might be a benefit."

"You mean more than just you, Elaine, and Lenire?"

He nodded. "I think it would go a long way to establishing more trust with Renka and the other …"

"Troublemakers," Lenire finished for him.

Cora tutted. She didn't like using that word to describe them, but sometimes it fit. Renka's words from earlier, the ones that suggested Faron might as well have just stayed asleep since she was apparently walking all over him, surfaced in her mind. And with it came anger. But beneath the anger she held for Renka was fear. Their numbers were small after separating from the school. The last thing she needed was to inadvertently put her faction of dragon riders in danger. "I want to know more about what we're dealing with before we go involving the other riders. There are unknown elements at play here. I don't need a repeat of what happened to you in the mountains."

He smiled softly at her. "You can't avoid *all* risk in this kind of fight."

"Not all of it," she said. "Just the worst of it."

"Okay," Faron agreed, deferring to her decision. "Then we should get going. We're wasting daylight."

And with that it was settled. They mounted their dragons, Elaine settling behind Cora, and then they were skybound.

"Whoa!" Faron said as they landed in the mountains.

Cora hadn't wanted to bring the group too close at first, but even from a distance it was easy to feel the overwhelming magical charge radiating from the mouth of the cavern. Cora had grown accustomed to the feeling in the weeks she'd been tracking the Heart, but for Faron, whose last encounter with the river had been before the Blight had attacked him in the mountains, it was a lot of energy to contend with.

"Are you okay?" she asked him as he dismounted Wyn.

"I feel great," he said. "Like I'm supercharged. Sort of the way you feel right before you unleash Dragon Fire."

Cora knew what he meant. The same energy coursed through her. It was similar to being gifted energy through their dragon bond, only stronger, more potent. She supposed they were siphoning that right from the source of Tenegardian magic, so it was as rich as it could be. "Please promise not to overexert yourself. If you need to take a break or put some distance between you and the cavern, do it."

"Cora," Faron said. "Don't worry about me. Wyn and I won't push our luck."

"Okay."

"I wonder if the sensation of the Heart's energy is as strong for the others, or if our dragon magic makes us susceptible to it?"

"It's not just you," Lenire said, walking over to them. "I can feel it too." He lifted his arm, his sleeve pulled back. Goose bumps spiraled across his golden-brown skin and the tiny hairs there stood on end. Lenire replaced his sleeve. "This place is dripping in magic. I suspect even a non-magic wielder would be able to pick up on the energy."

"Did you see the way the trees were bent?" Elaine said. "It's like all living things are drawn to this place."

"A lifeblood," Cora said.

"It's fascinating."

"It would be even more fascinating if we could get near it," Cora remarked.

Lenire gave his shoulders a shrug, shaking off the cramps of dragon flight. "Let me give it a try, I have an idea." He marched toward the mouth of the cavern. Yrsa stayed where she was, lowering her head, watching Lenire's every move with sharp focus.

"You're just going to walk up to it?" Faron called after him. "That's your big idea?"

"Yeah. The gist of it." Lenire drew his sword from its sheath. Then he started running. Cora held her breath as he darted between spiked rocks. As he drew near, his sword came up, and Cora knew he was preparing to strike. Then all at once, his hand fell to his side, the blade of his sword striking the ground.

Lenire dropped his sword and tried to push forward, but that invisible magical energy kept him from advancing. He lifted his legs, over and over, staring down at them.

"Heavy, aren't they?" Cora shouted at him.

Lenire backed up a step, until he regained control of his weighty limbs, then twisted his hands in that familiar way. Cora knew he was conjuring Itharusian magic. She imagined more of those knots she'd seen the times she'd linked to Lenire's magic using the disk. He tossed invisible spells at the Heart's defenses, but judging by the look on his face when he turned around, nothing was sticking.

Finally, Lenire picked up his sword and retreated in their direction. "I'm not done yet," he said as Cora opened her mouth to speak.

"Okay," she murmured under her breath, her lips twisting to keep from smiling. Accessing the Heart was proving to be impossible, and though part of her was growing more anxious by the minute, she couldn't help but be amused by Lenire's darkening mood. His entire demeanor turned stormy as he scrambled up Yrsa's back. The two of them took off like a shot of lightning, exploding upward so fast Cora and Faron had to duck out of the way of Yrsa's wings.

"What do you think he's trying now?" Faron wondered.

Cora had one guess: Dragon Fire. They watched as a red hot stream of flames burst from Yrsa's mouth, clawing through the sky toward the cavern. But just like when Cora and Alaric had tried the same thing, the flames dissipated to nothing more than smoke before they got anywhere near the cavern.

"You already tried this, didn't you?" Faron guessed.

"Oh yeah," Cora said, watching Lenire and Yrsa spiral around the cavern. They approached from different angles: head on, behind, from either side, and even directly from above. But each time they were halted before they could reach their goal.

Lenire returned, scowling at his failed attempts.

"At least now we know it's impervious to all magic, not only Tenegardian," Faron said.

"Well, don't write me off just yet," Elaine said. She'd maintained a safe distance, staying perched between Alaric's shoulders, but now she made her way toward the cavern. Elaine was less physical than Lenire, more focused on testing the boundaries of the magic, but even her sophisticated Athelian powers had no effect.

Elaine returned, red-faced, and even though Lenire didn't show it as much, Cora could tell that they had both been overwhelmed by the currents of power coursing through the area just as she had.

"No luck?" Cora said.

Elaine sighed. "I attempted to bypass the magic, to gain entry into the cavern. That didn't work. Then I attempted to cast a protective spell over it but my magic was swept away by that current we can feel pulsing everywhere. You won't often find me admitting this as far as *life* is concerned, but I am too limited to influence a living force so vast."

The hair on Cora's arms prickled, and she shivered at Elaine's words. She supposed that's really what the Heart of Tenegard was—a thriving, magical life force. That didn't help ease the sense of defeat that swelled inside her chest. Cora hadn't had high expectations when they left the base camp, but between the four of them she thought there might have been a small glimmer of progress. She felt worse now than she had earlier when she and Alaric had failed to get past the defenses on their own.

"What about casting a shield around it?" Elaine wondered. "Like the one we cast around the school?"

"Using our magic in tandem worked for that," Cora agreed.

Lenire shook his head. He was perched higher up on a rock, scanning the landscape surrounding the cavern. "The surrounding terrain is too dangerous. By the time we found safe anchor sites for the shield, we'd be too far away from the cavern for the spell to stand. Besides, I have a feeling that any spell we try to cast over the cavern, no matter how high, will be brushed away. It would be a lot of work for nothing."

"There's something we're missing," Cora said, slumping down on a rock. Alaric came up behind her and nosed her gently. His warm breath on her shoulders mixed with the bead of hope he'd sent down the bond to her.

We'll figure it out, he promised. She leaned into him, soaking up his reassurance.

"Maybe there's something back at the school," Faron said. "Additional resources."

"The crystals," Cora said, "but I don't see how that helps us."

Faron kept throwing ideas out. "Maybe the council has started allocating military supplies to the school."

Cora thought she remembered Octavia mentioning that there were stockpiles of military supplies deep in the palace in Kaerlin left over from Onyx's reign. Again, she didn't see how that was helpful. The look on her face must have said as much because Faron frowned. "I was thinking about a weapon or something that might bypass the Heart's magic," he said.

"I know, I'm sorry." Cora reached for his hand. "They're good ideas. I just don't know what to think right now."

"You know, you don't have to be the only one solving this puzzle," Faron said.

Cora tried to smile. She knew that too. Only, it felt like her job. She'd carried this responsibility since the first dragon rider had succumbed to the Blight's sleeping sickness. And she'd come too far now to do anything but see it through.

"Perhaps I could return to the school and do some discreet investigating," Elaine suggested. "If there's anything that looks promising, we can figure out how to get it to the mountains."

Lenire had been quiet and Cora turned to him. "What's on your mind?"

"I was thinking … It's no wonder Tenegard's enemies want to destroy a source of such power."

Cora agreed, distressed by the thought. If Melusine and the Blight got to the Heart and figured out how to bypass the enchantments, that would be the end of the dragon riders. Cora would be responsible for both beginning and ending the second wave of dragon riders in Tenegard.

"I guess we can be comforted by the fact that if none of us can get close to the Heart, then maybe it's able to defend itself," Faron said.

"You only know some of what the Blight is capable of," Lenire told him. "I don't think we can dismiss it just yet."

Faron turned to Cora, looking for her support, but all she could do was agree with Lenire. "If you'd seen what it could do, you'd insist on protecting the Heart at any cost. Plus, Melusine and Zirael are both powerful sorcerers. There's no telling what they might be able to do if they make it this far."

"Then here's an idea," he said, looking at Cora specifically. "And before you dismiss it, hear me out. What if we test our hound against the barrier blocking us from the Heart?"

Lenire slid down from the rock he was perched on. "The hound's magical construction is radically unlike anything else we currently have access to."

Cora started to shake her head.

"If Melusine's hounds have the ability to get past the Heart's defenses, wouldn't you rather learn that from a hound we can control?" Lenire added.

Cora massaged the ache in her temples. She was about to refuse their idea flat out, but she hadn't even considered Melusine using her own hounds against the barrier. Her jaw tightened as she looked from Faron's eager face to Lenire's serious one. They had no other plan forward, and if this was it, Cora owed it to everyone to try. "I suppose, at the very least, we should test out the hound. It would be good to be able to eliminate them as a potential threat against the Heart's defenses."

Lenire and Faron shared a look, then jumped into action. As they prepared to head back to base camp to solidify their plan and retrieve the hound, Cora caught Lenire by the wrist and pulled him aside. "You don't think doing this poses a risk to the Heart, do you?"

"Cora, everything we try could be risky."

"I know," she said. "But not everything contains a fragment of the Blight." The last thing she wanted to do was be the person responsible for destroying the Heart of Tenegard.

CHAPTER 9
CORA

They brought Elaine back to the cavern the next day in case there was trouble. Cora really hoped they didn't need a healer, but she thought it was better to be prepared just in case.

"Set the hound down here," Faron called, waving Alaric over.

Alaric lumbered between the rocks to the outcropping and dumped the sack containing the hound down unceremoniously. For the moment the creature was only a lump of flesh. It wasn't until Lenire's magic took control of it that the hound came to life.

Everyone watched as his fingers twitched, like a puppet master, and the hound responded by trotting back and forth. "Just getting the hang of it again," he said when he caught Cora's eye.

Once he had smooth control over the hound, Lenire had the creature sit down on its haunches.

"What are you waiting for?" Cora asked.

"I have an idea. It might sound ridiculous—"

"We're standing outside a magical cavern that refuses to let us in," Faron pointed out as Elaine chuckled. "I think we're past the point of caring if something sounds ridiculous."

Lenire inclined his head as if to say, *okay then.* "I'm wondering what would happen if I lock my spells onto more than just the creature's limbs."

"What do you mean?" Cora asked.

"I think if I weave my spells into the hound's optic canal, we might be able to see through its eyes."

Cora frowned. It sounded tricky and potentially dangerous. Lenire gaining sight through the hound somehow meant it was also connected to his eyes. She glanced at Elaine who looked to be pondering the same concern.

"Why stop there?" Faron asked, his tone laced with excitement. "Let's try optics and auditory. Then the hound could literally be our eyes and ears."

Lenire lit up at Faron's support.

"Let's try it," Faron continued. "We won't know the limits of your control otherwise."

"Wait," Cora said, interrupting their discussion. "Don't we still have an issue with range? I'm glad you're excited to test this out, but shouldn't we focus on one problem at a time?"

"We think we've solved that problem."

"What?" Cora said. "How?"

"We might have stayed up last night and taken the hound for a few more test spins."

Cora pursed her lips to keep from saying anything she'd regret.

"It was perfectly safe," Faron insisted, holding his hands up as if to keep her from exploding. "I had the dragons supervise. If anything bad happened, they had orders to take the hound down."

Cora looked over her shoulder at Alaric. *Did you know about this?*

I might have stumbled upon Wyn and Yrsa supervising the experiments and offered my help.

You didn't think to wake me?

It was very safe, Cora. I assure you none of the other dragon riders were at risk. Besides, if we hope to make it past the cavern's defenses, a certain amount of proficiency is required when controlling the hound. There would have been no point attempting this today if Lenire and Faron couldn't maintain control over the creature.

Cora grumbled inside her head. She didn't like finding this out after the fact, but as she thought about it, she wondered if maybe Renka was right. Maybe she wanted too much control over everything.

Trust that I would have woken you if the need arose.

I know you would have, Cora said. She trusted Alaric implicitly. If he said there was no need for her to be there, then there was no need. When she broke from the conversation with Alaric, both Lenire and Faron were staring at her.

"Don't be mad," Faron pleaded with her. He came to stand beside her, his hands ghosting up her arms to anchor on her shoulders. "We're trying to help. I may not be the greatest dragon rider or warrior right now, but I *can* do this."

Cora caught Elaine's eye, saw the briefest of nods, then glanced back at Faron and sighed. She hated that she was inadvertently hurting his confidence. She was just going to have to let go of a little more control and hope everything would be fine. "I know you can." She summoned a supportive smile. “Now show me how exactly you and Lenire plan to increase the hound’s range.”

All at once they broke into a maddening explanation, talking over each other with so much speed Cora and Elaine were both lost. Cora held her hand up to call an end to the cacophony and requested they start again but keep it simple.

Faron let out a deep breath. “Basically it boils down to an anchor.”

“Like the one you created yesterday when you were trying to reel the hound in?”

“Something like that,” Faron said. “But instead of magicking a physical object for Lenire to hold on to, I cast my Tenegardian magic around one of his knotted spells. This allows him to essentially reel himself in and out, and gives me more control over how tight I hold onto him. Here, we’ll show you.”

Lenire drew an X into the dirt with his foot.

“This gives me a reference for where his spell will be attached,” Faron explained as Lenire cast an invisible knotted string at the ground. This time when Faron summoned the earth, he didn’t create a handle for Lenire, but instead piled the rubble and dirt around what Cora imagined was the invisible string of Lenire’s spell. “Does it feel secure?” Faron asked Lenire.

“Yeah, pretty good,” he said, tugging as if to assess the tension on that invisible spell. Lenire walked away from the anchor, looking behind him as if to see where he was trailing the string that Faron now anchored to the ground. Cora had to admit this would have all been easier for her to understand if they still had the disk. Then she would be able to see the world the way Lenire did when he was using his magic.

"Okay," Lenire said. "I'm going to try extending my spells to the hound's optic and auditory center."

Faron summoned more earth around his anchor point, strengthening the connection. "Ready!"

Cora couldn't see the invisible workings of the magic, but she noticed when something happened by the way Lenire and Faron both startled. It was as if something had raced toward them quickly and they'd been forced to duck out of the way. "Are you okay?" she asked as Faron straightened.

His mouth was open, and Cora heard Lenire say something in his own language — words she didn't understand.

Elaine approached quickly. "Faron?"

"By the stars," he said under his breath. "It worked. It actually worked the way we thought it would."

"You can see it?"

A laugh bubbled out of him. "I'm connected to Lenire's magic, so I can see what he sees through the hound."

"Fascinating," Lenire said, one arm extended toward the anchor, the other extended out toward the creature.

"Do you think if I—" Cora started to ask, reaching to place her hand on the anchor.

The second she touched it, the shift in her vision was stark and sudden. It was grainy, as if she were watching through a filter of glass. Maybe even two filters. She gasped, pulling her hand back, but the vision didn't fade. She was still connected to Faron's magic, and like when she'd shared memories in the past, they didn't need a constant physical link to experience it. Faron was sharing his magic with her freely and even now that she was disconnected from the anchor, she would continue to see through him until one of them severed the connection. Apparently, all that practice sharing magic and memories in the mountains before they knew about the Blight or Melusine's treachery was coming in handy now.

"That's us seeing through the hound's eyes," Faron said excitedly.

"And Melusine can't see any of this?" Cora said as an errant worry filled her mind.

"No," Lenire said with certainty. "That connection was severed when we used the hound to wake the dragon riders."

Cora stood impossibly still, watching the hound's foot strike the ground. Then the other foot shot out, clawing at the earth as it picked up speed. The hound raced around them, and a gloomy gray filter swam over everything. That was until Lenire forced the hound's head up and daylight highlighted the mountains. Cora saw herself and Faron and Lenire and Elaine through the hound's eyes. More than that, she could finally see Lenire's Itharusian magic again. She saw the thin strings of his magic coiling through the hound. She traced it back to his right hand where the strings knotted around his fingers or anchored into his palm. She traced the other string from his left hand straight back to Faron's anchor point. As he pushed the hound farther and farther away, the string between him and the anchor stretched.

"Will it break?" Cora wondered.

"It hasn't yet," Faron said, though he was making minute adjustments to the anchor with his own magic. Letting off slack. Holding tighter. They were like one being, working together to keep control of the hound.

"Are we ready to give this a shot?" Lenire called.

Cora felt Elaine at her shoulder. She'd left the relative safety of the dragons and come to observe. Cora reached down and found Elaine's hand, pushing her magic into the healer. The moment Elaine gasped, Cora knew it had worked. She'd extended the grainy image of what the hound saw.

"Ready!" Cora and Faron called at once.

Lenire broke the hound from its path and steered it toward the mouth of the cavern. As they approached, Cora expected the hound to run up against resistance. She'd no sooner thought it, then the hound crumpled against that invisible barrier.

"Wait, did you see that?" Lenire called.

Cora blinked, wondering if it was a trick of the light. Lenire nudged the hound against the barrier again and this time the previously invisible defenses blurred into a streaming floor of colorful elemental magic. It reminded Cora of the shield around the school. On a sunny day, at just the right angle, she could glimpse fantastic colors.

"This is the barrier we encountered," Cora called.

Lenire attempted to steer the hound through it again. The colors seemed to converge on the spot the hound nosed at. Then all at once the color shot out across the barrier like a flash of Dragon Fire and he cried out. Cora herself could feel the turbulent surge of magic sweep across the mountains. It was like getting caught by the river. Cora broke from Faron's shared magic and the sight line of the hound just in time to see Lenire struggle back to his feet. He wobbled from side to side, overwhelmed by the dizzying churn of that magical current. The hound staggered back and forth along the border, tangled in the same sweeping flood of magic.

Beside her, Faron worked frantically, spiraling the anchor of Tenegardian magic around Lenire's spell. Little by little, Faron pulled Lenire back, dragging him and the hound out of the magic. By the time Lenire reached the anchor, laying a hand on it, he was gasping.

"It's like a lifeline," Elaine said.

"At least we know it works," Faron added, bending down to take a look at Lenire. "How're you feeling?"

Lenire straightened up, shaking off the sensation of almost being swept away. Cora reached out to help steady him. "Glad the anchor was there. Looks like it was an important little innovation."

Faron grinned. "That's high praise coming from you."

Cora swelled with pride at how Faron lit up at Lenire's compliment. His confidence had clearly taken a beating since waking from the sleeping sickness and she hadn't done anything to help that. When he insisted they try again, she didn't have the heart to refuse him. "If Lenire thinks he's up for it," she said when they all looked at her.

"I am," he assured them, setting himself up again by securing his spells.

Faron released some of the tension on his anchor, letting Lenire stretch the range of the hound. This time Cora gave Faron a boost of her own magic to strengthen the lifeline that connected to Lenire.

"Elaine," she said. "Can you use your healer magic to give Lenire a boost of mental clarity?"

"I'll do you one better." Elaine put one hand on Cora's shoulder, linking herself to everyone. Cora felt that cold thrill of healer magic wash over her amid a burst of awareness. Elaine was providing mental clarity for them all.

"Here we go," Lenire called, sending the hound toward the barrier again. This time as the defenses attempted to brush the hound away, sending currents of magic sweeping over Lenire, he stood steady and strong. It was like he could finally see clearly through the onslaught of magic fighting to keep the hound out. Perhaps he was even steadied by Cora's added support. Inch by inch, Lenire forced the hound through the magical current to the other side of the barrier.

"Oh my stars," Elaine murmured.

Through the hound's eyes, Cora caught a brief, distorted glimpse of rivers of light and bridges of rainbow flecked stone surrounding a single pool of water. It shimmered and then the vision shifted. Disjointed slices of the cavern came into view, each one flashing by before she could grasp the whole picture. Even anchored by their combined magic, the effect was overwhelming, and after that short exposure, the hound was forced back through the barrier. Faron reeled Lenire in as fast as he could, pulling them clear of the flooding magic. The moment he reached them, Cora felt herself sag in relief. She hadn't realized just how tense she'd been trying to bolster Faron's magic.

Lenire sat on the nearest rock and for a moment they all just reveled in how spectacular the sight of the Heart of Tenegard had been. Cora replayed her thoughts over and over again for Alaric to experience, but something worrisome beat at the back of her mind.

Then Lenire cleared his throat. "As fantastic as that was, we now know that if our hound can make the journey across the barrier, Melusine and Zirael's hounds will likely be able to do the same. And unlike ours, they'll be able to summon the Blight to destroy the place and devour its magic."

"All they need is that brief glimpse inside and it's all over," Faron said.

Bile caught in the back of her throat and Cora struggled to swallow it down. "That tells us all we need to know, then. We have to find a way to get inside before Melusine shows up." The task of protecting the Heart was more urgent than ever.

CHAPTER 10

OCTAVIA

I*magine if Serafine brought all forty-eight senators to meet with you*, Raksha said.

Thankfully, there's not enough room to accommodate them all here. Octavia lifted the delicate cup of tea that was balanced on her lap and raised it to her mouth. She took a polite sip to disguise her sizing up the eleven senators who currently occupied the courtyard of the inn. Her eyes flashed between the elegant chairs and fancy settees spread around the sunny courtyard, studying the interactions between different senators. If being on the council had taught her anything, it was that in any group, sides were always chosen. All she had to do was figure out which of the senators' ideals aligned with her own.

It was a bit overwhelming considering the only faces she recognized were Serafine, Commander Dolan, and the smattering of Athelian soldiers who had been stationed around the inn since their arrival. Serafine had kept her promise, allowing Octavia the freedom to explore the square by pulling back her soldiers, but she felt sort of cheated. At the rest of the senate's insistence, the military presence was never gone completely—a dragon was too big a threat to leave unattended. It was another complication she was going to have to contend with if she hoped to be able to slip away long enough to do her bidding without alerting the soldiers or the rest of the senate to her movements. If Serafine was going out of her way to employ a spy, she obviously meant to keep her discoveries secret from the other senators until she had concrete information. Octavia was still waiting for the other woman to summon her to discuss the logistics, and she'd wondered if today might be a test or an attempt to familiarize her with persons of interest. Without knowing Serafine's true intentions, Octavia planned to use the meeting to her own advantage to determine key alliances between the senators.

"And you, Octavia, how are you liking the tea?"

"Oh," she said, breaking from her thoughts long enough to look down at her mostly full cup. "It's very lovely indeed."

"It comes from our northern parts. A remote region really, but beautiful. Most Athelians consider it to be one of our finer teas. I would think former royalty would have expensive tastes," one of the senators said. He was a bulbous man, balding from the center of his head. "That is what you consider yourself is it not—*former royalty*?"

Octavia wore her best placating smile. "I've been called many things since the fall of Onyx. Rebel princess. Dragon rider. Councilor. I find no one title suits me best."

"A woman who wears many hats," Serafine said, lifting her cup in Octavia's direction.

"But it must have been a difficult adjustment," the man continued. "Going from having everything to … flying around on dragonback."

His insinuation that she was somehow lacking now she was no longer Tenegard's princess irked her. But there was no explaining how fulfilling the bond between her and Raksha was, or how she would escape with Raksha from the palace one hundred times over if it meant they were together. She would wear the title of rebel happily because in the end, it brought her to her dragon.

Octavia opened her mouth to respond, but before she could, Raksha climbed to her feet. She'd settled outside the courtyard to avoid disturbing the senators during their visit, but she was well aware of the conversation thanks to the telepathic bond she and Octavia shared. Raksha made a show of unfurling her wings all the way before stretching in the direction of the senators, her sharpened claws grazing the stonework pathways beneath her feet. Octavia lifted her cup again, hiding her grin behind it. Raksha was just showing off now, reminding the senators who the biggest threat in the room really was. To prove her point, Raksha threw her head back and yawned, showing off each of her dagger-like teeth. Then she shook all over, curled up, and settled back down, perhaps a little closer to the courtyard than she'd been before.

Octavia heard the eager scrape of chairs as the senators attempted to put some additional space between themselves and Raksha. Most had settled under the shade of trees to get out of the sun, but with Raksha drawing closer, they braved the sun once again.

Clearly my presence here is making some of them uncomfortable, Raksha said.

Well, that's what happens when you threaten someone, Octavia pointed out.

I never threatened anyone, Raksha said, though her tone was amused. *I merely wanted to get more comfortable. Besides, I promised I would be nice, I never said I wouldn't show my teeth.*

I know you were just trying to stick up for me.

I will not tolerate old, ignorant fools who like to toss around their power to belittle others.

Nor will I, Octavia said. *But if we want to get some answers—*

You do not have to make yourself smaller in order to secure the information we need. You are *the rebel princess who helped bring down a tyrant. You* are *a dragon rider. And though you have been banished, you are* still *a councilor of Tenegard, and you are doing what's best for your country.*

Or trying to anyway, Octavia thought. She sipped her tea, noticing most of the senators were still either staring at Raksha openly or stealing nervous glances over their shoulders.

"You know," the bulbous senator said loud enough to capture Octavia's attention as well as everyone else's. "It's unfair of you to use your dragon to throw us all off balance." He chuckled as he said it, perhaps meaning it as a joke, but the shifty look in his eyes told Octavia his intention was serious.

Serafine sighed. "Liddel, can't you see there is nothing to worry about?"

Raksha responded directly to this, her low growls sending Liddel right out of his chair.

Octavia swallowed her laughter before translating. "Raksha merely wishes you well, Senator Liddel, and she wants to assure you all that she is merely here with the intention of representing dragon kind. She hopes to prove to you that dragons are really not as frightening as you've been taught."

"A diplomatic dragon," Liddel muttered as he took his seat again, one hand clutching his chest. "Now I've really seen it all."

A chorus of laughter echoed through the courtyard and Octavia caught Raksha's eye. *As long as Liddel doesn't keel over from a heart attack, I think that little display might have won some of them over.*

Did you ever doubt my charms?

Octavia returned her attention to the senators to find Serafine watching her. The woman didn't immediately look away, so Octavia smiled and picked up her tea, breaking eye contact. For someone who wasn't a dragon rider, it sure seemed like Serafine was interested in whatever conversation Octavia and Raksha were having.

"We apologize for being nervous," one of the senators cut in. She was tall and thin, with wispy hair that fell to her shoulders. "For most of us here, this is the first time we have seen a dragon, especially this close."

"No need to apologize, Senator …"

"Jangoor."

Raksha growled lightly and Octavia smiled at the senator. "Raksha assures you she is not offended. Dragons get much the same reaction in Tenegard."

That earned Octavia another chuckle from the group, though her attention was on Serafine again, who watched the exchange, smiling a little. She cleared her throat, capturing an audience with the other senators. "I could hardly have Octavia in Erelas as a guest and a refugee while denying her dragon the same courtesy."

Murmurs of agreement sounded and Octavia took careful note of which senators seemed to gravitate toward Serafine. Liddel chuckled until his face was red, muttering "Of course, of course." But Jangoor and the senators who sat with her only smiled politely at the comment.

I think I'm picking up on tension, Octavia told Raksha. *Especially between Serafine and Jangoor.*

It was bound to reveal itself eventually.

For the most part, the senators Octavia had met so far had varying reactions to Serafine's presence. Some had been embarrassingly obvious in their eagerness to please, while others maintained a cool neutrality. And then there were those who lingered on the other side of the courtyard, scowling each time Serafine spoke. If Octavia could pick up on the discontent, then they were doing a poor job of concealing their dislike.

"I think we can agree on the importance of a united senate when it comes to who we allow refuge in our country and more specifically in our capital." Mentions of a united senate received fervent support from the assembled senators, even those who previously looked to be in obvious opposition to Serafine. "We will not allow discord to divide us on the topics that truly matter, like those cursed pacifists, who are to be rooted out at all costs."

Serafine caught Octavia's eye then and did not look away. Was she trying to tell her something? Were there pacifists among them?

Liddel laughed boisterously. "'At all costs' is a little on the nose, don't you think? Considering the sums we've been pouring into the military coffers lately."

"Where else should the money be going when Athelia is threatened?" another senator cut in. He sat close to Serafine, making his loyalties clear.

Liddel lifted his hands up. "I only meant that the money we sank into those defective war engines might have been a mistake."

"Mistake or not, it sounds like you mean to stir up discontent."

"They're merely facts," Liddel said.

"True facts," Jangoor added. "Which we can discuss and debate at length among ourselves so long as the truth about how much money we've invested in the defective engines remains within the senate and away from the public."

Octavia's thoughts churned a mile a minute. Despite the division that existed within the senate ranks, it was clear most of the senators wanted to preserve the illusion of Athelia's military strength and prowess. She couldn't fault Jangoor for wanting that, especially during wartime.

"I don't question Liddel's loyalty," Serafine commented casually. Liddel rolled his eyes and gave an ironic little salute with his tea. "But he has a good point. A person's spending habits can certainly reveal embarrassing secrets. Though, of course, I'm sure nobody here has anything to hide."

Her comment lingered over the group like a weight. Even Octavia, who had nothing to do with the spending habits of Athelia's senate, felt called out for her deception. Yes, she wanted to secure alliances with the senators who may be open to a peace treaty between their countries, but she also still had to investigate her suspicions about Athelia's involvement with Melusine, as well as get to the bottom of Serafine's lies. Somewhere in the middle of all of that, she'd also become Serafine's personal spy.

"That's a lovely dress," Serafine said to one of the other senators, shifting the topic smoothly to something more inconsequential, blatantly ignoring the chill her words had cast over the group. Octavia watched as the senators avoided eye contact with each other.

Being afraid seems to be something they all have in common, Raksha pointed out. Octavia could tell she was a little disturbed by the turn of events.

"There was something I wondered about," Octavia said to the group. Now seemed as good a time as any to cut into the conversation.

Serafine cocked her head.

"When I requested aid to help Tenegard address the sleeping sickness at the dragon-rider school," she began, "what turned the vote against us?"

Jangoor cleared her throat. "In more peaceful times, perhaps …" Her words drifted into nothingness as Serafine shifted in her chair.

"We had no choice but to vote as we did," Serafine said. "Considering the intelligence we received about the Tenegardian military presence at our border."

Octavia swallowed hard. This was the same lie Serafine had originally sold to her. Octavia had never questioned her about it. "But that information wasn't true," Octavia said. "There had been no *Tenegardian* troop movements at the border." She let her emphasis on the word Tenegardian be slight, and she watched Serafine for any sign that might reveal she knew Athelian guards had been on the wrong side of the border when they'd captured Jeth.

Some of the senators shifted uncomfortably, looking anywhere but at Octavia and Serafine. Jangoor was most obvious of all, hiding behind her teacup.

"Yes," Serafine said coolly. "It's a shame our intelligence turned out to be premature. Though clearly it was true in spirit even if it wasn't yet true in fact."

I think she knows more than she's admitting, Octavia said to Raksha. *What if the information about the Tenegardian troops being on the border wasn't premature, but instead fabricated by Athelia? Did that mean they wanted this war?*

They're all hiding something about that vote.

Or maybe Serafine's premature intelligence came from a true enemy of Tenegard. Melusine could have fabricated a lie about troop movements. Maybe that's why she captured and interrogated Jeth with Athelian soldiers present. Melusine didn't need Athelia's help to capture one dragon rider. But by having them there, she could spin the interrogation out of control, making the soldiers think a dragon rider at the border signaled the presence of other Tenegardian military forces. Those Athelian soldiers would have immediately reported that back to the senate.

Of course, that's assuming Athelia isn't purposely working with Melusine, Raksha pointed out. *Serafine or any number of the senators could be exchanging information with her. We still haven't determined whether an allegiance exists there.*

What we need is proof that Melusine has been in contact with the senators, Octavia said. *For all we know, she might have simply used guards dressed to look like Athelians in order to spark rumors to incite Northwood.*

Clearly, there's more going on here than a simple miscommunication about the border. So we keep playing their game. Raksha growled out loud, drawing the attention of the senators.

Octavia paused a moment before translating, realizing Raksha was playing along. "Despite the unfortunate turn of events caused by that premature information, Raksha hopes to show Tenegard that they might one day find allies in the Athelian people."

"Yes, well," Serafine said, "that day certainly feels very far off."

None of the other senators challenged Serafine's statement, the group falling into uncomfortable silence as they sipped their tea and ate their biscuits.

Raksha returned to their private conversation. *The Athelian senate must be as bitterly divided as the Tenegardian council. They just work harder at concealing that fact.*

All the talk of unity is a farce, Octavia agreed. *I wonder what kind of blackmail or back-channel deals Serafine is using to keep the others in line?*

Well, there was that obvious dig about spending habits. So, she's got dirt on someone.

As the meeting came to a close, the senators began to bid Octavia and Raksha farewell. When it was just Serafine left, she flitted to Octavia's side. "So, what did you think?"

"Everyone was lovely."

Serafine laughed loudly. "You know that's not what I'm asking."

Octavia ran her finger over the edge of her cup. If she was going to uncover the truth of Melusine's involvement and Serafine's lies, she needed Serafine to trust her. So she took a chance to pick away at the cracks of division she'd noticed. "I wonder how sincere some of the senators' professed commitment to unity really is."

Serafine nodded. "You're quite right. I have suspicions about most of them myself, and their involvement with the pacifist movement, but I can't prove anything yet." She got to her feet. "That's where you come in. I'll call on you soon, and once you get me the information I need, it's only a matter of time before one of them makes a misstep."

The moment Serafine was gone, Octavia fled the inn. There was another formal dinner organized that night, and Octavia needed to clear her head. She set off into the market square, knowing she was being watched. However, the city seemed to be even more on edge than she was, and as she shuffled by people, someone shoved a leaflet into her hand. This was what the people were buzzing about. This anonymous leaflet being circulated through the square. Octavia smoothed the wrinkles from the paper, finding it to be a screed against the senate's corruption. It talked of the senate's willingness to feed Athelia's youth and resources right into the maw of war. It all seemed to be fairly harmless protesting until she saw the line about all the money foolishly spent on defective war engines.

So much for keeping that information within the senate.

CHAPTER 11

CORA

"Elaine should be back any moment."

"Is that why you've been standing here for the past hour?" Faron asked, climbing to the rocky shelf where Cora stood.

It looked out over their base camp, but it also gave her a perfect view of the horizon. She'd be the first to spot a dragon. "I want to make sure she gets back okay."

Although it was only the school, Cora sort of felt like she'd sent Elaine into enemy territory. She knew she was wrong for thinking it of the other dragon riders, but she couldn't help herself. Elaine had aligned herself with Cora's cause, and that might make her a target. Cora didn't need anyone getting injured on her behalf.

"The dragon riders wouldn't dare do anything to harm Elaine," Faron said. "Especially not after everything she's done to help keep the sleeping riders alive. Besides, Lenire's there to pick her up. If anything were to happen, wouldn't you trust a dragon knight to be able to rescue her?"

Her brows pinched together. "Of course I would. Sometimes I just worry things are slipping through my fingers." Lately, she was juggling all these important tasks: finding the Heart, overseeing Faron's recovery, keeping the troubled dragon riders content, monitoring for news of the school or Kaerlin or the war at the border, fretting over Strida and Octavia. These were all worries that beat at the back of her mind, and now she'd added getting inside the cavern to her list.

When they'd managed to get the hound past the magical border around the cavern, even for those few moments, Cora knew Melusine would have no trouble getting inside the cavern should she and Zirael create more hounds. All Cora's attention and focus had turned to figuring out a way for her group to get inside, and she'd finally taken Elaine up on her offer of returning to the school in search of information or even a weapon that might allow them to safely pass through the defenses. Clearly, no amount of magic they'd used so far was doing the trick, and Cora was getting desperate.

"Elaine is a skilled healer. She knows how to get herself out of a pinch. And Lenire will stay out of sight. Nothing will happen to them."

"Elaine said that before we showed up to rescue you and the other sleeping riders, they were expecting orders from Northwood. What if those orders were accompanied by soldiers?" Cora envisioned an army of marching men and women who'd been told that Cora and her friends were traitors. She imagined them taking up residence at the school—sleeping in their cabins, eating in their dining hall, rummaging through their classrooms—alongside the remaining dragon riders. "It might not be the dragon riders we have to worry about in the end."

Faron didn't have any nice words to dissuade her thinking, no matter how much Cora wished he did. Northwood moving troops to the school was a possibility they had to consider. The dragon-rider school was an important part of Tenegard. It would warrant defending should Athelia break through the border, never mind from Melusine and the Blight.

"She's only been gone a few days," Faron said finally. "Let's not panic until there's something to panic about."

It felt like it had been an eternity, and Cora was beginning to think that worrying about Elaine and Lenire's whereabouts would be enough to put her in her own sleeping coma.

"Come on," Faron said, tugging on her hand.

"Where are we going?"

"To get you something to eat."

"I'm not hungry," Cora protested.

"No, but I think it would be better if you stopped watching the sky. You know, kind of like that old adage, a watched pot never boils?"

Cora sighed, the corners of her lips fighting a smile, and for a moment, she let herself revel in the fact Faron was with her. She'd spent so many days and nights wishing she could talk to him, share his company or his confidence, and now she could. She had him back. She lifted her hand to his face, cradling his cheek, letting her thumb trace the dark circles under his eyes. For someone who'd been asleep for so long, it clearly hadn't been restful. She could trace the lines of exhaustion across his features, but behind it all was *her* Faron. No matter what happened, she wasn't ever going to let the Blight take him away from her again.

He leaned forward and pressed a gentle kiss to her lips. It was too quick for Cora to even close her eyes, but when Faron pulled away, he laughed.

"What is it?" Cora asked.

He turned her on the spot, so she was facing the horizon again, and there it was, the shadowy figure of a dragon. The way it slithered through the sky meant it could only be Yrsa. "If you squint really hard," he said, "I think you'll notice two distinct figures on dragonback."

Cora let out a breath that was giddy butterflies and relief all mixed into one. "They should arrive any minute," she said, taking Faron's hand and practically dragging him off the shelf. "Let's go meet them."

By the time Cora and Faron had made their way down to base camp and across to the clearing, Alaric and Wyn were already awaiting Yrsa's arrival. She glittered with that iridescent sheen as she approached, doing a loop around the clearing before touching down. She lay flat on her belly and Lenire helped Elaine dismount.

"Did you run into any trouble?" Cora asked.

Lenire shook his head. "Not the kind we were expecting, at least."

Cora and Faron exchanged a look of concern.

"There were hardly any dragon riders there," Elaine said. "And the ones who remained were so busy being run off their feet, they hardly took notice of my presence."

Worry boiled in Cora's gut. "What do you mean there were hardly any riders there?"

Except for Faron, they'd left behind all the riders who had been awakened from the sleeping sickness. The school should have been busier than ever.

"I managed to speak to my healer colleagues. Apparently, Northwood issued orders for many of the dragon riders to report to various military units."

Cora's worry flared, seeping between her ribs. It felt like acid, and she rubbed at the ache in her chest.

"That's not all," Lenire said. "They've also taken a hefty number of the school's crystals with them to these other locations to guard against possible Athelian attack."

"What?" Cora said. "That doesn't make any sense. The crystals and the shield are to protect the dragon riders from the Blight."

"I guess Northwood wants to cover all his bases," Elaine said.

"Or make sure Cora can't return and use the school as a stronghold," Faron pointed out.

"The remaining riders have managed to stretch the crystals that are left to keep the shield active," Elaine continued, "but only barely. If any more crystals disappear, so does that protection."

"I have to sit down," Cora said, already stumbling backward. Faron caught her by the arm, keeping her upright, and before she could protest, Elaine's hands were on her cheeks, her forehead, either side of her neck, that cold wave of healer magic assessing.

"You're running yourself ragged," Elaine said, leading her across the clearing to a fallen log.

"It's kind of hard not to." Cora sat down, already feeling better, and Elaine took a seat beside her. Faron and Lenire followed.

"Were there any weapons?" Faron asked. "Or anything that might help us bypass the cavern's defenses?"

Elaine shook her head. "It sounds like all the supplies are being hoarded in Kaerlin for the front lines."

"Strida must have fought tooth and nail against Northwood's decision to separate and relocate the dragon riders." The thought alone made Cora feel ill.

"At least she'll know where our riders have been deployed if we need to reunite them," Faron said. "If you're worried, why don't you try contacting her now?"

It would be a relief to hear Strida's voice, but reaching out via the anchor would put her friend at risk for something that wasn't yet an emergency. "It was my idea to exercise caution using the anchors. I can't break that every time I'm a little worried." Cora sighed. "Was there anything else?" she asked Elaine.

Elaine's shoulders lifted. "I'm not sure it's newsworthy, but before Lenire and I left, the school received word that the soothsayers were on their way."

"Ismenia?" Cora said. "Why would she be coming to the school?"

"You think Northwood deployed them there?" Faron wondered.

"Or do you think they've foreseen what's to happen at the border and decided to relocate somewhere safer?" Elaine said.

"I think there are a lot of other places the soothsayers could have taken refuge. If they're on their way to the school, it must be some sort of plan concocted by Northwood."

"Maybe Emmett can find out," Faron suggested. "I've heard he's good at that kind of thing."

Cora huffed. Figuring out what nonsense Northwood and the soothsayers were up to was not going to help with their current problem. "Defending the Heart of Tenegard is looking more and more impossible."

"Maybe we just need to change our strategy," Lenire said after a beat.

"You mean go on the offensive for once?" Faron said, eagerness bleeding into the question.

"How exactly do you propose—"

“The hound,” Lenire interrupted before Cora had even finished asking the question. “We can use it to spy on Melusine and Zirael.”

She resisted the urge to roll her eyes. She shouldn’t be surprised, really, that his plan involved the hound considering how pivotal the creature had become these past weeks, but alarm rang in Cora’s head like bells. “I know the hound has proven to be useful—”

“More than useful,” Faron said. “I’m living proof of that.”

“But,” Cora continued, uneasy, “our enemies are familiar with Itharusian magic. What if they can sense what we’re up to?”

“Without some sort of intelligence, we have no way of knowing what either sorcerer is up to,” Lenire countered. “We can’t afford to be that ignorant knowing how vulnerable the Heart is to their magic.”

Cora had her reservations, but she couldn’t argue the success they’d had putting the hound to work for them.

What do you want to do?

Cora looked up at him as Alaric broke through her concern, his question soft, his tone reassuring. She knew he would support whichever decision she made. *I can’t tell whether my fears are reasonable or whether I’m preventing our cause from moving forward*, she admitted to him. Maybe she was the biggest threat to the Heart.

There is no way to know for sure, he said. *Not even a soothsayer can see the way forward that clearly. I think in this case, you have to go with your gut.*

My gut says we’re running out of time.

Then we do what we must.

“Okay,” Cora said finally to Faron and Lenire. “We’ll do it your way. We’ll use the hound to sneak into Melusine and Zirael’s camp.”

CHAPTER 12

CORA

"I didn't think it was going to be this difficult," Faron said as he joined Cora around the campfire. Dawn was breaking across the sky, and though Cora felt as if she'd hardly slept at all, an entire evening had passed since she'd agreed Faron and Lenire could attempt to use the hound to spy on Melusine's camp.

The problem was that before they could spy on the camp, they actually had to *find* the camp.

"Well," Cora sighed, prodding at the hot coals of the campfire with a stick. "Melusine hasn't ever been one to make things easy for us."

"You said the last time you talked to Octavia, she mentioned Melusine hiding out along the border between Athelia and Tenegard?"

Cora nodded. "Before we parted, Octavia said one of the dragon riders was attacked along the border. It was part of the situation that prompted her getting banished from the council and Kaerlin."

"I guess we can't assume Melusine has remained there."

Cora had been up half the night pondering the same thing, and if she was going to try to shake her exhaustion, she was going to need to eat something. She added another log on top of the coals, waiting for it to catch before she strung a pot of water over the hungry flames. "If I were Melusine," Cora said, "following the hound battle in the mountains, I would have fled and regrouped. Then, I would have moved my camp closer to my ultimate goal."

"The Heart of Tenegard."

Footsteps crunched behind them and Lenire appeared, wrapped in a thick blanket, looking as bone-weary as Cora felt. His eyes barely opened as he sat down on the other side of the fire. "What are we talking about?"

"The fact that Melusine probably packed up and moved her camp after your last run-in with her," Faron said.

"It would make the most sense that she'd settle closer to the mountains," Lenire said.

"We could fly around," Faron offered. "And try scanning for other living things."

"That could waste days and energy we don't have," Cora said. "There are likely other remote village settlements in the mountains. Animals. Maybe even dragons."

"Stumbling upon the camp at that point would be pure luck," Faron agreed. "I wish there was some way we could get a glimpse of where they might be. At least it might give us a direction to focus on."

"I should have tried planting an anchor on her when we fought," Cora muttered. "I might have been able to eavesdrop on her camp somehow." At the time Cora wasn't really thinking about the future or the fact that Melusine would once again escape. She'd been focused on keeping Melusine distracted so Lenire could attempt to wrestle the Blight from her control. Now it felt like a wasted opportunity.

Lenire stood suddenly, the blanket falling from his shoulders. "An anchor," he repeated under his breath. "We have an anchor!"

"What?"

"The Blight fragment," he continued excitedly. "The one inside the hound. We can use it to help us locate the rest of the Blight. That's where we'll find Melusine."

"But how?" Cora asked. "You severed the connection to the main Blight when you woke the sleeping dragon riders."

"But that frayed connection is still there. The same way you could sense your damaged dragon bond with Alaric—"

"The hound can sense the frayed bond with the Blight?" Cora finished.

"Exactly. It just no longer has the autonomy to pursue that connection. But if I take control of the hound and lean into it, maybe I can rewire the hound's initial purpose from hunting crystal deposits to tracking down the Blight."

"Will this really work?" Cora asked. In her experience, Blight fragments were nothing to mess around with. She still thought of the Blight fragment possessing Alia's body, the girl from the last village they'd stayed in, before it escaped and contaminated a bunch of crystals. But maybe she was once again letting her worries overshadow a good idea. Frankly, their only idea.

Faron inclined his head toward the pit. "Only one way to find out."

Northeast.

That was the direction the hound had pointed. Like a needle on a compass, when Lenire had started to manipulate the Blight fragment, the hound had arranged its massive, mottled body to point the way toward Melusine's camp. At least, that's where they hoped it was headed.

"We should take the hound closer before deploying it," Lenire shouted up at them from the bottom of the pit. "Reducing the distance will help us keep the best possible control."

Faron picked up the giant sack they used to transport the hound long distances and jumped into the pit to help Lenire wrangle the hound into it. "How far do you think we have to go?"

"If our theory is right, and she's relocated to be closer to the Heart, her camp could be anywhere between here and the northeasterly foot of the mountains."

"Covering that whole distance is a three-hour flight," Cora said.

"If we come up on the camp too quickly," Lenire said, "they'll either spot us or we'll set off whatever magical defenses they've placed for protection."

"We'll go slow and scan the area using magic," Faron said. His initial plan worked much better now they had narrowed down a direction, but all Cora could think about was how much energy Faron and Wyn would expend scanning that much ground. Elaine had yet to declare Faron recovered, and Cora knew he tired easily despite him insisting otherwise.

"I'm coming too," Cora said. "As backup."

Faron looked up at her, his eyes reflecting the morning cloud cover. "I'm not sure it's a good idea for you to leave again so soon. The other riders are restless. They know a lot has been happening these past few days that they aren't yet privy to. Your departure might have a negative effect on them."

"They'll cope," Cora said sourly. She didn't mean to be so short with him; she was simply frustrated by the attitude in camp. She didn't have time to explain and justify her every decision regarding the hunt for the Heart of Tenegard or their enemies. And honestly, after what had happened with the sleeping sickness, she would have thought the riders would be more cognizant of the dangers she was trying to keep them from.

Faron climbed out of the pit and squeezed her shoulder gently. "I've said it before, but you know you don't have to do everything yourself, right? You've already spent so much time pursuing the Heart. Maybe getting some rest for once would do you some good."

Cora had to admit it was nice to have someone looking out for her again, but this wasn't something she was willing to budge on. "Thank you," she said, softening her tone. "But spending the whole day powerlessly imagining worst-case scenarios would be the exact opposite of restful."

"I figured you'd say that," Faron said. "Just thought I'd give it a shot. Guess it's time to round up the dragons."

"Meet you in the sky," she said as she crossed the camp toward Alaric. He'd returned from a successful hunt with Yrsa, and the pair of them had settled outside of camp to enjoy their meals.

Cora hurried between the tents where riders were now waking and prodding their own fires to life. Before Cora reached Alaric, a voice caught her attention. It was Renka, sitting on a log outside her tent, a fire poker in her hand. "Guess we'll hang around and wait for you, as usual."

"That's the job," Cora bit out. "Trainees and soldiers wait for orders." She kept walking.

Don't let it get to you, Alaric said. He'd picked up the tone of her thoughts and finished his meal in a hurry in order to join her. He drew near now, waiting at the edge of camp.

I'm not, Cora said as she reached him and climbed onto his back. They both knew she was lying, but Alaric kindly chose not to mention it again for the duration of the flight, instead pouring his energy into helping Cora magically scan the terrain for living things.

She channeled her frustration into the search for Melusine's camp, stretching her magic farther than she ever had before. But they were still nearing the three-hour mark before they came upon what seemed to be a camp buried in the woods at the northeastern base of the Therma Mountains.

"Let's double-back to that clearing we saw," Lenire suggested. "Before we get too close."

Alaric dove into a turn, sweeping below Yrsa and past Wyn, landing in a rocky clearing. If they climbed a short distance and perched on the tops of the cliffs, they would have a decent view of the woods. It was impossible to know what was going on beneath the canopy, but hopefully the hound would be an adequate spy.

"This looks like a good place to set up," Faron said as Wyn dumped the sack containing the hound at his feet. He pulled the sack free, and Lenire took control of the hound, carefully guiding it up the cliff face. Cora and Faron followed, and once they were situated at the top looking down, Cora started to doubt their plan.

"Navigating the hound down there is going to be tricky," Lenire said.

"We could try settling somewhere closer to the woods," Faron suggested. "At least we'd be on level ground."

Lenire shook his head. "We don't know how far their defenses extend. I don't want to risk triggering something before we've even tried to infiltrate their camp."

"Should I try scanning for living energy again now that we're closer?" Cora asked. When Lenire nodded, she let her magic flow down the mountain. It picked up small, warm-blooded animals. Mountain hares most likely. She read the edge of the woods, prodding with her magic. "I'm not picking up any kind of defense. That doesn't mean there isn't one, though."

"I think we should hold our position," Lenire said. "I kind of like the idea of keeping a mountain between us. If something goes wrong it buys us some time to flee."

Cora had to admit she liked that last part too. She didn't relish another battle with Melusine.

With that settled, they prepared themselves the same way they had when they used the hound to break through the barrier surrounding the cavern. Faron created an anchor around Lenire's knotted spell, connecting the Tenegardian and Itharusian magic in a way that allowed him to also watch through the hound's eyes. And through Faron's connection, Cora linked her own magic, giving him the ability to share with her what the hound saw. The only piece they were missing was Elaine's spell for mental clarity, but hopefully, it wouldn't be necessary this time since they were simply spying on the camp, not trying to break through an unknown, magical barrier.

The trip down the mountain was as hazardous as Lenire had suspected, and the hound slipped several times as it navigated between the sharp, rocky shelves.

Good thing the creature doesn't feel any pain, Cora said to Alaric. The dragons had remained in the clearing to avoid being spotted if anyone was looking up at the mountain.

Are you approaching the woods?

Just about. Cora held her breath, expecting some sort of magical alarm to go off as the hound slipped between the thick evergreens. Through the hound's eyes, she watched needled branches sweep by as the creature darted around large trunks. *Okay, we're in. Everything seems to be okay so far.*

I don't think their magical defenses will be triggered by a creature of their own making, Alaric assured her.

I hope you're right.

"There," Lenire said as they all caught sight of the same movement. This was farther than he and Faron had ever managed to pilot the hound.

"Look! There are other hounds," Faron said. "A whole pack of them. Running the border."

As Cora watched the hideous creatures race past, her initial fears that their presence inside the hound would be noticed proved to be unfounded. Clearly, Lenire was able to shield them and make it appear as if their hound was connected to Melusine's strange pack just like all the others.

Lenire steered the hound closer, slipping into the enemies' camp. They passed hastily strung tarps and cold firepits. It reminded Cora of their own base camp, except that in the center of the camp dozens of people were silently at work, building strange contraptions.

"Who are all these people?" Lenire asked.

"Clearly not on our side," Cora said.

"Or they're being controlled," Lenire said.

"A Blight possession?"

"Could be."

A chill ran through Cora, and she struggled to shake it off.

"What do you think they're building?" Faron asked.

"Just a second," Lenire said. "I'm going to try to get closer." He steered the hound back the way they'd come and ran behind the tents. Then he ducked the creature beneath a massive wooden worktable. The hound laid on its belly, inching along on its paws. When they were close enough to see the mechanics of what the camp was building, Lenire swore.

"What is it?" Cora asked.

"Looks like Zirael's been revealing more of Itharus' tricks of war. These are magically augmented weapons like the ones used to fight against the resistance in Itharus. It wasn't always just the Blight they used against the people. They outfitted their soldiers with weapons infused with magic to make them twice as deadly."

"Like what?"

"Imagine an arrow that never misses. Or a blade that melts through armor."

"But why would they need all these weapons if their plan is to get to the Heart and drain its power?" Cora asked.

"Maybe plans have changed," Faron said. "Can you angle the hound toward those trees?"

Lenire did and they spotted a roughly sketched map. The hound crept beneath the table until they were close enough to make out the image.

"That looks like Llys," Cora said as she studied the settlement that had been circled on the paper. Llys was the city where Cora and Faron had originally met. Back then, she and Alaric had flown to the city to rescue her father and Raksha while Faron, who was working as a military guard at the time, was helping fuel the underground resistance against King Onyx.

"It also looks like they're planning a magical attack on the city while the Tenegardian military is distracted elsewhere."

"Why would they waste time attacking Llys?" Cora wondered aloud. "It's a Tenegardian stronghold. Only another military would care enough to attack that city." As the words fell from her mouth, she thought back to the concerns Octavia had expressed when she revealed that the dragon rider had been attacked at the border. Octavia had worried Melusine might have aligned herself with Athelia. Discovering the truth of that matter was partly what prompted her to risk crossing the border herself. Now, seeing the augmented weapons and evidence of their planned attack, it looked like Octavia's theory was correct. "She's working with Athelia," Cora said, stunned at her own revelation. "Maybe she has been this whole time."

"Are you sure?" Faron asked.

"That's why she's been after the Heart from the beginning! We knew she was trying to destroy Tenegard's magic, but we could never figure out why or what her end goal was. This must be it. To give Athelia the advantage."

"But she hasn't managed to reach the Heart yet."

"No," Cora said. "That's true. Attacking Llys before draining the Heart would seem foolish, but that was before the Tenegardian council declared all-out war. The Athelians know it's probably now or never. If not, most of their forces will be tied up at the border as well."

"Plus, now they have all these magical weapons," Faron said.

Cora was dizzy thinking about it all. "With Llys in Athelian hands, the Tenegardians and Kaerlin especially will face attack from both sides."

"And any supply lines to the dragon-rider school will be cut off," Faron "aid. "The remaining riders would have to abandon the school. It'll keep our forces separated."

"Do you think the Athelian army can hold the fort?"

"Llys is well stocked with emergency food and other supplies," Faron said. His knowledge of the fort was vital. "If Athelian forces manage to take the city, they could hold out for quite some time without any resupply from their own army. And with added magical weapons, even if the dragon riders mounted a counterattack, the losses could be devastating."

Cora stared through the hound's eyes again, studying the map. Before she could say anything else about these daunting revelations, commotion in the woods caught their attention. Carefully, Lenire slipped the hound from beneath the table and navigated it deeper into the trees. There they found Melusine and Zirael mid-argument, and most disturbing of all was the Blight, coiling into a tight cloud of black mist, like it was preparing to strike.

When it lashed out at Melusine, Cora jumped despite being safely situated in the mountains. It was such a surprising gesture from a creature that had always seemed to obey her. Melusine commanded the creature back but it struck out at her again. She ducked out of the way, pushing her mop of long curly hair out of her eyes as she straightened.

"I told you your soft touch was going to give you problems," Zirael said. Cora could only see the back of him, but his tone was laced with amusement.

As the Blight reared up to strike again, Zirael lifted his hand and the creature recoiled, obeying him, though it seemed reluctant and sullen, as if it was resentful of the sorcerers.

“Clearly, I’ll be the one leading the creature against Llys since the weapons are almost finished and you don’t seem capable of it anymore.”

Melusine’s dark eyes flashed in the low light that filtered in from the tree-lined canopy above. “We both know the only reason the creature still bows to you at all is because of that disk in your hand.”

When Zirael turned, Cora spotted the disk Melusine was talking about. She recognized the polished stone instantly. It looked exactly like the one Lenire had used to try to wrestle control of the Blight away from Melusine before the disk had been destroyed. “I don’t think you’re comprehending the fact that I could now take the Blight at any time and leave you to this mess of a plan.”

“Don’t threaten me,” Melusine warned. “You might have that disk, but I managed to summon the Blight away from Itharus once. Don’t think I won’t do it again.” Cora knew Melusine wouldn’t let Zirael leave with the Blight until she’d destroyed the Heart of Tenegard. If Zirael wanted to flee back to Itharus without a fight, he was going to have to help Melusine finish her mission.

“The moment I can be rid of you can’t come soon enough.” Zirael pocketed the disk and marched away, clearly frustrated by the exchange.

Melusine flexed both her hands in his direction but curled them tightly without casting a spell. “You better hope that disk of yours doesn’t stop working one day!”

CHAPTER 13

CORA

"Did you know Zirael brought a disk with him?" Cora asked as they landed back at base camp with the hound. She'd known there were three disks total before Lenire's had been destroyed, but she was still surprised to see another one in Tenegard.

"No, but it makes sense that Zirael would have brought it with him from Itharus. I don't think he would have rested his ability to reclaim control of the creature solely on getting my disk back. And now the one I stole is gone, and Melusine seems to be losing her grip on the creature, he's getting close to achieving exactly that."

"But didn't it look like even Zirael was struggling to control the creature?"

Curious dragons riders had gathered when they landed, hoping to hear what news came of taking the hound out again. For days Lenire had been eager to prove the creature could be an asset, but he simply gave the riders a curt nod and brushed past, expressionless as he piloted the hound through camp and back to the pit.

"Lenire?" Cora called. She dodged a group of riders returning from a training exercise. "Lenire!"

"The disks were designed as a trio," he said, answering her question from earlier without looking at her. "They probably don't work as well as a pair."

Cora wondered if there was any way they could possibly get their hands on that disk. It seemed unlikely, given the way Zirael was guarding it against Melusine. But she couldn't help thinking about trying to seize control of the creature again or being able to help Strida repair her dragon bond. Then again, the last time they had access to a disk, controlling the creature still hadn't gone so well.

The way Lenire was acting, Zirael having a disk wasn't the surprise she thought it was. The Blight had always been out of their control. That was nothing new. "I suppose I shouldn't let myself be distracted from the real goal of protecting the Heart or even of figuring out how to stop Melusine from carrying out her plans against Llys."

Lenire hummed in response, and the hairs on Cora's neck stood up. Now she was less concerned with any of that and more concerned about the way Lenire was acting.

"Are you all right?" she asked, sitting on the edge of the pit, looking down at him. Lenire had history with the Blight and with Zirael. Perhaps seeing those weapons again, the ones that had been used against the people of Itharus, brought up bad memories. Maybe just seeing their enemies again and listening to their plans was enough to upset him.

"I'm fine," he answered immediately, hunched over the hound as he made it lie on the floor of the pit.

"Then why won't you look at me?"

Lenire dropped his hands to his hips and straightened to look at her. He did it all so quickly that he staggered to the side and finally Cora saw the exhaustion that left dark, drooping circles beneath his eyes. She slid down the wall of the pit and hurried to his side.

"You've run yourself ragged today," she said, using her shoulder to help prop him up.

"I've also been putting in long hours this past week trying to figure out the hound's secrets."

"And have you been sleeping?" Cora asked. She thought she was tired after a night of stressing about how to find Melusine's camp, but the exhaustion she felt was obviously nothing compared to Lenire's.

"Not much," he admitted.

"It's okay to take care of yourself," she reminded him. "You're allowed to rest." She felt him tense beside her as they staggered to the edge of the pit together.

"I'm not one of your students," he said, pulling away from her. "And you're hardly one to talk about taking care of oneself."

Cora knew he was right. She was terrible at taking her own advice, but this wasn't about her. "You're not the only one working your fingers to the bone with the hound," she reminded him. "You keep pushing for more. Faron has thrown himself into the project to help you do just that, but he's *still* recovering."

Lenire reached for the wall of the pit to steady himself, his eyes downcast. "I'm sorry, I wasn't thinking. I know how much Faron means to you." He sighed heavily. "You do have a point. Maybe we should slow down."

Cora smiled ruefully. "You also have a point and I *should* take my own advice."

"I got ahead of myself and when I saw the opportunity to use the hound against our enemies, I wanted to make it work."

"And you did."

"But it didn't help these feelings," he said, touching his chest. "This desire for revenge. I saw it as an opportunity to get back at Zirael—the man responsible for all my terrible experiences. When we were in the camp today, it didn't feel like success, it felt like failure. And that made me angry at myself."

"Why would it feel like failure?" Cora asked.

"Because here I am, playing with a hound like a child with a puppet. Meanwhile, Zirael's helping Melusine design the same weapons that caused so much death in Itharus."

"Lenire, without you and this hound, we would be no closer to knowing what Melusine's next move was. We also wouldn't know that she's likely been aligned with Athelia from the beginning. Information is just as useful as a weapon."

Lenire ducked his head. Cora wasn't quite sure he believed the compliment she was trying to give him, but she didn't want him to think his contributions to their cause were trivial. "Come have dinner with my father and Elaine," she said.

Lenire lifted his head then. "Thanks, but I think I'm going to take that advice you just gave me and go straight to bed."

"You're sure?"

"Yeah." He turned and climbed out of the pit. Cora watched him to make sure he didn't stumble and fall backward. "We'll talk strategy later?"

Cora nodded. "Sounds good." When he disappeared from view, Cora turned around to face the hound. It lay there, just a mass of flesh, but

Cora had a new appreciation for the creature. It had been created of magic with dark intentions, and yet it had been immensely helpful since the day it was captured. Cora supposed she really should be grateful Lenire had thrown himself into uncovering the hound's secrets with such gusto.

"Isn't it so nice that she gets to have her family and her partner and her little friend from Itharus?" a familiar voice said.

Anger flickered to life inside her, and Cora raced up the wall of dirt, hoisting herself out of the pit in time to see the back of Renka and her little group of disgruntled dragon riders.

"Meanwhile, the rest of us didn't have the luxury of sticking close to our nearest and dearest since choosing to follow her into these forsaken mountains," another one of the riders said. "I don't even know if leaving was worth it anymore."

Renka laughed humorlessly. "Guess we all chose wrong when Cora made her little speech in the meeting hall."

The group walked off toward their campfire. Cora wasn't sure if they'd even noticed her, or perhaps they had and said everything purposely so she would hear. Either way it felt as if their words would burn a hole in her chest.

Cora, Alaric said softly, calling her attention away from Renka and the others. He must have sensed the intense anger that flared through her. Maybe he even picked up on the hurt she was trying not to let show. *Tread carefully.*

I haven't done anything yet. She marched after them, a bubbling anger fueling every step.

We can't afford for the riders to truly become divided. Especially not after what we learned today. We are going to need help fighting the battle to come.

He was right. Of course, he was. Cora took a deep breath and kept walking, straight into the *troublemakers'* small camp. All eyes turned to her as she approached, and the conversations ended abruptly. The group exchanged questioning glances.

Anger would have been the easiest choice, but Cora knew deep down there was truth to their words. That's why it had made her so angry and uncomfortable in the first place. Regardless of past regrets or hurt feelings, they needed her and she needed them. Besides, acting in anger was what someone like Northwood would choose, and Cora didn't want to be that kind of leader.

"Can I join you?" she asked, keeping the question measured and calm. It wasn't anger that bubbled inside her chest now but nerves. "We clearly need to talk."

Renka, who was probably the most taken aback of all, made room for her on the fallen log they used as seating.

Cora crossed the camp and sat down. "I've heard your frustrations." Eyes darted around the campfire, refusing to make contact with her. "For weeks," she added pointedly.

"Well, you've sure taken your time addressing them," Renka said.

"I've been trying to balance my duties here as your leader and teacher with my responsibilities out there, dealing with Melusine and the Blight."

"You've all but abandoned us as a teacher," one of the riders pointed out. Cora could hear the frustration in her tone.

"We've given up a lot to follow you into the wilderness," Renka added. "Friends, comfort, a place to call home."

"We haven't heard from anyone at the school," another rider said, her worry eclipsing any frustration she might have felt. "When you told us to choose sides, I didn't think it would be so final. How could you even ask us to make a choice like that so abruptly?"

With a pang of regret, Cora realized she and Strida were right about how the deception of splitting up the school would lead to mistrust. Keeping the riders in the dark was only letting that wound fester, but she couldn't risk losing control of the secret, not while Octavia and Strida were still undercover in their roles. Cora wouldn't do anything to increase the danger they faced, even if it would have brought comfort to her riders, knowing it was all a necessary ploy.

"I'm sorry," she said instead. "You're right. I have been neglecting my duties as your teacher, and though there's a lot I can't share with you yet …"

Renka huffed and rolled her eyes.

"I'll at least make a point of leading drills every morning instead of leaving it to other faculty."

"What *can* you tell us?" Renka said. "We watch you fly off with Faron and Lenire all the time. We know you're doing something with the hound."

Cora sighed. She couldn't reveal the deception that caused the split at the school, but she could tell them this. She would have liked to address all the riders at once, but if it helped alleviate some of the tension, then it was worth making this speech twice. Besides, she knew her words would spread through the camp like wildfire. "We used the hound to spy on Melusine's camp today."

A rider jumped to his feet. "You found her?"

"We did."

"Then what are we waiting for?"

Cora held her hand out, asking for calm. "Her camp is well protected by hounds and the Blight and other magic. She is also still working with Zirael. Attacking without thinking it through first would be foolish."

"There's more?" Renka said, watching Cora closely.

"Yes." Though their relationship thus far had been marred by tension, Cora finally felt like she was taking a step in the right direction. "Melusine is creating weapons. Dangerous weapons that have been used against the people in Itharus before. We think Zirael taught her how to make them."

"And what are they going to do with these weapons?" a small voice asked.

Cora looked up at the fire-lit faces of the dragon riders who surrounded her. "Their plan is to attack Llys. But we're going to stop them."

She just had to figure out how.

CHAPTER 14
OCTAVIA

Octavia dipped her hand into her pocket, checking again to ensure she still had the leaflet she'd picked up in the market square. It had been almost a week since she'd last seen Serafine, but when the summons for lunch had arrived at the inn this morning, Octavia had washed and dressed and carefully tucked the leaflet into her pocket before setting off for the office suite Serafine occupied outside the senate building.

She'd expected to be called upon sooner, but senate business kept Serafine busy, so Octavia had kept herself busy by trying to carefully wheedle information out of Commander Dolan. He'd refused to speak of troop movements or the Athelian military with her, however, so she'd attempted to befriend some of the brave citizens who stopped by the inn to get a glimpse of Raksha. They proved to be even more wary of her than the guards who had been left by the senate to watch her movements, so she didn't have much luck getting answers to any of her burning questions.

I suspect Serafine's been keeping a close eye on you despite her distance these past days.

At Raksha's comment, Octavia spied over her shoulder, trying to pinpoint the guards who were never any farther than an arrow could fly. *I wondered if she was testing us. Waiting to see if we would try to pass information to Tenegard somehow. I truly doubt she trusts us any more than we do her.*

She trusts you enough to ask you to spy.

I think that has less to do with trust and more to do with seizing an opportunity. How often does she get to employ a Tenegardian dragon rider for her own devices? Octavia said as she turned down the busy thoroughfare leading from the market square to the stately office suites occupied by many of the senators. Though magic wielders were not permitted in the senate chambers, there was apparently no such rule on the company one could keep in their private offices. *I do think she is short on allies, though. The relationships between Serafine and the other senators are rocky at best. And despite the show of unity they try to put on, after all my experience with Northwood, I know division when I see it.*

If alliances are shifting, then it's best to leave our options open, Raksha agreed. *We'll continue to play Serafine's game until a better opportunity arises.*

Octavia agreed with a soft hum inside her head. Now that she better understood how the Athelian senate operated, she wasn't all that surprised her request for aid from the Athelian sorcerers was denied by the senate. It appeared there were underhanded, conniving bullies in power everywhere. Bullies who might be in league with Melusine and the Blight. She still hadn't found any evidence to prove that Athelia, or any of its senators, were connected to Melusine, but she wasn't ruling anyone out yet.

Octavia reached Serafine's office building and looked up. It was tall and square, carved from white marble, with an intimidating staircase and an ornately shaped door knocker. Though clearly lavish, it felt nothing like the palace in Kaerlin, and it was leagues above the accommodations at the dragon-rider school.

A shadow crossed one of the upper windows, and Octavia knew Serafine watched her. She hurried up the stairs, worried her hesitation would look suspicious, and stopped only when she was forced to by the guards who stood watch by the front door.

Many of the senators had a personal guard in Athelia. That struck Octavia as odd, considering how freely the Tenegardian councilors had moved around Kaerlin, but she kept those thoughts to herself as the guard asked her business.

"My name is Octavia. I have been invited to dine with Serafine."

The guards knew very well who she was. There was only one Tenegardian dragon rider currently running around Erelas, and her riding clothes and her softly braided hair, however neat and tidy she made them, would never allow her to blend in with the more stark, upscale Athelian styles.

"Wait here," one of the guards ordered before disappearing through the front door.

The other guard put his hand on the hilt of his sword. Octavia couldn't tell if it was out of habit or if it was meant to be a threat. For a moment, she wished she'd brought Raksha along to sit outside the building. That would have given the guard something dangerous to worry about.

Before she could come up with any other methods by which she might truly intimidate the guard, the door was flung open. Serafine stood there, wearing a pleasant smile of surprise, like she hadn't already been watching Octavia out the window. "Did you find the place, okay?"

"Yes," Octavia said. "Your directions were spot on."

"Good," Serafine said, sweeping Octavia inside before shutting the door on her two guards. "I hope you're hungry."

"Famished," Octavia answered almost rotely. Growing up at Onyx's table, she'd been taught never to decline hospitality, especially when alliances were being forged.

"Good. My staff have been cooking all afternoon. I'll have them bring up something to drink." Serafine linked her arm with Octavia, holding her tight enough that Octavia got the message. This wasn't going to be her opportunity to poke around in Serafine's life or linger over her things. This was a business meeting, and Serafine was going to get right to it. She led Octavia up a winding set of stairs and down a narrow hallway to an office. Octavia gaped. The room was filled with more books than she'd ever seen outside the palace libraries. Every wall was stacked floor to ceiling with shelves that held old, leather-bound tomes.

"You like to read?" Serafine guessed as she shut the door and returned to Octavia's side.

Octavia nodded, running her finger over the spine of a book. "Growing up in the palace in Kaerlin had its … challenges."

"I assume you mean Onyx."

Just as his name, Onyx the Deathless, implied, even in death his memory still lingered. "The palace had a wonderful library and I used to hide myself away with the books, reading for hours and hours, sometimes until I couldn't see straight."

"My sister also likes books," Serafine said. "Better than people most days." This felt like the first real bit of information Serafine had offered her. The first bit of information that humanized her. That made her appear more than the stark, unyielding senator.

For a beat Serafine shed some of her imposing armor and Octavia smiled. "We might have that in common. There were times when I would have preferred a good book over dealing with some of the Tenegardian councilors." Maybe Octavia could use the connection to further convince Serafine to trust her. "Did your sister find herself called to Athelian politics as well?"

Serafine chuckled. "Stars, no, she found her calling in the more mystical arts."

How interesting, Octavia thought. A senator and sorcerer. Two powerful positions within Athelian society. She wondered if Serafine's sister was half as cunning as she was. If she could speak to her, perhaps her sister might be able to shed more light on who Serafine really was and what she wanted. "Perhaps you could introduce us while I'm here," Octavia said. "I'd love to meet another voracious reader."

Serafine's brow twitched the tiniest amount. Octavia could tell she'd stepped on a nerve. Perhaps Serafine had realized what Octavia was trying to do. "Unlikely. My sister is quite busy."

"That works out well," Octavia said. "I find my schedule quite flexible."

"Unfortunately, she is not in the country at the moment. She's always been more of a free spirit. Enjoys her travels." Serafine gestured to an armchair. "Besides, you might find your schedule to be less flexible following our meeting."

By the time Octavia had sat down in the armchair, the sharpness of Serafine's features had returned, and it was clear she had no interest in making introductions with her sister. "How has your stay at the inn been?"

Octavia knew she wasn't really inquiring about the inn. She reached into her tunic and retrieved the leaflet, carefully unfolding it as she passed it to Serafine. "I was handed this in the market square about five days ago."

Serafine's eyes skittered over the page.

"They write of the defective war engines. You were right when you said someone in the senate is leaking information to the pacifists."

"Yes," Serafine said, crushing the leaflet in her hand. "I'm aware of these pernicious bits of illegal, unsanctioned propaganda. I've seen them before in the market squares. They've been allowed to spew their rhetoric for too long. But I've actually had my eye on a woman who I suspect might be the author. She is a printer and bookbinder in the city. She specializes in creating some of the posters you might have noticed around the market square."

"If you know who she is, why haven't you arrested her?"

"Because she is only the printer. If I remove her from the equation, another will pop up to replace her. In order to bring them down, I have to get to the top. And you're going to help me."

Octavia swallowed hard. She'd been a rebel fighter in the war to bring down Onyx. She knew how these things worked. She also knew Serafine was testing her loyalty. "What would you have me do?"

Serafine took a scrap of paper and scribbled something down. She passed it to Octavia. "The address where you can find the printer. Use her to make contact with the pacifists and convince them to give you a communication device to stay in touch."

"What will that help?" Octavia asked, pocketing the address.

Serafine took a vase from her desk, tipping out a black pebble into her hand. She held it up for Octavia to see. "This little device can track down any communication anchor's other half. If you bring me a pacifist's communication device, I can use it to finally make some useful arrests."

Octavia left her riding clothes with the clothier, exiting the shop in what she was assured was the latest Athelian fashions. Though she felt strange and a bit out of step in the unusual garb as she walked through the market square, her disguise was apparently working because none of the passersby looked her way. Some even bumped into her as they hurried past, as if she'd not even been worth their time. Octavia had never been so glad to be invisible.

You should change your hair too, Raksha suggested.

Oh, right. Octavia quickly untangled her braids, then twisted her hair into a knot at the back of her head in a style similar to the way the women in the market square wore their hair. When she was done, she pulled the paper with the address from her pocket, and hurried down one of the side streets.

It was bustling and crowded, the early afternoon sun hot overhead. Octavia peered in through shop windows, rubbing away grime with the sleeves of her new shirt to find the printer.

"Oh, excuse me," a young boy said as he stumbled into her, carrying a stack of flyers. He rushed off before Octavia could respond, but she traced the path he'd come from to a darkened doorway and made her way toward it.

Octavia passed through the entrance, moving aside a heavy sheet that had been hung instead of a door. Inside were six strings, each one stretched across the entire length of the shop, from which hung dozens of drying papers, large and small, each one smelling of fresh ink.

Apparently, she was in the right place.

"Excuse me," Octavia said.

The woman behind the counter paused her work, wiping her ink-stained hands on her apron. "Can I help you?"

Octavia lifted her hands, casting a shield wall of air that ruffled all the papers in the store.

The woman looked up.

"That's just to keep us from being overheard," Octavia said.

The woman's eyes narrowed, immediately suspicious, and Octavia couldn't blame her. It was clear to the printer that this wasn't a trick of Athelian magic. "You're the Tenegardian. The one who came on dragonback."

The woman lifted a finger and Octavia looked to where she was pointing. A stack of papers sat on the counter, an etched drawing of a dragon taking up most of the page. Apparently, her arrival had been newsworthy.

"What do you want?" the woman asked.

Octavia paused. Serafine wanted to bring down the pacifist movement, but Octavia suspected they might be the key to finally achieving peace between their nations. The same way the rebel fighters had taken down Onyx, the pacifists would help secure a brighter future for Athelia. All they needed was a little help. "You're being watched," she said.

"What?" the woman stammered.

"The senate suspects your involvement with the pacifist movement and they are watching you."

The printer rang her ink-stained hands together. The news had obviously come as a surprise. "I suppose everyone in Erelas is being watched these days," she said warily. "But why do you care?"

"All I want is peace," Octavia said. "And if any of your friends are interested in discussing that peace, I will be at the fountain by the inn in one hour. If it helps, I can prevent our conversation from being overheard."

The printer nodded once to show she understood, so Octavia headed for the door. Before leaving, she turned and said, "They should ask me how fast a dragon flies."

Then she stepped out into the street and dropped her shield, immediately scanning for the familiar faces of the guards. They'd gotten into the habit of following her around in civilian attire, so she couldn't be sure she was alone, but she was certain the shield had kept anyone from listening to her exchange with the printer.

Do you think they will come? Raksha asked.

I hope so, Octavia said, wandering back through the market space. She wasn't sure how else she would make contact with the pacifist group if not through the printer. That was all the information Serafine had provided her.

Just be careful.

Why do you think I chose to meet so close to you and the inn? If it all went south, Raksha would be right there.

By the time Octavia made her way back to the inn and retrieved a book from her room, the hour was almost up. In her new Athelian attire, she walked out toward the fountain and sat on the ledge, the supple sound of water trickling behind her. She cracked her book in her lap, letting her eyes drift between the words and the surrounding square as her heart began to race. There were people everywhere: flitting back and forth across the plaza with packages, leaving the inn after a late lunch, stopping to gawk at Raksha, feeding the pigeons that gathered to bathe in the fountain. It would be impossible for her to pick the pacifists out of the crowd even if she knew what to look for.

Then, from the corner of her eye, she watched a young couple approach, but it was only to toss a coin into the fountain. The man turned to the woman on his arm and said, "How fast do you think a dragon flies?"

Octavia's ears burned hot. The pacifists had come to meet her.

"Too fast for me," an older man answered, standing on her other side. He bent down, feeding the pigeons from his hand.

An elderly woman, bent over a cane, toddled past and sat on the edge of the fountain, facing away from Octavia. She tutted. "Even a horse is too fast for you, Erik."

The flush that had begun in Octavia's ears now painted her cheeks as she realized she was surrounded.

Across the square, Raksha acknowledged the arrival of the group with a slight dip of her head. Octavia lifted her book in her lap and used it to hide her hand as she cast a shield wall of air around them, pulling it tight enough to block out the clamor of the plaza.

"Clever trick," the elderly woman said. She turned a fraction so Octavia could make out spirals of gray curls. She was clearly the leader judging by the way the others deferred to her.

"I don't want anyone to overhear us," Octavia said.

"And what would you worry about them hearing?"

Octavia made a show of turning the page in her book in case anyone was watching. "You are the pacifists, are you not?"

The woman shifted her cane from one hand to the other. "What do you want from us?"

"I've been sent to spy," Octavia admitted. She watched the shifty glares the group shared.

"By whom?"

"Serafine. She's a—"

"We're well aware of who Serafine is," the woman said abruptly. "And what exactly is Serafine after?"

"She asked me to retrieve one of the pacifists' communication devices in order to use it to track you down and make arrests."

"But you've clearly deviated from that plan," the woman pointed out.

"It was never my intention to spy for Serafine. I've come from Tenegard in the pursuit of peace. To end the war between our nations." Octavia lifted her head then and looked at the woman directly. "From what I can tell, we want the same thing. So how can I help you?"

The man feeding the birds tilted his head in their direction, clearly intrigued. But the woman showed no emotion. She studied Octavia for a long moment, then slowly got to her feet.

"It is obvious you're deceiving someone," she said as she passed Octavia. "I just haven't figured out yet if it is Serafine or us."

CHAPTER 15

CORA

The news of Melusine's plan to attack Llys with the augmented magical weapons had spread through camp, just as Cora had suspected it would. Some of the riders were skeptical of the news, while others seemed to be relieved they finally had a target to focus on. In both cases the news was distracting, and Cora called an early end to morning drills. The last thing she needed was for a pair of dragons to collide midair or a rider to slip from their saddle because they weren't paying attention.

As Alaric touched down, Cora spotted Faron. He sat on the low hanging branch of an almost-naked evergreen. Wyn curled up at the base of the tree. She dismounted and walked in his direction. When she was close enough, he dropped from the branch. "Renka seems to be in better spirits today. Whatever you said to the so-called trouble-makers looks to be working."

"I promised to run morning drills, but I think I mostly just gave them something else to fret over."

"You mean Llys?"

Cora nodded. “I could tell their minds were elsewhere this morning.”

“They’re not the only ones,” Faron admitted. “Now we know what Melusine and Zirael intend to do, I think we have to seriously talk about shifting our focus away from the Heart.”

“We can’t abandon the Heart,” Cora said, shocked to even hear him mention such a thing.

“I never said abandon it. I just think we need to—”

“Don’t you see that it’s all connected? Protecting the Heart, saving Llys. We can’t sacrifice one goal for the other. That’s what she wants us to do.”

“Cora, there’s not enough of us to protect the Heart and somehow stop Melusine and Zirael from attacking Llys.”

“We’ll figure it out. Somehow. We always do.”

“Too bad we can’t see the future. Then we’d know where to invest our time and energy.”

“Yeah,” Cora agreed, but his comment about the future spun an idea to life in her mind, and she grabbed his hand, roughly pulling him to a stop.

“The future,” she repeated. “The soothsayers. Didn’t Elaine say she’d heard the soothsayers were on their way to the school?”

“I—yes. But what does that have to do with anything?”

“We can’t see the future, but they can!” When Elaine had mentioned it after her last visit to the school, Cora hadn’t thought anything of the news other than the fact Northwood was up to something. But now maybe they could use this to their advantage.

Faron scoffed. "You really think the soothsayers are going to help? They're at the beck and call of the council. If anything, they're going to get us into more trouble."

"I'm not so sure," Cora said. "I know the soothsayers relocating to the school feels like a plan concocted by Northwood, but while you were trapped in the sleeping sickness, Ismenia flew to the school's aid with Octavia."

"She what?" he said, startled by the revelation that Onyx's former seer would help those who'd overthrown him.

"It sounds crazy," Cora agreed, squeezing his hand in reassurance. His uncertainty reminded her of just how much he'd missed while he'd been unconscious. "But maybe if we ask them about the future, we can figure out what's going to happen. And if we know what's going to happen, we can better prepare for it."

"I don't know about this," he said reluctantly. "Ismenia helped Onyx terrorize an entire country for years. I don't see how bringing the soothsayers into our mountain camp, giving away our position to Northwood's forces and the countless others Ismenia has aligned herself with, is a good idea. She only seeks to serve herself. The moment it is convenient for her, she'll betray us."

"I know our history with her is complicated, but trusting Ismenia last time paid off. She helped us save the school."

Faron tipped his head back and forth, considering her words.

"Look," Cora said. "I didn't think using the hound was a good idea. You and Lenire had to convince me otherwise. And see how far we've come? This is the only plan I've been able to come up with. But if you've got something better, I'm all ears. If not, I think this is our best chance at figuring out the way forward."

“Okay,” Faron said. “You’re right. This is the only idea we’ve come up with, so let’s give it a try. I’ll fly Elaine back to the school myself. She can sneak in and connect with Ismenia. Then I’ll fly us all back here. Sound good?”

Cora grinned, then whirled and ran, dragging Faron along behind her all the way to the infirmary tent.

Faron returned from the school with Elaine and three soothsayers.

Ismenia had brought along two assistants, but it was still Ismenia herself who unnerved Cora the most. Her eyes were permanently clouded over, her long silver hair left unbound and stringy around her face.

When they dismounted from Wyn’s back, Cora was surprised to see Ismenia stumble. Despite her discomfort, Cora reached out to steady the woman. This wasn’t the soothsayer’s first time on dragonback, so she doubted it was the flight that made her dizzy.

“You found the Heart of Tenegard,” Ismenia said, gazing at Cora with those pearly eyes. Cora couldn’t tell if she was looking at her or through her.

“How did you know?” she replied before she could stop herself. What a foolish question to ask a soothsayer.

“I did not *see* it,” Ismenia clarified, almost as if reading Cora’s thoughts. “But I can feel it.” She gestured to her assistants. “We all can.” It was then Cora noticed the other two seers swaying gently, as if they might be carried off by an errant wave. “We’re close enough that the currents we usually navigate in our magic are much stronger.”

Just as Cora’s dragon magic came from the Heart, so did the soothsayers’. Only the soothsayers used the magical currents of that subterranean river to navigate their visions. Being this close to the source was clearly overwhelming as one of Ismenia's assistants grabbed her head with one hand, the other shooting out to steady herself against Wyn.

"Come," Elaine said, ushering the seers to the camp outside the infirmary tent. "At least sit down."

They went without protest. Cora, Faron, and Lenire joined them as Elaine stoked a small fire to life. A few other riders gathered close enough to listen in, and Cora even spotted Emmett hovering.

"You don't seem all that surprised to be here," Cora noted as Ismenia took a seat on a log.

"I'm not. Frankly, I was surprised it took you so long to reach out."

"You knew I would ask for your help?"

Ismenia clearly still had the presence of mind to be smug about that fact because she smirked at Cora. "I suspected you might be in need of our assistance."

"*That's* why you relocated to the school," Cora said, swallowing whatever remained of her dislike for the woman.

"You assumed we had been sent to spy?" Ismenia asked.

"Can you blame me?"

"I suppose not. Especially now Northwood has lost his liaison." Her gaze drifted to Emmett across the crowd. He grew uncomfortable under her scrutiny and fled across the camp. Cora wasn't surprised. Ismenia had that effect on people whether she was trying to or not.

"What's in it for you?" Cora asked. Ismenia merely blinked at her. "Why would you leave the comfort and safety of Kaerlin to trek across Tenegard?"

"We've left behind comfort, yes," Ismenia agreed. "But only because we worried our safety might be threatened."

"Is Kaerlin going to come under attack?" Cora asked.

"That future is not yet known, but we are at war with Athelia. You do not have to be a soothsayer to know Athelia will come for the capital if given the chance. We have done what we must to ensure our own survival if the border should fall."

"I don't think the border is the only thing Kaerlin has to worry about," Cora admitted.

Ismenia's blank, roving eyes settled on Cora once more. "What is it that you know?"

"The enemy means to strike Llys," Cora told her. "And if they are able to hold and maintain the ground there—"

"Kaerlin will be attacked from both sides," Ismenia finished for her. She exchanged a look with her assistants, and Cora wondered if they were reading futures with this new information. When Ismenia looked back at Cora, her mouth was set in a firm line. "What is it you want from me?"

"We want to know the future," Faron cut in, gesturing around the camp. "We want to know what happens in the next few days, weeks, even next month."

"That is asking a lot," Ismenia said, not unkindly but pointedly.

"Can you not do it?" Faron asked.

"Contrary to what some might think, it will actually be more difficult to direct our visions this close to the Heart. We've learned to swim in the magical currents of our visions, but they're so powerful here, we're liable to be swept off course if what you seek is too broad."

"Try," Faron insisted, the challenge strong in his voice.

"Very well." Ismenia took the hands of her assistants and all at once their cloudy eyes turned solid white. It was a chilling sight and made Cora dizzy to watch. Ismenia released her assistants' hands. The seer gasped as if surfacing from deep water.

Elaine touched her shoulder gently, but Ismenia just shook her head. She hadn't seen anything. Faron hunched over, propping his head on his hand. He was already wary of Ismenia, and now he didn't think she was capable of helping them. Lenire stood behind them, quiet, arms folded across his chest. He looked a million miles away.

"Maybe we're not asking the right question," Cora suggested over the murmurs of disappointment. "Maybe what we need to ask isn't what's going to happen, but what we need to do in order to protect the Heart and stop Melusine and Zirael from invading Llys."

Ismenia cleared her throat. "Is that your question?"

Cora nodded. "Tell me how to save the source of the magic we both share."

Once again Ismenia's cloudy gaze solidified as she peered into the future.

"Wait," Cora said, reaching out her hand. "Share it with me."

She'd done this before, taking memories from Ismenia. But this time she wasn't taking memories. She was asking to share in their creation. To be given a glimpse of the visions the seers swam through to find the future.

With another one of those knowing smirks, Ismenia snatched Cora's hand, sharing her magic, and Cora was dragged into the torrent of the seer's world. True to her word, the foray into the current of visions was chaotic and overwhelming. Glimpses of futures flashed by so quickly Cora thought she might be dragged away with them. Then, like they'd been caught in a whirlpool, the visions twisted around them before spitting them back into the current. A vision surfaced and Cora recognized the school. It was the moment Octavia had shown up to tell them to use the crystals to protect the school.

We're going backward, Cora thought to herself. *The current of magic has hurled us into the past.*

Suddenly, a thunderous echo sounded around her, and Cora spotted another fragment of a vision. A booming burst of magical energy rippled across the sky over an unfamiliar landscape. It reminded Cora of the energy that had radiated from the broken bond between the hound and the Blight when they'd woken the sleeping dragon riders, but on a much more massive scale.

Before Cora could wonder about the vision, they were captured in that twisting whirlpool and hurled out. Cora had the sense they were moving forward through time now, and as Ismenia navigated them through the currents, she locked onto another scene with a similar burst of magical energy. This time it was accompanied by a chilling scream and a striking pain, as if Cora had been wounded at close range. The vision trembled, growing shaky in the magical current, but Ismenia managed to hang on long enough for Cora to spot Melusine's hounds fleeing the source of the energy. One of them staggered to a halt, limbs locked, and fell to the ground.

All at once Cora was thrown from the vision. She found herself on the ground, Ismenia within arm's reach, their hands no longer linked. Faron's voice was in her ear, asking her a thousand things as he and Lenire helped them up.

"Ismenia," Cora began, her mind filled with a dozen more desperate questions after seeing the vision. But the seer wasn't paying attention. Her focus was locked on one of her assistants. The woman flailed backward clutching her head, and Cora knew the power of the magic they navigated had overwhelmed her.

"What can we do?" Cora asked, still reeling from what she'd seen.

Ismenia shook her head, her expression grim. "The proximity to the Heart has dragged her into an uncontrollable torrent." She turned to the other assistant. "You'll have to return with her to the school if there's any hope of stopping the visions."

"I'll take them," Renka offered, stepping forward.

"You're sure?" Cora said. "You can't let yourself be seen."

Renka nodded. "I can do this."

"Okay," Cora said, stamping down the part of her that wanted to argue. Letting any of the dragon riders out of her sight right now felt reckless, but she couldn't always send Faron. She was still concerned about him overexerting himself. Plus, she knew she had to start relinquishing control. If not, the progress she'd made with Renka's group the other night would boil down to nothing but words with no action. "Choose a partner to go with you. Fly safe."

Renka turned on her heel, rushing off to ready the dragons as Faron dispatched a few of the riders to help carry the thrashing soothsayer through the camp. Elaine followed, doing what she could, but a soothsayer's magic wasn't something she could heal.

As the commotion drifted away, Cora revealed what she and Ismenia had seen to Faron and Lenire. Alaric was already in her head.

I've never heard of such a thing happening in the sky, he said, referencing the glimpse of the past Cora had relived. *An event like that would have certainly been preserved in dragon lore,* Alaric said. *Unless it didn't happen in Tenegard.*

Or unless it was lost with Onyx's reign.

Alaric grumbled at the mention of Onyx. *And the other burst of magic you noted in the future part of the vision ... you said it was painful?*

I only felt a fraction of what the real thing would have been like, Cora said. *This was pain unlike anything I've ever experienced.*

I'll ask around and see if the other dragons know anything about either event.

Thank you, Cora said, dropping back into the conversation between Faron, Lenire, and Ismenia. Her concerns about the vision from the past were only outweighed by the vision from the future. Though Ismenia argued that the vision was obscure, Cora knew it had something to do with a plan to strike back at Melusine and Zirael. A plan they hadn't yet made.

Before she could even begin to contemplate their next step, a cry for help cut through the air.

CHAPTER 16

CORA

Cora raced through base camp with Ismenia, Faron, and Lenire on her heels, rushing toward the source of the commotion. It was Renka. The trainee had chosen another young dragon rider named Joi to accompany her on the journey to take the injured seer back to the school, but the soothsayer was thrashing so badly she kept slipping from Renka's dragon, who was crouched low, belly to the ground, so Elaine and the group of dragon riders could try to wrestle the seer into position.

"It's no use," Elaine said, taking her hand off the seer's forehead. "Even if we send more riders to hold her, she'll wriggle right out of their grip. We can't afford to risk anyone falling off."

"She can't stay," Ismenia insisted. "The power of the Heart will fracture her mind more than it already has. Her only chance at recovery is to get some distance from this place."

Cora's thoughts raced as the riders laid the seer on the ground again. They'd wrapped her in a blanket, but as her limbs seized and spasmed, she threw it off. The image sparked Cora's memory and she knew exactly what they were going to do.

"Cora?" Faron shouted after her as she raced back through camp, grabbing a tarp that had been strung between two trees to cover a firepit.

She returned to the others, dragging the tarp behind her.

"What's that for?" Faron asked.

"If she can't ride on dragonback," Cora explained. "Then she'll ride between them."

His brows pinched together in confusion, and Cora almost said, "Don't you remember?" But of course he couldn't remember. When she'd used this trick to transport Faron and his dragon from the mountains after they'd been rendered unconscious by the Blight, the only other people with her were Strida, who was currently in the capital, and Emmett. Cora scanned the gathering crowd. Emmett was never far from a scene of chaos, and just as she expected, he wormed his way through the gathering dragon riders, carrying a length of rope.

"This should be enough," he said. "The sling won't have to be nearly as big if they're not transporting a dragon."

"Thanks," Cora said, cutting the rope into pieces with her dagger. "I need another large tarp!"

The dragon riders scrambled, but it was her father who raced over with one, torn down from above a weapon's rack. He handed it over as Cora tossed some of the rope pieces to Faron.

"A sling?" Faron said, passing rope to Lenire.

"Tie the two tarps together," Cora said, already on her hands and knees, feeding rope through the holes in the tarps. Faron and Lenire crouched down next to her. "This is how we transported you after the Blight attacked you and Wyn. One tarp is probably enough, but I want the pocket to be deep so that even if the seer thrashes, she won't slip out." Cora, Faron, Lenire, and Emmett worked quickly, securing the tarps together while Renka and Joi attached the corners of the tarps to anchor points on their dragons. Ismenia attempted to soothe the seer with Elaine, but it didn't sound like it was working. Cora jumped up to inspect the anchors.

"I double knotted them," Renka said, the corners of her eyes twitching, almost as if she was working hard to contain an eye roll.

"I don't doubt that," Cora said. "But this is a woman's life. We can afford to be thorough."

Renka sighed but let Cora double-check her work.

"When you fly, you have to keep yourself level with Joi and her dragon."

"I figured as much."

"Not too fast. Not too much higher or else—"

"The seer will tumble out," Renka said. "I got it. I can do this."

"I know you can." She tugged on the final anchor point. "Okay, riders! Let's get her loaded up."

The same team who had carried the thrashing seer down to the dragons now lifted her into the center of the tarps. Renka and Joi scrambled into their respective saddles along with Ismenia's other colleague, and as Faron and Lenire waved the gathered crowd back, the dragons took to the sky.

The moment they were airborne, Cora walked beneath the tarp, inspecting it from the bottom.

"Are we good?" Renka called.

Cora shot her a thumbs-up. "All good!"

A blustery wind whipped around her as the dragons ascended, and Cora had to squint to avoid getting dust in her eyes. The crowd who had gathered slowly drifted away. Elaine wrapped her arm around Ismenia, guiding her to the infirmary tent, probably to assess her after what had happened. Cora remained, watching as the dragons became two tiny specks on the horizon. Watching them go made her feel like she still had a measure of control over what would happen next.

"Are we going to talk about this?" Lenire called.

"Talk about what?" Cora asked.

"The fact that the vision you and Ismenia saw clearly shows us attacking Melusine's camp."

"I never said it was *us* attacking the camp."

Lenire huffed. It wasn't quite a laugh. "Who else would go after the sorcerers?"

"I don't know," Cora said. "But we need to proceed with caution."

"We've been cautious," Lenire said. "We've been so cautious that instead of planning some sort of counterstrike when we found Melusine's base camp, we waited and waited some more. Now we've spoken to your soothsayers who also foresee an attack on Melusine's camp. If that's not a sign for us to coordinate and strike, I don't know what is."

Cora didn't know quite what to say. Was she hesitating in making this decision? Yes. But what if attacking Melusine went badly? "Something terrible happens in that camp," she reminded them, looking from Lenire to Faron. "What if it happens to one of us because we rushed this plan?" Sending the seer off in the tarp had brought up memories of the moment Faron had been injured. She'd just got him back from the sleeping sickness. She couldn't bear to lose him again. "I think attacking the camp is too risky. I'm also worried about our continued use of the hound."

"Not this again," Lenire said. "Cora, we've talked about this. Using the hound gives us the advantage we need against the sorcerers."

Cora shook her head. In Ismenia's vision, she'd heard that booming explosion of magical energy and felt some remnant of that striking pain. The shrill echoes of that wretched scream still lingered in her mind. And then there was the image of that hound. The one who'd staggered and seized as they were escaping the burst of energy. "I can't shake the thought that the fallen hound in the vision was *our* hound," she said to Lenire. "The one *you've* been piloting. And that scream! It was clearly one of agony."

Lenire shrugged, unconvinced. "Who's to say the scream isn't coming from Melusine? Or Zirael? How can you tell the hound wasn't one of theirs?"

Cora let out a heavy breath. She was frustrated with Lenire's indifference toward Ismenia's vision. Then again, Lenire was unfamiliar with soothsaying magic. Of course he wouldn't feel the warning as urgently as she did.

"I really think this is our chance to strike the sorcerers for once. Right now, we have the element of surprise. I vote that we use it."

Cora turned to Faron. He'd been quiet. "What do you think?"

"I think Lenire's right. We have the element of surprise on our side."

Cora groaned but Faron reached out, taking her by the shoulders before she could turn away. "Wait, hear me out. What if it's waiting too long to strike that works against us?"

Cora stood there, letting his words wash over her. She wasn't really interested in hearing them, but apparently, she was outnumbered here.

"I know what you saw and heard in that vision. But let's not pretend any of us really know how soothsaying magic works or how to properly read a vision like this. What you saw could be interpreted in different ways."

"Like how?" Cora muttered. It had seemed pretty clear to her.

"Maybe it's like Lenire said. Maybe the hound and the scream point to us successfully fending off Melusine's attack on Llys. The mission might just go our way."

Cora bit the inside of her cheek, reluctant to agree with him.

"Besides," Faron continued, "whatever this vision truly foretells might not be something that's within our control to stop anyway."

Cora knew Faron didn't want to give up on the hound. It would be giving up on his way to contribute to the battle, and she didn't want to be the one to take that from him. "I'd hate to risk everyone's safety by being optimistic about an ambiguous vision."

Lenire cleared his throat, drawing Cora's attention. "You always try to keep the dragon riders out of danger," he said. "It's one of the things I admire about your leadership. But now you have to let go of that control. Cora, we need you to let the riders take risks beyond what you think is safe. It's the only way this works. You heard Zirael and Melusine when we spied on them. Those weapons are almost ready."

Faron took her hands and squeezed. "If we let Zirael and Melusine finish their weapons and attack Llys, the fort will fall. If we strike now and destroy enough of their supplies, we could at least delay those plans. Give ourselves time to regroup and plan another attack."

"I don't know," Cora began but she was interrupted by Yrsa. She and Alaric and Wyn had gathered close.

"I am not interested in risking Lenire's safety any more than you are," Yrsa said. Wyn agreed on Faron's behalf. "But we know our vulnerabilities."

"I think they're right," Alaric agreed softly. "Now is the time for action."

With Alaric's words, Cora felt her arguments shatter. "Okay," she relented, despite the anxious butterflies that lingered in her chest. Worry dripped from every one of her words. "We keep talking about a strike, but what does that even look like?"

"We can't very well just fly in with a barrage of dragons," Alaric said. "Melusine will have prepared for that."

Yrsa nodded. "We have multiple enemies to contend with. The sorcerers. The Blight itself. The hounds."

"Let's not forget whatever Athelian forces are in camp at the time," Faron added.

Cora could feel the stress of Yrsa's words trickle down the bond from Alaric. Clearly, he was feeling as overwhelmed as everyone else looked. If their last encounter with Melusine and the hounds was anything to go by, this was going to be a dangerous attack. What they really needed to be able to do was somehow isolate their enemies. Make it easier to fight them.

But how did they get control of the …

"That's it!" Cora said suddenly. "We take control of the Blight."

"What?" Faron and Lenire said at once.

"Melusine's losing her control over the creature, remember? So what if we used our hound to sneak in and steal Zirael's disk? Then we would control the Blight *and* the hounds."

"Because the hounds are animated by fragments of the Blight," Lenire mused.

"Exactly!" Cora said excitedly.

"Is it possible to steal the disk?" Faron asked.

Cora deferred to Lenire, who was conferring privately with Yrsa. "It would be tricky," he finally said. "Zirael's obviously keeping a close eye on it because of Melusine. But I've managed to steal a disk from him before. I'm sure we could do it again."

"Plus, he won't be expecting the hound," Yrsa added.

"Melusine and Zirael are powerful, but alone they can't stand against all of the dragon riders," Faron said. "Without the Blight and their minions, they're much less of a threat. We could swoop in and easily destroy the weapons' cache they're building, saving Llys."

"And if we control the Blight," Cora continue, "then the threat to the Heart of Tenegard also disappears!" For the first time since seeing the vision, Cora felt a glimmer of hope. If they pulled this off, they could possibly defeat all their enemies at once.

CHAPTER 17
OCTAVIA

The people in Erelas were about to riot. Octavia could feel their anger in the tremor that rippled across the cobblestones from their marching feet. They'd gathered in the courtyard outside the senate building for a public forum, lambasting the senators about the allocation of resources for the war and the misuse of funds.

"Are you lying?" one woman screeched as she stood before the senators, holding up a wrinkled leaflet. "Is this what you're really doing with our money? Buying defective war engines? Meanwhile, I can hardly afford to feed my children!" A rousing cheer of agreement sounded through the crowd.

Octavia stood off to the side of the massive stage that had been erected in the senate square for this meeting. The area where she watched from had been cordoned off for the senators and select community stakeholders. They mingled and drank and nibbled on finger foods, almost as if they were oblivious to the concerns being shouted by the people. It made Octavia uncomfortable and she clutched her teacup tighter.

"You look troubled," Serafine said, coming up beside her.

It took everything inside Octavia not to jump at Serafine's sudden appearance. "Are the people always this … vocal?" she asked, drawing Serafine's attention away from herself.

Serafine huffed, seemingly unbothered by the entire display. "The pacifists have gotten them riled up. Once they've said their peace, Senator Jangoor will talk them down with her pretty words, and everyone will go about their business."

"Is that how all concerns are dealt with in Athelia—pretty words?" Octavia didn't know what made her say it. Genuine curiosity, maybe. Tenegard was far from perfect, but at least the issues brought to the concern of the small claims court were addressed with action. To her surprise, Serafine smirked in response to her question. "Sometimes the people do not know what is good for them. Was that money foolishly spent? Yes. Does that mean we are going to pull our troops back from the border? No." Serafine turned so her words brushed Octavia's ear. "The people know only a small fraction of what really goes on behind the scenes. They have no idea what it takes to wield the power necessary to run a country. So we let them moan and whine about the war until they're satisfied, and then we all go back to work, keeping Tenegard's military off our doorstep. Besides, when it comes down to it, the people are fools. Look at how easy it was for you to infiltrate the pacifists and bring me one of their communication anchors."

"Yes, that's true," Octavia said. After her initial meeting with the pacifists, they'd given Octavia a dud communication anchor to pass off to Serafine. That way the senator would start to trust Octavia, but the pacifists could lay false trails, ensuring none of their people were arrested. If they played their cards right, Serafine would pull Octavia further into her inner circle, and Octavia could carefully pass vital pieces of information to the pacifists to help them fight back against the warmongering.

Geri, their wizened leader, also promised to share any useful information they managed to uncover about the movement of troops at the border or Serafine's plans. Between that and her own sleuthing, Octavia hoped to uncover the truth of Serafine's deceptions.

"Everyone wants to believe they're doing the right thing for the right reasons," Serafine said lightly. "Even the pacifists. And that's what makes them the most dangerous of all." She turned at the sound of her name and drifted away.

What did she mean by that? Octavia asked Raksha.

Maybe just more of those pretty words she talked about, meant to distract you.

Or unnerve me. Octavia couldn't even finish her tea and looked around for a place to put her cup. She might be working for Serafine, but she didn't trust her any farther than she could throw her. She spotted a small table with used dishware and cut through the crowd of senators toward it. As she did, a young man took the stage. Octavia wasn't sure what exactly he said, but suddenly the crowd parted as half-a-dozen tomatoes crashed down on the cobbles. They exploded, spraying the nearby senators, looking like blood where they landed.

"That is all that will remain of the children you are sending off to war!" the man shouted.

A chill shot through Octavia. Her gaze lifted from the tomatoes to find Serafine standing there, wiping tomato juice from her beaded blazer, her face stormy and unreadable. Jangoor attempted to calm the crowd but the young man stoked their anger. The already agitated citizenry was on their feet, shouting slogans and hurling insults. One woman picked up a palm-sized stone from the street and wrenched her arm back, only to be seized by a guard before she could throw it. The crowd pushed toward the stage in response, threatening to overrun the guards who surrounded the senators' private meeting area.

Several of the senators had abandoned their finger foods and dashed toward the senate building where they would find solace behind the stone walls.

Serafine walked through the crowd, past Octavia, and whispered something into the ear of a guard. He nodded briskly, once, then melted into the crowd of angered citizens. The next moment four guards had ascended the stage and taken the young man by force.

"Please," Jangoor declared. "There is no need for that."

The guards did not heed her protests, instead dragging the man across the podium. He struggled, and the guards responded with a sharp kick to his ribs.

Jangoor's voice echoed as she gasped.

The man struggled some more, shouting obscenities directed at the senate, and one of the guards punched him square in the face, the metal on his armored glove breaking the man's nose with a spurt of blood.

The crowd's anger dissipated, replaced by whispered fear as the guards pulled the man down the stairs of the stage and across the cobblestones. When they drew closer, Octavia recognized him. He was there that day by the fountain with the other pacifists—posing as the young couple who meant to throw a coin into the water. She slipped between the senators, close enough she could speak with him as he passed, but spotting her, the man shook his head and she stopped in her tracks, frozen with her foolishness. What was she thinking?

She'd only wanted to help. To demand the guards release him. That they provide him with proper medical care. The demands surged through her like fire. But she wasn't a councilor here. She had no power. In Athelia, even being a dragon rider meant nothing other than the fact she was a liability.

If she spoke to him, the senators might think she was dangerous. Or worse. Serafine might realize he was more than just a man expressing his frustration. She might peg him for a pacifist.

"That was interesting," Serafine said, coming to get a good look at the man as the guards dragged him past the senators and into the senate building. She smelled strongly of overripe tomatoes. It was sweet and slightly acidic.

As the man disappeared, the crowd's anger returned, fueled by the guards' involvement. Members of the Athelian military surrounded the square, looking down from perches above the crowd, armed with crossbows, and from doorways, dressed in their armor and carrying their swords on full display. Now that Octavia was *really* looking, this forum felt more like the events held under Onyx's rule, when the people of Kaerlin had been gathered together in a farce meant to celebrate Onyx's reign. If any of the Tenegardians had spoken out against Onyx in this way, the reaction would have been similar, and the shiver she'd felt before returned. This kind of event was familiar to Octavia and not in a good way.

"Do you usually have to break the noses of the people at these forums?" she asked.

Serafine chuckled, the sound low, like it had been caught in her chest. "Don't fret. He'll sleep off the rest of his anger in a cell," she said. "And when he wakes up, he'll realize what a fool he's been."

The sight of the man's face, dripping with blood, made Octavia hesitate to respond.

"You don't agree?" Serafine asked.

"I don't think violence can pave the way to peace," she said.

Serafine blinked at her as if the words had been in a foreign language. Then she smiled, her lips stretching across her face. "You're right, of course." She left Octavia and cut through the crowd until she'd reached the stairs leading up to the stage where Jangoor was still desperately trying to call for order. Serafine leaned in, exchanged a few words with the other senator, and they switched places.

Serafine lifted her hand, telling the crowd she meant to speak. They responded as expected, with jeers and cruel taunts. Serafine did not cower away from them, but stood firm, her shoulders back, her gaze steady as she made eye contact with the crowd. "I know you are afraid," she began. "And angry. But we cannot tolerate violence against each other. Especially not when Tenegard is poised on our doorstep, waiting to strike. That is the real enemy. They are the ones who deserve your vitriol and your rage."

Serafine's voice carried over the crowd, her words turning the angry jeers into murmurs that dissolved the tension Octavia had felt earlier. It shifted into something that felt oddly like agreement.

The loyalties in this crowd blow faster than the wind, Raksha noted. She was seated against a brick wall on the far end of the courtyard where she would be out of the way.

Serafine does have a way with words, Octavia admitted. It took a special kind of person to be able to calm an angry crowd. *Apparently, uniting them in anger against Tenegard is the way to win back favor.*

"For decades Tenegard has threatened our border, made us fear for the lives of our children, but no more!"

The crowd cheered, surprising Octavia and several of the other senators. Jangoor looked astonished and somewhat concerned as she whispered to a colleague.

"Athelia will not stand by as Tenegard continues to bully us and betray our trust," Serafine continued. "We will fight back against our enemies. Even those who come from *within.*"

Uh oh, Octavia said to Raksha. *Do you think she knows we're working with the pacifists against her?*

Octavia stared across the courtyard, past the stage and crowd, to where Raksha sat. It was a long way to run. Plus, she'd have to fight off multiple guards. Raksha would help, of course, but Octavia wanted to avoid casualties. She wasn't here to kill Athelians.

Why wouldn't she have confronted you earlier?

I don't know. Octavia said, starting to make her way through the crowd of senators. *Maybe she wanted to make a show of it. Use us as an excuse to further rile up the crowd against Tenegard. Blaming us is a lot easier than the senate actually owning up to their mistakes.*

I think Serafine is smart enough to know not to threaten a dragon rider when her dragon is watching from the wings.

That's a good point, Octavia said. Serafine wouldn't risk her life or those of the other senators by antagonizing a dragon. But as the woman's voice cut back into Octavia's thoughts, she froze next to the stage.

"These pacifists continue to threaten the very foundation of our society," Serafine declared. "They call for peace while our border is being attacked. They would have us stand by and allow Tenegard to destroy everything we have become."

The crowd shouted along.

"These pacifists are not true Athelians! Do not be fooled by their words!" Serafine held up a leaflet and crushed it. "They are trying to deceive you to disguise their true nature as Tenegardian sympathizers! But I have something that will turn the tide in favor of true-hearted Athelians."

Octavia squinted at the communication device Serafine held up in puzzlement. It looked like the one the pacifists had given her to hand over, but why was Serafine revealing it here?

"This communication anchor was recovered from a rebel pacifist sect in Erelas," Serafine told the crowd.

Be ready to run, Raksha said. Octavia was already shoving her way past people when Serafine gestured to the guards. But instead of rushing in Octavia's direction, they seized Senator Jangoor.

"What is the meaning of this?" Jangoor demanded.

"Search her pockets!" Serafine shouted.

The guards seized her belongings, holding up another communication anchor. They activated it. Serafine spoke into her anchor, and to everyone's surprise, her voice came through the device taken from Jangoor's pocket.

"That's impossible," Jangoor said as the crowd booed her. "That's not even mine!"

"Arrest her and take her away," Serafine declared. "There is no room in the senate for those who confer with these pacifist rebels!"

"You're making a mistake!" Jangoor shouted as the guards locked her hands behind her back. "You all are! The senate will serve your children to the maws of war. They will destroy us and everything we stand for! Peace is the only solution!" The senators around her were dumbstruck, some of their mouths open in shock, others sputtering with outrage, though whether it was over her speech or her arrest, Octavia couldn't tell. The guards dragged Jangoor toward the senate building, in the same direction they'd taken the young man with the bloody nose. Only, this wouldn't be a matter of sleeping off the events of today in a cell. From the looks of it, the now-former senator was going to be locked up for a long time.

Octavia turned back to Serafine, who stood with her back to the crowd, a look of smug satisfaction on her face as Jangoor was taken away. By the stars, what was happening?

That can't be the communication anchor the pacifists gave me, Octavia said to Raksha as her heart hammered in her chest. *Ours was meant to lead Serafine to a dead end.*

Maybe Serafine only wanted a pacifist anchor so she could recreate an identical one and plant it on Jangoor.

Is that even possible?

Communication anchors are Athelian magic. Who knows?

That was true. She didn't really know the extent an anchor could be manipulated by Athelian mages. Octavia's nails bit into her palms. Had she played right into Serafine's hands without knowing it? Had Serafine suspected she would try to align with the pacifists? *I didn't even know Jangoor was working with the pacifists. They never told me.*

They were obviously trying to protect her.

Octavia ran her hands over her head, shocked by the show of violence and how closely it resembled Onyx's reign. The truth was, Serafine had been taking shots at Jangoor from the very first meeting Octavia had observed. Maybe she had been waiting for the opportune moment to make the arrest. A moment that would gain her favor with the public and the other senators.

I don't think we're in the clear yet, Raksha said.

What do you mean?

Arresting Jangoor in public like this was meant to gain the public's trust and turn them against the pacifists. But I think it might have also been a message for us.

What message?

By getting rid of Jangoor, the one senator we might have been able to align with to build peace between Athelia and Tenegard ...

Serafine has just made it that much harder for us, Octavia finished for her. Had this been a message to Octavia to watch her step?

"Due to the recent turn of events," Serafine called across the courtyard, "we will have to postpone the remainder of the forum until further notice. I would like to direct my fellow senators into the building for an emergency senate meeting."

As the crowds began to break up, both the senators and the citizens, Octavia used the distraction to slip away from Serafine and her own guards. She was still reeling from the way the guards had stormed the stage, hardly paying attention as she shouldered her way into an alley. She needed to find a quiet place to think where no one would find her. Gathering her focus, Octavia used her magic to scan for living things nearby. Finding no one, she turned to the brick wall and used her magic to crumble the earth that held the stone together. She shoved her way through the loose stone, tumbling into an almost empty storeroom. Then she turned around and used her magic to seal the hole.

It's lucky the Athelians aren't aware of the full extent of Tenegard's newly rediscovered elemental magic. Otherwise Erelas would surely be shielded against it.

Octavia hummed in grim agreement as the final brick fell into place. The last thing she needed was to have Athelian mages added to her personal guard. She sank back against a sack of flour, replaying the events from the afternoon. Until this point, Octavia had done everything Serafine had asked of her, even foolishly providing the anchor that had been used to set Jangoor up. The real problem was that if Serafine suspected Octavia of attempting to work with the pacifists behind her back, she could easily be the next one dragged off to some

Athelian prison. If she tried to flee now with Raksha, they might get away unscathed, but then all the effort they'd put into reaching Athelia would be for nothing. Octavia still hadn't proven if Melusine was truly allied with them. She also hadn't figured out why Serafine had originally lied about Tenegardian troops being stationed on the border. And the only thing she'd done for the pacifists was accidentally help get one of their members arrested.

Still, if she managed to escape, she could more safely convey the information she did have to Strida, who could relay it to the council. She could share that there was a pacifist movement and a senator under arrest for speaking out against the war. She could tell Strida about the public unrest and the funds sunk into defective war engines. But if she abandoned the pacifists now, didn't that make her the same ignorant girl who'd turned a blind eye to all the people who'd once suffered under Onyx's rule? Could she really do that?

CHAPTER 18

CORA

"I don't sense anyone," Cora said, using her magic to sweep for life forms like she did the last time they were here. Her magic drifted from the cliff peak where they were perched, to the edge of the woods Melusine was using to conceal her camp. "Or anything. Not a mountain hare or even a bird in a tree this time." She let the scan drop. "Do you think that's because of a spell?"

"The hounds have probably chased everything out of the area by now," Lenire said. He was crouched down on her left, Faron on her right. "If I were an animal, I wouldn't hang around with those things patrolling."

"You've been able to sense Melusine's spells in the past," Faron pointed out.

Cora shrugged. "Only when she was manipulating Dragon Tongue. She could be using different magic, or maybe she's gotten wise to my tricks since then. Plus, I have no idea what kind of protective enchantments Zirael could be using." She sighed heavily. They'd managed to sneak the hound into the woods last time undetected, but she was afraid they wouldn't have the same luck again.

"If we could set up with the hound on the edge of the forest, we'd have much better control of the creature than from up here," Lenire said. "Last time we only wanted to spy. This time we need the hound to respond to physical commands."

Cora wanted to give them every advantage she could, and that meant getting as close to Melusine's camp as possible without ruining the element of surprise. Ideally, Cora would like to get in and steal the disk before Melusine, Zirael, or the Blight realized they were there. "But there's no way to know how close we can get to the boundary without testing it with an actual person. Last time it was only the hound that got that close."

"What's the plan here?" Renka whispered. She'd crept along the cliff face to join them. "The riders are getting antsy."

"Someone needs to go down there," Cora said. She swore under her breath.

"Send Joi," Renka suggested. "She's fast."

Cora shook her head. "It should be me."

"No," Faron said. "I'll go. You're the only one with a scan that can reach that far. If a spell is triggered and someone or something approaches, you can alert the riders and dragons up here. Wyn will let me know to get out of there."

"We're not sending you," Cora argued. "You're not back to full strength yet, and I need you to reserve what you do have to help Lenire." She couldn't send Lenire because she also needed him to be at full strength in order to pilot the hound.

"Send Joi," Renka said again. "You talked about trusting us to do our jobs, so let us help. She's the fastest on foot."

Cora bit her lip, still uncertain.

"Why are we always training if you're not going to actually let us do anything?" Renka complained.

"Fine," Cora said. "Joi can go."

Renka grinned and crept back along the mountain to deliver the news. While Cora waited for Joi to climb down the mountainside and approach the edge of the woods, her heart rate gradually increased.

She's almost there, Alaric pointed out. *Everything's fine so far.*

Cora couldn't see him or the other dragons since they were hidden farther behind the cliff point, but she knew Alaric could sense her anxiety like no one else. There wasn't much use in denying it. After the sleeping sickness, she couldn't bear to see any more of her dragon riders stretched out on infirmary cots.

You don't need to feel guilty about needing their help.

Cora frowned. So much for keeping that to herself.

You should know by now that there's not much you can hide from me.

I know. I just feel like every decision might be the wrong decision and I can't let other people risk their lives without knowing the consequences.

Cora, these riders are here regardless of what the consequences might be. They chose to follow you. They know the risks.

Cora wasn't certain they did, but that didn't matter anymore because Joi had reached the base of the mountainside. Since Alaric and the other dragons all shared a telepathic connection, Cora used Alaric to communicate with Joi's dragon who then communicated telepathically with Joi. The process was a little convoluted, but it allowed them to speak without actually being near each other.

What does she see? Cora asked Alaric as she watched Joi poke around the edge of the woods.

Nothing so far, Alaric responded.

Does it feel any different? Cora tried to clarify as she summoned her magic and scanned the area again. She didn't want anyone or anything sneaking up on Joi without them knowing. *Does she sense any kind of magical disturbance?*

Cora was so involved in the scan that she didn't notice her foot slipping until Faron snatched her back from the ledge. She snapped out of the scan, her heart hammering, and watched a couple pebbles tumble down the mountain.

"I think we're in the clear," Faron said after a beat, talking about Joi and not the fact Cora had almost pitched herself off the cliff.

Joi wants to know if you want her to head inside the woods? Alaric said.

Let's not push our luck, Cora responded. *Lenire said he can set up at the edge of the woods. That's good enough for now. Tell Joi to hold her position until we can join her.*

Cora held her hand up, silently calling for the attention of the dragon riders. Renka snuck forward again to hear the instructions. "Faron, Lenire, and I are going to sneak down with Wyn, Alaric, and Yrsa. The dragons will relocate to the cave there," she said, pointing to an outcropping at the base of the mountain. "A small group of riders will accompany us for backup as we prepare the hound. Their dragons will remain up here with the rest of the rider pairs and await our signal. Is that understood?"

"Understood," Renka said before skittering off. She returned a moment later with four other riders. "This will make nine of us down there total including Joi. If things go sour, Alaric, Wyn, and Yrsa should be able to easily get the nine of us out of there."

Cora nodded, appreciating how much thought Renka had put into the plan. With the dragons on board, they flew down the side of the mountain. Alaric, Yrsa, and Wyn moved into the cave and the rest of them hurried across the field carrying the sack with the hound in it to meet up with Joi.

"Take positions behind those large trees," Cora said to Renka and the others, pointing them to hiding spots. "If Melusine's hounds take notice of us before we've retrieved the disk, I want you to keep them busy and away from Lenire and Faron."

"Got it," Renka said, rolling up her sleeves. By the time the riders were in position, Lenire had animated the hound and Faron had dropped an anchor to ground him.

Cora reached out, touching the anchor, and was immediately granted access to the hound's sight through Faron's connection to Lenire. "All right, everyone," she said. "Here we go."

Under Lenire's control, the hound trotted through the woods. They'd done this part before without raising suspicions. Now that they were better positioned, getting the hound into the camp should be the easy part. Getting it out again with the disk and control of the Blight would be another story.

As Cora watched the hound pick its way between berry bushes, a dark figure swept past, and she gasped, only to realize it was another hound.

"It's scouting," Faron reminded her.

"We must have just passed the border of their camp," Lenire said. "I'm going to try to maneuver our hound in with the scouters and come out the other side."

Cora watched as the hound responded, trotting along a worn path. It ran the edge of the camp, past hastily built shelters where Athelian armor was carelessly tossed into piles. They raced past smoldering fires and those weapons they'd seen the first time they spied on the camp. The hound made an arching turn then and the Blight came into view. It was roiling uneasily, confined to the clearing by the remaining strength of Zirael's disk.

"Over there," Cora said, indicating the tent behind the Blight. It was more opulent than anything else in camp and had to belong to the sorcerers. "Can we check in there for the disk?"

"Yeah," Lenire said, carefully guiding the hound away from the outskirts of the camp. He led the hound beneath the Blight and paused by the entrance to the tent, poking its nose through the doorway. Slowly, he inched the creature inside, freezing the moment he saw Zirael.

"He's asleep," Faron said, whispering despite the fact Zirael wouldn't be able to hear him.

"I see it!" Cora pointed even though neither of them were looking at her. "On the table."

Lenire piloted the hound across the tent and stretched until it leaned its front paws on the edge of the table.

"Grab it," Cora said, practically jumping up and down with excitement. They were so close.

Lenire managed to get the hound to pick up the disk. With the disk secured in its jaws, the creature sat back on its hind legs. Cora was about to ask Lenire what he was doing when she realized Lenire was looking at Zirael, asleep on a fur-lined cot.

"Lenire?" she said, trying to get his attention.

"I could kill him now," he said.

He sounded a million miles away. "Lenire!" she snapped again. "Get out of there!"

"I could end it all right here."

Cora felt a surge of magic as Faron poured energy into the anchor.

"And then Melusine will take control of the hound again and this will never be over," Cora told him. "Stick to the plan."

Before Cora could break from the hound's sight to go shake some sense into Lenire, a spell ripped past the hound, slicing a hole in the side of the tent.

Zirael bolted upright, looking past the hound to Melusine. "Turning those creatures on me won't get you what you want!"

"That wasn't me!" Melusine cried. "It was that thing!"

"Go!" Cora shouted as Lenire scrambled the hound into action. It dove for the side of the tent, fumbling out the hole that had been left by the spell, accidentally dropping the disk as it went.

"The disk!" Faron shouted.

Lenire tried to go back but Melusine came running out the front of the tent, baring her teeth in fury as she cast a spell in their direction.

"Dodge it!" Faron shouted again.

Lenire pulled his arms back, tugging on the Itharusian strings that controlled the creature, and the hound came to a jarring stop. Melusine's spell soared past.

"They're in the camp!" Melusine crowed as Zirael raced out of the tent beside her, holding the disk. "We're under attack!"

"Pull back. We've got to regroup," Faron said.

Lenire moved his arms, dodging another spell. "First I've got to get away from these two."

Cora turned around and waved her arms above her head, signaling the dragon riders on the cliff. *Alaric, tell them I need them to fly over the woods and cause a distraction.*

Moments later, six rider pairs came surging down the mountain. They flew overhead with so much speed it made the trees around them tremble. Through the hound's eyes, Cora watched as a huge ball of Dragon Fire fell through the leafy canopy, setting the sorcerers' tent on fire. The next ball burst between the trees, setting the stack of weapons intended for the attack on Llys alight. The Itharusian magic they contained crackled and popped as it was consumed by the Dragon Fire.

Melusine howled with rage as Lenire poured all his control into getting the hound to run. It raced straight through the camp as fire-balls rained down from above. Zirael cast a spell and the Dragon Fire crashed against it, crackling and dissipating without reaching the camp.

"Get ready to go," Cora told Renka, Joi, and the other riders. They weren't getting near the disk now.

As the riders scrambled from their hiding places, a dark growl issued from the woods. Cora peered between the trees to see the glow of beady, inhuman eyes.

She cast a shield spell just as one of Melusine's border hounds pounced. It crashed against the spell, knocking Cora off her feet.

"Cora!" Faron shouted, turning to help her up.

"No!" she said. "Stay with Lenire!"

Cora rolled over and sprang up. Renka and Joi had taken her place, fending off the hounds.

"Burn out their crystal hearts," Cora ordered.

"We can do better than that," Lenire called as their hound came dashing out of the woods. He maneuvered the creature around, using it to attack the other hounds. Lenire sank their hound's teeth into one of Melusine's and when it pulled away, she saw it had latched onto the dark remnant of the Blight that controlled the hound. He was using the same trick he'd used in the infirmary to separate the hound from the Blight in order to wake the sleeping dragon riders.

Melusine's hound collapsed as the bond between the Blight and the Blight fragment was separated. Cora caught the resulting burst of magic with a shield spell, and redirected it into the woods, blasting most of the approaching hounds back.

"Now burn the heart!" Lenire shouted. Renka and Joi did, channeling their magic into the crystal heart. It shattered and the hound exploded into nothingness.

Another hound lunged out of the woods, but Alaric landed next to them just in time to catch it between his jaws. He tossed the hound against a tree, giving Lenire enough time to sic their hound on it again, severing the Blight fragment's bond. As before, Cora caught the burst of magic, while a rider burned the heart out. Alaric and the other dragons had joined the fight, appearing from the cave and flying down from the cliff.

Then a dark, seeping mist bled from between the trees accompanied by a brace of Athelian soldiers. "Retreat!" Cora shouted to Renka and the others. Joi hopped on her dragon and soared past, attempting to beat the Blight back with Dragon Fire. Cora cast a shield around Faron and Lenire, waiting for the Blight to absorb the attack and redirect it at them, but it never happened. Cora spotted Zirael walking between the trees, teeth gritted as he attempted to control the Blight. The creature seemed disinterested in attacking them. In fact, the Blight seemed much more interested in investigating the hounds with the broken bonds, those smoky tendrils lashing out to poke at the collapsed creature.

Cora wondered if it could sense the separation of its fragments. If it was drawn to the bursts of magic it released. For a moment, she even wondered if it hurt the Blight. Then Lenire managed to snap another hound bond. No one was there to catch the burst of magic, and it ricocheted out in all directions, effectively distracting the Blight. Cora's hair ruffled as the newly freed magic swept past her. She started running, casting a protective air shield in front of Renka and Joi, as they burned out another crystal heart, to protect them from the soldiers' crossbows. Melusine also threw a spell at them, and Cora planted her feet, fighting to keep her shield in place.

Instead of throwing another spell at them, Melusine pulled a black talisman from one of her pockets. She pushed her long, unruly hair from her eyes, and held the talisman out. It shimmered like it was made of a similar stone as Zirael's disk. She lashed out with a bolt of barely contained magic that raced out of the woods and struck Renka's dragon, Erisa.

Renka screamed in pure agony. Cora's blood ran cold as she reeled from the moment of déjà vu. Melusine's spell had shattered Renka's dragon bond, leaving both Renka and Erisa staggering. The resulting burst of energy exploded across the field like the mountain itself had cracked in half. Cora was blasted off her feet by the shock wave that followed, so strong it threatened to knock the dragons from the sky. This was what Ismenia had seen in her vision. This was what the seers had been warning them about, and they'd run right into it.

CHAPTER 19

CORA

"Get her out of here!" Cora croaked as she rolled over. She was still spinning after being thrown off her feet by the shock wave of magical energy that exploded from Renka's shattered dragon bond. She blinked the bright, sparkling stars in her vision away as she pushed herself to her feet. "Go," she shouted, stumbling forward. "Go!"

Joi and her dragon touched down in the midst of the chaos, grabbed Renka, and took off again to help Erisa fly up the mountainside. The rest of Melusine's hounds had recovered from the blast, and though Cora didn't see Melusine, she knew the sorcerer wouldn't be far. She reached for her sword but found the sheath empty.

She gasped and turned in place, scanning the ground. Her weapon lay in the dirt a few feet away. It must have come loose during the explosion. Cora raced for it just as a charging hound entered her peripheral. Cora dove for the sword and rolled over, preparing to impale the creature, but Alaric smashed into it first, knocking the hound away. He reached down and snagged Cora by the front of her tunic with his teeth, hauling her back to her feet.

"Thanks," she stammered, her gratitude immediately overshadowed by a wave of horror as the Blight shot upward, twisting and turning, the long tendrils of its smoky shape lashing out into the sky. "What's it doing?"

"Absorbing all the magic dispersed by Renka and Erisa's shattered bond," Alaric said.

"No," Cora muttered under her breath. The magic contained in a shattered dragon bond would only make the Blight more powerful. And Zirael was barely keeping the creature under control as it was. "We have to get out of here before the Blight can take advantage of its increased strength."

Alaric bent down so Cora could scramble onto his back. "Or before Melusine can recover enough to repeat her attack," he added.

"Make a loop," Cora said as Alaric took off into the sky. He flew so low Cora could have slid from his back to the ground and not been hurt. "Retreat!" she yelled as they swept past the remaining riders. "Get out of here! Fall back!"

Cora summoned her magic, raising shields of earth to block the hounds so the riders had time to get away. A few of their dragons didn't even bother to land, snatching their riders up with their talons before flying hard for the mountains.

Screams and grunts and growls all mingled together. Bile rose up the back of Cora's throat. This was exactly what she'd been afraid of.

"Cora, help!" Faron cried from somewhere below them.

Her heart leaped into her throat. Faron was in trouble! Alaric dropped to the ground so she could roll free. Sword drawn, she tried to pinpoint him in the chaos. "Faron?"

"Over here! Help!"

Cora bolted in the direction of his voice, skidding to a halt as a hound ran toward her. But it didn't attack, instead stumbling and falling just as Ismenia's vision had foretold. It lay at Cora's feet, unmoving, and Cora knew she'd been right. This *was* their hound.

And it was all coming true.

All the terrible things she'd seen in the seer's head.

Bile burned at the back of her throat, and Cora wanted to be sick. She pressed her hand to her mouth and surged forward, past the fallen hound, spotting Faron hunched over Lenire.

"What's wrong?" she asked, rushing up to them.

Lenire's eyes were closed, his teeth clenched, both hands clutching his head.

"The Blight got in," Faron said. He lifted his arm, throwing up a shield wall to keep the small army of Athelian soldiers from pressing their advantage.

Cora dropped to her knees beside Lenire as Alaric, Yrsa, and Wyn gathered around them, fighting off the army of hounds closing in, surrounding them. "What do you mean it got in?"

"Zirael used the Blight to repossess our hound." Crossbow bolts chipped away at Faron's shield until he grew weary and it finally fell away. "It reached back through Lenire's connection to try to possess him." Faron tried to pull up a wall of earth to stop another round of crossbow bolts. "Lenire lost hold of my anchor. I don't—" He faltered, falling to his knee.

Cora reached out to steady him. She wouldn't let Melusine or the Blight take Faron from her again. They were going to figure this out. Lenire was too distracted by whatever mental battle was happening against Zirael and the Blight to take hold of Faron's anchor. Even if

Cora poured her own magic into the anchor, making it even stronger, it meant nothing if Lenire couldn't take hold.

"We have to pull him out," Faron said.

"With what?"

"A thread of magic."

"Itharusian magic?" Cora said, a desperate, panicked laugh surging up her throat.

Faron nodded. "Lenire's been helping me practice."

"What do you want me to do?" she asked.

A nervous grin tugged at the corner of Faron's mouth. "Keep those crossbow bolts from striking me in the head."

"Don't even joke," Cora said, jumping to her feet. She summoned her magic, combining earth and air to pick up a slab of rocky ground and throw it at the Athelian soldiers who had taken shelter in the tree line.

She looked over her shoulder, watching Faron make a similar hand gesture to the one Lenire always made when he created Itharusian spells.

"It's working!" Faron shouted, clutching his hands around some invisible thread. He rolled his wrist, almost like he was unwinding the thread in Lenire's direction.

"Can he sense it?" Cora called.

"I don't know," Faron answered. Suddenly, he lurched forward as if he'd been snagged by something on the other end of the thread.

Faron reached back, separating his hands, and Cora realized he was reaching for the anchor. She raised a wall of earth to protect them from stray crossbow bolts and then poured her magic into Faron's original anchor, strengthening the hold. Then she reached out, took

Faron by the arm, and forced his hand onto the anchor point. Cora felt all their magic connect in that moment, and she caught a glimpse of that woven tapestry of Itharusian magic before she felt the surge of raging power as Zirael and the Blight fought for control. Lenire wouldn't be able to hold them off much longer. Cora directed her magic through the anchor point and into Faron. She could see the thin tether of Itharusian magic Faron had cast. It trembled and shook, but slowly, Faron reeled it in, pulling Lenire out of the Blight's psychic clutches.

A burst of energy surged down the dragon bond from Alaric and into Cora. She directed it straight to Faron, giving him the strength to finally wrench Lenire free. They all went tumbling back, heaving and gasping as the magical connection was severed.

"Where's the hound?" Cora gasped, staggering to her feet to pinpoint their fallen hound.

"What are you doing?" Faron called from where he was leaning over Lenire, attempting to rouse him.

"Burning out the heart," Cora said, exposing the creature's crystal heart and directing her magic into it until it shattered. She wasn't going to risk letting Zirael or the Blight use that connection again.

"I can't wake him," Faron said as Cora returned to his side.

"We have to get him to Elaine."

Yrsa charged through a row of hounds, rocking her massive head back and forth to throw the creatures off. She snatched Lenire in her great, curved talons, and launched into the sky.

"C'mon," Cora said, tugging Faron to his feet. She used her magic to hold off the hounds as Faron scrambled onto Wyn's back. Then she and Alaric conjured a flame of Dragon Fire to push their enemies back. Cora had barely settled in the saddle when Alaric took off, and it was all she could do to hold on. Alaric swerved as a tendril of black smoke lashed out at them, but it wasn't the Blight that pursued them. It was still occupied fighting Zirael's control. Instead, the army of hounds charged after them, scurrying up the side of the mountain.

"Stop!" Cora shouted.

Alaric slowed as Yrsa and Wyn pulled ahead, soaring back toward base camp. "Cora, there are too many for us to fight alone."

"I know," she said. "But we can't afford to lead them back to our camp. It's too close to the Heart. They'll sense it and lead Melusine right to it. We'll lead them along the mountain range instead."

Alaric flapped his wings and dove to the right. He swept close enough to snatch a hound from a rocky ledge and throw it to the ground. "That should get their attention," he said as the hounds regrouped and started chasing them. "Now what?"

"I'm thinking," Cora said, squeezing her eyes shut. Adrenaline surged inside her. It was so strong she couldn't get her thoughts straight. They were being crushed by the rush of blood through her veins. Crushed … *Crushed?*

"That's it!" Cora shouted. "We'll crush them." She looked up the mountainside at the same time Alaric did, scanning for an unstable, rocky point. "There!" She gestured to a place where the cliff jutted out. "Can you get me close?"

"Hold on to something!"

Cora dug her hands into the leather of the saddle as Alaric flew straight up the mountain. The rush of wind created by their flight was so strong it bit at the skin on her cheeks and the tops of her knuckles. As Alaric leveled out, Cora climbed from the saddle and launched herself at the cliff face. She landed hard, scraping both her knees.

She glanced over her shoulder. The hounds gathered at the base of the mountain, growling and grunting. A few of them began the long trek up the cliffside as Cora scooted into place. When she reached the rocky overhang, she blasted the ledge beneath her with a bit of magic.

"Be careful," Alaric warned, hovering close.

"I just need to get it started," Cora said, blasting the rock again. A crack appeared beneath her feet, shooting out in all directions. Perfect. She closed her eyes and let her magic seep into the rock the same way it had when they'd been tracking the river. But this time, instead of pulling back, she latched onto the stone with her magic and shoved it outward.

The mountain thundered as a massive crack exploded down the cliff face, echoing across the valley and through the surrounding woods. Cora was momentarily deafened by the sound but she felt the tremble of the ledge beneath her feet. Alaric was inside her head, shouting at her to *jump* and Cora did, seconds before it collapsed. She free fell through dust and debris until a massive claw snatched her out of the air.

From where she dangled, she watched as the rock slide gathered speed, boulders hurtling down the mountainside faster than a dragon could dive, smashing into the hounds and burying them beneath a granite prison.

CHAPTER 20

CORA

By the time Cora made it back to base camp, the entire group was still reeling from the aborted mission against the sorcerers. Riders scurried back and forth, tending to minor wounds, lamenting their failure, but most of all, they whispered in panicked voices about the new and mysterious weapon Melusine had used on Renka and her dragon.

Cora glanced away as she passed pale faces streaked with dirt and filled with fear. She couldn't look at them knowing she'd allowed them to walk into this mission when all along she'd known how it would end. Emmett and her father ran between the tents, taking stock of injuries and all the supplies being used. Her father grabbed her the moment he spotted her, wrapping her in a tight hug. Cora wanted to sink into that Viren Hart hug and never emerge.

"I'm okay," she said, breathing him in—woodsmoke and herbs.

"I know," he replied. "I just need one more moment to remind myself."

When she pulled away, the reality of the situation came crashing down on her. "I'll update you later about the hit to our supplies," Emmett called as he ran past.

Cora swallowed hard. She had no doubt he would, but right now she didn't even want to think about all the damage they'd taken. She left her father and walked past Ismenia. Judging by the solid white hue of her gaze, the seer was navigating through the future again. Cora wanted no part of what she saw now. Not only had Cora foreseen this disaster alongside the soothsayer, but in reality, it had been so much worse. The explosion she'd heard had been the shattering of a dragon bond. The hound collapsing had been Zirael and the Blight attempting to possess Lenire.

"What happened to you!" Faron demanded as he spotted Cora in the crowd. He grabbed her by the shoulders and pulled her into a tight hug, squeezing all the air from her chest. "One second you were behind me and the next thing I knew, we were halfway back to camp and you were gone."

"We had to deal with the hounds. We couldn't let them follow us and find the Heart."

"How did you—"

"Rock slide," she answered immediately. Faron looked impressed. "Did you get Lenire to Elaine?"

"He says he's fine now. Wouldn't even let her look at him."

Cora brushed the stray hairs back from her forehead. "What?" The last thing they needed was Lenire trying to put on a brave face. "He needs proper medical care."

"Are *you* okay?" Faron asked, not letting her go. He touched a spot by her temple that stung suddenly. "Looks like a ricocheting spell might have gotten you."

"Of course," she said, brushing him off. "I'm fine. It's everyone else who suffered."

"Cora," Faron said. "This isn't your fault."

"How is it not my fault?" she said, louder than she anticipated. The riders near them looked over awkwardly, then away. "I said yes to this mission."

"A mission we all willingly agreed to," Faron said. "If anything, I think we pushed you into it."

A humorless laugh escaped her throat. "I'm the leader of the dragon riders. If I can't put my foot down when I know something is too dangerous, what business do I have standing up here and giving orders?"

"You've earned that right."

"Not today," she said. "Today people got hurt and I could have avoided it."

"It wasn't a total waste," Faron said. "We might not have gotten the disk, but the Dragon Fire destroyed the cache of weapons they were amassing in the woods. For now at least, we've put a stop to their plan of attacking Llys."

"Okay, so *one* good thing came from today." Cora still didn't know if it was worth it. Was Renka's destroyed dragon bond the price they had to pay to save Llys? To stop Athelia from gaining ground within Tenegard? The sacrifice shouldn't have been Renka's to make. "Where did they take Renka?"

"Yeah, come on," Faron said, wrapping his arm over her shoulders. "Elaine was tending to her the last I saw."

Together they crossed through the camp, almost colliding with Elaine as she came through the flap of the infirmary tent carrying an empty bowl. "Oh, good!" she said to Cora. "You're back. Your father was worried when you didn't return with the others."

"I saw him a moment ago."

"Can I help?" Faron said, gesturing to Elaine's bowl.

"*You* should be resting," his aunt told him, but she thrust the bowl into his hands. "Bring me some fresh water from the stream."

Faron turned and hurried off, leaving Cora facing Elaine. She didn't know why but she suddenly felt like bursting into tears as Elaine dragged her into a hug. Part of her knew Elaine was testing and prodding with her magic to assess the extent of Cora's injuries, but since Elaine had married her father, the healer had become the closest thing to a mother figure that Cora had since she'd been little. And for some reason, it was too hard to hold herself together when faced with that knowing stare.

"Come," Elaine said, whisking Cora into the tent.

She sat her down on an empty cot and had a cup of tea in her hands before Cora could even think to protest. She wasn't the patient here.

"Drink up," Elaine insisted. "You look like you could use it."

"What is it?" Cora said.

"Something for your nerves."

Cora looked down at the dark, fragrant tea. She didn't need something for her nerves. She needed something for the guilt currently eating its way through her chest.

"I know," Elaine said, gently squeezing her forearm and looking at Cora as if she could read her mind. "Drink it. Trust me."

So Cora did, taking small sips as Elaine tended to the cut on her forehead that she hadn't even realized was there until Faron pointed it out.

Next Elaine's cold healer magic washed over the scuffs on Cora's knuckles from when the cliff had exploded out from under her during the rockslide. All the while, Cora tried not to glance across the tent to the other cot where Renka was laid out. She could hear her deep, even breathing. Cora tried to soothe her conscience by telling herself Renka didn't seem to be in any physical pain, but it didn't work.

Faron poked his head into the tent, moving slowly as he carried the now full bowl of water.

"Thank you," Elaine said, relieving him of the bowl. She crossed the tent and laid it by Renka's bedside as she prepared another tea.

Faron plopped down on the cot beside Cora. "How are you holding up?"

"She looks like you did," Cora said quietly, her eyes finally lifting to look at Renka. She couldn't avoid it any longer.

"Like me?"

"When you were caught in the sleeping sickness. There were moments I would look at you and imagine you'd never wake. That you'd grow old and die, trapped in unconsciousness."

Faron reached down and grabbed her free hand. "It's not the same thing," he whispered gently. "Her bond was broken, she wasn't attacked by the Blight. It didn't feed off her."

And as if proving his words, Elaine reached over with a cup of tea, helping Renka hold her head up. The girl's eyes fluttered open as she sipped from the cup. Cora's gasp got trapped in her throat. Renka was very much conscious. This wasn't like the sleeping sickness at all. When she was strong enough, when she'd recovered from the sudden loss of magic, she'd be able to walk out of this tent.

"She's going to be okay," Faron said. "And together, we'll figure out how to restore her bond with Erisa. There has to be a way."

"Lenire repaired my bond with a disk," Cora said, setting her teacup aside. "And yours was restored with the returned magic from the shattered hound bond. Our bonds weren't broken though, only frayed." Her shoulders slumped, disappointment making her entire body heavy. She didn't know if it was possible to fix a shattered dragon bond. Cora remembered how difficult it had been when she was losing her ability to communicate with Alaric. She couldn't imagine no longer being a rider. The thought made her want to be sick. This was all her fault. She wouldn't blame Renka if she completely despised her now.

"Lenire's had good luck figuring out how to help us so far," Faron pointed out. "I say we talk to him. See if he has any ideas about where to start." He stood and helped Cora to her feet.

"Try to convince him to come and see me while you're at it," Elaine called as they ducked through the entry to the tent.

Faron smirked. "We'll give it our best shot," he called over his shoulder.

It took them longer than she thought it would to find Lenire. For several long minutes, Cora actually started to wonder if something had happened to him. Maybe he'd passed out in the woods from exhaustion. Or slipped into the stream trying to grab a drink. Even Yrsa didn't know where he'd gone because he wouldn't respond to her.

When they finally found him, it was at the bottom of the empty pit they'd once used to store the hound. "*Stars!*" Faron swore as he climbed down into the hole. "Do you know the fright you just gave everyone?" He reached back to help Cora down.

She took his hand, sparing a moment to reach out to Alaric so he could let Yrsa know they'd found him.

"Hmm?" Lenire said. He sat there, legs pulled tight to his chest. He swayed and tipped his head to look at her.

Cora couldn't help but notice a glazed sheen to his eyes. It's like he was far away somewhere, dazed, or perhaps still trapped in the hound's sight. "Hey," she said, kneeling and putting a hand on his shoulder. "Are you all right?"

He snapped out of it, shrugging her hand off his shoulder. "Like I told Faron earlier, I'm fine."

"You don't look fine," Cora pointed out as she sat beside him on the muddy floor. Faron sat on Lenire's other side. "Do you realize what almost happened to you?"

"*Almost* being the key word there," Lenire said, even as his cheeks darkened with color.

"The Blight tried to *possess* you. That's a big deal."

"And Faron pulled me out before it could." Lenire let his head thump back against the dirt wall. "That was a nice bit of Itharusian spell-work, by the way."

Faron almost smiled at the compliment. "Learned from the best."

"Don't change the subject," Cora said. This was a dangerous near-miss with a Blight possession. They'd both been there to see how it affected Alia, and after Lenire'd told her of how his sister had died, her mind taken by the Blight, she knew how badly this could have ended. "You have a lot of people worried. Yrsa included. You really should go see Elaine."

"I don't need another healer. I *am* one," Lenire said, holding his arms out as if to prove that he was fine. "I had the situation under control."

“Did you?” Cora said. “You had it under control fighting against Zirael?”

“We got out, didn’t we? We destroyed the weapons. Maybe we didn’t get the disk like you wanted, but our enemies are weakened. This is a victory. We should be celebrating.”

For a moment, he didn’t sound like the Lenire she knew at all. But then she wondered if he was embarrassed. It had been his decision to linger in that tent with the hound, talking about how he could kill Zirael while he slept. Perhaps he thought if he’d just used the hound to grab the disk and run, things might have turned out differently. Maybe guilt was eating at him the same way it was eating at her, and he was trying to absolve himself of it.

“This wasn’t a victory for everyone,” Cora said plainly. “Renka’s bond with her dragon was broken.”

Lenire blinked at her like he was hearing the news for the first time. Maybe he didn’t realize what had happened in the field when they were blasted off their feet. Maybe he’d already been locked in battle with Zirael. Either way, Cora knew he needed a healer. Having to mentally battle Zirael and the Blight had taken a toll on him. He was beyond exhausted. That’s probably why he was still in this pit—he didn’t have the strength to climb out—and why he wasn’t answering Yrsa’s telepathic summons.

“That’s actually what we came to talk to you about,” Faron said.

“The broken bond?”

Faron nodded. “You’re the one who ended up repairing my bond and Cora’s. We thought you might have another idea for how we can help Renka.”

The task seemed to focus him, and she told Lenire about what she’d seen in the field before the attack. Melusine had used the same tactic

Lenire had used to break the hound bonds. She'd watched and observed Lenire's spellwork and then used that same kind of magic against the dragon riders to do something much worse. Cora was sure of it. But Melusine had also had some sort of talisman or weapon to direct the magic. Cora had seen it in her hand. The device amplified the spell, allowing her to break something as strong as a dragon bond.

"I'd have to take a look at Renka and her dragon," Lenire finally said. "Before I could see if there's a way for me to help."

He didn't sound very sure of himself, and Cora couldn't blame him. As far as she knew, no one had ever come up against a weapon like this.

"If Melusine can destroy a dragon bond that easily, she could take on an entire army of dragons," Faron said.

"And if that's the case," Cora added, "then the Heart of Tenegard is in even more danger than before. I stopped the hounds but they're likely not destroyed. As soon as Melusine and Zirael manage to dig them out or make more, they'll come for the Heart, especially now we've interrupted their plans to attack Llys."

Silence fell around them like a suffocating blanket. Cora couldn't shake the feeling that by bringing the soothsayers to the camp in the first place, she'd somehow made everything worse. Something else bothered her too. "I don't understand how Melusine was able to create that kind of weapon so quickly."

"I'm guessing she's been picking up things from Zirael the same way Faron has from me," Lenire said. "Mixing Itharusian magic with her own power might have allowed her to develop such a weapon."

"I wonder if she was trying to create a weapon capable of bringing down dragons to prevent a counterattack at Llys. But instead of using it on us then, we got a taste of it now," Faron added.

"That would make sense," Cora said. "She'd want to ensure they maintained the advantage, even against the dragon riders." She imagined Melusine striking the dragon riders with this new weapon mid-flight, and the damage that would result from the dragon bond shattering across the sky. Cora's thoughts suddenly spiraled back to Ismenia's vision. "*Huh.*"

"What is it?" Faron asked.

She shook her head, trying to organize the thoughts before she spoke. "I was just thinking … The pain I felt during Ismenia's vision was clearly the pain Renka felt when her bond was destroyed. And the booming explosion was the energy from the broken dragon bond rippling across the field."

"Okay?" Faron said.

"That explosion was very similar to the one I witnessed in the sky during the earlier part of Ismenia's vision. That part seemed to occur in the past."

"You think the explosion in the sky was the result of a broken dragon bond as well?" Lenire said.

"It could have been, right?" Cora didn't wait for their acknowledgment. "When we broke the hound bonds, or even when Renka's bond was broken, that released the energy into the air. It's there for anyone to harness. What if the explosion I saw in the sky was from someone harnessing the power of a broken dragon bond and using it for some terrible purpose?"

"Maybe," Faron said. "But what were they trying to accomplish?"

"I think I know," Lenire said, surprising her as he stared at the opposite wall of the pit, lost in his thoughts again. "In Itharus, when the Blight first appeared, it came through a terrible rip in the sky."

"Why didn't you say anything before when Cora first described Ismenia's vision?" Faron asked.

"I didn't put it together until just now. I saw something when I was struggling to fend off Zirael and the Blight, but it didn't make sense until Cora made the connection to the earlier vision."

Cora grasped his shoulder. "What did you see?"

"It was almost as if I could sense the Blight's thoughts. And the moment that burst of energy from the broken bond surged across the field, the Blight turned to it like a dog hearing its owner calling. I think Zirael's Order used a broken dragon bond to crack open the sky and summon the Blight. That's what you saw in the vision."

"The arrival of the Blight in Itharus," Cora stammered. *Of course*, it made sense. Itharus had their own dragons. If the Order was as powerful as Lenire had described, and if they had figured out how to break the dragon-rider bond, it would have been easy enough for them to do. "But wait," she said, wide-eyed. "If we can figure out how to open a portal like that again, maybe we can send the Blight back where it came from."

CHAPTER 21

OCTAVIA

Octavia pressed her ear to the door of the storeroom where she was hidden. There were no voices on the other side which boded well. It meant no one had seen her magically disappear through the hole she'd created in the wall to slip her guards. But that also meant her guards were probably looking for her. *Serafine's likely waiting for confirmation that I've returned to the inn.*

We should figure out our next steps before you show your face again. If we decide to leave, it would be easier if I didn't have to knock down the inn.

Octavia smiled despite herself, knowing Raksha would do just that if the occasion called for it. It wouldn't be the first time she'd had to knock down walls in order for them to escape. *I suppose I could blame my absence on the crowds. Say I got turned around in the chaos as Jangoor was arrested and the forum ended.*

The courtyard is still packed with people, so I don't think Commander Dolan would question you getting lost in the shuffle. He might not look too kindly on the guards who lost sight of you, however.

Explaining her whereabouts was a problem for later. Right now, Octavia still didn't know if she should go back to the inn at all. There was no reason for Serafine to let Octavia walk around Erelas, a free woman, if she had any inclination that Octavia was deceiving her. So what was today all about? She replayed the other woman's words in her head as she'd stood up onstage, addressing the Athelians: *"Athelia will not stand by as Tenegard continues to bully and betray our trust,"* Serafine had shouted. *"We will fight back against our enemies. Even those who come from* within.*"*

Even now the words made her shiver. Octavia had been certain Serafine was hinting at her double-agency within the pacifist group. When she had produced that communication anchor and had Senator Jangoor dragged from that stage, Octavia should have realized she really had no idea what games the other woman was playing. Octavia had to expect there was more than one spy under Serafine's employ. And for all she knew, the same person who had exposed Jangoor, had also exposed the fact Octavia was trying to help the pacifists by working against Serafine. Even if her cover remained intact and Serafine still believed her to be an ally, Octavia now had to worry about what Jangoor might reveal if she was interrogated by the guards. Did Jangoor know Octavia was involved with the pacifists beyond what Serafine had ordered?

This was exactly the kind of mess Octavia had worried about getting caught in when Serafine first proposed the idea of spying. The senator was playing with her … testing her.

I think the forum today was meant to test us. She backed away from the door and slumped against a barrel of mead. *We're only one piece in Serafine's puzzle, and she wanted to make sure we fit. That we were on her side. I think she meant for us to have a front row seat as Senator Jangoor was forcibly removed from the stage and taken into custody. She wanted to see how I reacted. If I was as blindsided as everybody else in that crowd.*

The fact that you really had no idea Jangoor was working with the pacifists probably saved your life today.

But if we go rushing out of Erelas right this second, Serafine will know I was trying to play her. She'll know that I really traded sides when I met up with the pacifists, and that I fled for my own safety.

So, we're staying? Raksha confirmed.

Yes, Octavia said uncertainly. If she had any hope of unraveling Serafine's deceptions or figuring out whether Melusine's attack on Jeth at the border was at all related to Athelia, she needed to stay. If she wanted to achieve peace between their nations, she had to maintain her cover. That might include pulling away from the pacifist group for now, until she could determine Serafine's next move. Maybe she was also waiting to see what Octavia would do next. Or maybe she was trying to determine how she might use Octavia before calling her bluff. The woman always seemed to be two steps ahead of her, and that was reason enough for Octavia to pull out of Erelas.

But if Octavia left, what would happen to the pacifists who were fighting to protect their country? Would Serafine prune them away, one by one, until she was free to manipulate the other senators and the people without opposition? A rebellion was only as strong as its members, and by convincing the pacifists to hand over that communication anchor, Octavia had given Serafine enough evidence to use against members like Jangoor. Members who might have been able to sway the rest of the senators and make real progress toward ending the war. Octavia had been trying to do the right thing, trying to maintain Serafine's trust while also aiding the pacifists in their pursuit, and it had all backfired in her face.

Now she didn't know what the right move was.

All she knew was that this was somehow her fault.

She'd gotten involved in things way over her head, and now innocent people were going to pay the price. She couldn't fully step away from the pacifist group yet, not without trying to help them. She might not be able to keep them apprised of Serafine's plans, since she had no idea what the senator was really doing, but she might be able to offer them a way out. A way to escape Serafine's wrath before she could round them all up and throw them in prison.

We have to try to get the pacifists out of Erelas, Octavia said suddenly. If she could help them escape, they could regroup and come back stronger instead of waiting around for Serafine to pick them off.

Have you lost your mind? Raksha said, unnerved by the plan. *What if there are other spies among their ranks and they reveal you to Serafine?*

I've thought about that, Octavia said, the reality of Raksha's words turning over uncomfortably in her gut. This would be putting her and Raksha in an even more dangerous situation, but wasn't that what she'd forced upon the pacifists? *I made this worse for them. I can't just stand by and do nothing while they're rounded up and imprisoned or executed.*

It was a risk she was willing to take in order to fix this mess. In the end, this one choice could ruin everything. It could destroy her chances of uncovering the truths she'd been hunting since she got here, and force her and Raksha to flee, but if she managed to get the pacifists out of the city first, maybe there was still some hope for peace. It was time to stop being a spy and to start being a dragon rider again.

How will you even find them now? Raksha wondered. *The courtyard is still chaotic. If they're anything like the Tenegardian rebels were, they'll have made themselves scarce.*

I know, Octavia said. She only had one easy way to make contact with the pacifists. *I'll leave a message with the leaflet printer. She can get it to them.*

And what if you get caught? By a guard or an agent for Serafine?

Then we'll have to be ready to fight our way out.

Octavia picked up a ragged blanket from the floor and tossed it over her shoulders, pulling it over her head like the hood of a cloak. Now she smelled of stagnant water and stale bread. Any guard looking for the rebel princess from Tenegard wouldn't glance twice at her.

Be careful, Raksha warned as Octavia pressed her hands to the wall, using her magic to shift the earth and the bricks once more so she could escape back into the street. She kept her head down as she scurried down one alley and into another.

Octavia was jostled into a wall as a rowdy group shoved their way through the door of a tavern, speaking loudly. "Did you see the way they just dragged her off? Not even the senators are safe these days."

"I reckon they'll throw her on the front lines. Let her face the Dragon Fire first," said a young man. He was tall and skinny, his face marked with spots.

"I don't know," one of the older men said. "I've had dogs more vicious than that dragon out in the courtyard. Didn't even bat an eye when the crowd broke out."

"They probably pick their teeth with our bones," the young man said.

"They don't eat people, kid!" someone said, laughing.

"Know a lot of dragons, do you?" was the last thing Octavia heard as the door to the tavern swung shut. News of Jangoor's arrest was making its way through the city. The words whispered between neighbors were catching, traveling faster than a flame on kindling. Even those who didn't attend the forum would soon know what happened.

Octavia pressed on, using empty doorways for cover when she thought she heard chain mail, and slipping between old, rickety buildings using her hole-in-the-wall trick. She held the edges of her tattered rag under her chin to keep her face well hidden. When she magically exited another empty storeroom, it spit her out on the street and the first thing she spotted was the steel of a sword on a hip. Without thinking, she turned and veered left, coming into an unfamiliar alley. As she tried to get her bearings again, she bumped into a woman who wrinkled her nose and backed away from Octavia with a sour stare.

"The print shop?" Octavia asked.

The woman lifted her hand, pointing. "Two streets over that way."

Octavia didn't thank her, just rushed in the direction she pointed. The moment she reached the shop, she slipped inside. Ensuring it was empty, she shucked off the rag before the woman could throw her out.

"What are you doing here?" the printer hissed the moment she recognized her. "Girl, do you even know what's going on out there?"

"That's why I'm here," Octavia insisted, walking right up to the counter. "I was there when Senator Jangoor was arrested."

The printer hushed her with a finger to her lips, her eyes skittering to the dingy windows and back. "Keep your voice down."

The rattle of armor caught Octavia's attention and she ducked against the far wall, standing in the shadows. The printer flitted to the door to watch a pair of guards disappear down the street. "The soldiers will be out in force now to tamp down any uprisings."

"So you've heard already?"

"I saw it with my own two eyes," the printer said. "Where do you think all this information comes from?" She pulled a handful of leaflets from under the counter and shook them at Octavia. "Do you think I just come up with this stuff sitting in that dark room back there?"

"You can't write about this."

"What?"

"I mean, not right now. I need you to get a message to the pacifists for me."

"I already made the introductions. Now they'll find you. That's how this works," the woman said, waving her hands as if the motion would banish Octavia from her shop. "I can't help you."

"Please, you have to speak with them."

"What's so important you'd ask me to risk making contact with them at a time like this?"

"Serafine is going to start hunting down the other pacifists." She knew Jangoor was only the beginning in a long line of arrests to come. Today was meant to spark fear and fuel doubt in the pacifist movement. "Everyone involved should lie low or even leave Erelas if they think they can."

The woman scoffed, a humorless laugh falling from her lips. "And where exactly would we go? Never mind that getting out of Erelas while there's a war brewing on our border is going to be next to impossible."

"Maybe I can help with that," Octavia said. She remembered what Jeth had once told her about Tenegardian traitors fleeing to the wilds of Athelia. That it was better for them to take their chances in a foreign country than to let Onyx and his shadow soldiers get a hold of them. Now it was time for Tenegard to return the favor.

The woman looked uneasy. "I will relay your message, but I can't promise it will be heeded. This is a determined group of people you're trying to help. Some of them are willing to risk their lives to end this war."

"I understand," Octavia said. "But if anyone does choose to leave, I can get them out of Erelas."

"How?" the printer asked.

Octavia glanced over her shoulder to make sure there was no one lingering at the window, then she summoned a bit of magic, shifting the bricks the way she had in the alleyways. The printer gaped, peering out the newly created hole in her wall. It looked into the next room where her printing press sat among a pile of fresh parchment. The entire space reeked of ink.

"Fascinating," the printer said. "I had no idea dragon riders were capable of such things."

Octavia closed the stones over once more. It wasn't much, but hopefully it would make up for the damage she might have done to their cause by getting involved. "If anyone needs to make an escape, they should send a messenger to deliver a pamphlet directly to me at the inn. I will know what it means. Raksha can take to the skies to provide a distraction, and I will meet the pacifists at the fountain where we had our first meeting. We can use my magic to funnel everyone through the city walls without having to pass through the main gate. If we're careful, Serafine will never know what happened."

The printer looked at her, eyes wide, too stunned to speak. All she could do was nod. Octavia had done a good job of concealing her true power from the senate thus far, which might have worked out in their favor. With a small, hopeful smile, she picked up the foul-smelling rag she was using as a cloak, and tossed it over her shoulders once more before rushing back into the street.

She stuffed the raggedy cloak into a trash bin as she exited the alley and made her way across the main courtyard. The forum stage was being torn down. Octavia stared at it, remembering the moment Serafine had revealed the anchor to the crowd. It might have only been wired to lead to a dead end, but somehow she was going to use it to track down more of the pacifists—Octavia just knew it—planting fake evidence on them the way she did with Jangoor. Octavia thought back to the meeting she'd had in the senator's office, remembering the little magical tracking device. That was it! Knowing what she did of Serafine's character, Octavia wouldn't be surprised if the senator had lied to her even then; that tracking device must do more than lead to an anchor's other half. For all she knew, it could track down anyone that had ever come in contact with a particular anchor.

We need to sneak into Serafine's office and get a hold of that magical tracking device she showed me. If it goes missing, it's going to make it a lot harder for Serafine to track down members of the pacifist movement.

Wouldn't it be smart if we played it safe for a week or so?

A week could be long enough for her to make a dozen arrests. We need to find that tracker and destroy it.

Raksha grumbled her doubts. *Well, if you want to stay in Serafine's good graces long enough to get access to her office, you better hurry and get back here. Dolan and his men have arrived, and it seems like they're starting to ask about your whereabouts.*

Octavia picked up her skirts and ran for the inn.

CHAPTER 22

CORA

Cora slept in fits and starts, dreaming of the battle at Melusine's camp, but mostly of the moment Renka's bond with Erisa had been shattered and of the piercing roar that had ripped from the dragon's mouth. Every time she woke up all she could do was wonder what would have happened if she'd never seen Ismenia's vision. Other times when she closed her eyes, all she saw was the moment just before Alaric snatched her in his claws, the torrent of boulders racing down the side of the cliff to crush her.

Eventually she got up and dressed, sitting outside her tent in the bitter morning chill, waiting for dawn. When she could make out the shadowed figures of the dragon riders rising from sleep, Cora found Joi and asked her to spread the word: morning training was canceled. The riders were to tend to any remaining injuries and recover their resources. She wanted to make sure they had enough food and fresh water prepared should they need to react quickly. "Clean and sharpen your weapons," she said to Joi, her breath fogging in the cold. "Tell your dragons to hunt in shifts. And make sure your saddles are flightworthy."

“Is there going to be another fight?” Joi asked, her eyes drifting across the camp to the infirmary tent where Renka remained.

“I don’t know yet. But can you pass on the instructions for me?”

For a moment, Cora worried Joi would refuse. That she would ask *why*? Why should they trust her—why should they listen to her—when all she did was put them in dangerous situations? No one wanted to end up like Renka and Erisa. None of the riders or the dragons wanted to risk their bonds on a foolish mission. Cora couldn’t blame them. She would have had the same thoughts if she were them. Stars, she *was* having the same thoughts.

She had no idea what Melusine’s next move was or when she would strike next. All she had was the knowledge that if they could somehow open another hole in the sky, they might be able to send the Blight back where it came from. And though Cora was still no closer to a plan, she wanted the dragon riders to be ready. She wouldn’t let them be surprised by a counterstrike.

“I can do that,” Joi finally said.

“Thank you,” Cora said quietly. She left Joi with her task and moved back through the camp as silent as a ghost. When she returned to her father’s tent, she found him outside stoking the fire. A plume of thick smoke bubbled from a pan that had been thrust into the flames, and he attempted to waft the heavy green-gray smoke from his eyes. The pan was filled with herb clippings that smelled strongly of sulfur as they burned. “What is that?” Cora coughed, waving her hands in front of her face.

“Medicine, I think,” her father said. Cora couldn’t help the laugh that bubbled up from her chest. Viren Hart looked about ready to keel over from the fumes. That couldn’t be medicine.

Elaine exited the tent with a towel wrapped around her hand. She used it to carefully pull the pan from the flames. With two deft fingers she plucked a pinch of the sizzling herb from the pan and placed it on her tongue. As she mulled the bite over, she nodded her approval. "For the nerves," she said in response to Cora's raised brow. "I ran out of my tea stores."

"Ah," Cora said, sitting on a felled log. She let the warmth of the fire leach into her boots and warm her toes. "There's a lot of that going around."

"They're just overwhelmed at what happened with Renka. It'll pass," Elaine said. Her words did little to assuage Cora's own worry that her riders might pack up and flee. At least on the front lines between Tenegard and Athelia they'd be away from Melusine and her new weapon. "I think it was a surprise to us all to hear that something like that could happen."

Cora hummed. Her riders weren't afraid to fight, they were afraid to lose their bonds with their cherished dragons; these sacred, special kinships that filled them with destiny and purpose. Cora felt a sweeping wave of calm reassurance bleed down her own bond with Alaric. It wrapped around her like a hug. She leaned into the feeling, letting Alaric know she appreciated his support. *How is Renka's dragon holding up?*

There's a lot of confusion and hurt, Alaric said. *It's hard for most of the dragons to relate as we've never lost a bond before. I can understand a bit, but even when our bond was frayed, and I had trouble communicating with you, I never once felt like I'd lost you.*

Cora didn't know what to say and her stomach flipped uneasily. She wasn't sure if it was the stench of Elaine's herbs or if it was knowing how much Renka and her dragon were suffering that did it.

"Cora?" her father asked. "Are you okay? You've gone green."

"Fine," she said, swallowing hard. She glanced from her father to Elaine, who was already walking round the fire to assess her. "Really, I'm okay."

Elaine laid her hand on the top of Cora's head, smoothing down her hair. "You know, I never believe you."

That earned Elaine a smile. "How is Renka doing?"

"I gave her a tonic so she would sleep through the night. I checked on her not that long ago, and she was at peace."

"When she wakes, I'm hoping Lenire can have a look at her. See if there's anything he can tell us about her broken bond using his Itharusian magic."

Elaine nodded. "That's a good idea. And if he's in the infirmary tent, he might just let me have a look at *him*."

"I wouldn't count on it. He's being stubborn," Cora muttered. She turned to her father. "I've asked the riders to be ready for a counterstrike. I can't be sure how Melusine will respond now, but I don't want to be caught off guard. Will you help them prepare their weapons?"

Viren nodded eagerly. "Of course."

Cora was suddenly grateful for his knowledge and skill. He might not have all the tools from his forge out here, but he was still a blacksmith, and she could tell it pleased him to be able to contribute in this way. Footsteps sounded behind her, and Cora tipped her head back as Faron put his hands on her shoulders.

"How are you feeling?" he asked squeezing her shoulders.

"I should be asking you that," she countered as he sat down on the log next to her.

“Well I’m asking you because it looks like you haven’t slept at all.” He let his thumb ghost beneath her eye, likely rubbing at the dark circles he saw there.

“If I try to sleep, all I think about is Ismenia’s vision and that hole in the sky.”

Faron sighed. “I wish I could say that I had some brilliant revelation overnight but I was mostly worried about Lenire. Did he seem off to you yesterday after the attack?”

“Yeah? But doesn’t everyone seem a bit off?” Cora said.

“I just … When we found him sitting at the bottom of the pit, it almost felt like he was mourning the loss of the hound.”

Cora shrugged. He’d been exhausted and magically drained and as stunned as everyone else as they unraveled the pieces of Ismenia’s vision. The fact that he’d been sitting in the bottom of the pit was really the least of her concerns. “Maybe he was mourning losing something you both worked so hard on. Or maybe he was feeling guilty about getting distracted by his desire to kill Zirael. If he’d just taken the disk and run from the tent before Melusine showed up, maybe things would have turned out differently.”

“But do you think he—”

Faron’s voice dropped off suddenly. Lenire came into view, trudging across the camp toward their firepit. He looked as tired as she felt.

“Morning,” he said.

“I’m guessing you had a rough night too?” Faron commented.

Lenire snorted. “Do I look that bad?”

“Do you want the truth or would you like me to lie to you?”

"Lie to me," Lenire said, crouching down and holding his hands near the fire.

"You're positively glowing."

An hour later, when the sun had dragged itself over the horizon, Cora, Faron, Lenire, and Elaine piled into the infirmary tent. Ismenia was there too, occupying a cot, a frequent visitor as Elaine worked to keep the strength of the visions from overwhelming the seer.

But it was Renka they were all there to see. The girl glanced between them, her expression grim. "I don't understand how being poked and prodded with magic is going to help me."

"Lenire's Itharusian magic has been useful in the past for repairing dragon bonds," Cora explained. She could hear the devastation in Renka's voice. It was difficult to stand here. "He helped me fix my own bond with Alaric not that long ago. Just give him a few minutes, and maybe together we can figure out a way to restore what you've lost."

Renka sat up. "What do I have to do?"

"Just sit still," Lenire said. Cora wondered if it was easier for him to find what he was looking for because he'd seen a Tenegardian dragon bond before. Lenire weaved his hands together, tying those invisible Itharusian knots.

"I don't feel anything," Renka said quietly.

"You shouldn't," Lenire said. "I'm assessing right now, not attempting to heal anything." After a moment, his face screwed up like he was looking at something particularly complex.

"What is it?" Cora asked. Without the magic of the disk or some kind of connection, there was no way for her to see the mishmash of Itharusian threads that ran between them and the rest of the physical world. "Did you find the bond?"

"I found the thread," Lenire said, standing and following something that only his eyes could see. He sighed sadly. "I can see what's wrong. The thread wasn't just cut. It's more like it's been burned through. The remnants look more like dead branches than the frayed weaving we saw when I healed your bond," he said quietly, glancing at Cora, then away.

"There's nothing you can do?" Elaine confirmed.

"I'm sorry," he said, releasing his spells as his hands fell to his sides. "I don't know how to repair permanent damage like this. Even with a disk I don't think it would be possible. But I'll think on it."

Renka's head dropped to her chest, her eyes locked on the blankets that covered her legs. "I understand."

"Don't be discouraged," Cora said, immediately dropping to her knees by the cot. "We'll figure something out."

Renka nodded, though Cora could tell she didn't believe her. And despite their difficult relationship these past weeks, Cora was still her teacher. She remembered Renka arriving at the dragon-rider school and quickly becoming one of the most promising trainees. She'd watched the bond between Renka and Erisa grow. Though Renka hadn't once blamed Cora for what happened yesterday, Melusine's attack only reminded her that no matter what she did or how she tried to lead, the people who followed her always ended up getting hurt.

And now—

The ground trembled around them. Cora stood and poked her head out of the tent to find Alaric. He didn't say anything, just gestured with his snout. He craned his long neck in the direction of another dragon. Erisa.

"Oh," Cora said. "I'll get her." She popped back into the tent, looking past everyone to Renka. "Someone's here to see you."

Elaine helped Renka to stand. She was still weakened by the sudden loss of her dragon magic, and she'd been battered by the shock wave that had exploded across the field. As they exited the tent, Cora heard the soft gasp that left Renka's throat the moment she laid eyes on Erisa. It must have been terribly strange for her to lay there overnight, her mind eerily quiet.

Elaine helped Renka stumble forward until the young rider was close enough to touch her dragon. Renka reached out, laying her hand against the scales in the middle of Erisa's chest. Her fingers slid down the scales like she was saying goodbye. When Renka turned around, her entire face was lined with sorrow. Her chin trembled and tears rolled down her cheeks. "There's nothing there," Renka said, touching her own chest. "It's completely empty. How can that connection we shared just be gone?"

For the second time that morning, Cora wanted to be sick. Elaine gathered Renka into her arms, guiding her back to the infirmary tent.

Lenire huffed loudly and turned on his heel, marching away from them. Cora knew he was frustrated that he couldn't help. If he felt half of what Cora did, then a burning rage was eating him up inside at having to witness what Melusine did to Renka and Erisa, but he couldn't take it personally. He couldn't let the anger and the guilt distract him from what really mattered.

She and Faron hurried after him.

"This is Melusine's fault, Lenire," Cora called out. "Not yours. No one blames you for not being able to repair the bond."

"None of us knew she was capable of this," Faron said. "If we did, we would have taken better precautions."

Lenire turned on his heel. "I know that!" he snapped.

Cora flinched at his tone.

Lenire grimaced, rubbing at his eyes. "Sorry. I didn't mean to yell."

"What's going on with you?" Cora asked.

"It's nothing. All this magical exertion is making my head hurt."

"Maybe you should lie down."

"I don't need to lie down!" he snapped again. "I'm sorry. I just ..." But whatever Lenire's emotions were, he couldn't seem to get the words out to describe them.

Cora looked to Faron for help but he seemed to be at a loss as to Lenire's shifting moods. "Well, you're obviously not okay. Is this because of the close call with Zirael?"

"No, of course not. I told you, I'm fine."

"*Lenire*?" she persisted, knowing he was hiding something.

"It was a hard fight," Lenire finally admitted. "I wasn't prepared for how difficult it would be to fend off Zirael and the creature without the help of my stolen disk. And with the Blight trying to assume control of the hound, I was much more aware of it."

"Aware how?" Cora asked.

"I just … It's like I could sense what it wanted. I wasn't guessing anymore. I could feel the living, hungry presence trying to get close to me. I could even sense some of its frustration with Zirael. It was strange to think of the creature as something capable of feelings. Something I might even feel sorry for despite all the devastation it caused. It's … unnerved me a bit." He blew out a breath, running his hand over his face, massaging the exhaustion away. “I wonder if it was anything like that for my sister before she died.”

Cora didn’t know how to respond to that, but she didn’t have to. Lenire carried on.

“We have to stop Melusine and Zirael at any cost.”

“Don’t you think I know that?”

He grabbed her by the arms, looking into her eyes with an intensity she hadn’t seen since the moment he’d convinced himself that she’d been possessed and he’d tried to kill her. “I mean it. Whatever it takes.”

Cora shrugged free. “Another broken dragon bond is too high a price to ask.”

“It won’t come to that,” Faron chimed in. “We’ll find another way.”

Lenire grew quiet, the intensity gone, his voice bizarrely calm. “Sparing another bond might not be your choice to make.”

CHAPTER 23

CORA

Cora woke with a start. Whatever had pulled her from sleep was so strong she actually rolled off the edge of her cot, her heart hammering against her ribs as she groaned and propped herself up on her elbows.

Cora!

Alaric? So she hadn't been dreaming. It really was Alaric's voice in her head. She pushed up on her feet, shucking the heavy fur that had fallen from the cot with her. *Is everything okay?*

It's Lenire. Come quick!

Where are you? Cora asked, grabbing her weapons belt and stringing it around her waist as she raced through the mouth of her tent. She yelped as she collided with a body, and she would have fallen backward, her hands still clutching her belt, if not for Faron's hands shooting out to steady her.

The moon was high and the stars were out in abundance, letting her see the panicked tilt of his brows even in the darkness. "Wyn woke you?" she guessed.

He nodded. “Lenire’s in trouble. They’re down by the stream.”

He took Cora’s hand, and together they raced past the tents and the stifled dinner flames, toward the sound of water trickling over stone.

They passed Lenire’s solitary bedroll, abandoned in the clearing at the edge of the camp. That wasn’t unusual. Lenire often preferred to lay out under the stars than to be huddled under some tent. Itharus was a cold country. He was used to the chilled nights. Perhaps he even preferred it. Or maybe it reminded him of home. But none of that mattered as Cora ran toward the hulking figures of the dragons. Lenire lay on the ground between them, on his back, his body limp, his arms sprawled above his head.

“What happened?” Cora gasped as they skidded to a stop. She sucked in a lungful of brisk air, trying to catch her breath, and it burned all the way down. “How did he get all the way out here?”

“I dragged him from his bedroll,” Yrsa said.

Cora spotted the tear at the end of Lenire’s pant leg where Yrsa must’ve pulled with her teeth.

“Something is wrong with him,” Yrsa exclaimed. “I sensed a strange psychic absence from him as he slept and when I tried to rouse him, I couldn’t.”

Faron bent down by Lenire’s head, grabbed him by the jaw and gave him a shake. “Lenire, can you hear me?”

Cora knelt down on his other side, her thoughts churning as fast as her heartbeat. This looked like the sleeping sickness all over again. But then Lenire mumbled something unintelligible.

“Lenire!” Faron barked.

Cora gently lifted his eyelids. His pupils were glazed and misty, almost like a soothsayer's. His eyes flitted back and forth, like he was watching without seeing.

"He's still in there," Faron said with certainty. "We just can't make contact. I don't understand it. Should we get Elaine?"

Cora tilted her head back to talk to Yrsa. "You can't reach out to him at all?"

She shook her head. "There's no response. I could feel him pulling away as he slept. That's what worried me. It would be like that when he piloted the hound. I could always feel a small part of him pulling away, traveling with the hound. But I knew we left the hound back in that clearing." Yrsa's voice was desperate. "I've never lost sense of him completely like this."

"The hound?" Faron repeated, looking up at Cora. "Do you think that's what he's doing? Somehow projecting or piloting."

"But where?" Cora asked. "And with what?" The old hound corpse had been destroyed.

"I don't know, but if Yrsa says it's similar, then he must have gotten trapped inside his head somehow." Faron jumped to his feet. "We need to pull him out. The same way we did when Zirael and the Blight got a hold of him. Be my anchor?"

"Of course," Cora said, summoning her magic. She pulled an anchor from the earth and Faron linked it to his Itharusian thread of magic. His face was screwed up, the unfamiliar magic requiring all his concentration. Cora twisted the earth around his spell. She couldn't see the Itharusian thread at first, but she could feel it tangled in her own magic, like walking through a spiderweb. It clung to her and Cora poured her magic into the anchor. She wouldn't risk losing Faron to whatever magic had trapped Lenire, so she used Alaric's strength to boost her own, grinding her teeth as she felt Faron's Itharusian spell pull taut.

He cast the invisible magic at Lenire, swearing under his breath.

"What is it?" Cora asked, all her focus on maintaining the integrity of the anchor. When she opened her mind to Faron's own magic, she felt the connection immediately, as if she was looking through his eyes. Using Itharusian magic gave him the sight Cora lacked when it came to the foreign spells. Her vision expanded the same way it had when she'd held Lenire's disk to repair her own bond, a tapestry of woven Itharusian magic fluttering around them. She'd only gotten a glimpse of it when they'd rescued Lenire from Zirael and the Blight. But Faron's vision tugged her deeper, past the threads, and Cora could feel him moving dangerously far, chasing Lenire's presence through individual strands of magic.

"I've found him," Faron bit out, and Cora felt the strain on the anchor. "I'm trying to pull him out like we did last time, but he's stuck."

"Is it Zirael?" Cora asked, worried that the sorcerer had somehow found a way to invade Lenire's mind again.

Faron grunted. "It's like he's pulling against the lifeline. He's fighting me."

Something was really wrong. Faron's arms began to tremble. The last time an Itharusian spell had rebounded, Lenire had been severely injured. Cora knew she couldn't let that happen to Faron. She left the anchor and stood beside him. "Let him go."

"What?" Faron cried.

"Let him go and teach me the spell. The simple knotted one Lenire taught you. Maybe the two of us together can pull him out of the mental hold."

Faron gritted his teeth, pulling against an immovable force. "Cora, I can barely cast it myself."

"I don't know what else to do," she admitted, desperately trying to avoid looking at Yrsa. What would happen if they couldn't pull Lenire out of this nightmare? What if they couldn't save him?

Faron gave a sharp nod, releasing the spell. Lenire's limbs trembled against the ground, like he was recoiling from the release. "Here," Faron said, taking Cora's hands in his own. He guided them in strange patterns, pressing down on her fingers in a way that reminded Cora of pressing on the organ keys as a girl back in the tavern in Barcroft. "Lenire said to imagine it's like tying a knot on your boots."

Cora repeated the pattern using Faron's hands as a guide. She did it again and again until he lowered his hands. "Is this right?"

"As right as I can teach you."

"Now what?" Cora asked.

"The moment you finish the knot, you have to grab hold of the thread it creates. Only then can you manipulate the spell."

"Grab hold of what?" Cora muttered, repeating the spell. It felt like trying to pluck a starburst of dust from the air. Whatever she was trying to grasp was too small or too flimsy to grab hold of. This was nothing like the innate feel of her dragon magic. She didn't have to *think* about her dragon magic. It just bled from her fingertips. But this was foreign magic. This was a magic that required practice and patience and even then she wasn't certain she could learn it. How was she supposed to grab hold of an invisible thread at exactly the right moment?

What if she didn't grab it with her hands? Cora repeated the pattern, casting another Itharusian spell, but instead of trying to pluck an invisible string out of thin air, the moment she finished the pattern, she reached out with a wisp of air magic, curling it around the space in front of her and drawing it back toward her hand. The moment she felt that spiderweb-like consistency against her palm, she closed her fist. A chill zipped from her hand, up her arm, and across her shoulders, leaving her skin buzzing with unfamiliar magic.

"You did it!" Faron said as the thread materialized between them. Holding the magic, the Itharusian tapestry returned. She could see everything. Faron recast his own thread. More deft with the magic, he looped it around himself and Cora and the anchor before directing it at Lenire. Cora could only cast her thread in Lenire's direction. When she compared her thread to Faron's or even the other threads around her, it looked weak and thin. As fragile as spider silk.

"We got him!" Faron said, pulling back on his thread.

Cora was worried one hard tug would sever the magic, but she copied Faron, planting her heels, and giving the thread a hard tug. Surprisingly, the string held, suddenly feeling as strong as metal in her hand, and Cora began to wind the taught thread around her hand.

She could feel the resistance, but it was working. She could sense Lenire's presence drawing near as they hauled his mind back into his body. When everything connected, the thread in Cora's hand shook and snapped. She lost sight of the tapestry and was thrust back into the chill of the night.

"What are you doing?" Lenire roared as his eyes shot open. "I was trying to *see*!"

"Great wandering stars!" Yrsa cried down at him, just as angrily, her fear sending spirals of steam from her nostrils. "You're lucky to be alive!"

Lenire sat up suddenly, thrusting his arms out as if he meant to shove them away. But Cora and Faron stood just out of reach. Instead of physically pushing them, it was some kind of Itharusian spell that hit them, square in the chest, like being shoved. The next thing Cora knew, she was airborne. The spell stole her breath, and she caught a wink of the stars above as she flailed. But she didn't hit the ground, at least, not the way she expected. Alaric had whipped his tail around, breaking her fall. She bounced off the side of the hard, scale-lined extremity and fell to her knees, wincing.

Are you okay? Alaric asked, his large, galaxy black eye landing on her as he lowered his head close enough for her to touch.

Fine, she assured him. *Thanks for not letting me hit the ground.*

She could hear the hum of his uncertainty in her head. She lifted her hand and stroked it over his snout. The heat billowing from his nostrils was warm enough to fight off the mountain chill.

I really am fine.

The fall wasn't painful, but the landing had been awkward, and she knew her knees would protest later. Her head snapped up as Faron groaned. Wyn hadn't been as quick to help, and Faron had landed hard on his back.

Cora climbed to her feet. She was willing to give Lenire the benefit of the doubt for a lot of things, but if he was going to start shooting off spells like that, they were going to have issues. She marched toward him. "You want to tell me what that was all about before I start firing off my own spells?"

Lenire huffed angrily.

"I'm not kidding," Cora said. She raised her hands and the earth beneath Lenire trembled. He snapped his head back and forth, then sprang to his feet as if the ground might open and swallow him whole.

The movement seemed to jar Lenire from his earlier anger. He lifted his hand to scratch at the back of his head.

"What in all the lands is going on here?" Faron asked, finally back on his feet.

"I was seeing," Lenire said.

"Dreaming?" Cora asked.

Lenire chuckled, the sound light, unburdened. "I was not asleep."

When he met her stare, Lenire's eyes were so round and glazed that she could see the glow of the moon reflected in them. "Then what were you seeing?"

"I don't need the hound anymore." A smile stretched across his face. It was so unlike Lenire to smile like that or to speak with that lithe, musical tone. For a second, Cora thought it was a completely different person standing before her.

"What do you mean, Lenire?" Yrsa asked. She blinked down at him.

"I understand it now. I can see everything."

Faron's hand slowly made its way down to his sheathed sword like he thought they might have to fight and restrain Lenire. Cora didn't know if Lenire was in his right mind, but she'd fought him before. Dragon knights from Itharus were skilled in battle and swordsmanship. This wouldn't be easy.

"The Blight is no longer out of our reach," Lenire continued. He tapped his chest. "Because I know it well enough now to reach out to it myself. I've been learning its secrets."

Cora gasped, but the sound was overshadowed by the hideous sound that tumbled between Yrsa's lips. "Please tell me that's not what you were doing! Lenire, do you know how dangerous that is?"

He waved off her concern. "I know exactly what the risks of psychic contact are."

"Really?" Faron barked. "Because I think you're forgetting the way we had to rip you out of Zirael's psychic grasp back in the middle of that clearing!"

"Zirael has nothing to do with this," Lenire said, grinning like he was finally besting his enemy. "He didn't even know I was there."

Faron wheeled around, marching back toward camp. "This is insane!" he called over his shoulder.

"He's right," Cora added. "After the last close call I would think you'd be smarter than this."

"It's dangerous," Yrsa said. She nudged him with her snout.

Lenire's smile faded. "Don't you at least want to hear about what I saw?" he called loud enough to catch Faron's attention.

"I don't know," Faron said, turning around. "You don't really seem like you're being a team player right now."

"You'll be glad I took the risk when you find out what I've learned."

Though Cora could tell Faron was still angry by the way his fist clenched and unclenched around the hilt of his sword, he marched back toward them. "Go on, then."

The corner of Lenire's mouth twitched. "Using the Blight, I was able to spy on the camp. I saw that talisman she used in the clearing to break Renka's bond."

"Okay," Cora said. So far none of this was new information.

"It's not some sort of strange magical device," he explained. "It's a disk."

"Like what Zirael has?"

"Better than what Zirael has," Lenire said. "She's making a master disk. One that can assume total control of the Blight and the remaining two disks: the one here and the one still in Itharus."

"One that can break dragon bonds," Cora whispered under her breath. It made sense now. It wasn't a weapon that she'd seen, it was the beginnings of a disk. Because surely if a disk could be used to repair dragon bonds, then it could be used to break them too.

Lenire shrugged. "It can break any kind of magical bond, I would think."

"She's trying to take her power back from Zirael," Faron said. "She's done working with him."

"And if she succeeds in finishing this disk and seizing control over the creature, the Blight will be more dangerous than we could ever imagine."

Cora's heart beat at the base of her throat. She didn't know if she wanted to scream or be sick.

"When Zirael's Order held all three disks, they used them to manipulate the Blight into destroying entire cities. You've seen a Blight possession before," Lenire said, catching Cora's attention. "This will be worse. It will be possession on a massive scale, turning citizens against each other. I've seen this terror play out in Itharus."

Cora remembered when the Blight had temporarily possessed a handful of dragon riders in the mountains, forcing them to fight against each other. "It'll be a bloodbath," she said.

"Even in Itharus, the three disks were distributed between three members of the Order to ensure no one sorcerer held too great an advantage over the rest. The idea of one person wielding that full power alone is beyond terrifying. It's horrific."

Cora studied Lenire. For someone delivering this kind of news, he was oddly serene. "How long do we have before she finishes the disk?"

Lenire rubbed his jaw. "Using it to cast the bond-breaking spell against Renka while it was still incomplete will have damaged it. Sort of like the way lightning damages a tree. Melusine will have to spend some time repairing it."

"The fact that she could cast that spell at all suggests the disk wasn't far from finished, right?" Faron asked.

"We're running out of time," Cora said as the realization dawned on her. She'd been so worried about how Melusine would again target the Heart of Tenegard now that her plan to move against Llys had been interrupted. But this was worse. If she finished that disk, Melusine would use the Blight to terrorize Tenegard. And then when she was done destroying everything, she would waltz right into the cavern protecting the Heart. There would be no one left to stop her. "We have to open that portal as soon as possible."

Lenire's lips flattened into a thin line. Is this why he was acting so oddly? Had he reached the same conclusion? He avoided her gaze and Cora suspected she was right. He knew what had to be done now, and he was steeling himself to sacrifice his dragon bond in order to create the portal that would save them all.

If that's truly the case, Alaric said privately, *then I don't think Yrsa knows it.*

Cora was shocked to hear it. She'd told herself that they wouldn't sacrifice any other dragon bonds to rid Tenegard of the Blight, but how could Lenire be planning such a thing without consulting his dragon first? *Surely he wouldn't break their bond without Yrsa's full cooperation?*

I'm certain she would have told me if that's what they were planning.

Then it sounds like Lenire hasn't formulated a plan yet. She frowned up at Alaric. It didn't make sense. Lenire still had a devastated kingdom to return to and set to rights. That would be a strong incentive not to sacrifice his own bond without conferring with the rest of them. He would need his magic to help his people rebuild. He was a knight, a healer … He couldn't be the one to do this. Cora couldn't ask it of him, or anyone for that matter. There's no one else that she could ask to bear the required sacrifice.

Alaric, she said gently, catching sight of the moon in his eyes. *When the time comes, it has to be us.*

Her entire chest constricted at the implication of losing him, but there was no other way. She'd already seen the devastation in Renka's eyes. She couldn't do that to another. The guilt would eat her alive.

I know, he said softly. Sadly. *You're right. And it will be.*

CHAPTER 24

CORA

"Keep your shields up!" Cora shouted as she and Alaric pursued a group of dragon riders across base camp. Alaric twisted in the air, and Cora summoned a wall of water from the stream, casting it at the riders. There was a disgruntled cry as it crashed over the riders and left them soaked through. They slowed their escape, hovering in midair with their dragons to argue with each other. *Can you get us up there*? Cora asked Alaric, but he'd already launched toward the riders.

"What in the stars was that?" one of the rider's yelled. He was a tall, lanky boy named Henry with freckled cheeks and hair that fell into his eyes. "Why did you drop your shield?"

"I didn't drop my shield. You were supposed to have the flank covered!" Joi shouted back.

"Yeah, the left flank!"

Joi rolled her eyes. "That's not how it works. The flank is the flank. You're supposed to cover both sides of it!"

"What's going on?" Cora called as she and Alaric swept around the group. The six riders were trembling in the morning chill, their tunics and shawls drenched from Cora's training attack, but their faces were red with anger, their fists clenched around their saddles.

"Henry isn't covering his assigned part of the section," Joi said.

Henry's nose wrinkled. "Joi wasn't clear when she gave directions. If she wants to be section leader, then she's doing a pretty terrible job of it."

"He's just mad that he can't keep up with the rest of us."

"Cyan was injured during the battle!" Henry cried, defending his dragon and their sluggish flying. "Give me a break. At least my shield doesn't crumble every time a bit of wind hits it. Maybe if your friend knew how to cast better shields, she'd still have her dragon bond!"

"Shut up!" Joi snapped. For a moment, Cora thought Joi was going to launch off her dragon and onto Henry's in order to throttle the boy. "You have no idea what you're talking about."

"You know what, you can cover your own flank! I'm not working with you anymore."

"That's enough!" Cora barked. The riders fell into silence, but she could tell by the way Joi and Henry were huffing and puffing that they weren't done shouting at each other. "I know things are tense right now, but turning on each other is not going to prepare us for the battles ahead. This is a training session. This is where we're supposed to make mistakes," Cora said. "That way we don't make them out there," she gestured toward the mountains, "during the real thing."

"I don't see why you keep having us practice shields anyway," Joi said. "Shouldn't we be honing our other magic? How else do you expect us to fight against Melusine?"

"If Melusine uses the disk she's making to try to sever another dragon bond," Cora said, "the only thing protecting you might be a shield."

"We don't even know if our shields are strong enough to stand up to her disk," Henry complained. He shivered and Cora sighed.

"That's true. We don't know if they will be strong enough to rebound the spell, but it's the best defensive magic we have. Actually, working together, being able to layer your shields mid-flight, in the middle of action, is the best we have. That's why we're practicing now, so that if it really comes down to it, you're ready to work together to defend yourselves."

Joi and Henry glared at each other, looking guilty, but neither of them relented their earlier arguments.

"All right," Cora said, calling an end to their session. They clearly needed some time apart, and they also needed to get out of their wet clothes. Having a bunch of sick riders on her hands would only put them at a disadvantage if Melusine attacked suddenly. "Get yourselves in front of a fire," she ordered.

One by one, the riders and their dragons flew off, back to their respective corners of the camp to change and calm down. Cora hoped that some part of the lesson had gotten through to them.

They'll remember it when it matters, Alaric assured Cora, diving for the ground so they could wrangle up the next section of riders.

I hope you're right.

They're scared. Renka and her dragon's loss is still very fresh.

And they're stubborn, Cora added. She knew that losing a dragon bond had unnerved the group, but there was no way to stop it from happening again unless they worked together.

All you humans are a little stubborn, Alaric said softly.

Hey!

He chuckled, the sound like a balm in her head as they landed. *I never said it was a bad thing. I actually think your stubbornness is where your courage comes from.*

Cora squinted up at him as she slid from his back. Though she couldn't tell if he was teasing or not, she smiled anyway. Alaric reached down and nudged her with his snout. She wrapped her arms around his head as far as they would go, her fingers brushing against the smoothness of his midnight blue scales. Sometimes it still left her in awe that this was her life. That Alaric was her dragon and she was his rider. Despite everything else going on, that much remained true and it always would.

Though, of course, if they sacrificed their bond, it wouldn't really be true, would it? Alaric blinked at her and nuzzled against her palms, almost as if he could sense what she was thinking. But Cora was careful not to share her thoughts. They were terrible enough without making Alaric suffer with them too.

Alaric pulled away, lifting his head so that he towered over her once again. Cora turned to see where he was looking. *Oh*, she said to him, surprised.

Renka and Erisa approached.

They want to participate in morning drills, Alaric said.

Cora opened her mouth to tell them that probably wasn't a good idea without a bond to communicate with, but she was cut off by Renka's plea.

"It doesn't matter that we can't communicate psychically or that our magic has been cut off," Renka insisted. "We can still contribute."

"Renka," Cora said, formulating an argument.

"Please! We can still fly and we can still fight. Shouldn't we also train, then?"

She's not wrong, Alaric said.

Cora let out a heavy breath. She knew the pain of a damaged dragon bond—not a broken one but a frayed one—and she didn't have the heart to refuse them. Renka was right, anyway. There must be a way for them to help the group. It's not as if they'd suddenly forgotten how to flap their wings or pick up a sword. Maybe with some practice, they would find a new way to communicate. Sort of the way she and Alaric had. The difference was Cora had a bit of time to adjust to the disintegration of her bond. As communication with Alaric waned, they'd relied on charades and simple words and, at times, Dragon Tongue symbols carved into the ground. Renka and Erisa had lost everything all at once. There was no slow acceptance, this was just the way it was now.

"Okay," Cora said. "Join the next session. We're about to fly."

Renka's smile was so wide Cora almost felt bad about it. This was her fault. She'd put them all in the valley that day. She'd agreed to the mission despite the vision's warning. Renka touched Erisa and pointed to where the others were gathering for take-off. They hurried away together and Cora shook off the wretched guilt that clung to her.

Ready? Alaric asked.

She nodded and climbed onto his back. They waited for the section of riders to take off and sort themselves out. They positioned Renka near the middle so she would have the support of the other riders and be able to follow the lead dragon. They did a couple laps of the area.

They're not doing too bad flying in formation, Cora noted.

Erisa still has a psychic connection to the herd. That will never change. So it's easy enough for her to follow along.

Maybe this could work. The bond may be gone but maybe Renka and Erisa could still figure out a way to be part of the team.

Take us up, Cora asked Alaric.

They coasted on the wind beneath the section for a time. Cora cast gentle spells at them and to her delight, they ricocheted off the shield walls surrounding the group.

This is an improvement on the last group, Alaric noted.

Let's hide out in the trees, Cora said as the group made a sweeping pass over the woods on the other side of the stream. Alaric dove for the trees, pulled his wings tight, and disappeared from the sight of the group. He hurried between the trees as Cora kept her eyes on the fragments of sky that appeared between the branches.

Tell me when, Alaric said.

Steady, Cora said. *They've almost passed us.* She watched a dragon tail swish by overhead. *Now!*

Alaric launched himself straight up in the air, exploding through the treetops, and Cora cast a spell. Their emergence startled the section of riders. But instead of staying together, the section scattered, leaving Renka exposed. Cora's spell hit her shield hard and Renka was bowled over. She slid from the saddle and across the slick scales, slipping over the edge of Erisa's back.

Get us over there! Cora said hurriedly.

Renka managed to grab hold of one of the straps that secured the stirrups to Erisa's saddle, but she was unable to communicate with her dragon, who thrashed frantically in the air trying to reach her. Renka screamed as her grip loosened. The sound reminded Cora of the attack.

Before Cora could reach them, another dragon whipped by, and Cora spotted Joi. She and her dragon swept under Renka, pulled her to safety, and took off again for the ground. Erisa followed close behind.

When Cora landed, Renka was slumped on the ground, her head in her hands, sobbing. A chill ran through Cora's entire body. Without the special awareness that came from their magical connection, Renka and Erisa would have to work doubly hard to find a way to be coordinated and in sync. It would make everything they ever tried to do more dangerous. It hurt Cora to watch the rider be so defeated, but she also didn't want her to die because of it.

Erisa walked over, curled around her, and let out a high keening. The sound was so jarring and sad that everyone in the camp froze. It was unnerving and disheartening, but Cora felt the weight of it most of all. This is what she and Alaric would become by sacrificing their bond: they would have a shell of a connection. Would they mourn the loss like Renka did now? Would they ever be the same?

She cleared her throat awkwardly as Joi knelt down to comfort Renka. "That's enough training for today."

Slowly, the riders disbanded, leaving Cora alone in the field with Alaric. When she turned, she spotted Faron leaning against a tree, his lips puckered, his arms crossed. He looked stricken. Cora walked toward him, needing his comfort, but at the last moment she realized she couldn't tell him what she and Alaric were about to do. He would only try to stop her and she'd already made up her mind.

"You tried," he said as she reached him. "You gave Renka the opportunity. That's more than a lot of people would have done."

She nodded sharply. "I'm going to take the scouting detail for the afternoon. I'll see you later."

"Wait," Faron said, rushing after her. "I'll go with you."

"You should stay here," Cora said as she made her way back to her tent. "Rest up."

"You're not even saying that for me," he said. "You're only saying it because something is troubling you."

"Nothing is troubling me." She swapped out her cloak for a heavier fur-lined one that was good for scouting in the mountains. She also slung her weapons belt around her waist, the weight of the sword on her hip comforting.

"Then you won't mind if I come," Faron said. "We both know Wyn and I can manage the flight. I think we proved that on the battlefield."

Cora couldn't argue that. Using the sleeping sickness excuse no longer worked when Faron was obviously close to being back to his old self. And she couldn't push him away without confirming that there *was* something troubling her. "Suit yourself," she said, heading back to the clearing to meet up with Alaric.

At the edge of camp, Faron caught her hand, pulling her to a halt. "You know what happened to Renka just now wasn't your fault."

"I know," she said.

"You don't sound like you believe it. No one expects you to foresee every possible risk."

She shook her head. "They asked me to loosen the reins, to give up control, and I did. And then Renka lost her dragon bond. I'm not surprised there's tension and fighting among the riders. I would be frustrated too if I didn't think I could trust my leader."

"Cora, they're not asking you to loosen your control because they don't trust you. They want you to do it to show that you trust *them*. Even now they want to know that you trust them to fight alongside you in the battles ahead. Renka wants that, too. Somehow, she wants to prove to you that she can still be useful."

"How do you know?"

"Because it's what I would want if it happened to me and Wyn. I'd want you to look at me and still see a capable dragon rider. I wouldn't want your pity." He ran his thumb over her knuckles. "Now I know something else is troubling you. Please tell me."

Cora was grateful for his words, and she wanted to confide in him, but saying out loud that she was willingly going to give up her dragon bond made it too real. She couldn't admit to everything she was about to lose, not knowing what she'd gained since stumbling upon Alaric in the mountains back in Barcroft for the first time. It was more than a bond. It was the most special of friendships. A friendship Cora had never had in her life until Alaric. It brought her Faron and the dragon riders. It gave her a community where she finally felt like she belonged. It was everything and she wasn't quite ready to say goodbye yet.

"I'm sorry," she said. "I just can't."

"Cora?" he began, but she pulled away, frowning as something tugged at one of the pouches on her belt. She pressed her hand to it, feeling the magical tug again. "What is it?" Faron asked.

Realization struck Cora and her eyes widened. She plunged her hand into the pouch. "The communication anchor! There's a message trying to come through."

She fumbled the anchor out of the pouch and activated it. "Yes, hello!"

"There you are!" a familiar voice growled. "I've been trying to reach you all morning."

Cora couldn't help but grin at the disgruntled sound of Strida's voice. Faron grinned too. Stars, it was good to hear her. "Sorry, we were in the middle of training." Her momentary joy faded. "Is everything okay?"

"That depends on your definition of okay," Strida grumbled. "Am I alive? Yes. Is Northwood running Tenegard into the ground? Also yes. Look, Cora, I know you wanted to protect us by keeping the silence unless it was dire, but enough is enough. I'm breaking the *emergencies only* agreement because I can't take it anymore. Northwood is out of control."

Cora almost choked up, overwhelmed with emotion. She was elated to be in contact again but worried that Strida might be discovered.

"I know my news isn't great, but I thought I'd receive a happier reception."

"We've really missed you here," Faron cut in as Cora recovered.

There was a momentary pause, then Strida let out a breath that sounded almost like a laugh. "I know the riders at the school are awake, but it's still weird to hear your voice." Cora could almost hear Strida's smile. "For a while there, I wasn't sure we were ever going to get you back."

"I'm not going anywhere," Faron assured her.

"Well, that's good because the dragon riders need all the help they can get."

"What's happening out there?" Cora asked. She had so much she wanted to update Strida on, but she let her speak first.

"According to my sources at the school, they've completely torn down the shield."

"What?"

"Northwood's had the crystals moved and deposited to random outposts along the border."

Cora had already heard this from Elaine when she'd gone back to the school, but she hadn't shared this with Strida yet.

Faron frowned, then asked, "Why would he do that?"

"I don't know. Apparently, he thinks we can just throw shields up wherever he demands it," Strida said.

"That shield was constructed to keep out the Blight," Cora said. What was he thinking?

"*I* know that, but he's a pompous, cantankerous fool."

"It was also constructed with the help of the healers and Lenire."

"So you see the problem," Strida said. "He doesn't understand why we can't just make it happen. And since there are no shields, he's separated and ordered most of my remaining dragon riders all over the countryside. I'm having a hard time keeping track of them. But that's not what worries me the most, though."

"What does?"

"Now they're awake, Northwood's turning his sights on the weakened dragon riders left at the school as the solution to his problems. He's losing control of this fight with Athelia, and if it comes to needing reserves, he won't hesitate to send them to the border. Cora, most of those riders aren't ready to be in combat yet. If he orders them to the border without proper recovery, they're going to be slaughtered."

CHAPTER 25

CORA

Cora woke the next morning, still thrumming with adrenaline from Strida's call. Hearing her voice after everything they did to divide the school renewed Cora's hope that they would be reconnected in person one day. The war with Athelia couldn't go on forever, and this fight with Melusine had to end. She just prayed to the stars that when it did, they were the victors.

After hearing, again, that Northwood had divided Strida's dragon riders throughout Tenegard and was using the crystals in disastrous ways, she'd felt uneasy. Learning that Northwood might come for the weakened dragon riders left at the school next had made her furious. But once she and Faron had updated Strida on locating the Heart of Tenegard and the loss of Renka's dragon bond, they'd all decided it was more important for Cora and her team to keep their focus in the mountains. Strida also agreed that creating a hole in the sky and sending the Blight back where it came from might do away with their enemy for good.

"Without that creature at her beck and call," Strida had said, "I bet Melusine will skulk off back to where she came from."

Once she'd mentioned Melusine going back to where she came from, Cora had to tell her about the Athelian soldiers who had been in Melusine's camp. Melusine and Zirael had obviously been planning to take control of Llys on behalf of Athelia, which meant they were in alliance with the Athelians.

"What if this is all Melusine's doing?" Strida had said. "The war. The Blight. By using the creature to get rid of Tenegard's magic, it would make it easier for Athelia to invade us. Maybe that's how it's all connected."

"I still don't know what she hopes to gain," Cora had responded. She'd thought back to the very first time she'd met Melusine, the girl with the wild hair and the bare feet. The girl who'd saved injured rabbits in the mountains and who'd healed Cora's wounds.

Strida had only hummed in response, theorizing that Octavia might know, but it was still too much of a risk to contact her and ask. They left the call with nothing but questions about Melusine's true motives, but Cora had bigger concerns than the crisis at the border. Strida would have to handle that. Cora needed to figure out what to do about the Heart of Tenegard, sacrificing her own dragon bond to send the Blight back, and this new bond-breaking disk Melusine had almost perfected.

By sacrificing her bond she could possibly get rid of the creature, thus protecting the source of all Tenegard's magic. But that would leave her weak and defenseless against Melusine. And though there'd be no Blight for the sorcerer to control, she'd still have her disk, which could do significant damage to the rest of the dragon riders. Was that a risk Cora was willing to take?

When faced with the option of letting the Blight remain in Tenegard any longer, Cora knew what she had to do. She would have to give up her bond and trust Faron, Lenire, and the others could handle Melusine on their own.

Cora prodded the coals of the firepit in front of her with a long stick, trying to get them to catch. While she waited, her eyes drifted across the still slumbering camp to the massive dark blue hill out in the clearing. Alaric rested, wrapped in a tight ball, the ridges on his back rising and falling with each deep breath. She longed to reach out to him for a bit of comfort, letting her mind seek his own. Not knowing how much longer she would be able to do that made her palms sweat. She wiped them on her pants, retrieving a cooking pot and thrusting it over the small, crackling flames. Waking him just for some reassurance would be foolish. Soon there would be no more bond for her to fall back on, so she was going to have to learn how to soothe herself.

"Morning," a gravelly voice said.

Cora twisted to find Lenire standing there, his eyes squinted against the pale morning light like he'd just rolled out of bed.

"Morning," she said, her eyes flicking up and down his form like she might be able to identify the cause of his strange behavior the other night. They still hadn't really talked about it. Yesterday had been filled with training and Renka's breakdown and the call from Strida. Frankly, Cora had almost forgotten about the strange episode of having to wrench Lenire away from his psychic connection with the Blight.

That thought still gave her the chills. Cora would much rather have him linked with Zirael than with the Blight itself.

"I heard Strida reached out," Lenire said, coming to sit by the small fire.

"She did."

"It must have been a relief to hear from her."

The corner of Cora's mouth turned up. "It was. I'm making tea. Would you like some?"

Lenire nodded and went silent. It wasn't unusual for him to sit in silence around her. She'd grown used to his steady, observant nature, and after the other night, hearing him sound like his old self brought her a measure of comfort.

"I'm sorry," he mumbled when she handed him a warm cup.

She raised a brow but kept quiet, forcing him to continue.

"For scaring you like I did."

"It wasn't only me. It was Faron and Yrsa too."

Lenire sighed. "Yeah, Yrsa's already given me an earful."

A chuckle escaped Cora as she sat down, cradling a cup of tea between her hands. "Good. It's the least you deserve." It had been out of character for Lenire to engage that closely with the Blight, but she supposed he'd grown more used to the creature now that he'd learned to sever the Blight's bonds with the hounds. Maybe his odd, erratic behavior these past few days was all due to the stress of the failed attack. She could understand why he would have wanted to do everything in his power to help after what happened to Renka.

If Cora could have reached out to spy through the Blight, she might have done the same, despite the risk. But she wasn't going to tell Lenire that. She didn't want him making more rash decisions like that without consulting her and Faron and the dragons. They were already down a dragon-rider pair. She didn't need to lose him to some sort of Blight possession.

"I've been thinking," he said.

"About what?"

"The hole in the sky. I know you said you didn't want to break another dragon bond."

Cora looked up from her cup and into his eyes. She'd worried Lenire was planning to sacrifice his own bond, but she'd never mentioned she was prepared to do it herself.

"And I think you're right," he continued.

"Oh?"

"We should exhaust every possibility we have before contemplating a step like breaking bonds."

Cora tried to keep her face neutral. She'd love to explore another possibility, she just didn't know how else they could create a hole in the sky of that magnitude. Something that could traverse realms.

"What if we tried harnessing the power of the Heart itself to open a portal like the one in Ismenia's vision? If we can get a hold of some of the Heart's magic, all we have to do is get near enough to the Blight that it would be attracted to the portal."

"If the Heart is powerful enough to keep us out, I don't know if we're strong enough to harness that kind of magic."

"But shouldn't we at least try?" Lenire said.

Cora wasn't sure it was smart to take this idea seriously. She wasn't even sure she could trust Lenire after how foolish he'd been the other night. Still, the lure of a solution that wouldn't risk destroying her dragon bond was impossible to resist. "We couldn't get in last time," she said. "We barely managed to get the hound past the barrier even when we combined all our magic. And that only lasted for a short time."

"But I think we were on to something," Lenire said, jumping to his feet. She could tell by the way he paced and used his hands for emphasis that he'd been thinking about this for a while. "Combining our magic got us through once."

"We don't have the hound anymore."

"So we'll have to try it ourselves."

"That sounds like a really bad idea," Cora said.

He shrugged. "Maybe. But I've learned recently the dragon riders aren't the only ones in our camp that draw their power from the Heart."

Cora frowned.

"We might have only gotten a glimpse of the inside of the cavern last time we tried to access it. But last time we didn't have Ismenia."

"No," Ismenia said the moment Cora asked her to accompany them to the Heart.

"Ismenia, please." Cora's knees bit into the rocky earth where she kneeled in front of the soothsayer.

"You saw what happened to my colleague. I'm barely able to cope with the currents of magic from this distance. You want me to travel even closer to the Heart?" Her pale brows furrowed and her glassy eyes narrowed, making Cora feeling foolish for even asking.

"What if this is exactly what you're supposed to do? What if this is why you're still here? You could have left with your colleagues," Cora said. "But you decided to stay. There must be a reason."

"I've remained here with your camp because that is what I felt called to do." Cora opened her mouth but Ismenia cut her off. "That is not saying I feel called to put myself in danger."

"I think you're our only hope."

Ismenia cackled. "Child, don't pull that line on me. I'm far too old and wise to fall for that."

"Then you know we need you." Cora climbed to her feet. "We've only succeeded in getting a hound past the Heart's defenses for a few moments by combining all our magic. Dragon magic. Healer magic. Itharusian. But it wasn't enough to stop the Heart from forcing us out again. We need the magic of the soothsayers. We need you to be our guide. You're the only one who can swim through the currents that pushed us out last time."

Ismenia sucked in a sharp breath. "I've grown used to navigating the intensity of my visions here," she grumbled. "But I don't know what condition I will be in if I go with you. I may be more of a hindrance than a help."

"We won't leave you behind if that's what you're worried about," Cora said.

Ismenia looked up at her, and the stretch of her smile and the knowing look in her eyes made Cora shiver. "No, I suppose you won't."

The soothsayer rose to her feet and marched across the camp toward the dragons. Cora looked over her shoulder where Faron, Lenire, and Elaine were assembled. "I guess we're going."

Faron shivered as he passed her. "She still gives me the willies."

"I heard that, boy," Ismenia called over her shoulder.

"Come on," Cora said, setting off. "Ismenia can ride with me."

"Cora's promised not to leave me behind," Ismenia chirped. "So I suppose I can count on the fact she's not going to let me fall headfirst off her dragon." She stopped next to Alaric, looking up at him as if she could peer through his pearly black eyes to his thoughts. "If you drop me you'll regret it," she said to him.

Alaric didn't even need Cora's translation to get the gist of what she said. He rolled his massive eyes, lowering to his belly so Ismenia could climb up his back.

If someone had told Cora she'd be aligned with the soothsayers when the rebellion against Onyx started, she would have laughed. She'd never seen them as anything more than Onyx's strange pets. Now she was preparing to defeat Melusine with their help.

People do change, Alaric noted. *However annoying they still are.*

Just try not to toss her, Cora joked. *I actually think she might be able to help us.*

They took off, first Cora and Ismenia on Alaric, then Faron and Elaine on Wyn, and finally Lenire and Yrsa. The day was clear but for the mountain fog, making their ascent over the cliffs quick. Alaric flew with speed and renewed determination. Cora felt hope bloom in her chest alongside her pounding heart.

They coasted on the wind, and Cora kept a close eye on Ismenia. She was seated just behind the saddle, hanging onto the leather seat, but Cora was acutely aware of every shift the soothsayer made. She hated to think it, but Cora was ready to grab Ismenia if she reacted to the power of the Heart the same way her colleague had and started seizing.

How's she doing? Alaric asked.

So far so good. Hey, Yrsa hasn't mentioned anything about Lenire to you, has she?

His concern turned to confusion. *Anything like what?*

I don't know. He seems to be behaving more like himself today. I just wondered if she'd said anything after the other night.

If she's worried, she hasn't brought it to my attention. And I'm sure she would have. We tend not to keep worries like that from each other if it might affect the group. I think the other night was a poor decision made after a long and taxing battle.

Right, Cora replied, smiling at how close Yrsa and Alaric had gotten since Lenire first arrived in that village all those weeks ago to save her from the hound. She heard him huff out loud and sensed his dismissal of her prying. *You poked fun at me when I realized I had feelings for Faron. Turnabout's only fair play.*

That's because you did a spectacularly poor job of keeping your thoughts to yourself, Alaric joked. *You still do.*

Cora flushed and she felt the teasing hum rattle through Alaric's chest as they approached the trail of bent trees.

Suddenly Ismenia groaned, and Cora looked over her shoulder to see the soothsayer clutching her head. "Should we turn back?"

Ismenia's loose hair blew in the wind, the white strands almost transparent against the mountain sun. "I'm all right."

"Are you sure?" Before Ismenia could answer, Alaric flew around a peak, and a burst of intense energy from the Heart surged through them. Cora could feel it pool and tingle in the tips of her fingers. Ismenia must have sensed it too because she clawed Cora's shoulder, making her wince. She twisted around in time to watch Ismenia's eyes roll back in her head. "Ismenia?" she cried, grabbing the woman.

What's wrong? Alaric asked.

Take us down. Quickly.

Alaric dove as Cora awkwardly reached around and clutched Ismenia. The seer's body slumped against Cora.

From the corner of her eye, Cora spotted Wyn and Yrsa, both dragons following Alaric's lead. They were within walking distance of the mouth of the huge cavern. This was probably a good place to set down anyway.

"What's going on?" Faron asked the moment they touched down. He jumped from Wyn's back, turning to help Elaine climb down.

"She just passed out," Cora said, her fingers tangled in the fabric of Ismenia's sleeve. Cora was at an awkward angle and she sighed with relief when Lenire ran over to take the soothsayer from her. "It was during that big surge of energy. Did you feel it too?"

"Lay her down here," Elaine said, digging in her pocket for a bottle of black dust. It almost looked like ground up charcoal. She pulled the cork and wafted the bottle under Ismenia's nose. "I think the surge of magic overwhelmed her," Elaine said. "But she's a lot stronger and more experienced than her colleagues."

With a strangled gasp, Ismenia shot up, her pale, empty eyes settling on them. Then a dozen wrinkles appeared on her forehead and she clutched her head. "I suppose we're here."

Cora nodded, moving out of the way so Ismenia could see the cavern. "How are you feeling?"

"Like I've been smashed over the head with a brick." She struggled to her feet with Elaine's help.

"Do you want to rest?" Cora asked.

"Rest isn't going to fix what ails me," Ismenia said. "Best we get this over with."

Cora glanced toward the cavern. Like before, the magic from the Heart spiraled around them so strongly she felt as if she could reach out and tangle it around her fingers like strands of hair.

The land was full of its power. The air was thick with its energy. Now all they had to do was get past the barrier and they might be able to harness some of it for themselves.

"What's the plan here?" Faron asked, coming to stand beside her. "Are we just going to hurl our magic at the barrier until something gets through?"

"No," Cora said. "We've done that before."

"You've also tried to cross through the barrier yourself," Elaine pointed out.

"Our magic needs to be combined," Cora said, certain about that. "But I also don't think our magic can be cast from a distance."

"What?"

"I think that's why when we combined our magic to get the hound through, we only caught a glimpse of what was inside before we were forced out. I think we have to travel through the barrier all at once while protected by our magic."

"You mean like a—"

"Personal shield." Cora nodded. All that talk with Strida about Northwood taking the crystals and leaving the dragon-rider school undefended had left her thinking a lot about that shield. "What if we stitch a shield around the five of us using dragon magic, Itharusian spells, and healer magic."

"Just like the one at the school," Elaine said, catching on quickly.

"And where do I come in?" Ismenia asked.

"You're at the center of it all," Cora said. "Your magic guides us through while the rest of us protect you from becoming overwhelmed."

Lenire made a noise of surprise and when Cora looked at him, he was beaming. "That's a fantastic idea. I think it might work."

"Or it's going to get us all killed," Ismenia said, her cloudy gaze stormier than Cora had ever seen it.

CHAPTER 26

CORA

"Do you really foresee our deaths?" Cora asked.

Ismenia studied the jagged, rocky points that hung from the mouth of the cavern. "There is darkness in this cave."

"You said you wouldn't be able to control the visions this close," Faron said. "Maybe you're not reading it right."

"It's not a vision," Ismenia clarified. "It is merely a feeling."

Lenire snorted. "No offense, but if we turned and ran every time we had a feeling, we wouldn't get very far."

Ismenia cut her eyes toward him. "Do what you will with the warning."

Cora was uncertain. None of them had taken Ismenia's last vision as seriously as they should have and look how that turned out.

What if the darkness she sees is just another trick of the Heart to protect itself? Alaric said, trying to reassure her.

What if it means we can't control the magic inside? Cora countered. Maybe that's why the Heart was working so hard to keep them out.

"There's no choice now," Faron cut in. "We have to push on. Every second we waste, Melusine gets closer to finishing her disk."

There *was* another choice, though, Cora thought. She could sacrifice her bond with Alaric. She glanced up at her best and most trusted friend in the whole world and remembered the desperate keening of Renka's dragon in the field after the disastrous training session. The sound haunted her still, sending a chill through her body. If there was even a sliver of a chance this might work, and she could save them from that pain—that loss—then she owed it to Alaric to try.

"All right," Cora said. "Faron and I will raise a wall of air around us. Lenire, you thread your knotted magic around the group, and then Elaine will stitch it all together. Got it?"

Cora lifted her hands, summoning a spell that she cast up and over the group. Ismenia huddled at the center, watching the shield take form. Faron stood on the opposite side of the group, and Cora felt the moment her shield butted up against his. Instead of jostling for position, Cora layered her shield over his, and Lenire began to cast those knotted ropes, almost as if he were weaving additional support around their air shields, like a net, to hold them steady.

"Ready?" Elaine asked.

Cora nodded, letting Elaine's cold healer magic flow through her as she knitted the seams of their spells further uniting the different powers they'd conjured.

Cora's magic tensed as it solidified. Suddenly, she no longer had to hold her own spell in place, and as she glanced up toward the sun, she could make out the faint rainbow reflection of the shield wall. It was like a giant soap bubble, she just hoped the strength of the barrier around the cavern wouldn't pop it.

"How do you feel?" she asked Ismenia.

"Better," the soothsayer admitted. "More steady."

"That's a good start," Faron commented.

Cora picked up her sword and slid it back into the sheath. "Then let's proceed."

They walked as a group toward the mouth of the cavern. Alaric, Yrsa, and Wyn hung back so as not to disturb the barrier. Cora could feel Alaric's anticipation trickle down their dragon bond as he watched them. She could also feel the steady stream of magical energy he sent her. Between that and the Heart's own magical energy, Cora was practically buzzing. The tiny hairs at the back of her neck stood straight up and goose bumps prickled on both her arms. This was the moment of truth.

As they approached the barrier, Cora's gaze drifted to Ismenia. The soothsayer rolled her head back and forth like she was listening to a tune only she could hear.

"Go slowly," she warned as they got closer.

Cora's heart beat hard against her ribs as the currents of magic swirled all around them.

"Don't stand too close to the edge of the shield," Ismenia snapped as Lenire pulled up the rear.

He scrambled ahead.

"This is the most dangerous part," Ismenia said as they began to cross beneath the giant stalactites that hung overhead.

Cora's entire body ached suddenly. It wasn't just from exertion of pressing through the Heart's defenses but a sort of magical ache, like the barrier was testing the strength of the shield. She imagined the bones in her arm rattling and splintering from the stress as she clutched her sword. She didn't know what they would find in the cavern, but she wanted to be prepared. A burst of energy coursed down the bond, and Cora could feel Alaric with her. She fought against the barrier's rejection as Ismenia guided them through, her cloudy eyes seeing beyond the wall of darkness that covered the mouth of the cave.

Elaine stumbled, and Faron reached out to help keep her on her feet. The barrier lashed out at them, the magic of the Heart crashing against the shield. Every time it did, there was a small burst of sparks in the darkness. Cora gritted her teeth as the Heart's magic threatened to overwhelm her. Somehow she knew that if she stopped walking, they'd be cast out of the cave.

Like she'd read her mind, Ismenia reached out and touched Cora's arm, pushing her ahead. It was a shock at first, feeling the way Ismenia was manipulating her magic, but then, all at once, it was as if the Heart's magic no longer crashed up against the shield wall, but slithered around it. The shield was passing through the thickest part of the barrier. Ismenia was guiding them through, navigating the currents. It was working!

Everyone gasped as they were released into the cavern. The crushing weight of the currents subsided, and Cora no longer felt as if they would be ejected from the cave. She suspected the shield was unnecessary on this side of the barrier and let herself relax. The magic that surrounded them now was so thick Cora could have fallen back against it and hung suspended in the air.

"By the greatest stars," Ismenia said, her jaw falling open. Elaine murmured in agreement.

The brief glimpse Cora had caught of the inside of the cavern through the hound's eyes did not do it justice. It was so much more spectacular. She studied everything, unsure which way to look first. She wanted Alaric to be able to see everything through her eyes. Magical rivers of light twisted along the cavern, glowing pink and orange, the colors of sunset. The rocky ground was not the gray stone Cora had become accustomed to in the mountains, but flecked with colorful filaments that glittered and cast rainbow reflections against the walls. As she walked forward, those reflections danced upon her skin. Above them, staircases of that same rainbow-flecked stone stretched, but it was the sparling arch ahead of them, followed by the intricately formed bridge that caught her attention. It led to a pool of water—the same pool Cora had seen through the eyes of the hound.

"That's it!" She pointed ahead. "That's the wellspring."

"The source of all Tenegard's magic," Ismenia said.

Cora set out immediately but she'd only taken a few steps before Faron grabbed her, his fingers biting into her shoulder.

Before Cora could ask what he was doing, Faron pointed to the ground where a dark chasm opened. Cora hadn't even seen it. She'd been so focused on reaching the wellspring. They crept forward, to the edge of the chasm, and Cora saw how far it plunged. At the bottom was another snaky river of light, and Cora's stomach dropped.

"Thanks," she whispered.

"Let's try that bridge over there," Faron said.

They moved as a group to prevent anyone from being left behind or accidentally slipping into one of the massive cracks in the cavern. A bridge of singular stones connected two sides of a wide cavern, but the stones themselves seemed to levitate.

Faron and Lenire bent down to investigate the first one.

"It's being held up by magic, there's no doubt," Lenire said.

"But can it take our weight?" Cora wanted to know. She didn't feel like falling to her death.

Faron sighed as he climbed to his feet. He squeezed her hand. "I think there's only one way to find out." He broke into a sprint, catapulting himself off the ledge and toward the stone. Cora shouted, the sound of her panic still ringing across the cavern even as he landed.

"*Stars*, Faron!" Elaine said. It was the closest to angry Cora had ever seen the healer get. "You could have killed yourself."

In answer, Faron bounced on his feet, and the rock held firm where it was suspended. "I think it's safe."

Lenire laughed.

"That wasn't funny," Cora muttered between her teeth as Faron jumped to the next stone. Cora jumped to the first stone, followed closely by Ismenia and Elaine. Lenire went last. Together they jumped across the massive divide. Cora tried not to look down, but it was almost impossible. Flashes of brilliant color winked below them and whispers of rainbow smoke twirled and danced in the depths.

They reached the other side of the bridge safely, approaching the arch she'd seen from the entrance. Another thin bridge of stone stretched over cataracts of magic, each of them spilling over a ledge like a massive, magical waterfall. The stone was slick with magic, and Cora's boots squeaked beneath her. She looked behind her at the colorful footprints they left behind in the magical runoff that collected in puddles.

That subterranean river she'd been following for so many weeks branched out in all directions, cutting paths into the mountain. The stalactites in this part of the cavern looked more like the crystals that grew in the caves they'd visited along the way—the crystals they'd used to build the shield at the school and fight off the Blight. The river was unusual, though, with some of the water running uphill instead of downhill. Cora followed it to that central pool she'd seen.

When they approached, the pool was perfectly still, not a ripple disturbed the surface, which glittered like starlight.

"Do you hear that?" Faron asked, looking down at the rocky crystals at the bottom of the pool.

"It sounds like they're singing," Elaine said.

"They're alive," Ismenia said. "This entire place is as alive as you and me."

The wonder Cora felt was only matched by her horror at the idea of the Blight greedily devouring the cavern's light and draining the thundering rivers down to dry bedrock. They had to do everything in their power to protect this place and send the Blight back where it came from.

Perhaps we should have brought Renka and Erisa, Alaric commented. He'd been experiencing the cavern through her thoughts. *Surely that much raw power could restore their bond.*

Cora posed the suggestion to the group.

"It could just as easily destroy us," Ismenia pointed out as she lifted her skirts to keep them from dragging in the pool of water. "Harnessing this much magic could be disastrous. Even riding its currents, as soothsayers do, is dangerous. Don't forget what happened to my colleague."

Cora looked down at the pool again. She couldn't forget the way the woman had thrashed about or Ismenia's warning outside the cavern. To think there was darkness here was almost ridiculous. Not when it was filled with so much light. Perhaps darkness had really meant danger and by trying to harness the Heart's magic, they were flirting with that danger.

"Then we'll only take a little," Faron said, uncapping his water flask. He knelt down and Cora's hand automatically shot out to steady him as he reached into the pool.

"Careful not to touch the water," Cora said. She didn't know what would happen if he did. Nothing? Everything?

A vision of Faron caught in the sleeping sickness, unconscious on a cot, flashed through her mind. She brushed it off, holding on to him tighter.

Faron pulled his sleeve back, then scooped the flask through the glowing, magical water.

Cora glanced around, half expecting the cavern to start collapsing in on them, but it didn't. Faron carefully capped the flask. He let a drip of magic slide off the end of the flask and drop back into the pool. He got to his feet, turning and grinning at them. Cora blew out a breath.

"That could have been very dangerous," Elaine commented. She cut a strip of her traveling cloak away and gave it to Faron to wrap the flask.

"We've learned to work with a fragment of the Blight thanks to the hound," he said. "Surely we can find a way to safely use a cup of undiluted Tenegardian magic."

"You're too sure of yourself, boy," Ismenia said.

"Oh, c'mon," Faron protested. "We can do this. Right, Lenire?"

There was no answer. Cora whipped around. "Lenire?" He wasn't standing with them. In fact, he was some distance behind them, on his knees, with his head in his hands.

"Are you okay?" Cora called, already hurrying to his side. But when he picked his head up, his eyes were not his own. He climbed to his feet, that unnatural, beaming smile stretching across his face, and reached for his sword.

CHAPTER 27

OCTAVIA

Octavia checked again to make sure the door to her room was locked. It had been a few days since the forum, and Serafine hadn't indicated she suspected Octavia's duplicitous involvement with the pacifist movement, but Octavia didn't want to take any chances.

As an extra precaution, she took a chair from the small writing desk anyway and shoved it beneath the handle. If someone should come looking for her, she didn't want to make it easy for them to discover she'd snuck out of the inn.

She shook the chair to make sure it was secure. *Well, that's the best I can do.* Octavia turned and watched Raksha's dark figure pass across the window. The afternoon sun was sinking, the city walls casting long shadows over the inn. It was shaping up to be a cloudless evening, the perfect night to flee Athelia, but Octavia had heard nothing from the pacifists in the days since she'd delivered the message to the printer. Apparently, none of them were concerned for their own safety. Or perhaps they didn't trust Octavia enough to get them out of the city. Then there was the even more likely answer: the pacifists were staying to fight.

Jangoor's arrest might have emboldened them, renewed their cause. Maybe the whispers spreading on the streets these past few days were the sparks of rebellion. The forum might have worked to draw more supporters to the pacifists' cause. So, until there was cause for Octavia to flee or a request for help from the pacifists, she was sticking to her original plan to retrieve and destroy the magical tracker in Serafine's office. If she couldn't help the pacifists escape, she could at least make it harder for them to be caught.

Your personal guard will switch out shortly for dinner. If they keep to their routine, the current soldiers will stop inside for a quick drink and a meal with the new guard before they take up their positions.

Tell me the moment they move. I'm ready. Octavia threw up the hood of her traveling cloak, tucking her blonde hair away. She drifted to the wall beside the window, careful not to let her figure be seen by people on the street below, blending into the shadows. She reached out and pulled the window an inch, letting the fresh air and the sounds of the street clear her mind. She'd been careful to make a show of retiring to her room after lunch. She didn't want to be seen leaving the inn. And she certainly didn't want armed guards to follow her through the square. The only way to accomplish that was to sneak out.

The whinny of horses and the sharp clatter of chain mail rang across the courtyard. Troops had been moving all day, marching for the border. Most of them were young men and women, soldiers who likely had no idea why they were even being sent off to fight. Octavia couldn't help but feel Serafine was behind today's troop movements. This was to anger the pacifists, to prove the senate had complete control and would not give in to a handful of rebels. It frustrated Octavia more than anything. Between the Tenegardian council and the Athelian senate, how many people were being ordered to the border to die in a needless war?

There they go, Raksha said. *If you're going to sneak out, now's your chance.*

Octavia moved at once, watching the guards' cloaks flutter out of sight as they walked into the inn. She shoved her window up higher. Then she ducked out beneath the frame and the glass, lowering it behind her, careful to stay flat against the roof as she crawled around to the side of the building. Raksha had sat herself at the entrance to the alley, her long tail stretching around the back of the building. Octavia dragged herself over the rough, wooden shingles. Everything smelled like a forest after a rainfall, as if the shingles were rotting. Patches of moss grew in the corners and Octavia was cautious not to slip on them as she maneuvered to the back of the inn.

Raksha lifted her tail, letting it lay against the roof where Octavia crawled. She took hold of the hard sides on Raksha's tail and suddenly she was airborne. Raksha lifted her from the roof, the strong muscles in her tail contracting and relaxing as she lowered Octavia carefully to the ground. The moment her feet hit the cobblestones, Octavia quickly ducked behind a rain barrel.

Do you see anyone?

The guards are still inside the inn, Raksha clarified. *And no one is coming this way. I doubt they will with me lying here.*

Then why do you sound nervous?

I simply wish I could accompany you across the city.

You know that will draw attention to my movements, Octavia said.

I would feel safer if you were within reach, Raksha said.

From the moment Octavia returned from the printer's shop, she'd stayed close to Raksha so that if they needed to make a quick escape, they could almost immediately. This was the first time they were to be separated, but there was no avoiding it. If Raksha left the inn's courtyard, people would wonder why a dragon was moving through the city. They would automatically assume Octavia was nearby, alerting the guards. The only way for her to sneak into Serafine's office was to go alone.

Don't worry, Octavia said. *I'll stay out of sight for the most part.*

I will always worry, but I know this must be done.

I'll be back before you know it, Octavia told her, getting to her feet while the alley was still empty. She gave Raksha's tail a pat, then turned and sprinted toward the end of the alley, darting around the corner before she could be spotted. She kept her hood pulled down over her eyes and her long traveling cloak pinched closed. When she came to a quiet stretch in the next alley, she summoned her magic, feeling it pool in her fingertips as she started to pull at the stone and the earth that held part of the city wall together. She slid through the jagged, uneven hole she created and crept along the wall's edge, sinking low between the ferns and wildflowers that grew with abandon against the stone. It took several minutes before she reached the square where Serafine's office was located.

She summoned her magic again, moving slower this time as she picked away at the stone. The last thing she wanted to do was tumble through in front of a crowd of people. She carved out a slit for her eyes first. A few people ambled by and she waited for a horse-drawn wagon to roll past, then used her magic to shift the stone and earth again to make a hole big enough for her to slide through. She spent less time on this hole, worried she would be seen, and it was a tight squeeze, the sharp rocks scraping against her belly through her tunic. She turned and quickly closed the hole, then hurried off down the street.

The crowds thickened as she crossed through the bustling market square to the row of stately senator office suites.

It looks like Serafine's personal guard is gone, she said to Raksha as she scanned the upper windows for shadows. *There's no one posted out front.* That meant Serafine had retired from her office for the evening.

You'll still have to be careful, Raksha said. *There are likely still staff inside.*

The corner of Octavia's mouth turned up in a smile. If it wasn't for all her practice sneaking around the palace in Kaerlin, she might have been more concerned. *I'll be careful*, she promised as she cut across the market square and walked briskly toward Serafine's office. Part of her regretted not scoping out the area, but at the time, she hadn't wanted to leave the inn in case one of the pacifists took her up on her offer for escape. Plus, she'd hoped her lack of activity would cause the soldiers stationed near the inn to grow bored with her lack of movement and stop watching her so closely. If their guard was down, it would make her getaway easier. Because of that, she didn't want to be seen ogling the front of the building looking for the best place to sneak inside, so she walked past and ducked into the gap between the offices and the neighboring structure. It was a tight squeeze between Serafine's building and the next, the brick walls closing in on her. Apparently, the gaudy marble stone had only been used on the building fronts, which worked in Octavia's favor. She suspected she would still be able to use her magic to pass through the marble, though it would have taken a lot more energy. The mortar that held the bricks together crumbled away with a flick of her hand, and she passed through the hole, stepping into the servants' quarters below the stairs.

It was damp and cold, like the cellars in the palace. There were no fineries or finishings upon the walls, and the floors were made of dirt. Octavia hadn't been down here before, but when Serafine had led her to the office filled with books, she'd taken her up a set of stairs at the front of the building. Octavia set off down the hall, listening for voices or movement. The only thing she could hear was the sound of her own nervous breathing.

A jolt of calm rushed down the bond and Octavia knew Raksha was trying to help. She let the feeling wash through her, right down to her toes, basking in the focus that came from the calm. She reoriented herself and hurried on. Footsteps sounded above and Octavia froze, her eyes lifting to track the movements. Another pair of footsteps joined them, drawing closer, coming down the stairs. Octavia darted into an alcove, willing herself to disappear into the shadows. She breathed in a lungful of dust, holding her breath to keep from coughing. Two young women skipped past the alcove, unaware, giggling to themselves. Hopefully, they were the last of the staff to leave for the day. Octavia released her breath, covering her mouth to stifle the sound of her choking on dust as she continued up the stairs. She spilled out into the upper hallway Serafine had walked her through. Octavia recognized the door to her office. It was shut, and she pressed her ear against it, eyes closed, just in case someone was inside. As an extra precaution, she let her magic flicker through the room, scanning for signs of life. She wasn't as adept at scanning as Cora and Strida or even Faron had been. They'd certainly developed a knack for it having tracked the river for so long, but she could manage to magically search a room as small as this.

Her magic swept through without incident. Assured now that she would be alone on the other side of the door, Octavia grabbed the handle, twisted it, and stepped inside. She was quick to close the door and lock it behind her. At least it would buy her some time to hide or escape if there were any other staff lingering in the building and they tried to enter the room, though Octavia had a sneaking suspicion Serafine's office was off limits when she wasn't around. And knowing the power Serafine carried within the senate, she knew the staff would obey that wish. For Octavia, that meant as long as she was quiet, she shouldn't be disturbed.

She inhaled deeply, overwhelmed by the comforting smell of old books. What she wouldn't give for a day here just to sit and read. The amount of knowledge this room must contain. Perhaps there was even knowledge of the Tenegardian dragons—tomes that had been lost to Tenegard for the generations of Onyx's rule.

Stay focused, Raksha warned her.

Right.

Octavia crossed the room, careful to stay on the plush carpets to avoid making loud footsteps, and lifted the vase on the desk the same way she'd seen Serafine do when she'd last visited. Octavia dumped the contents into her hand, catching a small stone—the communication anchor! She almost couldn't believe it had been so easy to find, or how smooth it was in her hand, like a rounded river rock repeatedly battered by the water. So this little thing was responsible for tracking down anchors or maybe even people? Octavia flipped it over, wondering how it worked. She was about to probe it with her magic when her fingernail snagged on something in the rock's surface—a shape. Confusion filled her immediately as she recognized the etching.

What is it? Raksha wondered.

Octavia stepped toward the window, catching the afternoon light against the pebble. *It's Dragon Tongue*, she told her. *The pebble is carved with a Dragon Tongue symbol!* How did Dragon Tongue come to be used here of all places?

Didn't Cora say Melusine used Dragon Tongue? Wasn't that how she summoned the Blight into their mountain camp?

You're right, Octavia said, astonished. Now that Raksha had reminded her, she remembered Cora explaining how Melusine had deceived them. How she'd manipulated the Dragon Tongue, first in the camp and later in the dining hall to lead the Blight to its targets. What a strange coincidence that both Melusine and Serafine shared an interest in Dragon Tongue. But what if it was more than a coincidence? Paired with the fact that Melusine had Athelian guards at her border encampment when she attacked Jeth, this evidence seemed to strongly suggest Serafine was the Athelian link to Melusine. *I know this is only circumstantial evidence, but I think this suggests Melusine and Serafine are working together in some capacity.*

Octavia turned the pebble over in her hand again, her brows drawing closer together. *I don't think the Dragon Tongue has anything to do with the spell*, she told Raksha. *It looks like it's carved over the top of the Athelian spell. Almost like a decoration.*

If Melusine had known enough to carve those Dragon Tongue symbols in the mountains, had she carved this one as well and given it to Serafine?

What does it say? Raksha wondered.

Listen and hear. Octavia frowned. That did align with Serafine's claim the device could track anchors, but with the Dragon Tongue decoration, this almost struck her as some kind of gift.

Can you destroy it? Raksha said.

Possibly, Octavia replied. But if I do, and it turns out Melusine and Serafine really are working together, this might be my only bit of evidence to prove that.

Octavia reached out with her magic, probing the tracker for weaknesses, when suddenly it felt as if she'd been caught behind the navel and dragged into a rocky riverbed. Her feet remained firmly on the ground, but her mind lurched, causing the room to disappear. Octavia gasped, clutching the side of her head as images swam behind her eyes. One of them surfaced, a hazy, grainy picture that wasn't fully formed. This was like the vision she'd once had of Cora reflected in the gleaming facets of a dozen crystals. That was the vision that had saved them from the Blight attack at the school. But there were no gleaming crystals this time. Instead, Octavia saw Serafine and Melusine, sitting side by side, their faces etched with filth, their clothes tattered, surrounded by rubble. Melusine was almost exactly as she remembered her from the battle in the mountains near the crystal cave—willowy, with curly, unkempt hair that dangled in front of her face. Though sitting there next to Serafine she looked frail, like the magic had been drained from her body. This sorcerer never would have been able to fight Lenire for control of the Blight and burn through his disk.

Octavia was expelled from the vision so quickly she lost her balance, falling to her knees beside the desk with a hard thump, the tracker rolling free of her hand. She crawled after it.

Raksha, she cried out in her mind. *Raksha, did you see that?* There was no denying it now. The vision had been as plain as day. Serafine and Melusine were clearly aiding each other in their pursuits. Maybe they'd been working together from the start, using the Blight and the war to destabilize Tenegard. And if so, that's why Serafine had lied to Octavia from the beginning, to cover her own tracks. Octavia's thoughts spun out of control.

The doorknob rattled suddenly, and Octavia wrapped her hand around the tracker, climbing quietly to her feet. Had there been other staff in the building? Had they heard her fall? She glanced around the office for a place to hide. *Raksha, someone's here.*

There was no answer.

Raksha?

Octavia's fear skyrocketed as their bond stayed strangely silent.

The office door burst open, the wood crashing to the floor, separated from the hinges. Octavia found herself face-to-face with a brace of Athelian soldiers.

"You there!" one of the guards bellowed, pointing a finger in her direction. "You are trespassing on senate property!"

She backed up until her shoulders hit the bookcase behind her. Did she try to run? To fight her way out of the office? No, not with Raksha's sudden silence. Her weapons had been seized when they'd arrived. She could use magic, but how far would she get before these soldiers summoned Athelian sorcerers?

"Turn around!" the guard ordered, unfurling a length of chain from his belt for her hands.

"Please let me explain," she said, lifting both hands.

One of the soldiers lurched forward, grabbing her wrist. She hissed in pain as the tracker dropped into the soldier's palm. He forced her arms behind her back, securing them with the chains, then shoved her out of the office. The soldiers escorted her out of the building and though Octavia's pulse hammered in her throat, the only thing she could think of was Raksha's eerie silence.

"Where are you taking me?" Octavia asked the soldier who had his hand on her shoulder. The metal edges of his armored gloves cut into her skin as they walked across the square toward the senate building. Last she'd heard, magic wielders weren't allowed inside.

The soldier didn't answer, but they veered left, toward a smaller building. This was the same building where they'd marched Jangoor. The moment they crossed through the wide, double-doors, Octavia was thrust forward into the arms of another soldier. He was burly, his gut protruding so far it seemed to lead him like a compass. He grabbed the collar of her traveling cloak, his fist gripping the fabric, tightening it around her neck until she was almost choking. He forced her down a set of stairs and into a dank, chilled room with a dozen holding cells. He swung open a barred door with a creak of metal and shoved her, hard. She stumbled and the next thing she knew she was on the ground. The door crashed shut behind her, the sound of failure ringing in her ears.

Octavia sat in the corner, her back to the wall, facing the door. She wanted to be able to see whoever approached as she poured her magic into breaking the bonds of the chains around her wrists. The chill in the room had seeped into her fingertips and her clothes clung to her like damp rags, but the heat of the metal behind her back was like a fire. Octavia felt the steel weaken enough for her to stretch the chains and pull her hands through. She dropped the chains and massaged the angry, red skin of her wrists. She'd had to burn herself to get free, but she couldn't bring herself to care. Her thoughts spiraled, her mind reaching out for Raksha, but there was still no answer. Their bond wasn't damaged, not like Strida's and Emrys's, but it was somehow blocked.

When the door burst open, Serafine descended the stairwell, followed by a handful of senators who Octavia recognized from the forum.

Octavia snatched up the chains, to maintain the ruse that she was shackled, then scrambled to her feet and stepped toward them. Serafine stopped in front of the cell. They were separated by only the bars. "Where is Raksha?" she asked.

"The dragon? We couldn't take any chances," Serafine said. "She's been subdued."

"Subdued how?"

"We can't reveal all our secrets, now can we?" Serafine chuckled dryly. "Especially not to Tenegardian spies."

Octavia growled. The only thing she'd ever seen that had managed to subdue a dragon were the magical chains from Onyx's reign. Only his dark creations could prevent her from being able to reach Raksha through the bond. Had the Athelians raided a Tenegardian supply stash? "I want to see her."

"I'm afraid you're not going anywhere." In her hand, Serafine held up the tracking device. "She was found with this," Serafine said to the other senators. "Do you see this symbol here? Dragon Tongue. Apparently, she sought to sow division among the senate using this magical aid."

"That's not true," Octavia said. "And you know it."

"Please, Octavia. I trusted you. I wanted what you said you wanted. Peace between our nations."

Octavia shook her head. That was the last thing Serafine wanted, but these senators would never listen to her. They were either in Serafine's pocket or dazzled by her words. They would never be convinced otherwise by a Tenegardian dragon rider, so Octavia didn't bother to waste her breath.

Serafine sighed. "I'm devastated to find you are nothing more than a spy trying to worm your way into Athelia's confidence." She turned to the other senators. "We are forever indebted to the citizen who reported Octavia's ability to pass through stone walls. It's truly inspiring to see how even a lowly pamphlet printer can contribute to the unity and security of our great nation during these dangerous times."

Octavia's jaw dropped. The printer had ratted her out? She'd suspected Serafine might have double agents within the pacifist group, but the printer? Were all those leaflets and pamphlets slandering the senate part of Serafine's games too? Had she forced the printer to push the rhetoric all so she could manipulate the inner workings of the senate? Or had the printer aligned with Serafine of her own free will? Either way, telling the printer she would help the pacifists escape had been her undoing. Serafine must have been watching her these past few days, waiting for an opportune time to make the arrest. And Octavia had played right into her hands by sneaking into her office, providing even more reason the war against Tenegard was justified. Serafine would label her a Tenegardian spy to the populace of Athelia and lie in order to wrench supporters away from the pacifists.

Serafine turned back to Octavia, wearing a darkly smug look. "We must have this device examined immediately by qualified mages," Serafine said. "And I know exactly who to entrust with a task so vital to Athelia's security."

"She's lying!" Octavia shouted frantically, realizing she'd never had any hope of uniting their nations. "Serafine is behind this war!"

Serafine scoffed. "You think I would subject my people to this?"

"She is!" Octavia insisted, calling out to the senators who would only glare at her. "She's connected to a dangerous sorceress who's been targeting the Tenegardian dragon riders. She's part of the reason we're in this mess. I know she is! I've seen it." Her cries bounced around the room but they were useless.

"More of your Tenegardian tricks?" one of the senators said. "Serafine is right. Tenegard's treachery and corruption runs even deeper than we knew."

"Agreed," someone else said. "We have no choice but to exercise emergency authority to root it out. After the forum and this incident, I'm confident we'll have enough of the vote to initiate emergency protocols during tomorrow's meeting."

"And in such times," Serafine added silkily, looking directly at Octavia, "there is no need for the formality of due process. You have wronged us, Octavia. Threatened to undermine the senate. Attempted to aid the rebel pacifists. And for your crimes, you and your dragon will be publicly executed tomorrow."

CHAPTER 28

CORA

Lenire lifted his sword and surged forward. Cora barely managed to dodge the blow. An alarming sense of déjà vu filled her. They'd once stood in a cavern, similar to this, surrounded by crystals connected to the Heart of Tenegard, and he'd tried to kill her. Back then she'd complained of a headache, and he'd been convinced she was possessed by the Blight. Cora didn't understand it then, and it had taken all her skill and Alaric bursting into the cavern to stop Lenire from killing her. Now she understood what had made Lenire so afraid. He was no longer in control, and that meant he was no longer himself.

Lenire whipped around and struck again. Cora threw herself out of the way, rolling across the hard, rainbow-flecked stone. She skidded to a stop alongside a massive crevice, scrambling away on her hands and knees as Lenire's sword sliced through the air. She felt the shift in the air as it came down where her head had been moments ago.

Footsteps pounded and echoed in the cave. "Cora!" Faron cried.

"He's been possessed!" she shouted back.

This wasn't anything like what had happened to Alia, the girl who'd been possessed in the mountain village. The Blight had only managed to take control of her body, leaving her movements stilted and jerky, like a puppet on a string. Lenire's possession was different. His movements were darting and graceful, and that's how Cora knew the Blight had seized control of his entire mind. Ever since Zirael and the Blight made contact with Lenire in the clearing, she'd been worried it might have attempted to harm him like this, but Lenire and Yrsa had been sure that he was fine. She should have listened to her instincts then. Instead, she ignored them, even after that night Lenire got lost in his own head, reaching out to spy on the Blight.

Lenire told her the Blight could seep into a mind without warning. Cora jumped to her feet and drew her own sword. Clearly, there was still a fragment of the creature left behind in his head. That might even explain his erratic behavior these past few days.

"Stay back!" she called, warning Elaine and Ismenia away. They huddled by the wellspring, wearing matching looks of shock.

As she shuffled to the left, keeping Lenire at a distance, she studied him. This was no empty shell of a body. This was the Blight made human and it fought with all of Lenire's own skill. Was this the darkness Ismenia had been referring to before they'd walked into the cavern? Had she sensed the Blight's presence? Had she foreseen Lenire's possession being fulfilled?

He darted forward, striking out, and Cora caught the blow with her own sword. They came face-to-face and for a moment, Cora swore she saw the dark shadow of the Blight swirling in his eyes. "Lenire, I know you're in there!"

He sneered, mocking her in a way that was so unlike him. She tried to shove him off, to put some distance between them again, but Lenire was too strong. As a dragon knight from Itharus, he was already a skilled fighter, but with the Blight in his mind, he'd become unfailingly strong. Cora's arms shook as the sharpened edge of Lenire's blade pressed closer to her throat.

A cry sounded through the cavern and the next thing Cora knew, Faron had jumped onto Lenire's back, getting his arm around Lenire's throat. He yanked with all his might, and Cora was able to shove Lenire off. Faron and Lenire went tumbling to the ground. As Faron tried to subdue Lenire, their swords scraped against the stone, creating rainbow sparks. She could tell Faron was trying not to hurt him, but Lenire drove his elbow into Faron's ribs repeatedly. They wouldn't be able to defend themselves from Lenire for long. He was cruel, remorseless, as if he'd been given one task, and that was to eliminate everyone in this cavern.

Lenire slammed his head backward into Faron's face, making him groan.

Cora dropped her sword and summoned her magic instead. She let it seep into the stone by Lenire's feet until the stone was malleable and she could wrap it up his legs. "Move, Faron!" she shouted. "Get out of there."

Faron released Lenire and crawled away. Lenire sat up and started to dig at the stone around his feet with his sword.

"Good thinking," Faron said, panting as he stopped by her side. "What do we do now?"

"I don't know," Cora said. "Lenire only ever told me that people possessed by the Blight had to be killed."

"All of them?"

"When it's in their mind. He said there was no cure. That they'd never been able to stop it before." Cora met his gaze. "His own sister had to be killed because the Blight infected her mind."

Faron shook his head. "There has to be a way. What if we pull him out of it like we did the other night?"

"I don't know if we can still do that if the Blight's in control."

"Well, we have to try something," Faron said. He dropped to his knee and started to form the beginnings of an anchor point.

He was right. Cora wasn't prepared to execute Lenire on the spot. They had to try to save him. She felt a burst of magical energy course down the bond from Alaric as she helped Faron create the anchor. Then she cast a thread of Itharusian magic using the simple spell Faron had taught her. They latched onto Lenire just as they had the other night, but immediately Cora's thread snapped. The momentary glimpse of the Itharusian tapestry that covered the landscape disappeared with the spell.

"It's like the Blight is burning away the spell," Faron said, trying again to cast the Itharusian magic.

"Your anchor isn't strong enough to support the spell," Ismenia said, coming up behind them.

"Get out of here!" Cora urged, pointing Ismenia back to the rock shelf Elaine had taken refuge behind.

"You need help against the creature." Ismenia held the flask Lenire had filled earlier with water from the pool. Carefully, she opened it and poured two drops of water onto the anchor point. Cora felt a surge of power zip through her. It was so strong her body vibrated.

Ismenia laid her hands on the anchor, her gaze cloudy with the magic of the soothsayers. Cora felt the vibrations ease. Ismenia was using the power of the Heart to strengthen the anchor against the corrosive presence of the Blight. "Cast your spells now," she insisted. "I can't hold this forever."

Cora began to weave her hands, creating the Itharusian magic. Faron threw his first, almost laughing as it connected. "It's holding!"

Cora was slower, less practiced, but she managed to take hold of the thread and cast it over Lenire's struggling form. Immediately, she was granted the sight of the Itharusian magical world. Her perspective shifted and she could suddenly see Lenire struggling against the shadowy, smothering grasp of the Blight. It was draining him, bleeding him dry of his magic. Soon he would be too weak to fight the creature, and it would take him over. The Blight continued to weave snaking tendrils across Lenire's body, holding him tighter, becoming one.

"He can't take hold of the lifeline," Faron said, swearing under his breath.

Cora's gaze drifted down the snaky form of the Blight. It hung off Lenire's body, stretched as if it was secured to its own anchor point. Perhaps if they could find it, they could sever it. But as she investigated, instead of finding the anchor point within the woven tapestry, Cora saw the faint outline of another figure. "It's Melusine," she gasped.

Faron and Ismenia both turned to look at what Cora saw. "She's caught in the Blight's grip as well," Ismenia said.

Melusine's presence was diminished. This wasn't her controlling the Blight. The Blight was feeding off her. Cora gasped. "Zirael must have turned the Blight against her to feed off her magic stores."

"I thought they were allies," Faron grunted.

"Perhaps she no longer serves her purpose," Ismenia said.

"They were fighting for control," Cora said. "That's why Melusine started making her master disk. Zirael must've realized he was in danger and taken action. She's extraordinarily powerful. Her magic alone would be able to sustain the Blight for a while."

Cora didn't know why, but her heart beat uncomfortably at the sight of Melusine's magical figure fraying at the edges as the Blight swallowed up her power. She shouldn't care that Zirael sought to destroy her. One less enemy for them to face should elate her, but it didn't. She felt queasy.

"Cora!" Faron cried as the Blight suddenly took hold of their lifelines. That grasping black mist sparkled with the faint silvery threads of Zirael's control. The darkness crawled down the thread toward them, and Cora could feel its rage and its hunger.

"Cut the thread!" Elaine cried, though her voice sounded like it was on the other side of the cavern.

"I can't!" Cora said. The thread was like metal wire all of a sudden. Even with Alaric's bursts of bolstering magic, it was too strong. Then she was blinded by a flash of light. When the spots in her vision cleared, she saw Melusine's diminished figure now glowed brightly.

"What's happening?" Faron asked as the Blight slithered back up the threads toward Melusine.

"I think she used our distraction to break free of the hold and grab her master disk," Cora said, watching the glow spreading from Melusine's figure lash out at the silvery threads that were still tangled up with the Blight. "She's fighting Zirael for control of the creature."

The magical thread in her hands lost some of the tension, and Cora shook it. Faron did the same, knocking the lingering tendrils of the Blight from their spells. Lenire cried out, clutching his head, the sound of his ragged voice ringing through the cavern.

"He's fighting the Blight," Cora said, hurrying forward.

Faron caught her arm. "He's still dangerous."

"Kill me!" Lenire shrieked, reaching out for them. "Please! Before it's too late."

"Lenire?" Cora said. They were finally talking to his true self again.

His face crumpled, that sickening sneer stretching across his features for a split second. Then he was back. "Cora, you have to do it," he said. He heaved, exhausted, his feet still trapped in stone. The Blight had consumed so much of his energy he could hardly hold his head up.

Faron's grip tightened on her arm.

"Do it," Lenire pleaded. "Before it's too late."

Cora shook her head. "Maybe we can help you."

"Kill me like I should have killed my sister." He slumped forward.

"He's losing ground," Ismenia said. "Once the last of his resistance is stamped out, the Blight will channel itself through him and devour the Heart."

"The same way it once used his sister to invade and destroy his city," Cora said.

"Don't let it happen," Lenire croaked, barely able to keep his eyes open.

But Cora couldn't do it. She'd led Lenire into that attack against their enemies. She'd allowed him to puppet the hound. She was the reason the Blight had a chance to grab hold of him. This was her fault. "Lenire, don't let the Blight win!" She sank to her knees, inching forward on her hands, trying to catch his eye. When she did, she saw only his pain, his fear, the torture he was being put through.

"Unless you kill me," he whispered, "the Blight will devour all of Tenegard's magic before you even have a chance to protect it. I'm sorry it must be you, but if my death prevents that outcome, it would be no victory for the Blight or Zirael. I came here to stop them, Cora. That was my mission. Let me die fulfilling that."

Cora's heart throbbed against her ribs so hard it was like being hit in the chest with a spell. Behind Lenire, in the mess of the tapestry, she could see Melusine and Zirael warring for control, but bile burned the back of her throat at the thought of letting Lenire sacrifice himself. Faron tugged at her, pulling her back to her feet. She couldn't keep a single thought straight until Faron pressed the hilt of her sword into her hand.

She looked at him and he nodded sagely.

"Please," Lenire begged, convulsing against the ground as he fought to hold off the Blight. "It's okay. Please, Cora. *Please*."

She looked from Lenire to Ismenia to Elaine, recognizing the truth of the matter. Lenire knew how this would end if they didn't put a stop to it, and still he was willing to sacrifice himself. She couldn't turn away from him now. He'd asked her to be the one to end it, and she couldn't let him suffer. Cora tightened her grip on her weapon, imagining the way Yrsa would scream once it was done. Once she killed her rider.

Acid burned through her chest as she advanced toward Lenire, steeling herself to deliver the death blow.

CHAPTER 29

CORA

Lenire bowed his head with what remained of his control, exposing his neck to Cora. She walked toward him at a steady pace, her grip on her sword growing sweaty. Her arm felt like it weighed a thousand pounds, and it was all she could do not to drag her sword across the glittering stone of the cavern. She adjusted her hold, using two hands to carry her weapon. She didn't want to hesitate, to draw this out for Lenire. What a sickening thought it would be to know death was coming and yet the person meant to deliver the death blow was taking their time. She didn't want Lenire to have to wallow in pain or fear. And yet, she couldn't make herself move any faster.

Cora fought every instinct inside her that told her to turn around and run. She couldn't be the one to do this. She couldn't raise her sword to Lenire and strike him down, even if it did mean saving the Heart of Tenegard. He was her friend, her ally. He'd helped her get this far. Without him, Faron and the other dragon riders would have remained trapped in the sleeping sickness for weeks or months. Perhaps forever. Without Lenire, Cora might have been bested by that first hound way back in that village.

“This isn’t right,” she murmured under her breath. “I can’t do this. I can’t. I *won’t.*” Who was she to decide Lenire’s fate? How had she become the leader of the dragon riders? She wasn’t qualified to be making these kinds of decisions. Everything she did got someone else hurt. First Faron, in the mountains with the Blight. She’d forced Strida to take the position in the capital and separated the students at the school, ruining friendships and loyalties. She’d allowed her riders to attack Melusine’s camp where Renka’s dragon bond was shattered. And now Lenire was dying because she’d allowed him to mess around with the Blight when she knew it was a bad idea.

She wasn’t fit to lead anyone.

It should be her head on the chopping block, not Lenire’s. Cora caught her reflection against the flat edge of her sword. She looked horrified, her eyes wide and glassy, her pale face caught with rainbow refractions that bounced off the stone walls. The sick feeling inside her had become torture. Her gut twisted and twisted, like it had caught all her organs up in a violent death roll, and Cora imagined herself dropping dead before she ever reached Lenire. It would be better that way. Then she wouldn’t have to make this decision. She suddenly understood his pain about his sister. He’d been tasked to kill her just like this, and in the end, he hadn’t been able to strike her down. More people had been killed because of his decision, but Cora couldn’t blame him for hesitating. It was an impossible task. The weight of it was suffocating.

“It’s okay,” Lenire said, his cheek pressed to the stone beneath him, his whispered words falling like pleas across the cavern. “I’m sorry, Cora. I’m sorry you have to do this. But I’m ready. It’s okay. It’ll all be over soon. You’ll see. Please. *Please.*”

Cora looked over her shoulder at Faron, her jaw trembling. He stood as still as a statue, his face caught in hard lines. He stood not like a dragon rider, but like a soldier: chest out, feet apart, his hands tucked behind his back. He was the picture of calm. The only thing that gave him away was the twitch in his cheek.

Cora looked to Ismenia next, who'd closed her eyes, either caught by a vision or choosing not to watch this reality come to pass. Cora was convinced whatever Ismenia caught a glimpse of outside the cavern was foretelling this moment. It might have been whisked away quickly by the strength of the magical currents that surrounded the Heart, but she'd spoken of a darkness. Cora didn't know what could be darker than what she was about to do.

Beside Ismenia, stood Elaine. Silent tears streamed down her face. This could have just as easily been Faron. Both he and Lenire had been messing with the hound these past weeks, poking around too close to the Blight. Cora's heart surged painfully against her chest. She wished one of them would stop her, that they would cry out and tell her they'd figured out a way to end this without killing Lenire, but it had never been done before. Cora knew that better than any of them. A possession of the mind was a death sentence, and today Cora was the executioner.

Alaric was talking in her head, but she was doing her best to block him out. He couldn't save her from this moment. He couldn't save any of them. And she knew he was with Yrsa, who was likely beside herself at the thought of Lenire sacrificing himself. Cora didn't want to hear any of those things right now. If she did, if she even imagined the way Yrsa was screaming, her keening dragon roar echoing between the cliffs, she wouldn't be able to lift her sword.

Cora walked through the woven tapestry of Itharusian magic, stepping past threads, watching the shadow of the Blight consume Lenire. He was almost completely lost to shadow, his entire body trembling.

His eyes lifted, finding hers. He nodded. "I'm ready."

Cora couldn't look at him any longer, pulling her gaze away. It drifted to the figments of Melusine and Zirael as they fought for control of the creature. Melusine was gaining ground again, her master disk forcing both Zirael and the Blight to cower before her. To her surprise, the Blight recoiled as the spells from Melusine's disk struck out against the black mist. It turned in on itself, roiling like it was trying to brush the spell away, mewling from somewhere deep in its ever-changing form. Cora didn't know what it was, but something about the way the Blight recoiled and whined reminded her of that injured rabbit in the mountains that Melusine had healed. The Blight was in pain. It was in distress.

Cora gave her head a shake. Surely a mindless force like the Blight couldn't feel distress. It was just an accumulation of raw magic. It didn't have thoughts or feelings. It only wanted to feed. Right? But then why was she reminded of the rabbit? Why did the Blight feel like a creature in need of help? Cora almost laughed at how ridiculous these thoughts were, but she couldn't shake this new perspective.

Zirael's faction had been manipulating the creature for years in Itharus, and now it was here, forced to obey Melusine's whims. She studied the creature again. It was holding on to Lenire, but it was also lashing out against Zirael and trying to dodge Melusine's disk. Maintaining its hold on Lenire was using energy the creature couldn't spare, but it wasn't the Blight that wanted Lenire, it was Zirael. This was Zirael's order, *his* control that was forcing the Blight to act. Now that she was looking for it, the Blight's anger and pain were much clearer. It was an animal, trapped in a cage, hissing and scratching to be free. It obviously wanted nothing to do with either Zirael or Melusine.

Even after all the years under Zirael's control, the Blight held no loyalty for him. If not for the threads of control the sorcerers had woven through it, Cora suspected the Blight would try to flee. It didn't want to be here anymore than Cora did; the creature was pulling away from the sorcerers. Ismenia's vision flashed through her mind. That magical explosion in the sky hadn't just brought the Blight into their midst, it had also ripped the creature away from its home world. It never wanted to devour the dragon riders' magic or haunt the mountains looking for the Heart or possess the people of Tenegard. Those were the machinations of Melusine, who was bent on helping Athelia take down Tenegard. The Blight was as much a victim of Melusine's plans as the dragon riders, and judging by the way it was hissing and striking now, it hated being controlled by the sorcerers. If Cora was this creature, all she would want to do was escape and flee home.

That meant they both wanted the same thing. A foolish idea sparked to life in her mind. Maybe it was time they stopped working against the creature. Cora dropped to her knees, abandoning her sword as she crawled toward Lenire.

"Cora, what are you doing?" Faron cried out behind her.

That woven tapestry of threads surrounded her, the misty shadow swirling up and down the threads that passed through Lenire's body. She reached out and lifted his head. "Open your eyes!"

Lenire did, his lashes fluttering. He was so exhausted, in so much pain. "Just finish it," he begged.

"No." He closed his eyes but Cora shook him back to attention. "Listen to me. Stop fighting it."

"What?" he gasped.

"Stop fighting against the creature and work with it instead. It doesn't want you, that's Zirael's doing. It hates them. It wants to be free. Use the insight you have, the connection. Maybe if you do, you can both be free."

Lenire struggled to stay conscious. "You want me to help the Blight?"

"It only wants to go home," she said. He looked at her like he thought she was crazy, and maybe she was, but nothing else was going to save him. Maybe this crazy idea would. "I won't be able to give you long. If this doesn't work, I'll have to kill you. I won't let the creature loose in here to destroy the Heart. Do you understand?"

"Yes," he breathed.

Cora let him go, watching Lenire's eyes roll into the back of his head. Whatever happened next would be up to Lenire, and she hoped he had the strength left to fight. A lesser dragon rider might not stand a chance, but she believed in him. His body twitched once, twice, then started convulsing, and Cora scrambled back, reaching for her sword. Before she could grab it, Faron was there, pulling her to her feet.

"What are you doing?" he hissed. "Stars, Cora! Are you out of your mind?"

"Maybe," she said, but then Ismenia was at her side.

"Look," the soothsayer said, pointing to the woven tapestry where a figment of light was spreading through the Blight. It sparkled with faint rainbow glimmers, as if Lenire was drawing strength from the Heart.

"It's Lenire's magic," Cora said, certain it must be. Melusine and Zirael were so caught up in their battle for control, neither of them had noticed Lenire infiltrating the creature.

"He's reaching back along the connection created by the possession," Elaine said, amazed. The tears on her cheeks had dried. "Is he trying to control the creature from within?"

"No," Faron said. "He's trying to help disentangle it from the sorcerers."

"Will it work? Does he succeed?" Cora asked Ismenia, desperate to know if she'd seen anything.

Ismenia lowered her head. "It's up to him."

Cora turned back to the Blight. Lenire's magic moved through the creature, though slowly, unraveling the threads of magical control cast by the sorcerers. "Maybe we can help him," Cora said. The magical threads they'd cast earlier were still intact. That's what allowed them a glimpse of the Itharusian tapestry.

"When we tried to reach through the threads last time, the Blight tried to use the threads to get to us," Faron reminded her.

"Because it could sense that we meant to attack."

"If this doesn't work you could end up possessed like Lenire," Elaine warned them.

Cora waited for a warning from Ismenia but it didn't come. The soothsayer remained silent. "We have to try," Cora said.

Faron nodded, already letting his dragon magic spiral down the Itharusian thread. Cora did the same, bracing for the moment her magic collided with the Blight. Through her magic, she could sense the Blight's distress more potently. It lashed out at their magic. Cora recoiled, then reached out again, trying to make her intentions known. *We're here to help*, she thought over and over again. She sensed a thread of Melusine's control and lashed out at it, severing the connection. Immediately, the Blight pulled back, but instead of attacking, it accepted her help, and turned upon the sorcerers again, pouring its energy into escaping their control.

With Cora, Lenire, and Faron burning through threads, the Blight gained more autonomy, and it lashed out at Zirael, whose disk was weaker. Through her magic and the connection they all currently shared, Cora could sense the startled surprise from the sorcerer.

"I think we've done enough," she called, hoping Faron would hear her. They needed to get out just in case the Blight turned on them. It was still a wild creature. They couldn't assume it would favor them with kindness.

Just as Cora started to retreat, she felt a sharp jolt of fear, and the image of Zirael disappeared, the tendrils of his magic blazed and vanished, like sparks extinguished in the wind. He was gone—and that was when Cora understood: the Blight had killed him. Lenire's magic continued to burn through Melusine's control even as Cora pulled away. They needed to get out now. There was no telling what the Blight would do once free. It struck out at Melusine next and she struggled to hold it off, the power of her disk failing as the Blight siphoned her magic. Cora sensed a burst of pain and the magic of Melusine's disk burned to ash. The Blight had destroyed it too, then descended on Melusine. Cora couldn't watch anymore, and she dropped the Itharusian thread, severing her connection to it all. The cavern appeared, and she blinked at the rainbow facets as she called out for Lenire.

He groaned and Cora surged forward, helping dig him out of the stone she'd magicked to hold him still.

"Is it you?" Cora asked.

"It's me," he said, breathing like he'd just run the length of the training field at the dragon-rider school.

Cora threw her arms around him. "I knew you could do it." When she pulled away, Lenire looked worried. "What is it?"

"I can still sense the Blight," he said.

"The possession?" Faron asked.

Lenire shook his head. "I don't think so. Just a link. The creature is after Melusine now. She used the last of her power to flee, but the Blight is furious. It won't stop until it's caught up to her."

"Then we should let it," Faron murmured darkly.

"That's not it," Lenire said. "I've seen the destruction the Blight can cause. Entire cities in Itharus fell to ruin. It won't hesitate to destroy everything in its path in order to find Melusine. Innocent people will be slaughtered."

Cora rose to her feet and reached down for Lenire's hand. "We have a flask of magic now. So we'll catch up to the creature and get close enough to give it something it wants more than Melusine: a portal home."

CHAPTER 30
CORA

They flew from the Heart straight back to base camp. Cora had a thousand thoughts rushing through her mind as she bent low to avoid the wind currents whipping past Alaric. He soared between the mountain cliffs, his mighty wings flapping urgently. Cora tried to get everything straight in her head: Zirael was dead, Melusine was on the run, and the Blight was free in Tenegard, seeking its revenge. They'd saved Lenire from the Blight possession, and he was okay. Right? She glanced over her left shoulder, squinting her watery eyes. Yrsa and Lenire flew on their left flank. The Blight had let Lenire live, but somehow Lenire maintained a link to the creature. He might not be possessed any longer, but that thing was still in his head, and the sooner they dispatched it from Tenegard the better.

How is Yrsa holding up? Cora wondered. She could only imagine the emotional turmoil Yrsa had been in, trapped on the outside of the cavern as her rider faced death.

She appreciates the fact you did not cut Lenire's head off. In fact, she feels indebted to you, but she's still shaken.

We have to end this, Alaric. Once and for all. She was done letting Melusine and the Blight destroy the people she cared about.

The burst of warmth Alaric sent down the bond invigorated her, and Cora savored every second of it.

As the dotted brown tents of base camp appeared on the horizon, Cora sat up straighter. *Can you put a call out to the other dragons requesting everyone's presence for an important meeting? Ask them to summon their riders to the clearing.*

Alaric went quiet for a moment, and Cora knew he was speaking psychically with the dragon herd. *They want to know if they should call everyone back? The scouts? The hunters?*

Everyone, Cora confirmed. This would be their last stand. She could feel it in her bones. This was the true battle they'd been preparing for and now was the time to fight. She would gather their forces and hunt down the Blight.

It's done, Alaric said.

Cora cupped her hands around her mouth, yelling across to Faron. "Stay airborne and head for the school. I'm going to rally the riders, then I'll catch up."

Faron nodded in understanding. He rode with Ismenia this time. Wyn peeled off in the direction of the school. Lenire rode with Elaine. They thought it best to have a healer with him after the incident in the cavern just in case. Yrsa hung back and followed Wyn just as Alaric fell into a dive. He swept over the camp, rustling tarps and putting out dinner fires as he coasted into the clearing by the stream.

The riders and dragons who were already waiting for them darted out of the way as it became clear Alaric wasn't slowing down. He let out a roar. It wasn't the bellowing, ferocious battle roar Cora had come to know. It was a call to action. More riders appeared on the hillside, running to join the group in the clearing as Alaric soared around them.

Once he finally touched down, Cora didn't disembark. Instead, she stood up in her saddle on Alaric's back, addressing the crowd as they gathered around. She spotted Renka, standing alone by a tree, and Joi, crowded in among the other riders who had been out scouting.

"What's happening?" a young rider yelled up at her.

"The Blight has escaped the sorcerers' control. Zirael is dead, and the Blight now seeks to destroy Melusine. She has fled and abandoned her hunt for the Heart in order to save herself. But the Blight is chasing her across Tenegard. We've collected magic from the Heart to attempt to open a portal to send the creature home, but we need to be close enough for the Blight to be attracted to the burst of magic," Cora shouted. She watched the riders exchange looks of surprise and whisper to each other. "We have to intercept and stop the creature or else it will destroy everyone and everything in its path. Grab your weapons and leave the rest. We fly for the school to strengthen our numbers!"

She dropped back into the saddle and Alaric launched into the sky. As they swept around the clearing, some of the riders immediately climbed on the backs of their dragons, soaring off after Wyn and Yrsa. Others raced for the camp, diving into their tents and retrieving their weapons. Alaric made a wide lap of the camp, roaring. His roar was answered by two dozen more, but still Cora knew this wasn't enough. They would return to the school, regroup, and gather the riders who remained there. Unlike Faron, who's strength and magic returned quickly because of how powerful he was before the sleeping sickness set in, most of these riders would still be weak. Cora knew it was a risk asking them to fly into battle against the Blight, but she needed their help and they deserved the right to choose.

Alaric zipped back to the ground. Cora reached down, took her father's hands, and helped him scramble up behind her. He hugged her briefly. "Is Elaine okay?"

"She's accompanying Lenire and Yrsa back to the school. He fought off a Blight possession."

Her father was speechless.

That's everyone, Alaric said, watching the last dragon rider take flight.

Catch us up to Faron and Lenire, Cora said. Alaric took to the sky and soared above the group, passing over dragons and their riders. The group fell into an arrow-tipped formation and when Alaric reached the front, he dropped into the first position.

They flew hard, racing the afternoon sun back to the school. Cora felt the moment they left the mountain chill behind and loosened the cloak from around her shoulders, tying it off to the saddle to keep it from getting sucked into the air currents that whipped around them.

She turned to see Faron doing the same. They'd grown accustomed to wearing so much fur in the mountains that now, even as the sun dropped and the air whistled past their ears, they were sweating. On her other side, Lenire was quiet, his face set in a grim line. When he noticed her looking at him, he urged Yrsa forward, close enough that she could hear him as he said, "The Blight is traveling on a clear and single-minded path. I think the same way I can still sense it, the creature is able to sense Melusine. It knows where she is and is headed right for her."

"Can you tell where it's going?" Cora asked.

"It's been there before," Lenire said, staring off into the distance, into the consciousness of the Blight. "It retains something like a memory of the place. A sprawling city. Courtyards. Market squares. Ramshackle houses and dark alleyways. White stone buildings."

"Kaerlin?" Cora said.

Faron flew closer. "Not Kaerlin," he called. "Erelas. The Athelian capital. The white stone buildings line the senate courtyard. It's where the Athelian senators have their offices since anyone with magic is forbidden to step foot in the actual senate building. We used to study the layout of the city when I was working with the Tenegardian military under Onyx's rule. He wanted us to be ready should we ever need to invade."

"Melusine must have transported herself right to Erelas when her disk was destroyed," Cora said. "If she's been working with Athelia this whole time, she likely has allies there."

"And while she's hiding out like a coward, the rest of the city has no idea what's coming for it," Lenire grumbled.

"Nor does Tenegard," Cora said. "The Blight will likely have to cross multiple Tenegardian villages along the way to Erelas. The people won't be prepared to fend it off." She was still too far away from Kaerlin to do anything about that, but maybe Strida could. Cora dug in her pocket for the communication device and activated it.

"It's me," Strida responded after a minute.

"Is it safe to talk?"

"I'm in my private quarters. Where are you? I'm getting a lot of wind resistance."

"We're flying back to the school," Cora said, quickly explaining what had happened once they reached the Heart.

"Stars!" Strida said.

"I need you to do whatever you can to rally the riders who Northwood's deployed across Tenegard to aid the civilians along the Blight's route between the mountains and Erelas." Cora heard the rustle of paper and the clatter of trinkets being knocked across a surface.

"I have a map here," Strida said. "If the Blight travels a direct path, it'll likely be passing just west of Kaerlin." She murmured something Cora couldn't hear, then swore. "There are a lot of villages in between."

"I know," Cora said, already imagining the devastation the creature would leave behind. "I need you and the riders you have at your disposal to gather as many of the crystals Northwood took from the school and prepare to intercept the Blight." For a moment, Cora racked her brain for the best place to plan a confrontation. It needed to be somewhere they could easily find in order to meet up with Strida's force. But it also had to be somewhere far enough from the populace to avoid civilian casualties. Cora just didn't know the area surrounding the Tenegardian capital well enough. She'd never spent a significant amount of time there.

"Cora?" Strida said. "Are you still there?"

"I'm here." Cora's thoughts raced. What if she chose wrong? What if the plan fell through because she didn't have enough knowledge of the terrain?

"What else can I do?" Strida asked.

Cora's racing mind stuttered to a stop as she remembered what Faron had said about trust days ago. The riders wanted her to loosen her control to prove she trusted them. Cora needed to believe she didn't have to do everything herself. And she trusted Strida with her life. She could let go of this one thing. "I need you to choose the best strategic location along the Blight's path for us to attempt to stop it without endangering too many civilians. Once we've regrouped at the school, we'll fly straight for the capital. With any luck, the dragons can outfly the Blight."

"Understood," Strida said. "I'll be in touch once we're in position."

"We're coming up on the school," Faron called over to her.

Cora nodded, recognizing the landscape. *Alaric, can you put out another psychic call?*

Already on it, he said. *I've asked the dragons and their riders to join us on the training field for an emergency briefing.*

As they approached the training field, Cora could see two distinct groups, the riders and dragons who had been awoken from the sleeping sickness, and those who stood before them like an armed guard: the last of Strida's dragon riders.

"What are you doing here?" a boy demanded as soon as they'd landed. Cora slid down Alaric's side and the boy jumped back, drawing his sword. "Don't take another step, traitor!"

Faron walked up next to Cora, his own hand going to his sword. "Watch where you point that thing."

"Or what?" the boy sneered. "I see you woke up and immediately scurried off to the mountains. You're no better than any of them," he said, gesturing to Cora's riders.

Faron stepped forward but Cora caught his hand. "Can you escort Elaine and my father to the infirmary so they don't run into any trouble?" she requested. "I'm hoping she can come up with something to revive some of Lenire's energy."

"I'm fine," Lenire started to say but then he caught Cora's stern gaze. "I'll go too."

Faron nodded, though his jaw twitched as he eyed the boy and his sword. He turned and marched off with Lenire and Elaine and her father.

"Hey!" the boy demanded. "Where do you think you're going?"

"How about we put the weapons away?" Cora said, but the boy rounded on her. So did another. The slash of steel rang out as the riders drew their weapons from their sheaths. Some of the noise came from behind her, and Cora knew her own riders were preparing to fight.

She held both her hands up, calling for peace between both sides. "I know this is going to be confusing, but Strida and I never wanted to force a division between the dragon riders. It was all a ruse so the capital would believe Strida was truly on their side. This was the only way we could ensure Northwood would seat her on the council once Octavia was banished."

"Liar!" someone shouted. "Don't believe her!"

"It's the truth," Cora said.

"Then why didn't you tell us that?" It was Renka who asked. She shoved her way to the front of the crowd.

"Because we needed you to believe it," Cora said. "It was the only way to keep Strida's ruse intact while she was actively working against Northwood to keep control of the dragon riders. To protect them from being ordered into war. It was too risky to involve anyone else. We couldn't chance Northwood realizing Strida's deception. We couldn't afford not to have eyes and ears on the council."

"But Strida *has* lost control!" the boy said. "The Tenegardian army took our crystals. They destroyed our shield. And riders have been deployed all over Tenegard!"

"But not all of you," Cora said. "If Strida had truly lost control, Northwood would have ordered the recovering riders to the border. That was his plan."

More shocked whispers coursed through the crowd.

"You can't just march back in here and expect us to believe you!" Voices rose in agreement.

Shruti, one of the riders who had taught with Cora at the school before Melusine and the Blight had showed up, stepped forward. "Enough," she cried. "Put your weapons away." The riders quieted and stepped aside. Shruti gave Cora a small, knowing smile, and she could tell Shruti was aware of the truth. Strida would have had to confide in someone the same way Cora had, especially while she was off in Kaerlin. "What Cora says is true. Strida told me the same thing. The division of the riders was planned. It was the only way to keep eyes in the capital and allow Cora to pursue the Heart of Tenegard at the same time. She's been fighting to save Tenegard's magic without the council's support."

An explosive whisper whipped through the school's riders. "You should have trusted us to maintain the ruse!"

"You should have known we could keep a secret!"

"I would have helped if I'd known!"

"You're right," Cora said loudly, waiting for the whispers to die down. "You're absolutely right. I *should* have trusted you. Thanks to the riders who followed me into the mountains, I've seen how in my fear, I've been holding on to authority and control too tightly. I've forced you to the sidelines when I needed you beside me. I don't want to lead you like that. I'd much rather the dragon riders of Tenegard choose to work with me than blindly obey me."

Cora looked around as the two sides started to spill into each other, her riders and the school's riders coming together as one. "So now I'm asking you to choose again. The Blight has escaped its captivity and is hunting Melusine across Tenegard. It makes for Erelas but before it gets there, it will trample and destroy all the Tenegardian villages in its path."

Cora watched the school's riders exchange looks of shock. They'd been cut off from everything that had happened in the mountains, and now she'd dumped this on them. Even Shruti looked taken aback. "That creature destroyed the dining hall. Some of our riders are still recovering from the sleeping sickness. How are we supposed to stand between the Blight and its goal?" she said.

Cora pulled out the flask Faron had collected inside the cavern. She uncorked it and let a single drop of water roll over the lip of the flask. The moment the drop hit the ground, greenery sprung up around the spot where it landed, radiating out across the training field until it was thick with clover and wildflowers. The dragons grunted in surprise all across the field, lifting their massive feet to study the sudden change.

Cora felt the surge of power that pulsed around them, and she was certain all the other riders could too.

"You found the source of Tenegard's magic," Shruti said, amazed.

"If we can use this small fragment of the Heart's power to lure the Blight, we might be able to get it to stop its pursuit of Melusine long enough to trap it in a shield like the one we used here at the school," Cora explained.

"And then what?" Renka asked.

"Then we open a hole in the sky and send the Blight home," Faron answered.

Cora turned to see that he and Lenire had returned from the infirmary. "He's right," she said. "With the Blight restrained, we'll have a chance to find a way to open the portal to its home dimension." She hesitated talking about the next part, but if she wanted her leadership to be based on trust, she had to commit to transparency. "But even with this new plan and the help of the Heart's raw magic, the task is still a dangerous one. If you choose to follow me, there is the risk you might be drained of your magic or lose it entirely." She looked at

Renka, who stood straighter. Her chin out. "And though I have hope the Heart's magic will be enough, opening the portal may also require the power that comes from breaking a dragon bond. If it comes to that, Alaric and I are prepared to make the sacrifice—just as you have all chosen to make sacrifices in the name of a peaceful, restored Tenegard."

Faron reached for her shoulder, the weight of his hand a comfort against the reality of her words. On her other side, Lenire shifted, his hand shooting up to clutch his temples.

"What do you see?" Cora asked, knowing it was the Blight drawing his attention.

"The creature is racing northward," Lenire announced. "There's no more time to waste."

Cora turned around, climbing onto Alaric's back. "I cannot force you to follow me," she said. "But I hope you do because I truly don't think I can do this without you all. This is the greatest threat to Tenegard since King Onyx, and only the dragon riders are equipped to end it."

Cora looked down at them from her perch on Alaric's back, and slowly, like a wave rolling up the shore, the dragon riders began to salute. It started with those nearest her, the ones who had been in the mountains, and then spread to Strida's riders and even those who'd woken from the sleeping sickness. Cora's chest tightened with emotion. It was almost too much for her to get her next words out. "You have fifteen minutes to arm yourselves. Then we fly for Kaerlin."

The riders dispersed quickly, racing off to their quarters. As they departed, Cora was startled to see Ismenia in the crowd, her hand held up in salute. Cora lifted a brow as Ismenia dropped her hand and scrambled up Alaric's side.

"Don't look at me like that," Ismenia said, settling herself behind Alaric's saddle.

"I didn't think you wanted to be anywhere near Kaerlin, with war at the border."

"I've been plagued with visions since the moment we left the cavern."

"Do these visions tell me what I'm supposed to do next?"

"Not everything is about you, girl."

Cora rolled her eyes.

"But I do have the overwhelming sense I'm supposed to go with you."

Cora tightened her weapon's belt as Ismenia took hold of it from behind. "You do realize we're flying toward danger?"

"Yes," Ismenia said curtly. "And before the end of this, you might even be glad I came along."

CHAPTER 31

CORA

B*e careful, Cora. Promise me.*

Her father's words still echoed in her ears. When they'd left the school hours earlier, he'd insisted on accompanying the dragon riders, but Cora had refused. She knew the risks ahead and she wasn't prepared to sacrifice her father to them. This wasn't his fight. Besides, Elaine had also stayed behind at Cora's insistence, and she thought it would be more prudent for her father to help out at the infirmary. She knew without a doubt they would find injuries in the Blight's wake. The creature was loose and enraged. It would feed on anything magical in its path.

She'd already discussed funneling back anyone who was stricken by the Blight to the school . The healers who remained there were now the most competent in treating symptoms of a Blight attack. Care anywhere else in Tenegard just wouldn't compare. Plus, when this was all over, it would be better to be close to the Heart, where Cora could figure out a way to restore any lost magic with its help. And she owed Renka an attempt to heal her dragon bond.

Elaine had still been concerned about the group traveling without a healer, especially if their intent was to use a shield to hinder and trap the Blight since healer magic played a large role in stitching the magic together. Nadia had offered to accompany them, and Cora agreed. She was the school's original healer and she was eager to help out on the battle line. Selfishly, Cora loved her father and Elaine too much and knew she would be distracted worrying if they were safe if either of them joined the fight, so she readily accepted the younger healer's request to join them.

Night had fallen now and a chill swept through her. She pulled her traveling cloak tight at the collar and tossed her hood up. Behind her Ismenia had gone silent. For a while, Cora had glanced behind her to find Ismenia lost in a vision, her eyes solid white. The sight made Cora queasy, so she'd stopped turning around. If it wasn't for the occasional comment, she might have thought Ismenia was asleep.

"There is darkness ahead."

The hairs on Cora's arms prickled uncomfortably. "There's darkness all around if you hadn't noticed." She said it flippantly, though she didn't forget the warning Ismenia gave them outside the cavern and what had transpired after. "I don't suppose you could be more detailed?"

Ismenia hummed in the back of her throat. "Not yet. The vision is still murky."

Cora immediately looked for Yrsa and Lenire. The night was clear, but even so, most of the dragons were nothing but glittering shadows under the stars. Yrsa, however, seemed to absorb the light of the moon, her white, translucent scales rippling like waves through the night sky.

Alaric, can you reach out to Yrsa and make sure everything's okay with Lenire?

He mumbled his acquiescence. A moment later, he confirmed everything was fine. *What worries you?*

Besides the fact we're flying into battle with the Blight? The last time Ismenia spoke of darkness, the Blight had been able to take over Lenire.

Yrsa says he's been more like his old self these past few hours than he has been for days. I don't think you have to worry about the Blight possessing him again. The creature seems to have its sights set on Melusine.

Knowing Lenire was free of the possession should have relieved her, but in light of what they were about to do, it almost made things worse. If that was not the darkness Ismenia referred to, then what was it this time? What new horror awaited them?

Cora tried not to think about the myriad of ways this could all go wrong. Instead, she focused on the task at hand: fly hard to reach the outskirts of Kaerlin, meet up with Strida, stop the Blight.

Ismenia's hand wrapped around her shoulder and squeezed. "Here," she said in a dreamy, far-away voice. "The darkness is here."

Cora whipped her head back and forth, like she expected to see the Blight surging up toward them. "You're sure?"

Ismenia squeezed her shoulder harder, and Cora caught a glimpse of something. Ismenia was sharing her vision. It was only fragments of a scene, like she'd been handed pieces of a puzzle. Distress. Pain. Everything bathed in darkness. "The creature has attacked," Ismenia said.

Alaric fell into a dive as Cora shared the news with him.

"Cora, what is it?" Faron called as Wyn swept down beside them.

"The Blight has attacked! Ask the riders to fan out. Have anyone proficient at scanning living energy look for a settlement in distress."

Faron didn't respond, but Wyn immediately shot upward, and Cora saw dark shapes peeling off the main group as they stretched out their search radius. The dark worked against them. Any number of settlements could have been in the landscape below. Even dragons, with their heightened senses, struggled to pinpoint unfamiliar things. They needed known landmarks to work off or they needed to fly a lot lower.

Take us down, Cora said and Alaric did. She heard as his talons brushed the tops of trees. The leaves rustled around them, making her shiver as she stretched her magic, letting it rise and fall with the landscape. *There should be dozens of creatures out at this time of night, but the forests seem empty.*

Perhaps the Blight has passed nearby and scared everything away.

"Over here!" a voice called in the dark. Cora stared into the night. "I've found something."

Alaric turned so swiftly Cora had to clutch at the saddle and Ismenia had to grab onto her. Alaric drifted along the tree tops until they spotted a couple dull lights near the ground.

"Lanterns," Cora said. "Someone lives here."

"Or they used to," Ismenia said as they neared the ground. Moonlight painted everything in shades of gray, but Cora could make out the rubbled remains of a building.

Riders were already on the ground, using their magic to dig through the stone. Alaric picked up rock between his massive teeth and tossed it out of the way.

"There are people under here!" a voice yelled. Cora squinted. It was Joi. Beside her, Renka dug through the debris. Without her magic it was a taxing job, but she didn't stop.

The lanterns Cora had seen from the sky lay upon the ground, still burning in the wreckage. Cora picked one up while other riders lit torches with Dragon Fire.

"Here!" Lenire called, running around the side of the crumbling building. He and Faron carried a young man between them. He was moaning, hardly coherent. Nadia rushed to their side and Cora stepped closer with the light.

"They look like mages," Cora said, noting the way the young man was dressed.

"The Blight must have attacked to feed."

"We're not that far behind it," Lenire said as more mages were carried from the remains. "This attack just happened."

Nadia's hand felt along the man's forehead. "You're right. They do have magic, and his has been critically drained. I'm not picking up any other injuries, thankfully, but there's nothing more I can do for him in the field."

Cora whipped around, looking for help. "Shruti!" she called, spying the young woman moving bricks. The rider ran over. "We need to get these mages back to the school, but the entire group can't linger. We're closing in on the creature."

Shruti nodded. "What do you need me to do?"

"I want you to assign some of the weaker riders to fly the injured mages back to Elaine," Cora said. "She'll stabilize them until we can restore their magic."

Shruti peeled off with a nod, shouting orders. Cora had been away from the school for too long to know which riders were best suited to stay with the group and which would be better escorting the wounded.

She trusted Shruti's opinion and let her handle that as she turned back to Faron and the others.

"Get this man to Shruti. Nadia, stabilize anyone you can for the flight. Then we're off." Faron and Lenire hurried off with their charge. Nadia picked up her skirts and ran after them.

Something cracked in the darkness. It reminded Cora of the mountains when she'd sparked the rockslide that buried the hounds. She turned quickly toward the standing remains of the building. "Watch out!" she cried, waving riders out of the way as she ran toward it, slipping on pebbles and dust as she went. The entire exterior wall of the building was about to come down. Cora summoned her magic, letting it race through the earth and up the stone, holding everything in place. "Move!"

She waited for the last riders to clear the area, then let the wall come down in a controlled fall. Better to bring it down now than to have it fall on someone later. When the dust settled, Cora called out to the riders. "Anyone who wasn't tagged by Shruti to stay behind it's time to move!"

She ran through the field to Alaric, climbing on his back. Ismenia hadn't even bothered to get down.

"Let's go!" Faron yelled, urging the riders back into the air.

Alaric shot straight up.

"Was this your vision?" Cora asked.

"The first of them," Ismenia confirmed.

A chill shot through Cora at her answer. Sure enough, less than an hour later, they came upon a village where a healers' school had been flattened. Nadia gasped when she saw the wreckage, and as soon as they touched down amid the destruction, she set about doing her best to stabilize the wounded they found. Again, Cora had Shruti select a small team to stay behind and transport the wounded back to the school.

“The fires are still hot,” Lenire said, reaching toward a pile of coals as they prepared to leave. “We’re catching up to the creature. It’s stopping only to feed when it senses magic in order to keep up its strength.”

Cora squeezed the flask containing the Heart’s magic on her hip. “Hopefully, that insatiable hunger helps with our plan.”

As they flew toward Kaerlin, the black of the sky faded to navy blue, and Cora could make out more of the shadowed landscape below. The farmland bore signs of the Blight, the crops torn up, the fields scoured down to the stone. *At least we know we’re going the right way,* Cora said to Alaric.

He didn’t say anything but she could sense his determination. He flapped his wings harder, carrying them toward the faint shimmer of turquoise that cracked across the horizon line. Cora’s pocket vibrated suddenly, and she shifted, digging for the communication device. “Hello?” she said, holding it up to her ear. “Strida, say again?”

“We’re ready,” Strida answered. She was breathing heavily, like she’d just finished lugging a heavy crystal into place.

“Where are you?”

“Just south of the city. I wanted to intercept the Blight before it gets anywhere near Kaerlin. I know Lenire said it was meant to pass to the west, but I think letting it pass by a city full of magic is too big of a risk to take.”

“That’s smart,” Cora said, grateful she’d put her trust in Strida’s judgment.

“The moment the Blight approaches, my team will throw up a shield in its path.”

"And I'll help distract the Blight with the Heart's power while my team and yours enclose the creature. Once it's trapped, that should give us time to figure out how to open a portal with the magic."

"Assuming you get here soon enough," Strida said. "How far out are you?"

"Alaric suspects we'll be there by dawn. We've been following the Blight's path of destruction through the night. It's not that far ahead of us now."

"Then I guess I'll see you soon," Strida said.

"See you soon," Cora replied.

"There!" Lenire shouted.

"I don't see anything," Cora said, squinting at the dark line laced with yellow daylight ahead of them.

"Right above the trees."

As they crested the next hill, Cora saw it. The Blight hovered ahead of them like an unnaturally dark and turbulent cloud. And beyond that, like tiny specks in the sky, Cora could make out Strida's dragon riders circling the crystals they'd placed.

"Strida, get ready!" Cora shouted into the communication device. "The Blight's almost upon you!" She watched those tiny figures dart to the ground before looking to Faron. She made a waving motion with her hand. "Get Nadia down there to stitch the magic together."

Faron nodded, held his right arm high above his head, and a line of riders soared off after him to encircle the Blight from the right. Cora turned to her left and saw a line of riders following Lenire's lead. She unclasped the flask from her hip, popping the cork. "Hold on tight," she told Ismenia.

The moment the soothsayer's arms wrapped around Cora's waist, Alaric dove so fast he could have overtaken the creature if it was a bit closer. She recognized the moment the Blight crashed up against the makeshift shields Strida and her dragon riders had magicked. It flattened out, looking for a way through. It slithered along the shield, that lashing smoke searching for cracks. They couldn't let it escape.

Alaric, get us closer to the ground.

Alaric spiraled beneath the black cloud, dodging tendrils of smoke as Cora let three drops fall from the flask. They hit the ground and immediately spiraled into living magic, turning the ground rich with foliage. The Blight, momentarily distracted by the raw magic, dove for the ground, seeking the source. Alaric barely managed to evade the edge of the mist.

They didn't get far before the Blight realized the source of the magic was in her hand, and it soared after them. The riders near her scattered as Cora waved them away. The creature roared and shrieked in a way that made Cora's skin tingle unpleasantly. It was like a feral animal, crying out to be fed. Cora let another drop fall from the flask, and the Blight chased it to the ground, buying them some time to get away. When the drop of magic sprang up in vividly pink flowers, the Blight shrieked and surged after them again.

Faron had dropped Nadia off with Strida and taken back to the sky. He led his team against the Blight, distracting it with streams of magic. Spells disappeared into the Blight as that massive black shapeless form devoured everything they threw at it. "Try not to actually touch the creature with your magic!" he called. "Or it will absorb and rebound the attack."

Alaric ducked a couple of errant spells, almost bucking Cora and Ismenia off his back.

"Strida, how's it going?" Cora asked.

"Almost done. Lenire's helping Nadia now. Give us a few more minutes and the full shell should be complete."

Cora could already see the glimmering walls taking shape around her. She tucked the communication device away as they approached Faron. "Start clearing some of your riders out," she said quickly as they passed. "The shield's almost complete."

Faron nodded and flew off with Wyn.

"Let's keep this thing busy," Cora said to Alaric. Ismenia tightened her hold as they went twisting in a spiral straight for the Blight. Alaric ducked at the last second, and Cora enticed it with a drop of magic. The creature hit the ground, gathering its strength again before bursting upward in a coiling cloud. Gangly tendrils struck out at them, but Alaric managed to dodge every single one.

"They're going to fall!" Ismenia's hand slammed down on Cora's shoulder, directing her attention to a rider moments before the creature struck out and knocked them from the air.

"Faron!" Cora shouted but he was already diving toward the falling rider, catching her. The rider's dragon crashed right through a thick grove of trees. "Help them!" she shouted at Renka and Joi who flew close enough to hear her order. They raced off after the fallen dragon.

"We're ready to close it now, Cora," Strida said, her words buzzing from Cora's pocket.

"Clear the field," Cora shouted at the remaining riders. Their dragons zoomed and dove and ducked the snaky bits of the Blight that lashed out searching for their magic. Cora dumped a handful of the Heart's raw power on the ground.

Hold position, she told Alaric as he hovered above the expanding greenery below them.

"Move girl," Ismenia hissed. "Or we'll be killed."

Wait, Cora told Alaric. *Steady ... steady ... now!*

Alaric exploded upward like a shooting star as the Blight hit the ground beneath them, trying to feed off the magic she'd left behind. All they had to do now was escape out the top of the shield and Strida and the others would close it around the creature.

"Cora, it's coming!" Ismenia said.

Cora looked over her shoulder. The Blight chased them, shifting its form until it had condensed into a ragged, dragon-like shape.

"Cora, get out of there!" Strida shouted through the communication device.

"Close it!" she said.

"You'll be trapped with that thing!"

"Do it now!" She watched that familiar rainbow shimmer stretched across the sky above them.

The Blight released a single, charged flare of magic from the spells it had absorbed, and Alaric let out a roar as it struck him across the chest the way a dagger might slice a palm. Cora immediately felt his pain as he swept to the right, avoiding a collision with the top of the shield.

The Blight didn't stop, though. It flew straight, releasing another powerfully charged bolt of magic that burned out a handful of crystals near the ground, creating enough of a weakness in the shield wall that it burst through the magic, enraged at the near capture. It shrieked in that unnatural, animal-like way, but instead of attacking again, it shifted into that shapeless, misty cloud and soared north for Erelas.

CHAPTER 32

OCTAVIA

"Tell me where Raksha is!" Octavia demanded as she was shoved down another hallway. Her hands scraped against the damp stone walls as she tried to stop herself from falling.

"Move!" the guard bellowed behind her. "Or I will make you move!"

Octavia's feet slipped down a short set of crumbling stone steps as the guard grabbed her by the back of the neck, forcing her forward. "Where are we going?"

This was the second time she was being moved. First from the cell where she'd spoken to Serafine. And now she was being moved somewhere deep and cold. Somewhere that reminded her of the dungeons in the palace in Tenegard. Octavia couldn't help thinking that she was being moved so much to stop her from attempting to escape. If they kept her uncomfortable, she would spend less time trying to figure out a way to get to Raksha. Or maybe they moved her because they hadn't liked her watching them through the tiny window in her last cell erect the stage for her execution. Maybe they thought she would plot her escape from there.

Frankly, Octavia didn't know how she was going to get out of this. Without Raksha, fleeing Erelas was an impossibility, not just because it would be difficult to escape alone, but because she wasn't willing to leave Raksha behind to be executed.

"Turn," the guard ordered.

She did, spotting a door at the end of the hall manned by another guard. The door swung open as they approached, and a third guard stood inside. The darkness beyond was unnerving, and Octavia knew if she let herself be shoved inside, she wouldn't be able to see or hear anything in the outside world until she was dragged out to the executioner's podium. She stopped and turned to her guard. "I want an audience with Serafine."

He sneered and shoved at her shoulder. "I don't know how it works in your country, but here criminals don't get to demand anything."

"I'm a councilor of Tenegard. I deserve the appropriate diplomatic immunity until a full investigation can be conducted."

The guard laughed. "Soon you'll be a diplomat with no head."

He escorted her through the basement prison, and a cold hand wrapped around her upper arm, dragging her through a series of foul-smelling rooms. When they reached some rusty iron bars, he swung a cell door open. He didn't shove her inside. All he did was flick his head and touch the hilt of his sword. Octavia understood the message loud and clear: *Don't make me run you through.*

She sighed and marched into the cell, turning to watch him lock it with a key. One on a ring of many. "Don't get any funny ideas," he said. "The walls are spelled, so there's no escaping. And even if you manage to best the guards down here, you'll be running straight into the sorcerers. Do yourself a favor and don't rush your death."

Octavia clenched her jaw, her cheek twitching. Was this his idea of kindness? The guard stalked away, and she turned around to inspect her new holding cell. It was larger than the last, with a thin layer of hay on the ground, making everything smell of sickly sweet dust. There were no windows. Bars surrounded her on three sides, heavy stone bricks on the fourth, with a small wooden stool in the corner. She walked toward the bricks, pressed her hands to the stone, and summoned her magic on the off chance the guard had been lying. Her magic recoiled against her, like a sharp slap across the palm, and she wrenched her hands away.

She kicked the stool across the cell and rubbed her face. This was really bad. She couldn't even call for help because her communication anchor was in Raksha's saddlebag. If she even had it anymore. Octavia was certain the bags had probably been searched, and everything of value would have been seized. It was small, though, and there was always the possibility a guard might have missed it searching with those big, clunky gloves they wore. If she could just find a way to get to Raksha, she could try to call Strida or Cora. One of them would come for her.

Something slithered in the darkness and the clank of chains echoed through the drafty rooms. Octavia shifted away from the bars, her back up against the stone wall as she squinted, looking for shapes in the darkness. Were there other prisoners down here? Is this where Jangoor had been taken? Maybe she'd been locked up with something more dangerous. She wouldn't put it past Serafine to play games with her. She seemed to like games.

Something flashed in the darkness, catching the lantern light. Octavia would know that glimmer anywhere. She surged forward, grabbing the bars, her heart thundering in her ears. *Raksha!* she cried in her head, certain she would hear her. But there was no answer. She frowned, looking for the glimmer of her scales in the dark again. Had she been mistaken?

"Raksha?" she said hesitantly. "Is that you?"

A shimmering wave moved through the darkness, closer and closer, like a massive snake. At the last second, Octavia realized it was Raksha's tail, shifting close enough for Octavia to reach out between the bars and touch her.

Octavia did exactly that, running her hands along the fine, tapered scales on Raksha's tail. She didn't understand why Raksha didn't talk to her, unless they had somehow blocked her voice, but as far as she understood, those chains would only block her magic, the same way they did when she and Raksha had first met in the courtyard in Llys.

Then Raksha's tail lifted, gesturing down the darkened hallway. Octavia understood at once. Fate had brought them together, but if the guards caught them talking, they would be separated again. There was only one way to know which guards were within earshot.

"Hey!" Octavia shouted. Raksha's tail receded into the darkness. "Hey, I'm talking to you! What, do you ignore your prisoners, is that it?"

She waited, straining to hear a response. The shuffling scuff of footsteps reached her before the guard did. "What do you want?" he demanded, coming into view.

"Water," she said, grabbing at her throat. "You wouldn't deny a dying woman water?"

The guard rolled his eyes. "Just lick the condensation from the walls."

"Please," Octavia said in her most desperate voice. "*Please*."

His features shifted minutely, almost as if he felt sorry for her. "One cup," he said. "I will bring you one cup."

Octavia nodded. "Thank you." She waited for his footsteps to fade. "Raksha!" she whispered. "Can you hear me?"

"That could have ended badly."

In the darkness, between the bars of another cell, Octavia saw the dark pearls of Raksha's eyes reflect the flame in the lantern on the wall. She let out a shuddering breath as she pressed her head against the bars. It felt so good to be able to speak with her dragon again. "It was all I could think of at the moment."

"How are you?" Raksha asked. "They didn't hurt you, did they?"

"No," Octavia said. "I'm fine. Or as fine as anyone about to be executed can be." In the lingering silence, a droplet of condensation dripped from the roof and hit the ground.

"I'm not going to let that happen," Raksha finally said.

Octavia heard the sharp scrape of metal and realized Raksha was rubbing the chains on her head against the stone floor. If she wore them down enough, she might be able to break them. If only they had more time. Octavia imagined the way Athelia would lord this execution over Tenegard. They might even deliver Raksha's head to the border just to prove a point. *Look what we can do to your dragons.* Octavia shivered all over, banishing those thoughts from her mind as anger surged through her. "*We're* not going to let that happen," she agreed. "We're going to escape and warn the Tenegardian council of Serafine's alliance with Melusine." She told Raksha of the vision she'd had in the office before being arrested.

"So the tracking stone is likely Melusine's creation. I think these chains are as well."

"They're not from the Tenegardian supply?"

"No, these are most definitely not what Onyx created."

Octavia grumbled. "They must have been planning this all along. With Serafine's political prowess and Melusine's advanced magical ability, they've positioned themselves to not only wage war against

Tenegard, but to take full control of the Athelian senate by winning that war."

"Two young women, vying for power," Raksha said. "What better way to gain dominion than to destroy the source of Tenegard's magic and rid their perceived enemy of the one thing that sets them apart."

"Dragons," she and Raksha said at once.

"Without Tenegard's magic, our dragons will cease to exist. We'll die out."

"Cora and Alaric won't let that happen," Octavia said with certainty. Raksha went quiet and Octavia knew she was worrying over her son. Octavia might be up against Serafine, but Cora had to contend with Melusine *and* the Blight. "I'm sorry I brought you here," she said. "I know you never wanted to come and play spy in the first place. We should have fled right after the forum."

"Do not blame yourself," Raksha said. "I do not. We had to do what we could to help Tenegard, and once we realized the deception taking place here, we had to stay and do what we could to help those in Erelas resisting Serafine's oppressive rule. It was the right thing to do. And if I know anything about you, Octavia, it's that you always try to do the right thing, even at the detriment of your own personal safety."

Octavia smiled a bit and opened her mouth to respond, but footsteps approached and they both grew quiet as the guard appeared. "Who were you speaking to?" he demanded.

"What are you talking about?" Octavia said lightly.

"I heard voices."

"I was talking to myself," Octavia said. "Who else would I have to converse with?"

"Well, knock it off!" He thrust the cup into her hand. Water had slopped out as he walked, leaving only a third of a cup. Octavia guzzled it down greedily before the guard yanked the cup back.

"Wait," Octavia said, trying to eyeball the ring of keys on his belt.

"What?"

Their eyes met but before she could think of something else to say, the entire prison shuddered around them.

"The dragon!" the guard hissed, drawing his sword.

"That wasn't Raksha!" Octavia insisted. "Trust me! That came from outside."

Another trembling blow rocked the prison. Dust rained down from the ceiling and Octavia lifted her hand to protect her eyes. If the shock waves were reaching them all the way down here, then whatever was happening outside would be enough to bring down buildings.

The door to the prison burst open and half-a-dozen guards marched toward them. At their helm was Commander Dolan, his eyes wide and wild, like he'd just witnessed some unexplainable horror. He paused outside her cell, helmet tucked under his arm, his hair limp, his forehead beaded with sweat. "What devilry have the Tenegardians unleashed upon us?" he demanded, spitting the words with so much venom Octavia was forced to take a step back.

Alarmed, she shook her head. "I don't even know what's happening out there! If someone would explain, maybe I could help."

Commander Dolan drew his sword and leveled it at her. If he rammed it between the bars, it would drive straight into her chest and she would bleed out on this prison floor. "I'm the one asking the questions!"

Octavia held her ground. "The dragons are the deadliest weapons Tenegard possesses. And I know they would never attack a city full of innocent people."

"I know what a dragon is!" Dolan almost screamed. "I want to know what this creature is that's bringing down buildings!"

"Creature," Octavia repeated. Raksha shifted, her chains clanking, and the horde of guards surrounding her jumped.

Octavia stepped closer to the bars. "Is it a swirling black smoke? Like a storm cloud that's capable of rendering people unconscious. Of making them turn on each other."

"You *do* know what I'm talking about!" Commander Dolan cried.

"Only because it is the same creature that's been attacking Tenegard and the dragon riders. This is why I came to Serafine in the first place."

"What is it?" Dolan hissed.

"We know it as the Blight. The Itharusian dragon knights call it the Shagrukos. It has been wreaking havoc through Tenegard under the control of someone named Melusine who uses cursed Dragon Tongue symbols in her magic. Just like the symbol I found on the device in Serafine's office, which none of you will listen to me about!"

The armsmen behind Commander Dolan exchanged stricken looks. Even Dolan looked alarmed.

"What is it?" Octavia asked. "Do you know something about the symbols?"

Dolan shook his head. "No, but Serafine has an invalid sister named Melusine, though she's hardly ever seen in public."

"*A sister*," Octavia gasped. Serafine had mentioned her sister during their first meeting in the office. That meant she'd been talking about

Melusine. It was as if all the pieces had finally been uncovered. Her vision had been of two sisters sitting side by side—that's how they were really connected. Raksha growled and the guards jumped. "Serafine's been working with her sister this whole time to try to tear down Tenegard. When that didn't work, they attacked a dragon rider at the border, forcing Tenegard to declare war. We never wanted any of this. It's been the two of them, plotting together, all this time."

Dolan gaped at her.

The ground trembled again and a horn blasted somewhere above them as rubble started to crumble from the roof. "You have to let me out," Octavia insisted.

"How do I know what you say is the truth?" Dolan asked.

"Look around," Octavia said. "What other choice do you have but to trust me?"

The door to the prison slammed again and a pair of guards raced across the room. "Commander, the Tenegardian dragon riders have arrived in Erelas!"

"To finish their attack?" Dolan said, eyeing Octavia.

"No," the young, trembling guard said. "They're fighting to protect Erelas. They just shielded a section of guards who had taken up position in the north tower."

"What further proof do you need?" Octavia said. "We're not here to fight you, Commander Dolan. Serafine has filled your head with lies."

"Go back to your posts," Dolan said to the guards.

"Sir, we can't go back out there. It's like a hurricane has come to life, flattening buildings and sending deadly debris hurtling through the air."

"Let me out!" Octavia said, moving across the cell to look Dolan in the eye. "Your men are no match for the Blight. But I am."

Dolan scowled at her. Raging winds sounded outside.

"It's your job to protect the people of this city," she said. "So let me help you. Set me and Raksha free. *Please.*"

Dolan looked down at her, his face stiff. She could see the uncertainly in his eyes still. "Release them," he said.

"Sir?" The guard who had brought Octavia water balked at the request.

"Now!" Dolan bellowed. "And unchain the dragon."

The guards hesitated. "I'll do it myself," Octavia said the moment she was free. She took the key ring, grabbed a lantern, and approached Raksha in the dark. The chains around her were secured by massive locks. Octavia flipped through the ring for the biggest key. It slipped into the lock easily and she hauled the chains away. Raksha turned her head and nudged Octavia with her snout.

It's good to have you back, Octavia said. *Now let's get out of here.*

"Wait!" Dolan cried as Raksha began shifting between the prison cells the way she'd been brought in. "How do we fight this thing?"

The roof trembled, and Octavia cast a shield over the guards to keep the roof from caving in on them. "Evacuate anyone you can from the city," Octavia said. "And whatever you do, stay away from the mist." She turned then and chased after Raksha, catching up just as Raksha reached a set of large wooden doors. She pressed against them with her snout, but they were clearly bolted from the other side. Octavia climbed up Raksha's side and settled into her saddle. Then, with all the pent up fury she wanted to direct toward Serafine, she and Raksha unleashed a spire of Dragon Fire that blew the doors off their hinges.

CHAPTER 33

CORA

The Blight howled worse than any mountain storm, the sound carrying across Erelas as Cora, Ismenia, and Alaric swept over the city. From the air, Erelas could easily be mistaken for Kaerlin, from its stacked houses and market squares to its tall watchtowers and stately capitol walls. There was no palace, but the senate building sprawled across an entire street. The rest of the block was filled with those white stone offices Faron had talked about. People screamed below, ducking into buildings as the Blight destroyed everything in its path.

"It's chaos down there," Strida called as she and Emrys flew up to meet them. Of all the riders, Strida was still dealing with a weakened bond from their time in the mountains, but it was impossible to tell with how well the pair had adapted. Cora watched Strida tap Emrys' scales, similar to the way she and Alaric had when they'd been struggling to communicate before Lenire repaired their own bond. "If we don't do something soon, there won't be anything left of the capital."

Cora nodded, thinking on the fly. She hadn't anticipated the Blight breaking free of their shield trap and escaping to Erelas. She hadn't planned to defend an entire city. "Okay, this is a lot of area to protect, so take a group of riders and focus on shielding the residential streets and the market squares. That's where most of the population will be contained."

Strida nodded.

"Have the other riders shepherd those close enough to the city walls away from Erelas. Everyone else needs to be directed toward the safety of your shields. Can you pass on the orders?"

"On it!" Strida called, tapping Emrys again. The pair fell into a sharp dive. Alaric did the same, sweeping toward the edge of the city.

How are you doing? Cora asked Alaric as he tucked his wings to avoid a collision with a crumbling city wall. The spell that had caught him earlier when they were trying to trap the Blight with the shield had cut deep.

I'm fine, he said. *It's barely a scratch.*

Cora knew that wasn't true. She could also tell he was lying about his pain. Even though he was trying to block her, to keep it from her, she could sense it almost like it throbbed in her own chest. He was okay, and that's what mattered, but the second they were done here, she was going to see if Nadia or Lenire could tend to his injury.

Another dragon came into view suddenly, and Alaric swerved upward along the path of the city wall to avoid hitting them. The dragon roared as it swept below them, and Cora's head snapped around. "Raksha?"

And Octavia, Alaric confirmed, relief flooding through him at having seen his mother. *They're both okay.*

Since the day they'd all decided to go their separate ways, there'd been no communication from Octavia, so to find her alive and well was a balm to Cora's fraying nerves. The city was falling apart but at least the dragon riders had all been reunited.

Do they know what's happening? Cora asked Alaric.

Octavia had started to suspect one of the senators was working with Melusine. Alaric ducked beneath a crumbling archway, pulling his wings tight. *She found a device with a Dragon Tongue symbol. The senator's name is Serafine. They're sisters, apparently.*

Sisters? Cora said, as the puzzle pieces finally fit together into a clear picture. That was Melusine's connection to the Athelian military. That's why she'd been trying to destroy the Heart of Tenegard and move against Llys. The sisters were working together to bring down Tenegard, but it had all backfired, and if the dragon riders didn't do something soon, the Blight was going to leave Erelas as nothing but a pile of rubble.

"Watch out!" Ismenia called, drawing Cora's attention to a collapsing watchtower.

Alaric dropped to the ground and Cora cast a shield wall of air, keeping the structure standing as a group of guards surged out the bottom of the tower, fleeing with their hands held over their heads to protect themselves from falling debris. "Is anyone else inside?" Cora called down to a guard.

"No," he said, hunched over, clutching his knees as he breathed hard. "I'm the last one."

"Clear the area," Cora told him. He straightened up, quickly ushering civilians out of the way as Cora brought the tower down carefully. The mountain of rubble trembled and Cora turned to see the Blight racing toward them. "Find cover!" she shouted. "Hurry!"

The people scattered from the street and Alaric shot into the air. Ismenia clung to Cora's weapon's belt, keeping herself seated. Cora turned and released a narrow blast of magic. It shot right by the Blight, not close enough to hit it, but close enough to enrage it.

The Blight turned and twisted, spiraling so fast it became a massive, black tornado chasing them through the sky. Cora sent another spell speeding past the creature. Then another. It was like herding a stray animal to shelter.

Alaric rose higher and higher, circling the Blight as Cora distracted it with magic. A group of dragon riders were stationed at the entrance to the city, funneling out evacuees. Other riders had used their magic to carve holes in the crumbling city walls to create temporary exits. People scrambled through, flooding away from Erelas in a massive crowd. It didn't matter how far they ran, though. Not if the dragon riders couldn't stop the Blight. Once it was done wrecking the city, it would attack every last person, feeding from the Athelian mages and sorcerers until it found Melusine.

"We need to draw it away from the city," she said.

"Or you could find the girl and give it what it wants," Ismenia said. "She's down there somewhere."

Cora was surprised to hear her say that. "Is that what your visions have told you?"

"That is what she deserves," Ismenia said. "This is her mess, and the city and the people are suffering for it."

Ismenia had come a long way from the seer who jumped at Onyx's beck and call and dealt in secrets to the woman now sitting behind her. And though Cora wanted retribution for all the terrible things that had befallen them at Melusine's hands, in her heart of hearts, Cora knew she couldn't do that. *I can't sacrifice Melusine,* she told Alaric. *However much she might deserve it. And maybe that makes me weak—*

It doesn't make you weak, Cora. It makes you one of the strongest people I know.

"I don't think the Blight would stop with her," Cora said to Ismenia. "It would still demand and take and destroy everything. We have to lead it away, to somewhere we can safely try to open a portal." Cora uncorked the flask of the Heart's magic as Alaric circled closer to the Blight. She let a precious drop of the magic fall and then another, leaving an enticing trail for the creature to follow. It surged after the first drop and then the second, but when Cora left another handful of drops, leading it toward the city's northern border, the Blight's attention wavered.

Impossible, Cora said to Alaric. *It's hesitating. It wants to find Melusine as badly as it wants this magical meal.*

The Blight was a far more complex creature than they'd ever considered. It was capable of conflicting emotions and it was obviously able to make difficult decisions. The blind, ravening force she'd come to understand as the Blight had never really existed. Not here and not in Itharus. It was the sorcerers behind the Blight who had been the true evil all along.

"It's turning away," Ismenia said, perhaps more amused than she should be, considering the circumstances. "Apparently, our magic is nothing compared to the thought of Melusine."

The Blight blasted through a stone house, the entire structure exploding like it had been hit with Dragon Fire.

Lenire and Yrsa soared toward them. "The Blight's grown suspicious of humans bearing tempting lures," he reported grimly. "It's thinking about the trap we laid with the shield. I don't think it's likely to be tricked into following bits of the Heart's magic. Its focus on Melusine is too strong."

"Truthfully, I'm not even sure how to manipulate the raw magic to open a portal. I thought it would be more intuitive, but the Heart's power just sparks life whenever I release a drop from the flask. How is that supposed to rip a hole in the sky? If we can't create a portal and the Blight is no longer attracted to the lure of the Heart's magic, I don't know how to get it out of the city."

"Maybe I should try using the link I maintain with the Blight to force it to cooperate," Lenire said. "Now that Zirael and Melusine are no longer controlling the creature, I might stand a chance."

Yrsa snarled and Cora was quick to agree with her disapproval of that plan. "You've already come too close to losing your mind to the Blight. That's what got us here in the first place. The creature will rebel hard against you trying to control it. And we're not like Melusine and Zirael. We won't impose such control just to save ourselves." She turned to look over her shoulder at Ismenia. "Have you seen anything?"

Ismenia laid her hand on Cora's shoulder. "It's time for you to do what you know you must. You may not know how to fully wield the Heart's magic, but you know how to wield your own, and you can use the raw magic left in the flask to amplify your power."

Was this her fate all along? Cora wondered. Is that why they'd succeeded in entering the Heart, all so she would have the raw magic at this moment, when she needed to break her dragon bond? Had Ismenia foreseen that her future would unfold like this?

"We all know where the Blight really wants to go," Ismenia continued. "All it needs is the opportunity."

We need to send it home, Alaric said resolutely. *It's time, Cora.*

Cora's heart almost stuttered to a stop. She'd prepared herself for this, but after reaching the Heart, she'd truly believed they'd found another way. But really she'd needed the Heart's magic all along to make her strong enough to destroy her own bond. Cora swallowed hard, letting the gravity of the situation settle over her. "You're right, Ismenia. Alaric and I are ready. It's time to truly free the creature."

A startling burst of warmth and affection and love tore down the bond, filling Cora to the very tips of her fingers. She savored every last second of the feeling, committing it to memory. She wanted to be able to remember this feeling always.

"Ismenia," Lenire said, holding up his hand for the seer as Yrsa hovered just below Alaric.

Cora helped Ismenia transfer to the safety of Yrsa's back. She had no idea what would happen when the bond broke. If what happened to Renka in the clearing was anything to go by, they might be blasted from the sky, and the last thing Cora wanted was to hurt anyone else. "When the bond breaks, be ready," Cora said to Lenire. "You'll have to direct the magic or this will all be for nothing."

"I can do it," Lenire promised. "And Cora?"

She looked down at him.

"Thank you."

She smiled at him, and he blinked the glassy film from his eyes. Then Yrsa nudged Alaric's head with hers before giving them some room.

Cora didn't waste another second, as the Blight whipped through the city square uncontrolled. She tipped the remaining liquid from the flask into her mouth. Part of her almost expected to combust the moment she swallowed the raw magic, but all she felt was a glowing warmth that coiled in her chest. Cora closed her eyes, focusing on her bond with Alaric. She waited until his voice filled her head, until she could feel his energy match hers, until they were fully connected. And then slowly, little by little, they started to tear themselves apart. Separating their link was the hardest thing Cora had ever had to do. Even with the Heart's magic bolstering their own greatly, she could feel the sweat bead along her brow, dripping down the side of her face and neck. Her teeth were clenched so tight she couldn't tell if the pain in her head was from that or because she was ripping apart her bond. It was like cutting through a thick rope. Each strand they separated made Alaric feel farther and farther away until she could hardly sense him at all. Then, finally, they tore through the last of their connection, and the bond shattered.

She was expecting pain, sorrow, grief. But instead of a scream ripping from her mouth as she lost her link to Alaric, the raw magic surged inside her. Cora felt like it had ripped straight through her chest, leaving a gaping hole behind, but when she placed her hand there, all she felt was the frantic beat of her heart. The energy from their shattered bond echoed like thunder around them. Cora's eyes shot open and she saw as Lenire and Yrsa were forced back by the force of the explosion. Lenire's arms were held wide, trembling as he tried to contain the magic. The image of them grew smaller and smaller, and only then did she realize she and Alaric were falling through the air. The breaking of their bond had zapped her energy completely. She could no longer sense him in any capacity, though she imagined Alaric felt the same. He flapped his wings, but he didn't have the strength to keep them in the air.

Something rammed them hard from the side and Cora almost flew out of the saddle. She tilted to see what had collided with them. It was Faron and Wyn. Cora rocked to the other side as Strida and Emrys arrived to help keep them aloft as well. They all surged upward as a group, toward Lenire, who was struggling to handle the force of the magic they'd released from Cora's bond. Ismenia laid her hands on Lenire's shoulders, and together, the two of them managed to direct the magic above them, creating a bellowing hole in the sky.

"The portal's open!" Lenire cried. He waved them away. "Watch out!"

The Blight rocketed up from the city, shrieking as it dove for the hole, escaping through the tear in the sky. The creature flashed like lightning as it passed through the portal, and Cora realized it was shedding all the magic it had stolen while in Tenegard, leaving the power scattered across the sky like glowing violet clouds.

CHAPTER 34

CORA

Cheers erupted across the sky all around them, and though Cora could no longer sense Alaric's presence in her mind or even speak to him, she ran her hand along his glittering, dark blue scales, hoping he understood how grateful she was to him. They'd done it together. The Blight was finally gone.

Dragons took to the air, sweeping through the sky in intricate formations, twisting and twirling, putting on a show of celebration. Sparks of Dragon Fire erupted like fireworks. The riders whooped and hugged their friends. They threw their arms out, laughing in a way that was so carefree it made Cora feel like their sacrifice was worth it all over again. As she processed the glowing happiness she felt even as the overwhelming loss of her bond with Alaric filled her chest, she took a deep breath. These emotions would war within her and that was expected. She was allowed to feel both.

It was okay to celebrate what they'd won and mourn what she'd lost.

Tears tickled the corners of her eyes, and a laugh bubbled free of her throat. She blinked the tears away as she looked around at her team, at Faron and Strida, who still held her and Alaric aloft, and smiled. Their enemy had been defeated. The Heart of Tenegard was safe once more. *Dragon magic* was safe. Even if Cora could no longer live that life, she and Alaric had ensured the dragon riders would persist for years to come.

Something like booming thunder rolled beneath them. Cora realized it was the cheering and stomping of the people of Erelas. Looking down, she spied the citizens emerging from their homes and hideouts in droves, looking to the sky, pointing and clapping. Children raced through the rubble-packed streets, flapping their arms like mighty dragons.

Despite the fact there was so much destruction, Cora couldn't help but feel they'd already succeeded in rebuilding something important between Tenegard and Athelia. They would hunt down Melusine and her sister. And then she couldn't wait to speak to Octavia and hear what the Athelian senate had to say. With the threat of the Blight eliminated, perhaps they could finally find a way to end this war. As Cora focused on the city below, wondering where Melusine could be hiding, a tangle of that free-floating magic drifted by her head.

Curious, she reached out for the misty cloud. It tangled around her fingers like a glittery, purple spiderweb. *Strange*, she thought to herself, thinking maybe she was still dazed from the bond breaking. Somehow she could still sense this magic even with her shattered bond. It pulsed against her hand, the energy familiar, the sensation warming her palm. How was it possible she could sense the magic without her dragon bond intact?

Alaric flapped his mighty wings, still struggling to keep them airborne after the sudden loss of energy. Cora could feel the heavy exhaustion, too. It permeated every cell in her body, and all she wanted to do was curl up on Alaric's back and nap. The sensation was so overwhelming, she fought against it even now as the magic clung to her skin, spiraling over her hand and around her wrist. Their bond was definitely severed. There was no doubt about that. Perhaps she was just imagining all this, wishing she could still feel the magic or living through a memory. But as more magic flowed down from the sky, settling over her in flowing spirals that danced across her skin, she knew she wasn't imagining anything. She really could *feel* this magic, and somehow, it sensed something in her even without her dragon bond.

Could Alaric sense it too?

She reached out for him tentatively again, not with her hand, but with her mind. She took a deep breath and closed her eyes, searching that empty space in her head where her bond used to reside, where her magic connected her soul to Alaric's. There was a sharp jolt, like Cora had created too much static and shocked herself. The hairs on her arms stood straight, sending gooseflesh across her body.

When her eyes flew open, the magical mist had thickened between her and Alaric, tracing an invisible line that almost met in the middle. It was the two halves of their bond. The magic was floating along the traces of the severed bond! Cora gritted her teeth, grunting as she desperately tried to funnel the magic all the way across, connecting the two halves. But she didn't have enough of her own magic. There was nothing inside her except desperation and hope.

Yrsa drew closer and Lenire slid from her back, landing behind Cora on Alaric. Faron leaped from Wyn's back, climbing up Alaric's side, joining them.

"It's my bond," Cora said. "It has to be."

"Maybe we can connect the severed ends," Faron said.

Lenire shook his head. "She has to be the one to do it."

"Then I give you my magic," Faron told her, laying his hand on her shoulder. "However much you need."

Lenire put his hand on Cora's other shoulder. She felt a familiar source of power as they funneled their magic into her. Cora reached out, summoning Alaric's half of the bond toward her. It fluttered there, surrounded by the twisting violet magic from the Blight. Cora imagined a thick rope and pulled at it hard with the borrowed magic from Faron and Lenire. She cried out, her arms shaking.

From the corner of her eye, she saw Yrsa swing by, dropping Ismenia behind them too. The seer touched the top of Cora's head, and a flash of a vision swam before her eyes. It was her dragon bond, united in the middle, flaring with bright, brilliant magical power. The vision fell away, but Ismenia's hand remained, lending her power, and Cora knew she could do it. With their help, she could manipulate the expelled magic from the Blight. She could weave her bond with Alaric back together. She used every ounce of strength she had, combining the innate knowledge of her elemental magic with the learned magic from Itharus.

She felt the power like tangible threads in her hands and began weaving the magic as she had watched Lenire do many times before. As Faron, Lenire, and Ismenia poured their magic into Cora, the ropey halves of the bond between her and Alaric grew stronger, the ends glowing like they'd been lit on fire, and she knew Alaric was working to bring their bond together again too.

Yrsa flew in front of Alaric, facing him, and touched her head to his. Suddenly, the two flaming ends of the bond began to unravel, every thread reaching out for the others. The bond lengthened until the threads could reach each other, and then they finally connected and knitted back together. Cora felt a surge of magic wash over her. It was so strong it almost blew them all from Alaric's back, and Faron and Lenire scrambled to catch Ismenia before she could topple off.

Before Cora's eyes, the violet magic dissipated, like it had been absorbed into the sky. Then all was quiet.

Cora?

Alaric! She laughed joyously. Then she leaned over and hugged him, pressing her cheek to his scales. *It worked. The bond is restored!*

When Cora sat up, wiping the tears from her eyes, Faron and Lenire were beaming. She threw herself at them, rejoicing in the help from her friends. Once they'd steadied themselves, Ismenia patted her on the shoulder, smiling smugly. "Didn't I say that you'd be glad to have me along?"

Cora shook her head and pulled Ismenia into the hug too. "Yes, you did, and thank you."

Strida and Emrys pulled away from Alaric now that he was flooded with magical energy.

"Strida," Cora called suddenly. "Your frayed bond—"

"Was repaired almost instantly," she answered with a brilliant smile. "Emrys and I got so used to communicating without it I almost didn't notice at first. Then I heard Emrys in my mind for the first time in what felt like months."

"I told her she could stop tapping on my head," Emrys added wryly.

Cora and the others all laughed. "I guess a frayed bond is easier to repair than a shattered one."

Lenire nodded. "There's so much free-floating magic it has to all go somewhere."

Alaric cut into her thoughts. *Cora, he's right! There's enough magic here to repair Renka's bond too.*

Cora whipped around, studying every dragon and rider in the sky. Renka had joined them on their quest, but had she come to Erelas or had she hung back with the last contingent in the village with the destroyed healer school?

"What is it?" Strida asked.

"We have one more bond to repair. Renka was the first of us to lose her bond. Honestly, without her, I'm not sure any of us would have realized it was possible to send the Blight back the way we did."

Something vibrated in Cora's pocket. She grasped at her tunic, confused. Strida did the same. Only when they'd both retrieved their communication devices did she realize it was Octavia trying to reach out.

Strida's entire face crumpled with relief hearing Octavia's voice. In the chaos of their victory against the Blight, Cora had forgotten to tell Strida she'd seen Raksha and Octavia—that they were okay.

"Strida? Cora? Hello, is anyone there?" Octavia chirped through the device.

"We're here," Strida said, swiping tears from her eyes. "We're all here. It's so good to hear your voice!"

"I've missed you so much," Octavia told her. "And I can't wait to see you. But before all that, I have to tell you the Athelian guards think they've located Melusine and her sister."

"Sister?" Strida said, her eyes comically wide. Faron and Lenire exchanged a look of confusion.

"It's a long story," Cora muttered.

Octavia cut back in. "I think one of you should be here to speak to the senate about Melusine's crimes against Tenegard. I only have second-hand information."

"On our way," Strida said. The device cut out. "Sounds like a job for you."

Cora glanced over her shoulder at the free-falling magic. They needed to use it to help Renka before it all disappeared.

"You head down there and help Octavia," Strida said. "Deal with Melusine. The rest of us will track down Renka and try to get her bond reestablished."

Cora glanced around at her friends. After everything they'd been through together, Cora knew they were more than capable of handling this. Trusting other people with these heavy, burdensome tasks felt good. What she'd said when she was trying to rally the riders back at the school was true. She didn't want to control them. She wanted the riders to work with her, as a team, not blindly follow her every command. And admittedly, it felt good letting go of her fear and giving up some of her authority. "Okay. Let's do it."

"Are you sure you don't want to rest first?" Faron asked her, catching her hand.

Cora's heart leaped at his concern. "I'm fine. Better than fine, actually. Which is good, because Erelas is going to need our help restoring the city."

"We'll start funneling riders down to help with the cleanup."

"Perfect," Cora said. And as everyone returned to their respective dragons and flew off in search of Renka, Cora and Alaric dove toward the city streets. "Where are you, Octavia?" she spoke into the communication device.

"The offices near the senate."

Those white stone buildings? Alaric said.

Whatever's left of them, Cora replied as Alaric swept across the ruined city. He landed in a courtyard near those white structures, crushing rubble beneath his feet. Raksha moved to his side, nudging him with her head.

Cora smiled up at them as mother and son were reunited.

"Cora! Over here," Octavia called. She stood on what looked like a carved balcony. It had been severed from the front of one of the buildings and now lay in the street.

Cora jogged over to meet her. They embraced for a moment. No matter what politics Octavia was navigating, she was always there for the dragon riders when they most needed her. "You found her?" Cora asked as she pulled away.

"Commander Dolan of the Athelian army sent out soldiers to search through the debris. They started with Serafine's office and found the sisters there, trapped under the rubble. They were just starting to dig them out when I called you and Strida." Octavia waved her over to the balcony.

Cora scaled it and followed Octavia down a rocky, crumbling path toward a dusty staircase that rose out of the ground. The building around it had been reduced to bricks and wood and ash. On the steps, surrounded by six guards, Cora spotted Melusine. Beside her was another young woman who Cora assumed was Serafine. They were filthy and scowling, but those qualities weren't their only similarities —they also had the same set to their jaws, the same high cheekbones.

"Melusine hasn't tried to attack or escape yet, but the guards are ready should she try."

"The Blight consumed a lot of her magic," Cora said. "I assume she used the last of it transporting herself back to Athelia."

"Commander Dolan!" Octavia called as they approached. A man as old as Cora's father turned around and greeted them. "This is Cora Hart. The leader of the dragon riders."

The commander stuck out his hand for Cora to shake. "A pleasure to meet you. We are forever indebted to Tenegard and the dragon riders for saving Erelas from that creature. And to Octavia for exposing the corruption within our own senate."

“Does this mean the war is over?” Cora asked.

Octavia grinned. “I think it does.”

“We’ve determined these two meant to provoke war between our nations,” Commander Dolan said, gesturing toward the sisters. “They planned for an Athelian victory they could take credit for, ensuring Serafine maintained her seat of power.”

“Melusine’s plan was to use that creature to drain all of Tenegard’s magic. It would have destroyed the dragon riders for good,” Cora said. “That’s how they planned to win.”

“What will happen to them now?” Octavia asked.

“Well,” Dolan said, “the senate will be pruned of Serafine’s followers. The majority of the senators have already been convinced of her treachery. They’ve ordered the sisters imprisoned until they can stand trial.”

“Tenegard will expect to be represented at that trial,” Octavia said.

“Of course,” Dolan agreed. “I’m sure relations between our nations will be much improved now we’re no longer fighting each other.”

Octavia nodded, turning back to Cora. “Let’s go.”

"Where?”

“Tenegard. It’s time to do some pruning there too, and I know just where to start.”

CHAPTER 35

CORA

The palace in Kaerlin was in an uproar when they arrived. The scullery maids raced back and forth, carrying supplies. The guards cleared the halls of visitors.

"Return to your homes!" one of the guards ordered. "Take immediate shelter!"

Each passing courtier craned their neck to the sky, almost as if they expected it to start falling at any moment. The tension was like a living thing, snaking through the air, and everyone was so spooked they hardly bothered to acknowledge the three dragons who had just landed in the main courtyard.

"What's going on?" Cora asked, climbing down from her saddle. She met Alaric's eye.

"Looks like we're being attacked," Strida said, her brows crashing together in confusion.

Cora glanced around. It was a bright, beautiful day. Birdsong sounded from the gardens. The fountains bubbled. Sun crept across the palace lawns. There was no sign of trouble, and yet the unease emanating from the palace was almost palpable.

"I suggest we ask one of these lovely people running for their lives," Emmett said as a man tore past them.

Octavia led the way into the palace, and they followed.

Stay vigilant, Cora said to Alaric as he, Raksha, and Emrys settled in the courtyard. *I'm not sure what's going on.*

Alaric yawned in response, curling into a ball. Cora couldn't blame him. It had been nonstop flying and fighting. She didn't remember when she'd last slept or ate anything.

I shall keep one eye open, he promised.

Cora smirked. *That's all I ask.*

They climbed a staircase and walked along the open-air corridor toward the council chamber. A young guard turned the corner, dropping his helmet in his haste. Strida picked it up and handed it to him.

"What's going on?" she asked. "Why is everyone running around like Tenegard's on fire?"

"Haven't you heard?" he said. "Erelas has fallen to a terrible creature. Word from the council is that it is coming here next." He trembled in his armor. "It comes down from the sky like a giant, black cloud and swallows people whole."

He shoved past Strida, and she watched as he ran down the hall. "Well, there's our answer."

Emmett hummed. "Sounds like news of the Blight's visit has preceded us. But it doesn't sound like they know the Blight has left our world yet."

Strida snorted. "Because they're too busy running around to check their facts. Northwood has everyone in a panic."

"I suppose we should clear things up, then," Cora said, hurrying down the hall. "Before the entire city starts to evacuate."

When they reached the council chamber, Cora didn't stop to knock. She threw the doors open to find the council chamber full. They must have been in the midst of a meeting. Their entrance went unnoticed, however, the sound of worried voices drowning out the creak of the door. The voices carried like waves around the room, but the loudest of them was Northwood himself. He stood in the middle of the room, holding a young guard by the collar of his armor, spitting words into his face.

"Why was I not informed the monster had passed so close to Kaerlin?" he bellowed. "Why are the palace guards so incompetent?"

"We didn't know," the guard stammered. "It was the dragon riders who confronted the creature outside the city, not us. We didn't get reports until later that the creature had leveled villages and destroyed crops."

"Then what in the stars' names is going on in Athelia?"

The guard lifted his hands, shaking his head. "I … I—"

Northwood let him go and the guard dropped to the floor. He scrambled back to his feet, his footsteps clattering across the floor as he retook his position at the edge of the room. "Can anyone tell me what's actually going on?"

"We might be able to help with that," Cora said, stepping forward. She was flanked by Strida and Octavia and Emmett."

"What are you doing here?" Northwood seethed, pointing a finger in their direction. The other councilors sputtered and whispered. Some, like the old rebel leaders who had fought against Onyx, looked intrigued. Others were concerned. And still there were those who turned their noses up at the sight of them. Clearly, Northwood still had his supporters. "Last I checked at least three of you had been banished. How did you even get into the city?" He glanced around at the guards who stood in the corners of the room. "I was to be informed immediately if any of them were to return!"

"Apparently, most of your military force is too busy running for their lives to monitor who's coming and going from the palace," Strida commented. "That might be something you need to address."

"You don't get to speak!" Northwood hissed at her. "You fled the palace during a crisis and redirected the dragon riders I'd stationed at the border without my consent. You're this close to joining your friends."

"Go ahead," Strida sneered. "Banish me from the council. I have no intention of bowing to your insanity any longer."

"Well?" Northwood bellowed at the small contingent of personal guards who remained. "What are you waiting for? These riders are trespassing. Seize them all!"

The guards exchanged nervous glances, then surged forward. Strida immediately drew her sword, the slice of steel ringing through the room. Councilors ducked behind their chairs, crying out.

"Stop!" Cora commanded the guards, putting her own hand on the pommel of her sword.

They continued to advance, though more cautiously now. Strida twisted her sword in her hand, the blade cutting through the air. "They're not stopping," she muttered under her breath. "What do you want us to do here?"

Cora gritted her teeth and let out a controlled burst of magic. The wall of air shoved the guards back a foot. "The last thing I want is for anyone to get hurt," Cora said. "But I have not come to bow before the council or grovel for your forgiveness. You can choose to listen to me." She turned in a slow circle, eyeing the guards, but also acknowledging every single councilor. "Or you can choose to walk out those doors. But know that if you do, we will consider it your resignation."

There was a pause in which no one moved. It was as if the entire council was holding their breath, waiting to see who would act first.

It didn't take long.

"You have no authority here," one of the councilors behind Northwood sneered. "You're nothing but children! Be gone from our chamber and let us continue our work."

Cora turned and blew him off his feet with another controlled blast of wind. "I'm tired of pleading and begging and hoping the council will listen to us and support us. The only reason Tenegard is still standing is because of the dragon riders. Without us, the Blight would have laid waste to everything." Just like Athelia was now doing with their senate, it was time to prune the bad seeds from the Tenegardian council. Cora was done. The councilor spiraled through the air, screaming as he hurtled toward the floor. Cora was tempted to let him hit the ground, but at the last second, and after a stern glare from Octavia, she cushioned his fall with another small air pocket.

"What is the meaning of this?" Northwood cried. "You cannot come in here and attack councilors!" He gestured frantically to the guards who hesitated to follow his orders.

"The dragon riders sacrificed too much to free this country from Onyx and Melusine and the Blight to leave a bunch of bullies in charge of running it. You have heard my terms. This is your last warning. Do not make me angry," Cora announced to the room, silently wishing she could blow Northwood and his followers out the nearest window.

Northwood stood there, blustering, while Cora waited for the other councilors to make their decisions. Surprisingly, none of them left. Not Northwood. Not even the man Cora had blown off his feet. He simply stood up, dusted himself off, and scurried back to his chair.

"Now," she said, "as I was saying, in answer to your concerns about Athelia, all is well. The so-called monster you're all now worried about was the same beast that had attacked and terrorized the dragon riders." She glared at Northwood. "The same creature you offered no support against."

"We were fighting a war," Northwood said.

"Our fight was the same fight," Cora argued. "The monster was summoned by Melusine, a sorcerer from Athelia, along with her sister, Serafine, who wanted to bait Tenegard into declaring war, and because this council was so obstinate, you fell for it."

"So Athelia did want to fight, then?" one of the old rebel leaders said.

Cora shook her head. "Most of the senate knew nothing about Melusine and Serafine's plan. I have been assured they will be punished for their actions. And as a result of the deceptions Athelia found within their own government, they are making the necessary changes to their senate. Their first order of business was to draft a peace treaty between our nations. The fighting has ended. Dragon riders have been dispatched to the border as we speak to pass on the news and put an end to the conflict. Our soldiers are withdrawing."

"That is not your decision to make," Northwood said. "*I* command Tenegard's military."

"I think you'll find that it *is* our decision to make," Cora said, stepping aside for Emmett to take the floor.

"You no longer represent me," Northwood said as Emmett walked toward him.

"No, I represent the dragon riders," he said, unfurling the length of parchment clutched under his arm and holding it up for the council to see. "And as the dragon riders maintain an active role on this council, they are capable of enacting this emergency removal order."

"An emergency what?" Northwood spluttered.

Emmett turned to the councilors. "According to the rules that govern Tenegard's military, in the event the commander of Tenegard's army is determined unfit to lead, they may be removed from the office they hold and stripped of all their working titles with a majority vote."

Northwood's face turned a deep shade of crimson as Emmett continued.

"Given Councilor Northwood's catastrophic failure to recognize the dangers posed by the Blight and its manipulators, not to mention his egregiously inappropriate abuse of council authority and resources, the dragon riders call to remove him as head of the military and to strip him of his role on the council."

"You can't do that," Northwood seethed, snatching the parchment from Emmett.

"We just did," Strida said, raising her hand. "All those in favor of the vote, cast your hands now."

The rebel leaders were the first to join the vote, followed by a trickle of their supporters. Northwood's own supporters were slower to respond, but one by one they did, lifting their arms in favor of his removal.

Emmett beamed, looking up at Northwood. "It's unanimous. And seeing as you no longer hold a position of authority here, you needn't ever return to the palace or even Kaerlin, for that matter." Emmett waved the guards over. Strida snorted and Cora couldn't help but chuckle. Emmett was having far too much fun with this.

"Please help Mr. Northwood pack his things and escort him from the premises."

"You can't do this!" Northwood cried, tearing the parchment into pieces. "They don't know what they're saying. Do you hear me? You'll regret this. You all will!"

The door slammed behind him.

Emmett picked up the pieces of parchment from the floor and tucked them into his pocket. "I think there was something else you wanted to say, Cora?"

She nodded, addressing the room. "As of today, you will consider appointing Octavia as the special ambassador between Tenegard and Athelia. She has proven to be an ally to both nations in a time fraught with suspicion and danger. And Strida will remain on the council as representative for the dragon riders."

"Does anyone have any objections?" Emmett called.

When no one said anything, Cora dipped her head. "Then I thank you all for your time. Now, if you'll excuse me, the dragon riders have a lot of work to do. I'll leave you to discuss the council's contributions to the restorative efforts required in the wake of the Blight's attacks across Tenegard. And," Cora added on her way to the door, "when you get around to it, I'll be very interested to hear about the council's plans for the expansion of the dragon-rider school."

She turned and exited the council chamber, feeling lighter than she had in months. When she reached the courtyard, she gulped in a breath of fresh air, hurrying down the steps to meet Alaric.

"Cora!" Strida called after her.

Cora turned to find Octavia and Strida running down the stairs.

"You really want me to remain on the council?" Strida said and gasped. "Don't you need me back at the school?"

Cora smiled. "You are welcome to return to your teaching position as soon as you want. I just thought it would be nice for you and Octavia to finally have some time together. At least for a little while. When you're ready to return, we'll swap you out with someone else. It might be a good learning opportunity for some of our recruits, especially with Octavia there to guide them."

Strida looked touched as Octavia wrapped her arms around her. "Thank you."

"You both deserve it. And a break if you can manage to get away from the council long enough."

Octavia laughed. "After everything we've been through, I'm sure we can figure out something as simple as time management."

"Where are you heading now?" Strida asked.

Cora sighed. She'd been making a mental list since they left Erelas. "First I'm going to dispatch a crew of riders to round up and destroy any remaining hounds from Melusine and Zirael's camp. Without the Blight to pilot them, they're likely harmless, but I don't think we need to risk leaving any of their creations hanging around. I've asked the riders who were sent to the border to regroup here at the palace once they've ensured the armies are withdrawing. When they arrive, can you dispatch them to the surrounding communities that are in the most need of aid?"

Octavia nodded. "I'm sure the small claims council is already receiving requests. I'll check with the clerks."

"There are going to be casualties," Cora said softly. "People we couldn't save. They should be laid to rest with honors."

"We'll visit the communities and make sure of it," Strida said.

"Good," Cora said. "And if you find anyone who requires care beyond the capacity of your healers, anyone who needs their magic restored, send them to the school. The healers there are the most experienced. I'm going to lead an expedition back to the Heart to retrieve some more of the raw power to be used by the healers in repairing damaged bonds and replenishing magic the Blight might have taken."

"And then what?" Octavia asked.

Cora met Alaric's eye across the courtyard. "Then we rebuild."

CHAPTER 36

OCTAVIA

"Hold still," Strida said, tucking away an errant piece of Octavia's hair. "Your braid is coming loose."

"Oh," Octavia said, turning her back to Strida so she could fix it for her. It must have blown free during the flight from Tenegard to Athelia. They'd spent all morning visiting the village with the damaged healer school, documenting the progress that had been made since the Blight's attack. With the help of the dragon riders' elemental magic and some good old-fashioned labor, the building had been restored to its original function. And according to Cora, many of the healers who had been flown away to the dragon-rider school for treatment had already made excellent progress and were quickly returning to full health.

Cora had taken a small team back to the Heart of Tenegard to retrieve more of the raw magic from the cavern, allowing Elaine and the other school healers to restore the magic of any magic wielder who had been depleted by the Blight. Many of the victims had fallen into a coma-like sleep similar to the sleeping sickness the dragon riders had experienced, but between the expert care they received and the

Heart's power, all the victims of the Blight's final attack recovered far more quickly than the dragon riders had.

Now it was just a matter of letting them rest and recuperate.

Octavia relished Strida's fingers, twisting the locks of her hair back into place, prodding gently against her scalp. When Strida's hands fell away, Octavia spun, catching Strida's palm and pressing a kiss to it in thanks.

"Good as new," Strida said with a smile.

"Thank you." Octavia was dressed the part of an ambassador today. She wore fancy robes with the medal she'd been presented by Athelia's senate for her bravery and dedication to the country pinned to her chest, just above her heart. She reached down to straighten it. Today was the first official peace conference between the Athelian senate and the Tenegardian council, and it was being held here in Erelas, and she'd hate to turn up looking windswept. "I want to make a good impression in this new role."

"You're going to be fabulous," Strida assured her. "You've been preparing for a role like this your whole life. I can't think of anyone better or more suited to bring two nations together in the name of peace."

Octavia's chest tightened with emotion. "You really think so?"

"Of course. You stood up to Northwood even though you knew it might get you thrown out of the council and banished. You risked your life to expose Serafine's manipulation of her country and the war. You protected this city even after they planned to execute you and Raksha. As far as I can tell, you've already been doing this job and you're great at it."

Octavia smoothed her hands down the robes. All she'd ever wanted was to find out where she really belonged and find a way to serve the people. To prove that she was different from Onyx despite being raised in his shadow. Now, finally, there was a role where she could facilitate peace and protect her people's interests. She could serve Tenegard by strengthening relations with their northern border. And best of all, while Strida remained on the council, they could be together.

She knew it wouldn't be forever. Eventually, Strida would grow restless in the palace, especially knowing the students at the dragon-rider school were eagerly returning to their training. As much as Octavia was born to play political games, Strida was born to lead and to teach. She needed freedom she wouldn't find cooped up in the palace, so Octavia promised to enjoy every second they had together now.

"Do you think we'll make it back to the school in time for the victory celebration tomorrow?" she asked as the sun beat down directly overhead.

"We'll have to fly hard, but we should be there for most of it," Strida said. "Plus, after everything, I think the dragon riders are bound to keep the celebration going well into the night."

Octavia chuckled. "I think we all deserve an evening off."

"That's what Cora said. And then it's back to work."

Octavia's lips twisted. "Sounds like Cora." She reached for Strida's hand again, tangling their fingers. "I'm glad you decided to stay with me for a bit."

Strida tugged her closer and pressed a soft kiss to Octavia's cheek. It was enough to make her blush. "I'm not going to let our duties keep us apart again. Even if I decide to return to the school to teach, I'm going to make sure we see each other as often as possible."

"I like the sound of that," Octavia said.

Raksha cut into her thoughts. *The peace session should be starting soon. I've spotted some of the senators making their way to the senate building.*

Octavia glanced up. Raksha and Emrys circled overhead, their massive shadows drawing the attention of Athelian children who chased after them, arms spread out. It was nice to hear their laughter after such devastation.

"I should head over to the senate building," Octavia told Strida. "Are you sure you won't reconsider attending the meeting with me?"

Strida laughed ruefully. "I don't mind representing the dragon riders' interests on the council, especially now Northwood is gone, but I've had enough peace talks and negotiations to last me a lifetime. Keeping Northwood and his lackeys from siccing the dragons on Athelia used up all the diplomacy I had."

Octavia's lips twisted. "You got thrown into the deep end with that one, but I understand."

Strida squeezed her hand, her tone serious. "I did want to apologize, though."

"For what?" Octavia asked.

"For making your job harder at times. I know I'm not the most patient person and I'd rather fight than listen to councilors drone on, but I was short with you a lot, and I never fully appreciated how much emotional intelligence and political savvy this job requires. Not until I started doing it myself. I'm sorry I upset you and that we fought. I'm sorry I ever thought your role in the capital was somehow less important than your dragon rider duties."

Octavia reached up and cupped Strida's cheek. "It's okay."

"It's not, Octavia. I stormed out on you on more than one occasion. I left you alone in the capital. And still you carried the burden of such an important role, risking everything to uncover the truth in Athelia. I truly am sorry that I hurt you."

Octavia's jaw trembled, moved by Strida's words. She'd never needed apologies from her. She knew they'd been forced into difficult positions. They were both trying to do what was best for the dragon riders and for Tenegard in their own ways. Yet, she couldn't deny how nice it was to hear Strida at least understood where Octavia had been coming from this entire time. That she'd experienced the complicated role of navigating affairs of state.

"Can you forgive me?" Strida asked.

"There's nothing to forgive," Octavia said immediately, blinking away the tears she could feel behind her eyes. She didn't want to cry. Not before having to meet with the senators. She cleared her throat. "But I do agree we need to prioritize our relationship, so before we left this morning, I asked Emmett to block off the next couple of days for me. He promised to guard my time with his usual zeal, and that there were no council meetings on the agenda. That way we can truly enjoy our time together. Maybe you can even teach me some more of that Tenegardian dance you started to show me during Cora's father's wedding." It felt like a million years had passed since then, but those few hours in Barcroft together had truly been the last uninterrupted moments of peace they'd spent together, and she hoped this victory celebration could be their fresh start.

Strida beamed. "I'm looking forward to it." She leaned in, and Octavia knew she was going to kiss her, but before their lips touched, footsteps sounded and Strida pulled away whispering, "Later."

"There you are," Commander Dolan said, appearing in the courtyard outside the inn where Octavia had roomed. It had fared well during the Blight's attacks. "I've been asked to escort you to the peace conference."

Octavia laughed. "Is that your way of telling me I'm late?"

"No," Dolan said. "I was actually hoping to show you some of the progress we've made on rebuilding with the help of the dragon riders."

"Lead the way," Octavia said. She and Strida fell in line beside him. They walked from the courtyard of the inn, down narrow streets littered with flyers and old posters protesting the war. They crossed between stone arches repaired with dragon magic and passed fountains once again spewing crystal clear water. "You'd almost never have known the Blight had flown through here."

"If we weren't holding Serafine and Melusine in custody, I'd be inclined to agree the whole thing could have been a bad dream," Dolan said.

"How are they liking their new accommodations?" Strida asked.

Dolan shook his head. "The bickering is unbelievable."

When they exited near the senate square, Octavia could see where the bulk of the restoration efforts were being concentrated. The offices that belonged to the senators were still just heaps of rubble. In a way, it was fitting that one of the last things to be repaired would be Serafine's old office. "I'm glad you prioritized the people's needs before this," Octavia said waving at the mess in front of them.

Dolan smiled. As they approached the white, stone remains of Serafine's building, a woman turned to greet them. Octavia's eyes widened in surprise. "Senator Jangoor?" she said, reaching out to shake the woman's hand.

Jangoor covered Octavia's hand with both of her own. "It's good to see you again."

"It's good to see you too!" Octavia would never forget the woman being dragged off the stage at Serafine's command. "I thought the worst might have happened."

The senator tugged her closer. "Honestly, that creature attacking might have saved my neck," she whispered. "Quite literally."

The corner of Octavia's mouth quirked. "Mine too."

Jangoor's lips twitched as she pulled away. "At any rate, construction is coming along well thanks to Tenegard's support."

"Will a new senator take over Serafine's office building?" Octavia asked.

"Actually," Jangoor said, "I've been toying with the idea of turning it into an exchange school. I thought we might discuss the possibility of hosting Tenegardian youth, allowing them to experience Athelia, learn how we function, how the senate works, about our culture. It might be a good way to help bridge the divide between our countries for the next generation."

"I think that's a marvelous idea," Octavia said. "And in return we'd host Athelian youth. I'm sure the council would be happy to convert part of the palace into a school."

"Excellent," Jangoor said, holding her hand out toward the senate building. "Should we go add it to the agenda?"

Octavia nodded.

Wait! Raksha called, sweeping down from the sky suddenly.

Octavia froze, watching Raksha descend and land in the square among all the workers. *What is it?*

I think there is something both you and Strida will want to see.

Now? The peace conference is about to start.

Trust me. You want to see this first.

Jangoor's brow arched to a point. "Is everything okay?"

"I'm not sure," Octavia said. "But apparently, there's something I must see before the conference starts."

Jangoor inclined her head toward the senate building. "I'll let them know you're running a few minutes late."

"Thank you," Octavia said. She grabbed Strida by the hand and hurried off in Raksha's direction. Emrys hadn't returned, so they both climbed up Raksha's back. Strida clung to Octavia as Raksha shot straight up in the air.

She circled the senate square, then veered left, past the city walls. *Where are we going?* Octavia asked.

You'll see.

Are you trying to be deliberately vague?

Raksha's chuckle drifted down the bond along with so much excitement that Octavia's pulse started galloping.

"There's Emrys," Strida said, pointing ahead. He was in the middle of a patch of farmland just outside the city. Raksha pitched into a dive. As they approached Emrys, Octavia caught sight of something else. In the field, on the ground, something glittered under the sun.

"They look like crystals," Strida said, jumping down off Raksha's back the moment they landed. She ran ahead to join Emrys.

Octavia followed. Upon closer inspection, the strange crystals were the same color as the free-floating magic that had covered Erelas following the Blight's escape—a pretty, violet hue. Then the crystal twitched. Octavia and Strida both gasped.

"It can't be," Strida said.

"It is," Octavia breathed, falling to her knees next to one of the strange shapes. They weren't crystals or stones. They were eggs. "Dragon eggs!"

Raksha laid on her belly next to the pile. "Indeed. And they're incubating a kind of dragon that I've never seen before."

"But that's impossible," Strida protested. "Athelia doesn't have any native dragons."

Raksha reached out, laying reverent claws against the crystal surface of the eggs. "According to dragon lore, this is how the Tenegardian dragons came to be. They were hatched from a union between magic and the land itself."

"Incredible," was all Octavia could say, watching the eggs twitch with new dragon life.

"There are more," Emrys said, gesturing across the field.

Exchanging a grin, Octavia and Strida scrambled into their saddles. Their dragons took to the air again, flying in a wider circuit around the city. This time, Octavia kept her eyes peeled, pointing out similar crystal egg deposits scattered about the land.

It looks like it won't be long before Athelia finally has dragons of its own, Raksha said.

Octavia smiled uncontrollably. *I can't wait to share the news with the senate.*

CHAPTER 37

CORA

"Do you think everyone's having a good time?" Cora looked around at the dragon riders, finally reunited again. It was wonderful to be back at the school, not as a traitorous outcast, but as part of the same team after so much time spent hunting the Heart through the mountains and then chasing after the Blight. She was looking forward to long days of training new riders and teaching classes on Dragon Tongue. In fact, she was eager to do some good old-fashioned chores. But before all that could take place, they'd decided to celebrate their victory against Melusine and the Blight with a feast.

The entire school had spent the better part of a day decorating the dining hall and preparing delicious foods. The smell of sweet honey ham and jam-filled donuts dusted in powdered sugar filled the air as the sun set, and Alaric had just lit a massive bonfire in the middle of the training field to chase away the darkness. Apparently, the dragon riders had no intention of ending the celebration when night fell, and Cora heartily agreed. She wanted this feeling of triumph to last forever. Or at least until they all fell into bed pleasantly exhausted.

"I thought every single person here was having a great time," Faron said, smiling down at her. "But now that they've broken out the second barrel of ale, I think they're having a *fantastic* time."

Cora giggled, spotting Strida and Octavia in the crowd, and Elaine and her father. She waved, smiling when they waved back, happy to see everyone safe and in good cheer. She looked around some more. Someone was missing. "Have you seen Lenire anywhere?"

"Not for a while," Faron admitted.

"I know he's not a huge fan of gatherings like this, but do you think he's okay? I mean, this is his celebration too."

Faron shrugged. "Last I'd heard, he was going off to find Yrsa."

Cora handed her cup to Faron. "Hold this for me. I'll be right back."

"Do you want me to come with you?"

"Just enjoy yourself," Cora called over her shoulder. "I'll only be a second, I promise." She walked around the side of the dining hall, searching the mingling crowds for Lenire's familiar face. She doubted she'd find him socializing, but she looked anyway. Laughter and good cheer bubbled from every conversation. It filled Cora's heart with glee.

She squinted into the setting sun, spotting a dark shape way out in the training field past the bonfire. There was a translucent shimmer, and Cora knew at once it was Yrsa. And she'd bet on her dragon bond that where Yrsa was, she would find Lenire.

She headed in Yrsa's direction. The heat from the bonfire warmed her as she passed, the flame licking up massive logs felled that morning. Riders had started to gather around the fire, toasting sausages and vegetables and all sorts of sweets in the flames.

"Hey there," Cora called as she spotted Lenire. He was sitting on the grass, tucked up against Yrsa's side, watching the last of the sunset fade from the sky. "I've been looking for you. Everyone else is at the celebration, but I noticed we were missing someone."

"I'll be there shortly," he said. "I needed a moment alone with my thoughts."

"People are going to forget what you look like if you never show your face," Cora teased gently. Lenire didn't quite smile, but his cheek twitched so at least he knew she was joking. "These must be heavy thoughts to pull you away from all this fun. Anything I can help with?"

"I was thinking about home actually," he admitted freely.

Cora was struck by how far their relationship had truly come since he'd first arrived in Tenegard. They'd started as reluctant allies, and somewhere along the way had become true friends. Cora sat down beside him in the cool grass. The sun's warmth had faded from the field and the soft blades tickled her ankles. "You want to go back to Itharus now," she said quietly. It wasn't hard to guess. He had a melancholy look.

"With the Blight defeated, unfinished business waits for me there. I've completed the mission I was given to make up for my failings. If I return now, maybe I can help turn the tide of the civil war."

"Now Zirael's dead, do you think you can defeat his Order of sorcerers for good?"

Lenire sighed heavily. "I honestly never let myself imagine it. For a long time, I believed I would die fighting the Blight. Victory wasn't something I ever expected. Sitting here now, knowing we won, feels a little disorienting. Getting to go home again was my wildest fantasy—maybe I should have packed up and left already—but it still doesn't seem quite real. I guess I keep expecting to wake up in my tent in the mountains, only to realize it was all a dream."

Cora could understand that. She'd spent the better part of the last few days trying to wrap her head around the fact that they'd actually won. "Sometimes it feels too good to be true," she said. "I hope when and if you do finally decide to go home, you're able to save Itharus the way you helped save Tenegard and Athelia."

"Thank you," Lenire said. Yrsa made a soft sound of agreement behind them.

"But for now I'm glad you stayed to celebrate with us. You deserve to bask in some of this happiness. And you know you'll always have a home here in Tenegard with the dragon riders, right? We couldn't have done any of this without you."

Lenire ducked his head, staring at his feet. "After you and Faron fought for me in the cavern, saving me from the Blight possession, you and your dragon riders have begun to feel like a true family to me." He lifted his head, his eyes glassy, filled with a flash of uncharacteristic emotion. "I can't abandon my country. But I will always think of Tenegard as a second home, and for now, tonight, I think we should celebrate that home."

Cora jumped to her feet and reached for his hand. "Come on, then. Before all the ale and pastries are gone."

Lenire snorted, letting Cora pull him to his feet. Together they walked back toward the celebration, meeting Faron just outside the dining hall. A few of the more musically talented dragon riders had retrieved their instruments from their bunks and struck up a lively tune, beckoning people out of the dining hall to dance beneath the stars.

It reminded Cora of her father's wedding, and she was suddenly caught by the memory of Bodi, crashing the wedding to summon them all back to the school. His small, round, smiling face filled her mind. He and his dragon, Mina, had been the first to fall victim to the sleeping sickness. Though they hadn't survived the intensity of the energy drain, Cora had promised to do whatever it took to wake the rest of the riders and stop the Blight in order to honor his memory and his sacrifice.

As Faron passed her and Lenire a cup of ale, she held hers up in a toast. "To Bodi and Mina," she said. "And all the others we lost along the way. May their spirits live on in the stars."

"Bodi and Mina," everyone chorused. Faron and Lenire clinked their cups against hers. As Cora took a swig of ale, she basked in the moment of peace that followed. She was looking forward to a long, quiet future restoring the heritage of the dragon riders with Faron and her friends by her side.

A group of giggly young women approached Lenire, asking him to dance. He shook his head, gesturing to his cup.

One of the women took it and handed it to Faron, who laughed loudly.

"Go on," Cora said to Lenire. "It'll be good for you."

Lenire rolled his eyes, but allowed himself to be steered into the field. Cora chuckled, watching the young riders attempt to teach Lenire some Tenegardian dance steps. He stumbled and blushed furiously the entire time.

"Maybe one day we'll be able to visit Itharus and learn some Itharusian dances," Faron said.

Cora sobered at the thought. "I think there is another battle to be won in Itharus before that will ever be a possibility." She quietly wondered if Zirael's Order would be turning their attention to Tenegard once they realized there was enough magic here to control a creature like the Blight.

Faron put the cups he held down on a table and wrapped his arms around her, kissing the side of her head. "Stop fretting. I can see your mind churning. Itharus is a problem for another day. And if the dragon riders are ever called to battle again, at least we know that decision will be made among respected equals. We won't be pawns for someone like Northwood ever again."

"You're right," Cora said. Things were different now. And Itharus and the battles that may come were truly a concern for another day. Tonight they were celebrating.

A loud cheer echoed across the field, and Cora turned to see Renka walking up the path from the infirmary, surrounded by her friends. She and her dragon had been recovering well after Strida and the others had managed to repair her dragon bond. Cora caught Renka's eye across the field and lifted her cup. Renka beamed, accepting a cup of ale from Joi, returning the gesture.

As Cora lowered her cup, she resolved from now on, she'd do whatever she could to keep her whole family of riders strong and content—even when it meant letting them fly on their own terms.

"I'm so sorry," Lenire mumbled as he stepped on one of the dancers' feet.

The look on his face was enough to get Cora laughing again. She put her cup down and turned to Faron. "Do you think you're feeling strong enough to keep up with me?" she asked teasingly.

Faron touched his chest in mock offense. "I'd like to see you try to outlast me."

With that, he took her hands, twirling her onto the field, surrounded by their friends and their dragons, laughing and dancing long into the night.

END OF DRAGON WARS

RISE OF THE DRAGON RIDERS BOOK SIX

Dragon Tongue, December 28, 2022

Dragon Scales, January 25, 2023

Dragon Fire, February 22, 2023

Dragon Plague, June 28, 2023

Dragon Crystals, July 26, 2023

Dragon Wars, August 30, 2023

PS: Keep reading for an exclusive extract from ***Pack Dragon*** and ***Dragon Link***.

THANK YOU!

I hope you enjoyed **Dragon Wars**. Please don't forget to leave a review.

Receive free books, exclusive excerpts and be kept up to date on all of my new releases, when you sign up to my mailing list at AvaRichardsonBooks.com/mailing-list.

ABOUT AVA

Ava Richardson writes epic page-turning Young Adult Fantasy books with lovable characters and intricate worlds that are barely contained within your eReader.

She grew up on a steady diet of fantasy and science fiction books handed down from her two big brothers – and despite being dog-eared and missing pages, she loved escaping into the magical worlds that authors created. Her favorites were the ones about dragons, where they'd swoop, dive and soar through the skies of these enchanted lands.

Stay in touch! You can contact Ava on:

facebook.com/AvaRichardsonBooks
amazon.com/author/avarichardson
goodreads.com/avarichardson
bookbub.com/authors/ava-richardson

BLURB

An orphan searching for her future unlocks a destiny she never imagined...

War has engulfed Destia, reaching even the remote country-side, where foundling Eva Thirsk lives. When army recruiters come to town, Eva sees a chance to find a place where she truly belongs—something she's never found on her adopted family's farm. She enlists, hoping for adventure...and perhaps a chance to learn what happened to her parents.

But when one of her missions goes disastrously wrong, a powerful enemy is accidentally freed. The Venistrare Warlock, sealed away eons ago to protect Destia, has been unleashed—and things begin to *change* for Eva.

Strange visions, an electric sense of energy, and an odd feeling of deep connection to Perrell, the pack dragon she's befriended… If she didn't know better, Eva would think she's somehow gained magic. Including the ability to bond to a dragon, but that's not possible at her age…is it?

As the war rages on, the stakes grow higher each day. Can Eva and Perrell figure out Eva's new powers in time—or will they be consumed by the fires of annihilation?

EXCERPT

Chapter One
The Daydreamer

The sun was slowly setting over the farmlands just outside the small village of Flaxton, casting rich beams of golden light across the Southern Destian plains and lending an air of warmth to the oncoming chill of the springtime evening. Eva Thirsk reveled in that light—or at least, what little of it came through the open doors and windows of the barn in which she worked, unhitching the plow from the horses that had been in the field all day.

"It's going to be a clear night tonight," she said to the two animals, as she deftly undid the various belts and buckles that harnessed them to the old equipment. "Not a cloud out there."

She reached up and rested her hand against one of the horse's snouts for a moment as he snorted, imagining for a moment that he had understood her. She smiled, and then began removing the noseband and bit attached to the reins. "Let's just get this all taken off for you," she soothed as she worked, "and then we'll get you brushed and fed for the night. How does that sound?"

The horse shook out his mane once freed from the bridle, letting out another contented snort and stamping his hooves a couple of times against the ground.

"Good," Eva said with a light laugh, petting the horse's snout once more. "I'm glad you like the idea."

She made quick work of the harnesses on both horses, leading them into their pens and getting them secured. But then she took her time with their grooming and feeding, the light fading away outside as she continued to speak to them in low tones, feeling the tension leave her own shoulders as she worked. Caring for the horses was perhaps her favorite thing to do here on the farm, and she always wanted to make it last as long as possible.

Unfortunately, her tasks finally came to an end. Eva sighed as she leaned against the stable wall, loathe to leave the pens. "Would it be alright with you if I stayed here for a while longer?" she asked the horses. "It's nice and quiet here."

As opposed to the house, which would be a den of noise and mayhem, overflowing with children playing and adults complaining and everyone bustling around to get dinner on the table. Scores of people, young and old, all cut from the same cloth…except for her. The one who didn't fit. No one was ever unkind to her, but since Danwell had passed, she felt like she'd lost the strongest link tying her here.

Although he had already been an old man when he'd adopted Eva at age five, Danwell and his wife had always treated her kindly. Loved her, or so she liked to believe. But Danwell's wife, Hana, had died two years ago, when Eva was fourteen, and now, Danwell was gone too.

"You like me still, right?" she asked the horses fondly. "But then, I know where I stand with you. As long as I keep you clean, keep you fed, and keep your coat brushed, you'll always be happy with—"

"What are you doing?"

Eva gasped, whirling away from the horse and turning towards the front of the stables, where Lain, one of Danwell's grandchildren, was standing in the doorway. "I—um, I was just…finishing my chores," she got out, turning back to the horse and grabbing the brush, running it a few more times through his mane. "There; finished!"

Her adopted cousin rolled his eyes at her. "You were daydreaming again," he accused.

"No. I was simply…distracted."

"What's the difference?" Lain scoffed. "You should've been done with this half an hour ago, and here you are dawdling and talking to the animals. What's going on in your head?"

If she told him, she'd just get more blank looks of incomprehension. The family had always been kind to her—but that didn't mean they'd ever really understood her or her dreams of a different life, a different destiny beyond the family's farm.

"Nothing," she lied, as she set the brush aside and left the pen. She latched the gate shut. "Let's just go."

“Oh, Lain, Eva, can you come here please?” called Carina when they reached the house. The woman, in her mid-forties, was Danwell’s oldest child, and as such, had inherited the farm—though all his children lived and worked here. Carina seemed busy as always. “I need a hand with something,” the woman called from out of sight. “What took you so long with your chores?”

Eva followed Lain into the candlelit kitchen, breathing in the rich scent of garlic and rosemary from their supper and instantly feeling the warmth of the cooking fires surround her, the sensation almost smothering after the fresh air outdoors.

“She was daydreaming again,” Lain reported to his aunt at once. “I found her in the stables, conversing with the horses.”

“Eva, how many times have I told you not to dawdle with your chores?” Carina asked, as she hurried to the stove and gave the stew a quick stir before turning to the woodfire oven to check on some golden rolls. “I’ve been working in here for hours getting supper ready for everyone when I have other things that need doing, and I could have used your help.” She turned to Eva more fully, looking down at her with tired brown eyes. “I need to know that I can rely on you to help me. I can’t do that if you’re off daydreaming in the stables.”

“Sorry, Carina,” Eva said quietly. “I wasn’t thinking.”

“No, you weren’t,” Carina sighed, though seemed ready to drop the subject now as she looked down at a piece of paper in her hand. “Now, mind the stove for me. Lain, go help your father with the firewood. I have to go to town.”

“Go to town?” Eva repeated, as Lain disappeared out the door again. “But it’s nearly nightfall.”

“Yes, and I could be back by now if you had come in from the stables earlier,” Carina said. “I have to collect the docket at the guildhall; it’s nearly collection day and I need to know how much produce we're due to hand over to the army this month."

"I could go get it," Eva offered, eager for the chance to redeem herself. "I'll run the whole way, to make up for lost time."

Carina paused, giving her a narrow-eyed look. "You won't get distracted?"

Eva shook her head. "I'll be back by the time supper's on the table," she promised.

"Alright." Carina handed over the notice from the guildhall. "If you're late, we won't wait for you."

"I won't be late."

Eva stepped out of the kitchen and back into the twilight. She wasted no time in setting off at a run down the old dirt road towards the village of Flaxton.

It was a lovely night for a run, and Eva relished the activity. There was something so magical about the feeling she got when she ran. Something strong, something powerful. Something freeing.

She didn't slow down until she reached the outskirts of the village. She took a moment to catch her breath and then began walking briskly towards the center of town.

"Eva?" She glanced around to see Lyla, an old schoolmate, exiting one of the cottages. "What are you doing in town so late?"

"Oh, hello, Lyla," Eva panted, as her friend closed the distance between them. "I'm going to the guildhall, to get the docket for Fa—" She cut herself off halfway through the word 'father,' a lump suddenly catching in her throat. She hurriedly swallowed it back down. "For Carina," she amended.

"I'll go with you," Lyla offered. "That is, if you don't mind the company."

Eva shook her head, trying for a small smile. "I don't mind." It would be nice to have some company for the short walk from here to the guildhall. Besides, it had been awhile since she'd seen Lyla. For farm kids like her, schooling ended at age fifteen, and she rarely had reason to come into town anymore.

"I'm glad," Lyla told her, smiling back and falling into step beside her. Despite the darkening night, the village was aglow with warm light, staining out onto the road from the windows of the cottages they passed by and casting shadows from the oil-lamp lightposts overhead. "How have you been, lately?" *Since Danwell died* hung in the air, even if it was unspoken.

Eva thought of brushing her off with a generic "I'm fine," but then caught herself. She felt like she had to talk to someone, *anyone,* or the things she'd been feeling would eat her from the inside out—and here Lyla was, as if by fate.

"It's...been difficult on the farm," she admitted to her quietly. "Carina is working very hard, trying to run the farm and the family, and everyone's doing their part to help, but...I don't know." She sighed, absently kicking aside a pebble in her path. "I don't think I'm doing it right."

"What do you mean?"

Eva shrugged a shoulder. "Sometimes I just feel..." She paused, glancing up at the starlit sky as she tried to think of the right word to describe the heaviness she felt. "Tired. Not actually *physically* tired, but listless. Like I'm trying to wade through water against a current. Does that make sense?"

Lyla rubbed at the back of her neck, glancing at Eva sympathetically, but somehow looking less understanding than the horses. "That...

must be difficult," she said, after a few minutes of searching for a reply.

Eva managed a half smile. It was kind of the girl to try to be understanding. "It can be," she agreed.

"It actually sounds like something my brother used to say," Lyla continued. "I think it's why he joined the military. He loves our family, but our life here seemed to fit too tight. He needed more space to breathe."

Yes, Eva thought. *That.* It made her feel a little better to know that she wasn't the only one who couldn't help dreaming of a bigger life, a bigger future than Flaxton could offer. Maybe now she could stop feeling so guilty for her ingratitude. After all, Flaxton had given her a home and a family after her birth parents had abandoned her in the Sanctuary when she was just five years old. She should be happy here, should *want* to be here with the people who had taken her in and raised her. And yet, she'd never quite felt like this was where she was supposed to be.

BLURB

For sixteen-year-old Nova Harris, the last nine years in Florida have been a constant stream of disappointment. With her father dead and her mother missing, she's been shuffled from one foster home to another. The only connection Nova has to happier times is the strange dragon pendant that makes her yearn to reunite with her mother and have a family again

Until a dragon lands at her feet—and offers to help find her mother.

Before they know it, Nova and her best friend Zephyr are whisked through a portal to Ragond, a realm sustained by powerful magic. Though Nova has no memory of this land, the fantastical inhabitants are well aware of her parents. Because of her family, in fact, Nova is invited to participate in the upcoming dragon rider trials, and Zephyr in the witch trials.

However, it soon becomes clear that various factions are threatened by the newcomers and want to send them back where they came from —by any means necessary. Further complications arise when Nova and Zephyr discover twin dragons…and unexpectedly bond with them.

Suddenly, Nova discovers she must choose between searching for her mother and protecting those she loves. And either choice risks embroiling them in an inter-dimensional war.

EXCERPT

Chapter One

Sometimes, the world is too loud.

As Nova Harris climbed out the window of the old two-story house she currently lived in, she left behind a cacophony of sounds: slamming doors from downstairs, loud music from the room next to hers, crying from a kid out in the hall, and, loudest of all, the screaming voices of her foster parents as they entered the second hour of their latest fight.

It was a big one, this fight. Nova hadn't heard what had started it, but they'd already touched on the most popular talking points. There were too many kids in this house, and Stephanie hadn't wanted to take the most recent addition, but Todd felt like they'd had no choice, so Stephanie 'needed to get over herself' and do her job anyway. Stephanie wondered if Todd would feel that way if *he* had to spend all day taking care of 'snot-nosed brats,' which launched Todd into a tirade about how he slaved away all day at work to put food on the table and all he got at home was complaints that he was gone too much.

Nova had heard it all before and would hear it all again, but that didn't make listening any easier.

It had been going in circles like this for a while, but it had been when they'd brought up Nova herself, and started listing all the problems *she* caused, that she'd finally decided to make her escape. She already knew her grades weren't as high as they could be, thanks. She was aware that she had an attitude problem. And if Stephanie and Todd didn't want her to break their rules, maybe they shouldn't make such stupid rules! She was sixteen—she didn't need a *9PM* curfew! She was more than capable of existing outside after dark; she'd done it before and she'd do it again—in fact, that's what she was doing now. She slipped out onto the roof and turned, closing the window most of the way behind her before crossing to the corner of the gable. Outside the view of the living room windows, she lowered herself over the edge until her feet found the banister of the back porch steps. She climbed down the porch easily, as she often did, and left the house behind, stepping out of the light flooding the area from the windows and porch lamp, into the darkness of the nearby woods.

The warm, mild breeze of winter in South Florida was comforting compared to the hot, stuffy house. The silence of the night, accompanied only by the chirping of crickets and katydids and the occasional hoot of an owl, seemed to Nova like a sort of lullaby after leaving the noises of the foster home. It was almost like a completely different world, and it was only when Nova was out here in the woods at night that she felt truly at peace—or, at least, as close to 'at peace' as she could likely manage.

She sighed as she walked, adjusting her light jacket and the backpack she'd slung over her shoulders before leaving. It wasn't packed or anything, as she didn't really intend to run away. Not yet. But she liked to keep it with her at all times, just in case, as it contained most everything she could call her own. A couple of books, some headphones, small trinkets she'd collected over the years, and an old sweater and a change of clothes, as well as her wallet and a few keys from old foster homes that she'd never bothered to fish out of the bag.

As Nova walked, she felt a brief twinge of panic and put her hand to her neck to check for a leather cord attached to a pendant, breathing a sigh of relief upon finding it. She hadn't felt it for a moment and had thought she might have left it in her room—despite the fact that she never took it off. But it had simply shifted under the collar of her jacket, so she adjusted it carefully, looking it over for the hundredth time. The pendant was unique, made of a silvery sort of metal and streaked with colors of green and amber. She didn't know what kind of material the triangular pendant was carved from, but it was pretty, and it had a dragon etched on the front and 'NOVA' carved into the back.

Her thoughts were interrupted as she heard a few branches snap behind her. She didn't have to turn around to know who was following her, just pausing in her walk and waiting for the girl behind her to catch up. Zephyr, one of her foster siblings and her best friend, appeared beside her after a moment, giving Nova a knowing look as they walked on together.

"Thought I heard you leave," Zephyr said. "Sorry I'm late, but I had to sneak out the back door like a normal person."

Nova chuckled a little. "Thanks. I definitely don't mind the company."

Despite them being the same age, the two girls contrasted each other in nearly every way, from their appearances—Nova being taller and leaner, with darker skin and dark brown curly hair, while Zephyr was shorter, curvier, and pale, with straight blonde hair—to their personalities. Nova was stubborn, prone to anger, and got into trouble for talking back too much, while Zephyr was more shy and didn't like to cause trouble, and kept her head down because of it. Not that Zephyr's shyness kept her from speaking her mind, though, especially to Nova. She seemed to tell Nova everything while Nova preferred to keep to herself. She didn't like the idea of being vulnerable, of having someone else know the things she thought or the things she felt. She honestly didn't understand how Zephyr *could* be so honest about things. She was only leaving herself open to being hurt.

"I thought you wouldn't," Zephyr said, speaking quietly, as if trying not to disturb the peace of the swamp woods. "Though, we can't stay out all night. Again."

"I know."

"After all, you're on thin ice with them already," Zephyr continued. "If you get in trouble again, well… I don't want to lose you."

Nova scoffed a bit. "It's not like they care what happens to us anyway," she grumbled, shoving her hands into her pockets. "They're too busy fighting with each other to even notice we're gone."

"But if they *do* notice, they might send you back," Zephyr told her bluntly. "And where would that leave me? I don't want to end up on my own again, wondering if I'll see you in school or if you're gone for good, hoping it won't be too long before we maybe end up in the same house again."

"I know," Nova said again, softer this time. She and Zephyr had been in the same house once before, when they'd been younger, and they'd been friends ever since. Nova still remembered when she'd first met Zephyr. They'd both been nine, and it had been Zephyr's first foster home after losing her parents. The girl had been scared and confused, emotional and vulnerable, with no idea how to handle what was going on or what had happened to her folks, and somehow it had fallen to Nova to protect her and help her get used to her new life. They'd been together in that house for about two years before Nova had gotten moved to a new one, and although they'd still gone to school together, it had been hard for Zephyr at home without her. They'd both been shuffled around for a few years after that, and then, when they'd ended up at Stephanie and Todd's a year ago, together at last, Zephyr had made Nova promise not to get into trouble and leave her again.

Honestly, it was the only reason Nova had lasted this long.

They reached their destination, which was Nova's favorite place in the woods—at least, in this area. She had to find a new favorite place after every move, which was another reason to avoid being sent away, albeit a less important one. This space was a large clearing, maybe more like a rather small field around thirty feet from one end to the other, the foundations of an unfinished or mostly dismantled old cabin lying half-buried in the dry ground. Here, they could lie down without having to worry about getting muddy or finding unexpected bugs crawling on them most of the time, and from the center of the 'house,' on nights like this, they had a perfect view of the stars above them. They got settled, Nova using her backpack as a pillow while Zephyr took off her jacket, wadding it up for her own pillow, and for a while, they just watched the sky.

"Hey…" Zephyr spoke up after a bit.

Nova turned her head to look at her friend, noting a deep, thoughtful frown on the girl's face. "What's up?" she prodded when Zephyr didn't continue.

"Do you remember your parents?"

Nova froze, turning back to the stars and frowning herself. "I…yes," she said quietly. "Well, my mother. I don't remember my dad, though. Why?"

"Just wondering," Zephyr said. "I miss my dad. My mom, too."

WANT MORE?

WWW.AVARICHARDSONBOOKS.COM

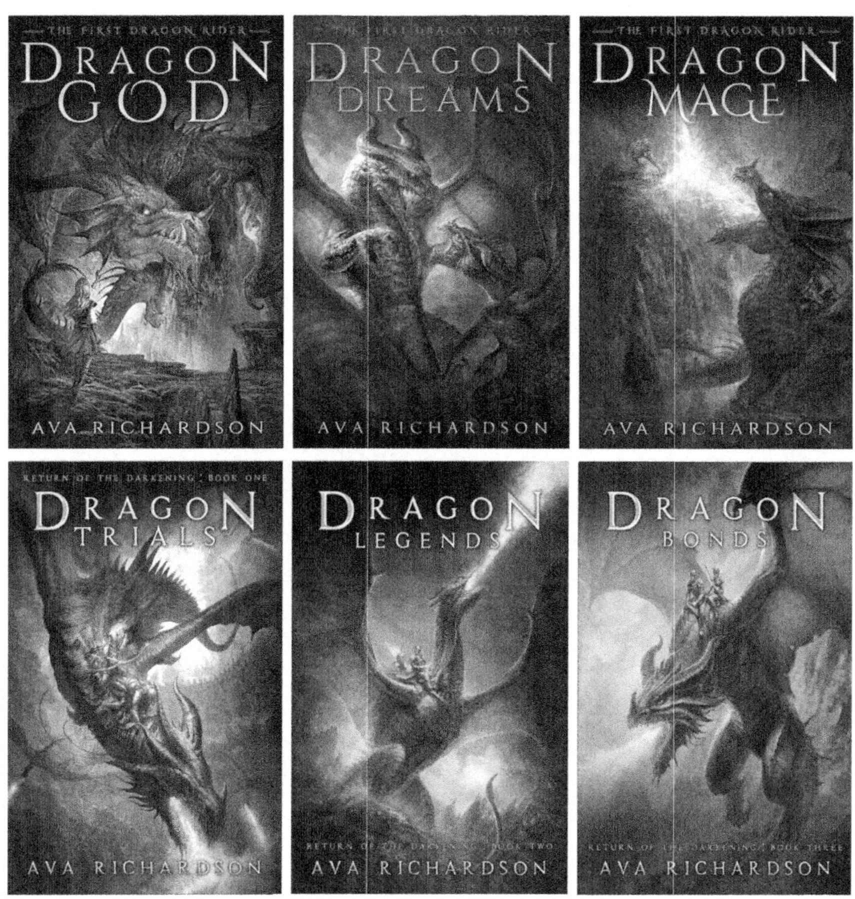